SPIRIT TALKER

THE LEGEND OF NAKOSIS

TOM COLES

Erebus Society

Erebus Society

First published in Great Britain in 2018
by Erebus Society

1st Edition

Copyright of Text © Tom Coles 2014
Cover & illustration copyright © Raven Hawk 2018
Editor: Constantin Vaughn

ISBN: 978-1-912461-10-3

www.erebussociety.com

www.tomcoles.ca

TABLE OF CONTENTS

Acknowledgments I
Introduction...V
About The Techniques Described Within This Book.......... VII

Prologue..1

Chapter 1 - Nakosis...7
Chapter 2 - White Mist Village...............................15
Chapter 3 - Dream 21
Chapter 4 - Loka's Story 25
Chapter 5 - The Cave 35
Chapter 6 - A Visitor.. 45
Chapter 7 - History 57
Chapter 8 - The Storm 69
Chapter 9 - Preparation 77
Chapter 10 - Black Faces 89
Chapter 11 - Aftermath 109
Chapter 12 - The Quest...125
Chapter 13 - Deer River And The Beyond 137
Chapter 14 - Shining Lakes.......................................157
Chapter 15 - The Tale...191
Chapter 16 - The Lost Village 207
Chapter 17 - To The Mountain 217
Chapter 18 - Sheenka's Story.................................. 233
Chapter 19 - Homecoming 251
Chapter 20 - Retribution.. 273

"A human being is a part of the whole called by us universe, a part limited in time and space. He experiences himself, his thoughts and feeling as something separated from the rest, a kind of optical delusion of his consciousness. This delusion is a kind of prison for us, restricting us to our personal desires and to affection for a few persons nearest to us. Our task must be to free ourselves from this prison by widening our circle of compassion to embrace all living creatures and the whole of nature in its beauty."

Albert Einstein

ACKNOWLEDGMENTS

There are many times in one's life when, often least expected, someone comes along and imparts a pearl of wisdom that can have profound impact on your world view. It isn't always in the context of personalized instruction in the tradition of pupil and master. Often it may come in the form of a passage in a seemingly unrelated book, a phrase overheard in a movie or the telling of someone's experiences. In these situations, something speaks to a part of you that instinctually seems to 'know' the deeper truth to the words. I am blessed to have had these wonderful occurrences often in my life and to have had that part of me that acknowledges them somehow kick into auto file and recall mode. In such situations, it is that deeper timeless part of our being that responds as though having met a dear old friend. It is the inner spirit being roused from its slumber.

To make a list here would be to give an injustice to the many people I would, no doubt, (due to my own forgetfulness) neglect to include. I must thank my parents, for as a child I was given the opportunity to experience some solitude among nature and that rekindled the primordial fires of connectivity - what Nakosis would call the 'Great Connection' - within me and lead me to constantly strive to live as closely integrated with and respectful of the Sacred Mother Earth as much as possible. I have had wonderful teachers throughout my life, within a number of spiritual traditions and I owe a tremendous debt of gratitude to them. Some have now passed on to other incarnations. I would like to thank my wife, Sandy, for her patience, suggestions and her help with proof reading my manuscript, and I would like to thank Nakosis, for having freed himself from the recesses of my psyche, to flow outward and enable me to make more concrete the wisdom of all those wonderful people who have helped shape my spiritual view.

The wisdom of Nakosis is not mine, nor is it confined to a character in a fictional tale. It is lying there within each of us, awaiting that spark of introspection that fans the fires of spiritual understanding.

INTRODUCTION

While 'Spirit Talker -The legend of Nakosis' is a work of fiction, it none-theless presents some spiritual perspectives that are universal among the world's indigenous peoples and among many who now embrace the Sha-manic tradition. The very words 'Shaman' and 'Shamanism' have been adopt-ed by most practitioners of this ancient practice of connecting to universal spirit and, as such, no one ethnic group, race or culture can claim proprietor-ship over these techniques. The word actually comes to us from the Tungusic word *saman*, native to Siberia and central Asia. It has even been suggested that this was itself a derivative of the word *samana* in the Pali language of ancient India. Shamanism is unquestionably the oldest spiritual tradition in the world, hence it's occurrence in virtually every culture. As these various cultures spawned religious traditions, some aspects of the more ancient Sha-manism continued to appear within all world religions. Consequently, the two overlap as is evident in the designations we now see, such as 'Buddhist Shamanism, African Shamanism, Native American Shamanism or Celtic and Wiccan Shamanism,' etc. If anything this reveals the universal appeal to a spiritual tradition that knows no bounds.

The many so-called advances of modern society have come at grave costs, the results of which now place us at the brink of a global environmental and climatic dilemma of catastrophic proportions. This is due, to a large degree, to our having lost the vision of our planet as a living, sacred entity of which we are but a part; an inter-connected fragment of a great circle of spiritu-al energy. This is the animistic perspective of the Shamanic path. It is the one great lesson that Nakosis, the young man who's story these pages reveal, comes to embrace fully in his great quest for wisdom. This view enables us to see our planet, once again, as the 'Sacred Mother'. It is my hope that this book will present this perspective through a story that is informative, yet captivat-ing and intriguing. It weaves adventure and fantasy with deep spiritual truths about the interconnectedness of all things within the 'great circle' of life and the need to preserve this natural balance. These are the lessons learned by the young Shaman, Nakosis, as he matures and experiences the unfolding of his power amid the spectacular wilderness of his primordial world. Na-

V

kosis embarks upon an adventurous quest that brings him encounters with fascinating people and beings both within the 'waking' world and the realms of his spirit journeys. He will come to know loss and hardship beyond his imagining and ultimately he will experience the deepest love and the inner tranquility of spiritual awakening. The young man comes to comprehend the life-changing experience of being one who is fully integrated with the spirit of all that is; of finally knowing his true identity as a spiritual being that is a part of that vast unlimited cosmos of inter-woven energies, the sum of which is none other than the Great Mystery.

This book is not meant to be a treatise on Shamanism, nor is it a factual account of pre-contact era first nations. It is a work of fiction that is intended to, hopefully, instill in the reader, young and old alike, the knowledge that we have within us the capacity to develop a spiritual awareness of ourselves, others and the world around us that many never dreamed possible. This story could have taken place within any number of ages and geographic locations. Nakosis bears similarity to the story of the Buddha, of Siddhartha. As such it could just as easily have taken place in the foothills of the Himalayas. He could have been a child upon the grasslands of the Mongolian plains, the Siberian taiga or the African savanna. But I chose the North American wilderness of the pre-contact era for the telling of the tale because I believe that in this turbulent time of environmental degradation, of exploitation, of vast economic disparity, poverty and violence that the world needs to hearken the ancient and reverent teachings of these marvelous people about the sacredness and sanctity of our earth and all the beings with whom we share it. I believe that it is the prophesized time of the 'rainbow nation' when we must turn to our native brothers and sisters for their help and spiritual guidance to, hopefully (with the spirit's blessing) undo the folly of millennia of greed, covetousness and irreverent attitudes toward our 'Sacred Mother'. I do know that Nakosis would agree and I hope you do too.

Blessings, Tom Coles

ABOUT THE TECHNIQUES
DESCRIBED WITHIN THIS BOOK

I have taken a few liberties in describing the methods that Nakosis uses to induce the trance state of Shamanic reality. However, it is important here to state that there is absolutely no incorrect way in which to do this, as it is an individual expression of spiritual ecstasy and, as such, may be achieved in a variety of methods. Technique is not as important as intent. If one's heart is open and one's intent is sincere then whatever techniques work for you is the 'right' one. The use of a drum and rattle is universal however among all cultures. Likewise, the prayers and invocations are of my own devising and are not meant to accurately reflect those of any particular culture of ethnic group. Those of you wishing to pursue the Shamanic path are strongly encouraged to do so and either adopt one of the many formats currently in use or use those ways and words that best express your deepest spiritual self.

PROLOGUE

She was growing tired, weakening with every step her great paws made upon the wind-crusted snow. This would make her ever more vulnerable. Instinctually aware, she dug deeper, seeking the strength to make the rocky outcrop silhouetted on the horizon. Dawn approached and the thin pale line of morning light illuminated the low ridges of mountains now purple and blue in the faint glow. The outcrop was close but not much of a prominence, yet it might just afford the security of height in this otherwise flat plain of snow and ice. She might find a crevice, or hole perhaps, in which she could conceal her hunger-wracked frame. It had been three days since she'd last eaten, since she had gnawed the rib cage of some indistinct creature thrust up from beneath the hard crust of snow. She labored hard, her powerful jaws challenged by the frozen bones. Still she managed to crush out a bit of life-saving marrow, enough to sustain her another few days to arrive at the point where she now stood. She had spent the previous night curled up in the snow beneath some scrub brush beside the riverbank as the mountains howled a blizzard down upon her. Now climbing the wind swept rock she could see across the barren expanse to the distant mountains, but there was no shelter among these rocks. Soon, she knew, she would curl in the snow, her back against the wind, her head tucked under her bushy tail and dream of warmer days of rabbit filled meadows and she would sleep the lasting sleep.

Her eyesight was not as sharp as it once was, nor her breathing as deep, yet her sense of smell told her that something was about - and it was close. It was right beneath her, beneath the snow under the very outcrop on which she perched! Her body lowered, from nose to tail, every muscle rippled and tensed preparing to lunge. Her eyes never moved from the spot her nose directed her to. Her ears flattened and her back arched slightly above her powerful hind legs. Something was stirring beneath the blanket of white only her body's length beneath her. Slowly, almost imperceptibly at first, the snow began moving, not in one place but in two. From out of the whiteness there emerged what looked like a pair of large bones. The great cat hesitated, trying to make sense of the apparition and whether it represented a threat. Suddenly a great flake of the crusted snow shook loose and a large shaggy head with great curved horns thrust up, free of the bank in which the ram had spent the night of the previous blizzard. Normally, taking on such a beast in her weakened state was a dangerous proposition, but she knew it would be her last chance at surviving as she drove her body down with the last of her reserves. Her claws dug into the thick mane as she struggled to get her jaws onto the ram's neck. It bellowed in shock but instinctively thrust it's powerful horns back at the attacker while bucking high out of the snow and trying to slam onto its back. Pain raged through her as she took the blow against her ribs but she never let go – she could not let go no matter what, lest she loose her only chance of survival and risk a bloody and painful death under sharp hooves and mighty horns. As the ram bucked once more it's back arched and for just a moment it's head lowered and she dug her teeth deeper with one last exhausted effort. Hot foaming blood poured into her mouth and she knew at that moment that it was over. The huge ram buckled, legs kicking uselessly for one last valiant effort then collapsed in the blood reddened snow.

The great cat hung on for what seemed like a long time, partly unable to extricate herself from sheer exhaustion, partly wanting to make sure the struggle was indeed over. When at last she let go it was to fall into the snow panting desperately for breath, her lungs bellowing frosty clouds in the cold morning air. She was in pain but she knew she had to ignore it and eat quickly. Soon others would find their way to the kill. The cold winds of this high plateau would carry the scent a great distance. At first she was too weakened to begin the task of ripping the carcass open and feasting upon the nutritious flesh, so she simply lay in the snow licking up the blood from the ram's neck. This seemed to stir some primal strength in her and she quickly tore into the beast with a ravenous urge.

The large black birds had already begun to arrive, circling above her watching, testing as they always do. Their caws would soon broadcast the location to other adept predators – some who would easily outmatch her in strength and numbers. She ate quickly, devouring the organ flesh and ripping away at the haunches. Then she quickly rolled her head and shoulders in the softer snow using her paws to wash the blood away from her fur. She knew once the carcass had been discovered the scent would linger on her enough to draw attention. This was the domain of the dire wolf. Their packs were the unchallenged masters of this world. As well, even more cunning and more sinister creatures haunted this wild land. She'd been lucky so far to not be detected, especially in her weakened state. She knew she had to make the mountains before the sun fell below the horizon. There, at the mountain's base, was the tree line and hopefully small game to hunt and a high rocky rise to climb to safety. She gave a cautious glance back as she sped on her way. Out of the scene of struggle and death and back onto the hard crust she could make good time as the strength of the ram coursed through her. As her pace picked up and her breathing once more returned, her nose picked up something on the wind – something strange, something unfamiliar to her and yet whatever it was it gave her a sense of foreboding. Westward, toward the trees she now moved at a steady running pace!

Nothing, not even food seems more important to the lone traveler than a fire, and in the cold of a winter's night it means life itself. Nakosis struggled with his fire drill - a small bow of bent willow and sinew strung around a wood shaft that rested in a depression adjacent to a notch in a small plank of wood. Back and forth relentlessly he worked the bow, the shaft spinning it's base against the wood getting hotter with the friction until a tiny bundle of shavings and grasses would begin to glow. Then with the greatest care, his hands cupped gently around the precious glow he would raise it to his mouth and softly breathe life into the bundle and watch as it miraculously became a tiny flame. He had arranged his small pile of dry twigs under which to place this precious flame, adding larger ones from the pile he had meticulously gathered.

'High wood is dry wood, Nakosis.' His father had once told him. He was just a small boy on the first of many trips he would accompany his father on. As his father gathered wood for a fire, young Nakosis rummaged among the driftwood wedged within the rocks of the river's edge but couldn't seem to find any that was dry enough to meet his father's critical eye. Nakosis was beginning to get upset when his father took him onto the riverbank, lifting him up under the boughs of a great tree. He helped him easily snap off some dead twigs. Nakosis was delighted. 'See how many good dry branches there are little one? And the tree shelters them for us too. Always have the wood ready first Nakosis. Start small then add. Don't make a huge pile and then try to light it. Even dead trees should not be wasted', his father told him.

What would father think of me now, thought Nakosis as he huddled against the approach of another bitter cold night in this strange and mysterious landscape. His tiny fire would provide little warmth but much comfort for a young man alone on this journey. His fire now crackling, he placed a tiny pinch of the offering plant from his shoulder satchel into the glowing embers and whispered 'thanks' to Aan'ga, spirit of all fire. He arranged a few branches and what sticks he could find as a bit of a windbreak then pulling off a small piece of the rabbit meat he prepared to meet the dark.

He recalled his father's words again, 'It is tempting for a man to want to look into the fire, Nakosis, for there one can sometimes see many things that are a mirror to your deeper self. But when you are alone you must also keep an eye to the dark of the woods at your back.'

'Why is that father?'

'Once when I was a young man,' his father began, 'my older brother, Mangas, went hunting alone. He had been on the trail of game for a full day and had not had success. Not wanting to return empty-handed, he tracked some deer deep into the mountains of the white mist. He had made camp this night in a small clearing high up on the mountain in heavy woods. He had made a sleeping cover of branches and boughs and had made a nice warm fire. Mangas had too many things on his mind and was not being as alert as one should at such times. Whatever you do, Nakosis, you should do with all your being! Mangas was lost in the thoughts that should have been left in the village and he sat staring into the fire. He still wore his heavy robe and his hunting satchel over his shoulder. He thought he heard a slight sound or perhaps some spirit was yet with him and watching out for him. He rose and turned toward the forest just as a great mountain cat leapt at him from the dark. Mangas screamed as the great cat knocked him into the fire and he rolled still screaming on the ground trying to put out the flames. The cat disappeared into the dark at the edge of the clearing. The great cat had not cut him but his heavy robe was now burned so badly it was useless to him. He had no other to keep the cold away and the weather was getting worse. His hunting satchel with his food, knife and fire drill were lost to the flames. Mangas spent the night piling wood on the fire lest the great cat should return and trying to fend away the bitter cold. In the morning he was forced to head home quickly as bad weather was fast moving down upon him, as is the way of the mountain. In the thick cold mist Mangas lost his direction for two days with no food or fire for warmth or protection. Another hunting party found him not far from the village near the Quick Water River just as the rain was becoming snow and they made fire and warmed him and gave him food. He survived, Nakosis, but it nearly cost him his life.'

With a sense of urgency Nakosis built up his tiny fire. His back against the rock he could now face the fire and would make his sleeping place between the two. Taking his pack off his back and the small bag off his shoulder he laid them beside him and placing his spear in reach he relaxed somewhat. If any great cat or other creature comes for me tonight, Nakosis thought aloud, at least it will have to go through this little fire. The thought of just how ridiculous a defense this really was caused him to chuckle. He thought of the tracks of just such a great cat in whose steps he now tread.

"Thank you, Mangus," he said aloud, partly in the belief that the spirit of Mangus would be pleased and see fit to help or guide him and partly just to hear a human voice – even if it was his own. As he too became lost in the enchanting world of the dancing flames he thought again of the strange and magical portents that appeared in the dark night skies above his village and the long chain of events that ultimately led to his being on this lone and fearful journey.

CHAPTER 1
NAKOSIS

It was during the winter of the popping trees, in the time of the moon's hiding, when the skylights are at their brightest that the first sign appeared. A young boy gave the first cry deep in the night when he left his robes to relieve himself. The whole village awoke at a start fearing some enemy had descended upon them in the darkness. Men ran from their lodges only half dressed, weapons in hand. As families gathered in the crisp air the boy needed only to look skyward for all gathered to see the great and frightening sign. A light, as had never been seen in all the people's memory was now journeying overhead across the blackness. Even the greatest of the skylights paled in comparison to this apparition. No one could speak for a moment and Loka, the village Shaman, shouted out to it asking what sort of spirit it was and what it wanted of them, but it did not answer.

The people wrapped their big sleeping robes about them and spent the entire rest of the night watching the fire in the night sky as it moved over the village, journeying to where no one, not even Loka, could say. The sky-fire vanished in the light of the morning, never to reappear. It was on this night, just before the great sky-fire left that Nakosis was born. Loka said at the time that this held great meaning, not just for the village, but for all the people, even the animal brothers and sisters, the rocks, the trees and rivers.

"All of what was known would one day be changed by this," he said, but how or when he would not tell. "In time" was all he'd reply when asked and all knew not to push Loka for an answer. It was understood that he listened to many different spirits and moved in different time and his words were to be respected.

The second sign appeared when Nakosis was fifteen summers of age. At his grandfather's beckoning, he had taken the bark container down to the river to fetch water. He did not know why or what moved him, but he suddenly found himself walking away from the village over the many dead trees piled up at the rivers edge, leaving the bark bucket in the gravel of the riverbank. Nakosis recalled later that it was as if he were dreaming, but awake, and unable to resist the urge that moved his body forward. As he crawled up and over a large dead tree he found himself staring, unblinking into the deep yellow eyes of a great mountain cat. The powerful animal froze and although Nakosis said later he was worried it would certainly kill him right then and there, still, he did not, could not move and all fear left as suddenly as it had risen and the great panther and he locked gaze with each other for what seemed like an eternity. Then just as quickly it was gone. The cat backed away, slowly at first, never removing its eyes from Nakosis, then turning it vanished into the dense forest like smoke into a fog. It was only when Nakosis heard a cry that he regained his senses and looked to see Taku, a young village woman, standing in shock at the edge of the clearing. She was returning from gathering sweet fruit when she happened upon the scene of Nakosis and the great cat and froze in terror, unable to move just as the two of them broke their stare and the panther vanished. When the two came running into the village with Taku yelling out, many men ran out to them scanning the surroundings for what surely must have been eminent danger. As Taku began revealing the story, the entire village expressed their relief that Nakosis came to no harm from the great beast - all except Loka. He stared at Nakosis in much the same curious way that the great cat had done but said nothing.

The next day, as Nakosis was helping Grandmother with reed bundles for her basket making, Peeka, Lokas' young niece, appeared in the doorway and shyly indicated that Nakosis was to follow her. Loka, she said, had beckoned! He followed the young girl through the village, past the curious eyes of the other young people, to where the Shaman made his lodge, in a clearing some distance from the lodges of the people. He wondered what the old Shaman could want with him.

Nakosis had lost both his parents to the wasting sickness that ravaged the villages of the Three Valley clans during his tenth year. Grandfather and Grandmother took over his rearing and to a large degree Loka stepped up and seemed to take a renewed interest in the young boy. Around the evening fire, his grandparents would often regale him with the legends, stories and myths of the people. He would listen over and over again never tiring to the tales of heroes, demons and spirits and of the ancestor's great exodus from some far off distant land; it's whereabouts lost to time. But it was Loka who would often seem to turn up at times when Nakosis was sitting alone, distracted, watching the passing course of the river or looking into the flames of grandmother's cooking fire and Loka would elaborate on the stories in ways his grandparents did not. He would tell him, for example,

"There were levels to each story and that to most people they were merely tales to entertain and pass away the long dark of the winter nights. But, they are like the sweet fruit of the low mountains – there was a greater richness beneath the outer layer. Every story has a deeper meaning, Nakosis," he said. "When we talk of the power of our animal brothers and sisters it is understood that each in their own way possesses a strength and a wisdom unique to them. But deeper is the spirit that each animal represents. And this is their true power Nakosis. The same is so with every one of the people also. When elders tell stories of how the ancestors spoke in the same tongue with the animals, it was the spirit of the people listening to the spirit of the animals. This is not just a story. It was the way things really were and for a very few it still is today. Some of us have been chosen to see and hear into the world of the spirits, this is why I am a Shaman. It is not just that I know the magic of the plant world that at times can help heal sickness, but I know that everything is as one – everything in all the worlds – people worlds, plant worlds, rock worlds, animal worlds and even the spirit worlds are joined Nakosis. To be a Shaman is to know this connection and to dwell in it at all times, even when doing the simplest thing in the world of people. At times, such as when the great sickness came, the Shaman must make the journey into the spirit world and there seek a certain guide and bring back a special power to help the people. Also, when in the everyday world of the people it is easy to remain stuck. The greatest challenge is to try to remain between the worlds, or more correctly, equally of the worlds at all times. That is why I must make my dwelling removed from the rest of the people, so that I can 'hear' the other worlds when spirit chooses to talk to me."

Loka opened wide the tiny door of his simple dwelling, letting in the fresh air. Nakosis was silently relieved as the dank odor of various plants hanging everywhere and pungent smoke were becoming overpowering. Other than a small smoke hole in the roof, the door was the only opening in the dark and cluttered hut. In the faint light he could discern a vast array of seemingly wondrous items used in Loka's magic. Drums and rattles of different sizes and adorned with patterns as old as the people themselves, whistles of bone and many fans of feathers, hide and bark packages tied with lacing and adorned with talismans of antler, precious stones and bone.

"Nakosis!" Loka called loudly, obviously disappointed at the boy's distraction.

"Sorry Uncle." Nakosis replied, using the title not as a relation, but in the respectful way that all younger people addressed elder village men. Loka nodded to the folded hides across the fire and Nakosis obeying, took a seat.

Loka spoke, "The great portent of the sky-fire marked your birth night Nakosis. This we all know and the coming of the sky-fire has become one of the many popular stories of the people. No one knew what it meant or what message it had for our people. I have always known that the sky-fire meant something very important to our village, but even I was not sure of just when the spirits would reveal it's mystery to me, until now, Nakosis. When I spoke of the animal spirit I was thinking about the great panther that appeared to you yesterday by the river. This was not just some great cat like all other of the great mountain cats. I believe, Nakosis, you understand what I am saying. I believe you also felt the presence of a powerful spirit when you looked into the face of that panther, the moment you knew not to fear it. Tell me, Nakosis, at that very moment, what did you see, hear or feel?"

"It was just...well... like a deep silence Uncle. I can't really explain. It is hard to find the words," sputtered Nakosis.

Loka reached behind him and brought a small bundle of sweet smelling smudge leaves to the coals of the smoldering fire. As the fragrant smoke rose he raised a feather fan and began softly directing the smoke over Nakosis and around the hut. Under his breath, almost inaudibly, he muttered soft words, sacred words. He told Nakosis to breathe and to close his eyes and once again to be at the river and to recall the moment. The smoke swirled about them and became as one again and rose out of the roof toward the sky. Somewhere in the trees above them, Raven called. Nakosis felt heavy at first like he was settling into the very earth of the hut's floor. He could hear only the now distant sounding chanting of the old Shaman, and the cry of Raven as though it was echoing off a high canyon wall. Loka had picked up a small drum and began a soft steady tap, tap, tap. Everything seemed to Nakosis to slowly become in time with the rhythm of the drum. The cry of Raven, the half muttered sacred speech, the cracking of the wood in the fire and even the beating of his own heart and his very breath were now also the drum. He knew Loka was speaking to him, telling him something but it no longer mattered. It was as though he understood without needing words, as though words made no sense and were left behind.

Once again Nakosis was climbing over the logs at the river's edge, but it was also as though he was an observer of his actions from within himself. When he met the eyes of the panther all fear vanished. The external world faded. The river became silent; the trees ceased their movement in the wind and light dissolved around him. There was only the yellow deepness of the great cat's eyes. It was sheer beauty, bliss and wonder. These eyes too dissolved like ice in a fire and only a vast glowing yellow expanse remained. Soon a scene appeared before Nakosis, a foreboding and unfamiliar scene of ice and snow and the blue, blackness of a cold winter night. Then faces of strange people speaking to him in a place now different, warmer, and with

10

rocky ground the color of the setting sun. Then once again very suddenly the great cat's face appeared before him. It was not just its eyes, but it's face staring into his and this time it was different. It seemed somehow changed, wilder, primal, and no longer safe. The beast flattened out its ears and a deep growl rose from its throat and Nakosis felt as though he had fallen hard to the floor and awakened as if from a dream. Loka was holding his shoulders and looking into his eyes. Nakosis glanced about him panicked, getting his bearings and piecing together in his mind just where he was and what had happened. Had he fallen asleep in the Shaman's hut?

" I...I... what happened?" Nakosis cried and almost as quickly remembered the Shaman's magic upon him. Loka had a perplexing look, not displeasure but something like a mixture of both satisfaction and concern. Nakosis did not know what to say or how to act. He felt lost.

Loka broke the silence, "Nakosis, do not fear this. You have just had a wondrous experience. The great cat spirit has chosen to speak to you, to show you its power, to bless you with its understanding. This is why you did not have fear yesterday, because you were being chosen to receive a message of great importance."

Nakosis had managed to bring himself up onto the cushion of folded hides from where he'd fallen back onto the huts dirt floor.

"I still don't understand uncle. What is the meaning of what just happened?" Nakosis begged.

Pulling his cushion next to Nakosis and in a caring, parental tone Loka explained. "The panther we all know is a powerful creature. Even the great bears will avoid our hunters and we fear them little. But the great cat makes even our best hunters ever more aware in the forest when they have been sighted, for, if hungry, they have no equal in threat. They are stealthy, fast and silent. They hunt equally as well in day or night. All can agree that there are no hunters among our animal brothers to match them. But the panther's *true* power is its spirit power. The spirit power of the great cat is one of knowing, unveiling of deep spiritual understanding – to know yourself, Nakosis. It is the panther spirit that can show your spirit self to you. It is the panther spirit that can guide you in a quest of the deepest knowing that a Shaman can have. I have been a Shaman for three times your young life and I spent many years learning in secret from Quansa, the old Shaman, and he taught me many great things. I learned how to seek out the portals to the underworld, the sacred places, the holes in the earth that are open to a Shaman, how to descend and seek the guides and recover the talisman and how to safely return, how to ascend upon a rainbow or waterfall or smoke to the upper worlds. Yes, I have learned many wondrous things in my many years with old Quansa. But you Nakosis! You have been chosen by the spirit world! You were taken by the panther spirit to see things from its world that only you were to know and then it returned you safely also. This with only my simplest of help Nakosis. Few Shamans, even ones of great power have this blessing. You are destined for something very important, very great. It now remains for us to see further what it is you are being chosen for, Nakosis. From tomorrow, you will spend your days here with me and we will begin the task of preparing you so you might know your path. We will prepare you for your journey Nakosis. Now, you must tell me everything you saw. Tell me everything - then you must repeat it to no one. Do you understand?"

His mouth open with shock, Nakosis simply nodded. He felt a little embarrassed revealing the feelings he had during his 'dream'. Remembering and repeating things that to him seemed silly and of no consequence, but the old Shaman listened intently to every word, grunting approving sounds, shaking his head. Loka walked Nakosis back through the village to the lodge of his grandparents. He placed his hand on Nakosis' shoulder as they walked and looking at him he smiled and said,

"Soon you will undergo the warrior ceremony, after which you will be known to all in the village as a man, Nakosis. You will not be looked upon as a boy any longer. I know all the young men look forward to joining one of the warrior societies after their ceremony but you will not join a warrior clan. You have a greater calling and at the ceremony when I give my blessing to the rite of passage I will inform the village of my decision and of your different calling. How do you feel about this, Nakosis?"

"So, then I am to become a Shaman, like you uncle? Asked Nakosis.

Loka stopped walking and removing his hand he laughed. "Like me? No, Nakosis. You would find it boring, I think. It would require many years of learning all the plants and sacred words and such and you do not have time, Nakosis. No, you are to be a seeker after wisdom, yes, but your path is already Shaman, already you are partly walking within the spirit world and I cannot say where it will lead you. But you will either become a story to be told around the evening fires - or you will perish! I simply want to help you not to perish!" Loka laughed hard at his words.

Nakosis obediently continued to be tutored at the fireside of the old Shaman. The seasons changed and came and went, each presenting opportunities to embrace the teachings he'd received. The cold dead of winter yielded to the radiance and life of the returning spring. The full blossom of summer then gently turned into fading colors and eventual decay that was autumn and the cycle would begin again, not new different seasons, but a steady progression of energy and power manifesting it's many aspects over and over again. Time began to hold less consequence as Nakosis began to embrace much of what Loka was imparting, preparing him for the great adventure he would soon embark upon.

CHAPTER 2
WHITE MIST VILLAGE

Nakosis watched the dust dancing in the thin shaft of light penetrating the darkness of the tiny hut. The smoldering fire sending tendrils of blue smoke wafting skyward through the blackened roof hole. There was something intoxicating about the fragrant mixture of pitchy wood, smoke tanned hide and the offering smudge of sacred leaves. Loka set the smudge aside and slowly stirred the coals, looking into the renewed flames as though pondering his next words.

"There are many things that cause the people to suffer. There is hunger, bad weather and there is war – but Nakosis, much suffering is the result of not seeing properly. People fail to see behind the cover of the waking world just as you cannot see through the wall of this hut. They are blind to the world of spirit that is about them at all times. They are like a man blind in one eye that only sees half of what is. You, Nakosis, have seen a little of the spirit world and even though our people learn such things from the time of a child, still most people only *see one* reality. They offer thanks to the deer spirit after a kill and make an offering of sacred plant or leave a small possession, but they do so out of fear. Fear of old tales. They have been told that the deer spirit will not present itself to be taken in the hunt if such customs are not followed. Yes, this is true, but how many actually know the deer spirit? How many truly know that just as they have their feet here on mother earth so too they walk in the spirit world everyday? When this forgetting becomes too common among the people, Nakosis, then the people suffer. Hunger comes because the hunter forgets to see spirit in his quarry. Bad weather comes when people forget to see spirit among the mountains and the sky. War comes, Nakosis, because people fail to see spirit among each other. To walk the Shaman's path is to be fully in both worlds at all times. This means to see or to remember always that there are two sides to everything in this world. Everywhere is spirit - every drop of water, every leaf, every bird, fish, animal in the sky and even in the rocks, Nakosis. For now I will help you to learn to see the spirit world separate from that world that you live in each day, but soon you will begin to see this spirit world alive and present all around you and in you at all times. You cannot live separate from one world or another, Nakosis. When people do this they live a life not in balance. This is when they can bring in sickness. Sometimes they deny their own spirit so long that it weakens and another spirit can take them over, or part of their spirit becomes lost and a Shaman must enter the underworld to seek this lost piece and return it to them so the balance can return and sickness has nowhere to reside. These things you must experience. Soon I will take you to the cave on the White Mist Mountain. There you will continue the journey."

As proud as Nakosis was at having become the new object of interest of someone of such standing in the village as wise old Loka, and the looks of approval this brought from the others, he was none-the-less somewhat relieved to be free of the responsibility of learning for a while. He was happy to once again be among the familiar surroundings of his grandparent's lodge and they too were delighted to have him back again. Once again he was gathering fish with his grandfather and once again he would do myriad small chores for grandmother, bringing her wood for her cook fire and for the fish smoking hut and materials for her weaving fine mats and baskets. He went with some of his childhood friends, other young men his age, to hunt and to the arrow rocks. Here, they would quarry pieces of rock on which they would spend much time chipping them into fine arrow and spearheads. Such work was meticulous and time consuming but essential to survival. Those who were adept at it made it seem easy, but Nakosis knew from experience it was a difficult task not easily mastered. His father had been gifted at chipping the hard stone into perfect points.

As a boy Nakosis spent a full day trying to duplicate the precise moves his father demonstrated to him. They sat together, a piece of heavy hide laid across their knees, a hard pointed river rock in one hand and a piece of arrow stone in the other, carefully knocking away at an edge removing tiny crescent chards of arrow stone, each crescent the same length and depth as the last and each point of the crescent touching the point of the previous. Too little pressure and the sharp crescent edge would be too small and when Nakosis tried to make it bigger by pressing just a little harder it would shatter. Once he made the first point that actually resembled an arrowhead he held it proudly for his father's approval and then he tested its edge against his thumb only to slice it wide open. The ease and speed of which left him speechless.

16

His father, seemingly not at all surprised, simply threw him a small piece of hide to wrap it in and continued about his chipping. Nakosis understood the coldness of the gesture and quickly continued with the work. However, when he once again sliced his finger open on another satisfactory point, his father gave him a stern disapproving glance and said, 'Stop acting stupid, boy!'

Nakosis smiled broadly, chuckling softly to himself at the recollection, his happiness mingled with a tinge of sadness at the loss of his father. He and his companions filled their bags with the sharp stones and headed back to the village.

The coming of age ceremony that marked the official recognition of boys and girls into young men and women of the village had taken place. It was a grand occasion for gathering, games, story-telling and feasting. It was at such events that the young men and women sometimes made acknowledgement of their attractions for each other, not in a direct and open display, but as was most often through family members and friends. Then it was customary for these intentions to be shared between the two families, discussed and then, if mutually satisfactory, a period of chaperoned courtship could begin, the young man having to impress his worthiness upon both his potential bride-to-be and perhaps most importantly, upon her parents. Part of the prestige a young man held was his membership among one of the warrior societies. These fraternal orders comprised all fighting age men in the village organizing them into groups depending on the size of the village and the number of warriors. In time of war, these represented fighting factions that could be readily mobilized into battle formations or most often into guerilla units that could strike the enemy from different directions, or at different points in a battle rotating their fighting force to keep up a constant defense or offense. The warrior societies trained regularly and would improve and hone their skills in mock fights between the societies. Each society would elect a leader who would make the critical decisions of battle and the leaders would communicate among each other by runners, signals and the use of loud shrill whistles carved from the bones of birds. The one to win the contests was the reigning society until another took the position by defeating the winning group.

Nakosis' village was one of three villages among his people. They each occupied one of three valleys that comprised the low mountain plateau dominated over by the majestic peaks of the White Mist Mountain. Great rivers ran the course of each valley. Two of them, the Quick Waters River and the Deer River met the third and mighty Blue Fish River, just a day's distance apart from each other. Nakosis' village was close to the confluence of the lower Deer River and the Blue fish river, located on a high and very wide valley in the shadow of the towering White Mist Mountain. Here the three valleys formed the widest flat lands in the entire mountain region lending itself to fertile soils suitable to the growing of many crops. The lush growth was favored by many wildlife and water-foul. It was a bountiful world and so the White Mist people, Nakosis' village, was the largest of the Three Valley people. As such, they boasted three warrior societies. The other villages being smaller had one and two societies respectfully. This meant that each year all three villages would hold a huge contest among the warrior societies to determine who would be the reigning champions. If another village dominated the games it was especially embarrassing for the White Mist Village, given that they had the superior numbers of men and thus the greatest odds at winning. However, Deer River warriors had dominated the games the previous year and, so, the new warriors were especially keen on beginning their training and competing among themselves, lending an air of bravado and competitiveness among the young men. Most of the groups were equally divided as the many village lodges already belonged to one of the societies and so, the sons of these lodges would usually follow their father's societal loyalties.

Nakosis' father had been a member of the Bear society. His father had been a society leader for a time and earned much respect in this capacity. That was during a time of brief but bloody battles with a fierce people from the flat lands who occasionally raided in small but brutal forays into the mountains. These attacks improved the system of warrior societies and the military structure of the three clans and led to the Three Valley Peoples' victories over the flatlanders. The fighting superiority of the Three Valley People was not just due to their ability to mobilize, to fight as a cohesive group and to communicate in battle, but it was their expert use of many weapons, including the deadly stone sling. The enemy warriors had the usual weaponry – bows and arrows, spears, knives and war axes, but had never encountered the power, deadliness, range and accuracy of a well slung stone using the unique rawhide slings yielded by the well trained warriors of Nakosis' people. Using their tactical superiority of occupying the high ground and knowing the terrain, Three Valley warriors rained stones down upon the heads of the enemy with bloody accuracy, shattering skulls and bashing bones like twigs even out of range of the enemy's arrows. Then the retreating, panicked enemy came under a barrage of arrows from hidden warriors of the Quick Water and Deer River villages, their attack signaled by White Mist lookouts on the high rock bluff overlooking the path of enemy retreat. The flatlanders were decimated and the Three Valley People had enjoyed a peaceful life in the low mountain valleys. Many songs were sung and stories told of sacrifice and bravery and were repeated to the present day and regaled at every warrior's gathering.

CHAPTER 3
DREAM

Nakosis had known Taku since childhood, playing and growing together in the shadow of his grandfather's lodge. As they matured over the years their conversations would sometimes become awkward for Nakosis when their eyes would meet and something in his look would betray the deeper feelings he was experiencing. Taku seemed to somehow sense this in Nakosis no matter how he tried to conceal his thoughts and the two would shyly look away, Taku appearing slightly uncomfortable, yet attempting to hide her smile. Nakosis simply felt embarrassed at such times, thinking she may just be silently laughing at his obvious awkwardness around her. He would quickly excuse himself or begin talking to one of the other boys. Ever since Taku saw him with the panther and walked back with him to the village that eventful day, Nakosis felt differently about her. He no longer felt the old childhood embarrassment around her. Something deepened between them in that moment by the river. He had shared a momentous life changing experience with someone he held in deep regard and the bond was now ever stronger. He had so hoped to express these feelings, perhaps to his grandfather, at the warrior's ceremony and perhaps win favor to court Taku, but Loka, as he had promised, when overseeing the rites of the ceremony, announced to all present that Nakosis was henceforth to walk a different path than the men of the warrior societies.

For Nakosis, it had been an emotionally long and hard day. He wore a stern face as he thought of what was expected of him, seeming to onlookers at least, to be comfortable and accepting of the role fate had assigned him. Not being a member of one of the village societies was not especially upsetting, in that it did not exclude him from battle should the situation arise. In fact, everyone in the village able to fight would do so. The women of the Three Valley Clans were also very proficient in hunting and defending. Many were especially skilled in the use of the bow and the sling. No, it was not this that wore heavy on Nakosis' mind; it was the possibility that he would not be able to pursue the courting of Taku. He hadn't even bothered to make mention of his intentions to grandfather or grandmother as he still didn't know exactly what Loka even really meant by 'a different path'. Would he still be able to live a life as others and perhaps take a wife? These heavy thoughts and the festivities of the day played out in his mind as he pulled the heavy sleeping robe over his shoulders, looking deeply into the coals of the dying fire, drifting into troubled sleep.

The sacred words of the ancient song repeated over again and again, the rhythm of the old man's drum beating out a cadence to the muffled words. Swirls of dark tones, black and gray, formed a backdrop for a tiny smoky fire that threw very little light. It was a small room and a slight draft of cold air entered from somewhere creeping across the dirt of the floor like a slow serpent. Hushed tones came and went, their location indiscernible like distant animal calls on a fog filled night. The fire slowly began to glow with a renewed brightness. Perhaps the cold draft was fanning it, thought Nakosis. Tiny sparks started to rise, randomly at first but now began to appear to have form and pattern to the movement. From the fires glowing coals they would lift, spiraling around and up into the blackness above, as dust will sometimes do on a hot summer breeze. The sounds grew in volume with the pulsating swirl of the fiery sparks. A Raven's rough cry, three times, easily heard now above the soft drumming. As Nakosis looked into the fire, the tiny spiraling sparks now steadily swirling upward began to resemble the shape of someone dancing. Sparks radiated outward but not as from a campfire, much slower as though still attached to the fire from which they came. They looked to Nakosis a little like the feathered headdress of the bird dancers. Bobbing back and forth as the flaming figure began to form ever more vivid among the rising smoke of the fire. Was it holding something, a weapon perhaps? No, thought Nakosis, it was smaller, more like a stick or an arrow. The swirling figure of flame and spark now formed limbs that were quite visible. Yes, someone dancing in the fire. Was this Aan'ga, the fire spirit himself, come to reveal himself to Nakosis? As the dancing apparition brightened, Nakosis could now easily discern the flaming flute it held to its mouth and a haunting melody filed the dark chamber that was at once immediately calming and at the same time beckoning. Nakosis wanted to join the figure in its fiery celebration but found it hard to move his limbs. He struggled to raise himself but as soon as he lifted his body from the heavy robes it was as though he had no weight whatsoever - like a feather he rose to full height and then higher so that he was now looking slightly down at the mysterious fiery being. The flute never moved from its mouth and although it didn't seem to be playing it as a normal person would, the enchanting melody continued to fill him as though it was everywhere with no one source, even from within Nakosis himself. The flute spirit, for now Nakosis had no doubt it was a spirit, swirled and turned and his fiery yellow eyes focused on Nakosis. Powerless to turn away, Nakosis watched bewildered as the familiar golden glow of the mighty cat's eyes again formed on the face of the spirit and as the blackness closed in from all around only the golden glow remained and the flute, the muffled words and the drumming faded from the scene. Only those piercing yellow eyes remained and Nakosis began slowly falling back to the floor he thought, but it was more. He felt smaller, much smaller and was falling, but not so much down as backwards - into himself, was the only way he could think of describing the sensation. Like going into a deep hole and the light rapidly disappearing all around as you fall further down.

There was a slight pain suddenly in his ribs and then again and again still. He opened his eyes and a dim light returned to illuminate his waking world. He lay on the floor of his grandparent's lodge next to the coals of a dying fire. The silhouetted figure of Loka loomed over him, easily discernable in the pre-dawn light. He was holding his walking spear and had been lightly kicking Nakosis awake with his hide-covered foot. Loka, not speaking, simply turned for the doorway. Outside Nakosis, still wrapping the warm robe around him, looked questioningly at the old Shaman who curtly barked,

"It is time we left. Grab your things and hurry. Soon it will be light and we've a distance to go today."

CHAPTER 4
LOKA'S STORY

He daren't question the old man further, so Nakosis tried to pack his large bag for any contingency, hoping his doing so would thwart any rebuke from Loka for not being prepared later on. He packed quietly not wanting to awaken his sleeping grandparents, checking off in his mind the many items he squeezed into the heavy hide sack. A satchel containing the most important survival tools would hang over his neck after he had shouldered the heavier bag. Then picking up his walking spear he ducked under the door into the damp mist of the 'magic time'.

This is what Loka called this period that is neither day nor night. It was the time when night beings were returning to their lairs and the day beings waking from theirs. Loka instructed, the spirit world also is more open to a Shaman's respectful curiosity at this time.

Nakosis raised his head as he exited the lodge fully expecting to see the old man standing there as he had been only moments ago, but he was nowhere to be seen. Quickly, Nakosis gave his head a shake trying to remove the foggy residue of the night's dreaming and willed his feet to take him at run to the old man's hut.

When he arrived the first light of day was just appearing on the horizon and Loka was barking commands at young Peeka, who stood shakily in the cold morning air, trying to rub the sleepiness from her eyes and catch the commands Loka was giving her regarding the tending of his herbs and the loading of certain objects into the large bag and the small shoulder satchel. At first he was so consumed with the minute details, inspecting every item, that he seemed to not even notice Nakosis, what to speak of offering some explanation as to just where they were off to and what route they would be travelling, or for that matter for how long he could expect to be gone. It bothered Nakosis immensely at times to be treated with such indifference by the old man, but he knew to be respectful and that in time the old Shaman would confide in him. Later, he thought that perhaps it was Peeka to whom he didn't wish to be so open or reveal too much of his plan. Even if this was not the case, the thought made Nakosis feel somewhat relieved that he was perhaps somehow special, sharing a secret world with Loka.

They hurried out of the village, the noise of the village dogs and waking families fading into the song of forest birds and the gentle babble of the mountain stream.

"So uncle, to where do we travel?" asked Nakosis, believing the last moments of silent walking enough to begin his inquiry.

Loka stopped dead in his tracks so abruptly that Nakosis, under the momentum of the heavy pack, actually walked into him.

"Boy," said Loka "do you have no memory for the things I say? Did I not tell you we would go to the cave of White Mist Mountain?"

"Oh, but, of course uncle, it's just...that... well...I thought maybe we were going somewhere else for right now and that ah...maybe we'd be going there later on. I thought I'd have more time to ...um... see...others," Nakosis stammered then quickly added, "I mean see my grandparents."

"Are you sure you don't mean see Taku?" smiled Loka.

Nakosis could not answer but felt he must be blushing.

"I may be just an old Shaman, Nakosis, but I am still a man!" Loka laughed. "I have long watched the way you and Taku looked at each other – the longing in your eyes. Surely you don't think that no one knew?"

Nakosis was dumbfounded. He could not stop his jaw from dropping at this sudden revelation. Loka turned and resumed walking.

Without looking back he added, "The whole village knows, Nakosis!"

Strangely, Nakosis felt relief and a sense of empowerment at this revelation. It was, in a way, a sort of affirmation of his now being a man among his people, he thought. Somehow his decision to leave the village and Taku behind to accompany old Loka seemed to be not so final, nor to fill him with melancholy as it did before. With a renewed sense of optimism he hefted the big bag higher on his broad shoulders and with a fresh lightness to his step they walked silently along an old deer path climbing steadily alongside the clear mountain stream toward the mist of the peaks looming above them.

The two had been walking for most of the morning. Loka seemed a changed man amid the splendor of these mountains and commented many times to Nakosis on the beauty that surrounded them, proudly pointing out the majestic views that greeted them at every new bend in the winding narrow trail. Nakosis was quite amazed at the old man's stamina. There were many men as old and older than Loka in the village. Grandfather was about Loka's age and although a good hunter and provider and still very active, Nakosis couldn't picture him journeying up the mountain with such childlike abandon as Loka now seemed to possess. The old Shaman seemed much more personal now too, talking openly about many different things not related to the spirit world. The casual conversation was a welcome departure to young Nakosis and it helped to strengthen his connection with the man. The teacher can also be a friend, Nakosis thought. Loka enlightened him with the story of his life. Nakosis had dearly wanted to ask this of the old man and now without any beseeching or begging he heard the Shaman's story.

He told of his childhood, how he came to be under the tutelage of the great Shaman, Quansa, chosen by him much in the way Nakosis had been chosen, but at a much earlier age. He told of when he was a young man of Nakosis' age. In that time he said Three Valley people were one large village before coming to the lush valleys of the White Mist Mountains. In those days, Loka said, we hunted more in the flatlands and we made our village in the benches of the low foothills overlooking the great wide expanse of plains below. Hunting parties also ventured higher up into the forests near White Mist Mountain but the terrain was very hard going. It was not until one group of hunters discovered the narrow canyon near where the arrow stone is that we found a way through and into Three Rivers Valley. No one would have guessed that this world existed beyond the steep rock and thick bush of the high foothills. This is also why we are safe here. The narrow canyon is the easiest way into the valley and easily defended and our lookouts there can see anyone for a great distance. But when the flatland people raided, it was through this little pass. Our people had encountered few others when we hunted the great beasts of the plains and brought much meat and thick hides back through the pass. We thought we were alone, safe, and didn't have lookouts at the far end of the canyon. A few younger men were camped at this end of the canyon by the arrow rocks when they first saw the enemy. They ran like the wind and still barely had time to alert the village. You know the story of the battle and how since then we always place lookouts at the entrance to the canyon. The last time the flatlanders tried to attack us, a raiding party snuck up the hills under the cover of the bush and trees. They were very good and hid themselves well but our brother Raven saw them and the lookouts heard their warning cries. Raven yelled like he does when the hawk comes and he swooped down near to where the enemy was hiding and the lookouts saw them but kept themselves concealed. We now had the runners between the two ends of the canyon and the village and so the warning was given and our warriors went out to trap the enemy. Our main fighters hid among the high rock and a small group took the narrow trail over the arrow stones and down the long winding way to come behind the enemy. Just when they entered the tiny opening to the canyon our warriors let out a cry and attacked them from cover with arrows, slings and spears. They fell like ducks on the water and when they tried to get back through the small opening our other fighters were waiting for them there also and easily cut them down.

"It was not an easy time for our people, Nakosis - the enemy, seeing their deaths, fought like cornered bears!" The retelling of this seemed to deeply sadden the old man.

"But," Nakosis broke in, "Didn't we defeat all the enemy and become better and stronger warriors ourselves? No one dare attack our people now!" he boasted proudly.

"Perhaps you are right, I certainly hope so, Nakosis. You have been spared the bloodshed of that time and do not know what it means to see such things. Many young men like to boast of the number of enemy they will kill, the heroic feats they will perform on the field of battle, the women who will swoon at tales of their bravery. We encourage such behavior because we know that young men will need to have their bravery strengthened and encouraged should they really have to do battle. But, Nakosis, they don't realize the truly terrible thing they may do in taking the life of another human being. In such boasting, in the frenzy that comes with the dance before the battle and in battle itself some men become like crazed things, detached from their spirit and in such a state, Nakosis, a man may become forever lost. I was your age when the attack came and I also had to run and defend the village at arrow rocks. I too did my part and fired my bow at the enemy and when it was finished we went among the injured and killed them all. Quansa was there in the thick of the fighting and I stayed close by him, partly feeling safer near him as I believed his spirit power would keep him from harm, but also I felt an obligation to defend him should I have to. His bravery and skill was a match for any of our best warriors. We took the bodies of the dead to the tiny cave we now all know of as the enemy grave. Really it was just a crevice in the rock just deep enough to put the bodies in. We covered them well with ash and piled dirt and rock on them and closed the crevice with stones in such a way as to conceal it should others come looking. There was a great celebration and it took many days for some of the younger men to loose the fever of battle. Some, I think, never quite loose this once it takes them. These people become changed by war. They are the ones who speak of raiding and fighting and must have the voice of reason from the elders and myself always in their ear to remind them they are still human beings. For such people we must ask the spirits for help to keep them on a sane path. We have always been a peaceful people and so the ways of the spirit world, of the connection to our spirit guides has always been very strong; but when people become warlike their sprit lessens somehow and they become less a human being. Some believe that such people become open to other spirits, bad spirits. Some whole peoples become this way. Among some of the flatland people I am told there are whole clans who live only for warring. They teach their young ones in such ways and so there is war for these people from one generation to the next. It becomes there way and hard for them to know the peace that our people have."

Nakosis thought well on the old man's words. By now he had learned to respect Loka's teaching of thinking before speaking out loud. When he tired of hearing useless questions designed merely to maintain a conversation Loka had said, 'Speak it in your head first and make sure what you say has meaning Nakosis. Then you will say what you mean and mean what you say.'

They stopped by a pool where the creek cascaded over mossy rocks under the shade of many small leafy bushes thick with red berries. The old Shaman dropped his bag to the mossy ground with a sigh of relief and arched his back raising his arms skyward. Nakosis, wanting to be sure Loka knew he as paying attention, did the same. As he stood there, arms reaching for the sky, duplicating Loka's exact positioning he looked intently at the old man waiting for the appropriate words of prayer, invocation or gratitude to the spirits. Loka glanced over at Nakosis and realizing what was happening said with poorly suppressed laughter,

"I'm only stretching boy! I hope you don't think every time I fart that it is a calling to the spirits?" Loka couldn't contain his laughter and Nakosis joined him until tears ran down his cheeks.

"If that were true," said Nakosis, "then our lodge would be filled to the roof with spirits – you have eaten Grandmother's root stew?"

Their laughter echoed off the forest and Nakosis began feeling much more comfortable with his mentor. They filled their cupped hands with the rich berries, each taking up a position on the large flat rock. For a while Loka simply stared into the clear moving water of the pool, popping berries into his mouth. Then, shifting he turned to Nakosis and resumed the conversation.

"You see that spider's web Nakosis?" he said, pointing with a stick to the perfect orb web in the twigs of a nearby bush. "That is like the spirit world. It is also like our waking world, every strand of the web is like every being, every animal, every plant and rock."

"And every person too." Nakosis blurted out, wanting Loka to know he remembered the earlier metaphor.

"Yes, quite right, everything is connected to everything else. It is not possible to say where it begins or where it ends. If you remove one or two strands of the web it is no longer perfect. It is no longer as strong. Our people know this and remember this when we harvest berries," Loka said, pointing now at the abundance around them. "We know not to pick every berry from the bush or collect every seed from a plant or it may die and there will be no more to harvest. We also know to leave enough for our animal brothers and sisters."

"But," Nakosis again interrupted, "mustn't we make sure we have an abundant harvest and have prepared enough dried food to feed us over the seasons until these things will grow again?"

"Yes, of course," said Loka, "but not more that we need! We must have respect for the other animals and for the plants also and this, Nakosis, comes from seeing spirit in all these things. We pray to the spirit of the deer before a hunt and we pray to the spirit of the plant when we grow and when we harvest them. This shows to them that we have respect and their spirit blesses us with plenty. This needn't be something done with grand ceremony. There are reasons for ceremonies and there are right times for such things, but in this case it is not good to make a show. It is something that is done out of deep respect and it is your intention to show that respect that you convey to the spirit. This you can do even without speaking it. Spirit does not need words to hear your intention. There are some Shamans who, it is said, live most of their lives without speaking to another human being. They dwell deeply within the spirit world and only speak a spirit tongue when necessary, such as when healing a sick person."

Loka popped the last of his handful of berries into his mouth and reaching down scooped up some cool water from the pool.

Nakosis took advantage of the pause to ask, "Uncle, I understand that spirit dwells in everything and that everything is connected and that we are to have respect for this, but then what of the enemy, such as these flatlanders who attacked our people? How can we kill them and yet have respect for them also?"

Loka looked at Nakosis, staring deeply into his eyes. He had a way of doing so that always made Nakosis feel uneasy and he'd turn away.

"Ahhh, a good question." He finally replied, "When the fight with these people took place at arrow rock canyon, as we described, we were defending our homes and our families. They came dressed to do battle, to kill us and perhaps to make slaves of our women and children as we have heard that this is the way of some peoples. We defeated them, yes. And when we sing the songs of our victory have you not noticed that we sing praise of our enemy also? How strong their warriors were."

"Yes, Uncle I have heard these songs, but once I heard my father say that sometimes these praises are sung of how strong an enemy was so as to make our warriors appear even stronger?"

Nakosis had never voiced these thoughts before. It was considered improper among the people to repeat words overheard between others or in confidence from another, especially a family member who was an honored warrior. He looked down at the pool embarrassed that he had spoken so openly. But Loka, seemed little bothered by any improprieties the question may have had.

"Yes, this is very true. It is one purpose of these songs and praise to keep the people trusting in the protection their warriors give to the village and to give the other warriors stories and examples of great bravery to look up to. But it also honors the spirit of the enemy, as they too are part of the greater web of all life, Nakosis. Do we not do the same for animals we hunt? So then why not honor the spirit of another human being even if we must kill them in defense? Let me tell you something that people do not know about that day."

Nakosis felt tremendous honor at being the confidant of any secret, spiritual or otherwise that Loka deemed him worthy to hear. He moved closer to him and Loka leaned in and continued,

"When the victory celebration was at it's fullest and our warriors were dancing and the whole village celebrated their good fortune at defeating the flatlanders, Quansa came to me. He was not joining in the celebration. I think the others believed that it was his way as Shaman to be somewhat apart, but I knew he was greatly troubled. He had been so ever since the battle and anyone who witnessed his fighting prowess and his bravery that day knew, as I did, that it was not fear, nor the after-battle type of trembling that settles in on many warriors. No, it was something else and even though I had not much knowledge of the spirit world then I knew things were troubling him. He took me away from the rest and he said that we had to go to the grave of the enemy warriors and that we needed to give rest to the spirits of these people and to help them on their way. He was so concerned that I dare not question him and so we gathered his sacred drum, rattle and other things and far from the people we descended into the small canyon to where the bodies of the enemy were hidden among the rocks. It was dark and a small moon lit the way. It was hard seeing down the trail and once we were on the ground of the canyon floor it was quite dark. The moon only lit one wall across from us and not all the way down so I had to walk behind Quansa as we groped along. There was a very strong power there and even I felt it and I can tell you, Nakosis, it gave me more fear than I felt in the battle."

Nakosis hung to every word. This was not like the stories told around winter fires to amuse the young. This was real. This was his mentor speaking, confiding of the spirit world and Nakosis realized at that moment that there was a very real and potentially dangerous realm into which he too was to journey and this made him share the fear Loka described in that long ago moment.

"When we rounded the rocks to where the canyon widens," Loka continued, "and the scene of battle, Quansa stopped. He reached for his bag and he told me to start a fire. I made fire as quickly as I could, as I was foolishly hoping the fire would ward off spirits as it does animals. Once a tiny fire was burning Quansa lit the tightly wrapped bundle of sacred herbs. He looked up the canyon walls and made offerings to the four directions, to the moonlit sky and to the blood soaked earth beneath our feet. He removed his ancient rattle and this and his drum he bathed in the sacred smoke. Slowly he began shaking his rattle, not back and forth as when in a singing way, but more in a front way as though throwing something away with it like this." Loka jerked his hand as though shaking water from them. "He spoke the old words to call on father sky and mother earth and the guardians of the directions to be present to protect us and to help us in our task. He then spoke to the spirits of the assembled warriors, of the enemy whose bodies were only a short distance from where we stood. As he did this, Nakosis, I don't mind telling you I felt cold, even though the fire was now growing well and this made me even more fearful. I knew, of course, that Quansa was a powerful Shaman and I had faith that he was up to any task. Still there was some fear with me. He threw more of the sacred herb into the flames and also seeds from his pouch mixed with a powder that made bright blue flames jump high above the fire. All this time he instructed me to beat my drum as he'd shown me. It was this task to which I turned all my focus and concentrated so as to not let my fear take me. This seemed to help me a lot. He directed the rattle all around us, all around the scene of carnage calling upon the spirits of those killed and then he directed it toward the crevice into which we'd put the bodies of the slain, calling forth with each direction of the rattle. At first I thought the fire had shot embers into the cold night air and they were now falling down, but I soon realized that I was seeing lights Nakosis! They were small and not very bright. They floated above the ground around the canyon moving ever so slowly back and forth slightly. Soon there were more of them, glowing a little brighter, some white and some a little blue, like the night sky fires but smaller. I could see them plainly and they were moving closer to Quansa and started to circle around him. There was a sound somewhat like many voices whispering in a wind. I knew that these must be the spirits of the dead. I kept tapping softly on the drum, chanting the words and I could not look away, although I felt great fear at that moment. The spirits began to swirl around Quansa as he also was turning to all directions, calling to them to come. A great owl suddenly appeared in the glow of the firelight, swooping down from the darkness and over Quansa as he shook the rattle toward the end of the canyon. In the faint moon glow I watched it glide silently through the scene and the lights began moving behind it like the soft down of reeds on a fall breeze. Down the small canyon the spirit lights flew, through the tiny pass and into the night sky they vanished. Quansa's arms dropped by his side as though they had been lifting a great weight and his shoulders fell while he let go a heavy sigh as he turned to face me. In the light of the fire I could see he was exhausted more than when he fought with the enemy. I stopped drumming and he motioned to me to remain silent. He once again faced the six directions, giving thanks and sprinkling the smoke offering plant in gratitude, then, without words he packed his sacred items into the bag and I sent an offering of sacred herb into the flames to Aan'ga for his help and we left that place. As we returned, climbing up the steep trail among the rocks of the canyon wall I could hear only our bare feet on the loose rocks and Quansa's strained breath. We rested at the top, standing in the moonlight, looking down on the canyon, and Quansa finally spoke.

'You did well this night, Loka,' he said to me, 'we have done what needed to be done. Now the spirits of these dead warriors will have peace even if we do not have it with the flatlanders themselves.'

"I had been with Quansa for a while and had witnessed him heal the sick, sucking the disease from a person's body and bringing rain to dry crops but until that night, there in the canyon, I had some doubt about the world of spirit, Nakosis. But in that moment, when the spirits swirled about him, I knew that if I was somehow worthy to understand this world then I would gladly make it my life."

CHAPTER 5
THE CAVE

Loka hefted the big bag up on his shoulders and picking up his walking spear he nodded toward the sun, indicating they should again start walking. Nakosis felt greatly honored by Loka's willingness to share the most poignant and spiritually pivotal moments of his life. He knew he must think deeply on these things before again speaking. He had much to ponder as they walked higher into the forested mountain. It was well past midday and they had not spoken since stopping at the pool. Nakosis was now walking ahead of Loka, following the path. Just ahead a huge rock shadowed the trail. It appeared like a giant slice of the mountain had broken off and dropped to rest. It sloped abruptly from alongside the now diminutive path to twice a man's height above where they stood.

Loka said suddenly, "We're here!"

Nakosis looked about eager to see what surely must be a wondrous place, but he could see nothing that seemed extraordinary. It must be concealed, Nakosis thought. Loka simply stood at the bottom of the large rise of rock smiling childlike at Nakosis. He is no doubt waiting to see if I can discover the secret location, Nakosis thought, as he rushed on ahead and bending low he peered into the blackness of the rocky overhang, fully expecting to find a cave extending into the mountain sheltered by the ledge of rock above, but the rock met the ground of the trail with no opening of any kind. Simple dirt greeted his inquisitive search. He spun back around to find Loka gone from where he had stood on the path only a moment ago. A movement drew his eyes up to find Loka walking, almost climbing, up the sloping side of the huge boulder.

"Where are you going? This way!" he yelled, as Nakosis, feeling the fool, scrambled up the rock after the old man.

At the top they brushed past a few small shrubs and gradually a tiny path emerged from the undergrowth and continued up along the mountainside rising gradually higher, up and away from the diminishing game trail they had been following below. No one would ever find this place, he thought, adjusting the big bag higher on his shoulders as the trail steepened. Soon they emerged from the trees beside a small pond where a spring or a series of springs sprouted from the earth and made their way down the mountain to become part of the many creeks that eventually combined to feed the big river now such a great distance below them. They came upon a wide and thickly forested bench. Their path took them through the middle of this bench then turned toward the mountain to emerge in a clearing. As they approached, a hut came into view nestled up against one of the large red-bark trees, its green flat boughs forming a protective canopy over the little dwelling. It resembled very much the Shaman's lodge back in the village. It couldn't have been more that three people's lengths wide and just as deep. Loka dropped his bag, satchel and walking spear on the ground beside a small rock-ringed fire pit with a sigh and air of finality.

"Ahhhh," he sighed as he began a short routine of stretching.

As Nakosis likewise unburdened himself of the heavy load, he took in everything in the small clearing. There was no cave to be seen, only the hut, the trees, the spring and the rock wall of the mountain behind them. Loka began moving the cargo into the shack. He dipped his head toward the fire pit, beckoning Nakosis to start a fire.

As the first small flames appeared, Loka emerged from the hut to stand across the fire from Nakosis, who was still kneeling tending the kindling and blowing into the coals. When he looked up, Loka was smiling at him in his strange childlike way, his hands on his hips. Saying nothing Loka reached into the fire and retrieving the best burning stick, he walked toward the back of the clearing.

Turning, he beckoned Nakosis with a wave of his finger. As Nakosis stood along side him the old man, near chuckling now, grabbed a handful of dead bushes against the rock wall and pulling them aside pointed with his burning stick to the base of the dead brush. There, Nakosis could clearly see a dark spot in the rock wall. Kneeling and working quickly, he cleared all the dead branches away to reveal an opening in the rock. This could not possibly be the 'sacred' cave! It was barely a badger burrow! He looked up as Loka nodded in the affirmative and pushing past him the old Shaman ducked low, holding his burning stick before him in the darkness. Nakosis followed, his curiosity peeked. After Loka had shuffled into the opening about the length of his body he pushed aside what appeared to be a reed mat and stood up, moving aside allowing the young man to enter past him. As he did so the old Shaman reached into the rock wall and produced a large bark and pitch torch, lighting it with the burning stick. The torch immediately burst into light revealing to Nakosis' astonished eyes a massive cave far larger than he ever imagined. He turned to Loka with what was undoubtedly a look of utter astonishment. Loka was giddy with delight at the surprise, his laughter ringing off the high walls. He handed a second bark torch to Nakosis and together they walked toward the center of what appeared to be a great hall. It was easily as wide across as one of the big village lodges was long – about forty paces distance and in the center, the remnants of many past fires contained in a ring of large river-stones. Nakosis wondered how Loka had managed to maneuver them into the cave by himself. As Loka dropped his sputtering torch into the fire pit, Nakosis could see that the smoke rose up to the high ceiling and appeared to exit through a wide fissure in the rock above. As his eyes grew accustomed to the dim light he could see that some light did, in fact, filter down from the opening overhead. Nakosis moved around the walls taking in the magnitude of this remarkable cave. He noticed sleeping platforms against one side of the cave adjacent to a natural flat rock ledge that protruded a considerable distance from the wall and about three hands width in height from the dirt floor. On this ledge was a large box made of red wood with the top adorned with the image of a large raven. Other images were carved on the sides but they were not discernable in the flickering torchlight. On another ledge were other red wood and bark containers. Bundles of firewood sticks of uniform length meticulously gathered from the floor of the surrounding forest were stacked neatly against one side as well as more torches. As Nakosis looked around he caught glimpses of many figures painted on the dark walls in faded white and ochre colors. They looked like animals and one appeared to be a human wearing a strange headdress. It was truly a place of power, Nakosis thought, a sacred place. It was obvious to Nakosis that Loka must have spent much time here to provision the cave so well. He turned to look at Loka who had simply stood like the proud creator of a work of great art, drinking in the obvious awe on the young man's face.

"This is not at all what I expected it to look like from the outside, Uncle," he said. Then turning toward a place at the back of the cave that appeared darker than the surrounding rock he asked, "Does it go further?" His voice echoed down from the high ceiling.

"Oh, you could say that." Loka answered.

Raising his torch higher, Nakosis peered closer at what was definitely a small crevice at the back of the cave.

"You could say it goes all the way to the underworld!" said Loka.

Nakosis thought he felt a breath of cold air and immediately stepped backward, still keeping his eyes on the black portal. He was visibly unnerved at the idea of being so close to what he perceived as a possible danger.

"Why does that make you so fearful boy?" The old man said as he stepped forward to rest his hand supportively on the young man's shoulder. "He's not afraid of a panther but the dark frightens him!" The old man laughed.

"It's just that, well...the panther I could actually *see*," said Nakosis.

"Ahh yes," answered Loka, "people do not understand that which they cannot see and fear what they do not understand. You, my young friend, I believe shall come to know much and fear little."

Nakosis was pleased that Loka should bestow such a compliment upon him. His having such faith in his abilities made him feel proud, encouraging him to do his best to try to please his teacher. It was the first time Loka had used the term 'young friend' and doing so greatly pleased Nakosis.

Loka nodded toward the door as the torches sputtered out and in the dim light the two men ducked once more out of the sanctuary and into the warm light of the clearing. As Loka breathed life back into the fire, Nakosis brought the fish they had gathered earlier in the day on their trek and they sat together watching their meal cook.

Loka spoke, "You remember what I said earlier about how all things, all life is connected? Well, it is somewhat the same with the spiritual world, Nakosis. We are body - flesh, blood and bone, yes, but we are also spiritual beings and you can no more separate them than you could remove your own head. So, as such, we live every day equally in both worlds. It is only that most people, even if they share in this understanding, go about their daily life as if they were mere bodies. They choose to ignore their spirit side and so when the spirit speaks to them they have no ears to hear. We, you and I, my friend, must choose a life in which we never forget, never loose that understanding, that connectedness. You must always remember that we are all a part of all worlds at all times - the spiritual and the physical and all nations- animal nations, fish nations, trees, rocks, everything is also within us as we are within them. So the underworld of the spirit is only a part of yourself as you are a part of it and you need not fear it, Nakosis. As with any journey, of course, one must be careful. You cannot be reckless. Undertaking such a journey takes time. It doesn't happen at once. You must be patient and I will help you."

Loka pulled more fish from the sizzling stick as Nakosis looked into the fire, appreciating the meaning of Loka's words.

"Uncle," he finally asked, "I was wondering, why is it that you went to such effort to build this hut when the sacred cave is just there?"

"Ahh, the *sacred* cave." Loka repeated the word 'sacred' rolling it about his mouth as though tasting it. "Tell me," he asked, "Why is it sacred?"

"Well," Nakosis began, "I suppose it is sacred in that all things are sacred. But, I suppose what I mean is that it has some *feeling*, something I sense that

I cannot place into words. Perhaps it is because of the journeying that you have undertaken there, Uncle." Loka smiled across the fire, almost beaming.

"Yes, yes, my friend, you understand well. It is both. All things are sacred but in the way of a 'sacred' or power place it is because people have undertaken spiritual practices at that spot sometimes for many, many generations. But this they do at a place that, for them, also has the 'feeling' as you call it. You have a gift for this *feeling*, this I have known for some time, since you were a child. This feeling as you say, is your connectedness to the spirit world. Tell me where else do you feel it?"

"Well, I suppose all of White Mist Mountain in some way." replied Nakosis.

"Yes, all mountains have this sense. It is because it is where Mother Earth meets Father Sky, where the power of both comes together and also it is home and shelter to many of our brethren in the other nations. It is like the offering we say at our ceremonies. 'To the earth our mother, the sky our father and all beings, our brothers.' Loka continued, "Please where else?"

Nakosis thought for a moment. "At the arrow rocks" he said, and then added, "But it was different. I only now know why, since your telling me about Quansa and that night. I used to think about ghost stories we told as children about that place and I thought that these affected my thinking about it, but now I think I understand why it felt a bit different to me."

"Yes," continued Loka, "You can tell the difference in the way places feel because of what happened there, this cave, where I have attempted for a long time to have a deeper understanding and experience of the web of life, and the scene where many poor people died tragically. Just as you leave a footprint in soft sand, so too these happenings leave a 'footprint' that exists in the spirit realm that you can feel Nakosis. This is why you are different, my friend, that is your great blessing and it is also your curse."

Nakosis looked up from the fire at Loka and his look needed no words.

"Because others will not understand this gift you possess and, as I said before, people fear what they don't understand and in their fear they sometimes will keep you at a distance. Oh, they will respect you and will readily ask your help when needed, but you will remain somewhat apart from others." Loka now looked deeply into the fire then he again spoke, "I think this is perhaps a good thing since it is when we are among these places of power, away from the world of men, that we gather strength. And, of course, with others like us." The two sat silent for what seemed like a long time, each simply looking into the fire before Loka looked across the smoke and said, "Finish up the fish, Nakosis, we will eat no more today"

That evening the two men entered the cave, Loka leading the way, a fiery brand in hand and the rattling of his necklace of bead, bone and claws the only sound. He struck a fire in the pit at the room's center and made an offering of thanks to Aan'ga. Then he brought forth a small, tightly wrapped bundle of the mixed offering herb and lighting this he then waved the flames out and began the offering to the six directions. Then he approached Nakosis who sat beside the fire and waving the sacred smoke with a feather fan he washed it over himself and over Nakosis. Turning to the carved chest on the rock ledge Loka brought forth a very plain and old looking rattle. The handle appeared to be carved in the shape of a raven but Nakosis couldn't be sure. Loka also washed this rattle in the sacred, cleansing smoke. He gestured for Nakosis to join him standing beside the fire as he then shook the rattle at various points around the cave and finally several times at the fissure in the rock wall at the back of the cave, all the while asking for the blessing of the spirit guides to help them in their task. Loka handed Nakosis the drum that he had Nakosis make under his supervision while back in the village. Nakosis was proud of his drum as, once it was completed, it met with an approving eye from the old man. He carefully unwrapped it from the hide bag in which it was permanently kept when not being used. Loka began swaying to the beat of his rattle, his eyes closed and chanting in the old tongue that Loka said was the language the spirits understood. Nakosis joined in with a somewhat reserved beating on his drum, not wanting to be a distraction, and not having had great experience he felt a little inadequate. But within a few moments his drumming automatically fell into rhythm with Loka and Nakosis closed his eyes and allowed the rhythm to take him over. Soon the world outside the cave began to dissolve. There was only the two men, the beat of their song, the chanting, the fire and the cocooning warmth of the cave. Nakosis had no way of knowing how long they continued. The reed door covering effectively blocked most light from entering the small doorway. Time, it seemed had no bearing on them. Nakosis knew he was dancing but it was not something he was in control of –he *was* the dancing! He was the primordial rhythm of rattle, drum and ancient words. He became aware of lying on the dirt of the cave floor. Did he collapse? How he got there didn't matter. He could hear Loka speaking as in an echo and his words punctuated by the shake of the ancient rattle. He instructed Nakosis to let his thoughts depart him, to melt into the space between his thinking and to become open to the spirit guides.

"When one of your guides comes it will tell you something, it may beg you to follow. Go with your guide, Nakosis. Do not be afraid. Your guide will protect you."

Then the rattle and chanting rose in accompaniment as the world became dark and Nakosis felt himself as small as an insect or perhaps a tiny mouse, he thought, as he fell forward toward the fissure in the dark cave wall. He could hear Raven cawing faintly at first then loudly in his ears. He looked up and Raven was looking at him. Raven seemed to smile. Funny he thought. How can a bird smile? Raven spoke without words and somehow Nakosis understood. Raven said, 'Lets go here.' They entered what seemed a tunnel in the mountain, taking them deeper at a speed no man could walk. They seemed to float very fast, down through dirt, roots, and rocks and dark. Small things scurried past getting out of their way and giving them passage. Soon a tiny spot of light appeared and they suddenly emerged into a thick, canopied forest and together they flew high into the treetops, past the highest branches and above the deep green into the clear sky. Nakosis was looking down on the landscape. Raven was somewhere. Nakosis could feel him present yet could not see him nor tell where he was. Perhaps Raven is within me or I within Raven he thought. In the distance he recognized the cloud-covered peaks of White Mist Mountain. He knew his village lay just beyond his sight, over the first line of a ridge. He delighted in looking down at the swirling bends and foaming waters of the Blue Fish River. The familiarity of the scene gave him confidence and he felt the free abandon of a child. He wanted to fly over his village calling out to everyone as he swooped down above their heads. Would they see me he thought? But something would not allow him. Something told him he must listen to Raven and go elsewhere. Was it Loka's voice? Nakosis now ascended ever higher into the blue sky and the green and blue of the world below grew smaller and he could no longer make out features like before. He could no longer get a bearing as to where they were- he and Raven. They passed through clouds and once again came to a place of clear bright sunshine and still calmness. No air moved and he was suspended as a fly in a spider's web, stationary in the sky looking toward a distant land. Slowly he floated closer in the direction. Now it was as though he could see a great distance to this far place. It was a high land, a foreboding mountain-ringed plateau of barren rock, snow and ice. Something moved across the bleak landscape. He couldn't make it out very clearly but somehow he instinctively knew it was Panther. The moment he had this realization it was as through he immediately crossed this great distance and was looking into the face of the great cat as she moved rapidly across the frozen dreamscape. It was like he was moving just ahead of her in the sky watching her. She bore a look of immense determination, steadfast in her travelling. As he watched her he was certain he was not visible to her. Suddenly she stopped and clearly locking her magnificent yellow eyes on his she spoke without words, loudly and clearly into both ears she said 'Nakosis!'

He sprang to consciousness as a man from a troubled dream. He was aware of being on his back on the cave floor and Loka, still gently moving his rattle, humming softly now sat beside him. His look was expressionless, giving Nakosis no cause for panic. Loka looked into the fire and standing he once again made the offerings and gave thanks to the fire, the directions, and to the spirit guides. Nakosis righted himself, clearing his throat and looked to Loka for some indicator as to what he should say or do. He felt somewhat out-of-place and a little disoriented. He realized he was sweating profusely but did not feel any excess heat. Loka circled the fire in a sun-wise path sprinkling the offerings of herbs into the failing flames as he past, chanting softly. He reached into the large sack by the sleeping platform and presented Nakosis with a large gourd vessel and told him to drink. Nakosis, only then realizing he was indeed parched, took a large gulp of the liquid only to realize that it was not water as he thought, but something sweet and burning. Surprised, he coughed but continued drinking. It quickly eased his thirst and also seemed to help him to re-orient. Silently, Loka handed him something indicating that he should eat. Nakosis accepted the handful of food and upon looking discovered it was, in fact, his favorite sweetbread. It was made from the combined flours of a grain plentiful and easily grown, and a much more rare flour ground from the tiny gray seeds of a leafy plant that only grows in the shaded meadows of forest clearings in the lower foothills. The seeds being so tiny that many are required to make even the smallest amount of flour. It has a very sweet and roasted nut flavor and is a highly prized delicacy among the people. How Loka acquired such a thing at this time of year and so fresh was indeed a mystery. But then, Nakosis thought, much about Loka was a mystery. Loka handed Nakosis a blanket and wrapping it about his shoulders he then followed him out of the low cave entrance. As Nakosis stood he was shocked to discover that the pale blue light of dawn was creeping over the horizon as a heavy mist rose up from the river valley below them, adding to the air of mystery and magic of the moment.

The two men stood together at the top of the trail, looking out over the blues and grays of the rising clouds of mist in the valley beneath them. The warming sun began his awakening directly behind them; a blanket of gold began illuminating the distant ridge of mountains across the valley. They stood together in silent awe as the warming light moved quickly down from the ridge bringing warm hues of verdant greens and new life to the dark forest. Birds were awakening around them, singing their greetings to the life giving sun. Nakosis looked upon the beauty of the world as if for the first time. His eyes now seemed to see everything with a new and a much deeper clarity. It was as though he knew everything in a personal way that he hadn't before. The birds were more familiar as if long time friends and Nakosis thought, as they flew past, that they too acknowledged this new sense of kinship. He looked upon a moss-covered log and saw beyond it's surface, beyond the many shades of green and brown to acknowledge the myriad life that called the rotting log home. He was aware of the mice running through the empty tunnel at the heart of the log, the beetles slowly devouring what sound wood remained and the army of ants meticulously removing minute particles to their underground colony. As he glanced about the surrounding forest he was now aware, as never before, of the splendid aura of life surrounding him. He at once knew what it meant to fully experience the connectedness to the web of life. As he turned to look at Loka the old man met his stare with a huge grin. Loka's eyes shone with a brilliance Nakosis had neglected to see before. They simply smiled deeply at one another, Loka chuckling and lightly nodding in acknowledgement of the wonderful experience Nakosis was now privilege to. This was indeed an experiential wonder for words could not describe it, Nakosis thought. He now understood what Loka had been trying to convey to him. He now knew, as Loka did on that long ago night within the arrow rock canyon, that his life would never be the same again. Nakosis and Loka stood together basking in the rapture of being one with the universe until the warm rays of the morning sun beamed directly upon them.

Loka said, "If you would be so kind to get us some fish from the pool at the river Nakosis, I will get the fire going." Nakosis smiled and began to gather his things when Loka added, "Oh, and Nakosis, if the opportunity presents could you please get a few extra fish today."

He then turned his attention toward the cold fire pit in front of their hut.

CHAPTER 6
A VISITOR

" Humankind has not woven the web of life.
We are but one thread within it.
Whatever we do to the web, we do to ourselves.
All things are bound together.
All things connect."
Chief Seattle

As Nakosis strolled down the mountain trail toward the river below he reflected upon the events of the evening past and marveled at how energetic and refreshed he felt after having not slept. Scenes of his journey played over and over again in his mind and he was determined to recall every minute detail as he knew Loka and he would discuss the evening's experience and together come to know the true meaning of what the journey meant. He found the prospect very exciting and was eager to return and to learn more. He tried to piece together what, if any, hidden meanings the images meant. He had heard Raven in the previous experience he'd had in Loka's hut back in the village and, of course, Panther, he was confident, was his spirit guide or protector and he knew there had to be a deep meaningful interpretation to the events beyond the more obvious.

The pool was deep and dark and the river here was wide and appeared to slow, but Nakosis suspected that beneath the water's still dark surface there was a strong current. Moving downstream to where the pool narrowed and again became the shallow faster river he climbed up on a large flat rock to where he could look into the clear waters without casting any shadow upon the surface and there decided to procure the days catch. In shallow waters he would wade in up to his knees and standing still with his bow and arrow he could take large fish. It took him some practice to learn to shoot not directly at the fish but to one side, as the water did not reflect the fish's true position. Here, however, the fish were very large and the water not too fast so he used his spear to much success.

Nakosis was always more guarded around water, something he'd learned from an early age from his father. Large and potentially dangerous predators also fed and came to drink at the same places as people and often their approach could not be heard over the noise of fast moving water. A surprise encounter with a great bear, for example, could be deadly. As well, one could not hear the approach of enemy when near water. The sound of moving water also created the illusion of distant voices, so Nakosis would sometimes duck for the cover of thick bushes and hide motionless scouting the terrain for the source of voices that never appeared. Then, of course, there was the threat of slipping on the wet rocks and being swept downstream. Even now as an adult, after learning to swim as well as any in the village and after many, many years of fishing he still took no chances near swift water. He shook away his distractions and focused upon being alert and cautious. He thought that in doing so the spaciousness and connectedness he was enjoying was somehow diminished, but when he closed his eyes for but a moment, focused on his gentle breathing and again looked about him he saw to his relief that all was as it had been. The world was an endless play of life, myriad beings all engaged in the interplay of co-existence. There was an indescribable power and light to the natural world around him. He realized as he speared the first fish and offered his thanks to the universe that it's life would continue within him and Loka, that the perpetual cycle of life would continue its revolution through boundless time again and again, every being existing for but a brief flash like lightning in the storm to die and be reborn again and again. He too, and Loka and everyone he now knew would play their roles in the dance of cyclical existence. As he pondered the revelation of this deeper understanding, he realized that death itself was only a part of life, that it was a necessary component for the continuation of every being's long march through endless time. Even so, he now felt an increased compassion and empathy for the beings he would have to kill in order to sustain his own life's source. Now when he offered his gratitude to the universe, to the spirit of the being that would sustain him yet another day, it had meaning as never before. He understood now what Loka had meant when he said that although most people make offering to the spirits they do not have the deeper understanding.

The spirits were truly generous this day and it did not take him long to procure enough fish for a very nourishing meal. He was somewhat curious as to why Loka suggested he get extra fish should circumstances allow. Perhaps, he thought, they would be undergoing an extra long journey in the cave and would require the additional sustenance. The prospect of doing so excited Nakosis and he realized he was very eager to be within the spirit world again. To him it had clarity to rival that of this, the waking world, if not more so. During the Shamanic journey he had a freedom unimaginable in the waking world. Where else could one become Raven and share his wings and soar to the heights of the mountain peaks?

As he made his way back up the long climb toward the cave his heart lightened at the thought of continuing his journeying. He paused upon a rocky ledge high above the river with a spectacular view of the valley below. Setting his fish and his spear down he sat crossed legged, feeling the warmth of the dark stone beneath him. He placed his palms upon the rock and as he breathed in he imagined the warmth and radiance of the sun filing his being through the gift of mother earth beneath him. With each breath he released he felt it becoming part of the intricate web of life, to become a part of the heavens, to be breathed in again by all other living things. He knew also that when he died his mortal remains would dissolve like his breath into the fold of mother earth, to become the means of continuation for other beings. This is what it meant to truly understand the universal 'connectedness' that Loka was intent on sharing with him. Truly it was a thing to be experienced, as words alone would never award this wondrous knowledge. Nakosis gave thanks to mother earth and father sun and to all the life around him who were now his brethren. Although he, like the others, had offered such supplications to the spirits many times, only now did he do so with full understanding and his heart filled with a joy like he'd never known.

Back upon the thin trail his passage was accompanied by the chorus of a multitude of singing birds, the high-pitched steady hum of countless insects and the rhythm of his breath. Today the sounds seemed to have increased strength and clarity and they pleased him greatly. Something though suddenly seemed out of place and Nakosis instinctively paused, lowered his breathing and crouching low he shifted his spear from walking staff to weapon. His ears strained to listen and almost as though sensing his apprehension the birds around him seemed to quiet their song. Voices! He was too far above the river to have his ears deceived by the sounds of rushing water. It was definitely the voices of men. Nakosis was now only a short distance from the cave clearing on a level portion of the trail that followed a wide bench. The trees and brush were thick. At least, he thought, it would thankfully conceal his movement. He cautiously moved forward, looking both ahead for any threat while scanning the ground to avoid stepping upon any dried leaves or twigs that might reveal his presence, his posture crouched and coiled, ready to respond. He could smell smoke in the air. As he neared the clearing he could clearly make out the voice of Loka and at least one other. There did not seem to be any urgency or threat in the tones and so Nakosis stood erect and cautiously, slowly, entered the clearing, his spear still at the ready. As he rounded the last of the bushes Loka and another, a somewhat older man, sat on either side of a small fire looking directly at him.

Loka smiled and pointing at the older man he said, "Nakosis please come and offer respects to my dear friend Chako!"

Still feeling a little unnerved Nakosis dropped the bag and his spear and stepping forward respectfully lowering his head toward the old man, as was the custom. The old man touched the ground beside him and with a great toothless smile he indicated for Nakosis to join them. Once seated Chako studied Nakosis' face intently then, still smiling he turned to Loka saying,

"Yes he does indeed have very good light about him. I am very pleased to meet you, young Nakosis."

The old man grabbed Nakosis by his right forearm and with his other hand he warmly and gently patted his arm in greeting. Nakosis felt an immediate liking for this fellow. All the while the old man never stopped smiling with a great, warming grin.

Loka retrieved the bag and removing the fish he exclaimed, "Oh, very good Nakosis, you did catch extra fish!"

He held them up proudly to Chako's approving nod. As Loka began preparing the fish he explained to an obviously still surprised Nakosis, "Chako is a dear friend of many, many years. He comes from the village of the Low Forest people, many days distant. He is a great Shaman!"

Nakosis just realized that when Loka requested he procure extra food he somehow knew that Chako was coming! Indeed there was much to the old Shaman Nakosis had yet to discover. It was considered impolite to question the motives of ones elders, especially a Shaman, and yet Nakosis just had to know how it was that Chako came to know they were there. Had Loka pre-arranged this meeting?

Amid tasteful bites of fish, Nakosis found the courage to break the sounds of their eating with his carefully worded question. Using the most respectful tone he could muster he asked, "Esteemed Chako, it is my honor to meet you. As you have known Uncle for many years I'm assuming that the two of you must meet here at this place often?"

Loka gave Nakosis a slightly curious look across the fire. Chako instantly beamed at the question, revealing that huge toothless grin that was such an endearing quality that it quickly made one feel at ease with him.

He giggled his response between bites of food. "No, no, my young friend. It was only twice before that we met here. The last time was long ago, just after that terrible fight with the flatlanders. Much balancing was needed in the world of your people then. At that time we gathered here with Quansa. He was growing very old then. I remember the journey here from your village was very hard for him at that time, and (giggling like a young boy) Loka and I were much younger."

Loka nodded in agreement and he too shared in the laughter.

"The first time," Chako continued, wiping his toothless mouth with the back of his hand, "was after the wasting sickness came to our villages."

"It came to your village also?" Nakosis asked.

"Oh yes." Replied Chako. "It swept from village to village like an invisible ghost, striking young and old alike." The two old men shared a brief silent moment, re-living the loss that the sickness visited upon them then Chako continued, "I had gone to see your people at Quick Waters village and also at Deer River village to see if the sickness was there also, as our people were suffering badly at that time and we did not know if it was only our people who were sick. Your village was suffering also, but not as badly as Deer River village and so Quansa and Loka had gone there to see if they could help. It was there that we met and together we did everything we could to help the sickness leave our peoples. Afterward, we came here to Quansa's cave to replenish our power and to further beseech the spirits to help our peoples. Since Quansa's passing many years past, Loka has continued to use this cave and now we call it Loka's cave," finishing his comment with his infectious giggling laughter which made even Loka laugh.

Chako then turned to Nakosis with a look of seriousness so uncharacter-istic that it actually frightened him. He said, "Now, my son, this time I have come because of you!"

Nakosis was speechless. He didn't know what to say and he turned to look across the fire for direction from Loka, but only received a smile that was somehow even more unnerving.

It was Chako who broke the uncomfortable pause. After more of his gig-gling he said, "Oh, not to fear my young friend, I didn't mean to scare you. I heard about you in your village and how Loka had taken you under wing and then departed. I then knew to look here."

"Oh you came from the village?" Nakosis asked in a relieved tone.

"Why, yes. I knew it was time to visit my old friend once again and last night in Loka's hut the spirits told me what I needed to know."

Nakosis looked at Loka half expecting some surprise that someone had actually been within the sanctuary of his hut in his absence. It was common knowledge among all in the village not to even go near his hut uninvited, what to speak of sleeping there! But obviously there was a much greater bond between these two old men.

Loka now spoke, "It was in my hut last night that Chako was aware of our journey. He was aware of *you* Nakosis."

It hadn't occurred to Nakosis that this magical world was not his and Loka's alone to explore. Not only could others see the spirit world, but also it was obviously possible that while doing so they too could share in another's journey. This revelation suddenly struck fear in Nakosis. So, he was also vulnerable in the spirit world as in the waking world.

"Ah, so you understand." Chako said. Looking into Nakosis' eyes.

Loka continued, "While we are few there are still many who can travel within the spirit world, Nakosis. Where do you think the guides come from? They too are many and each animal spirit also abides within this realm. Even the dreams of common people often times will take them into the spirit world, although they usually do not understand it as such and cannot control their journey. Still you are never totally there alone, Nakosis."

"Indeed," said Chako. "We have journeyed often and have learned, under the guidance of our teachers, how to journey safely, how to avoid danger and how to know when it is risky to remain there."

Loka nodded that he concurred. Then Loka continued, "Yes there are others who can also do harm to you in the spirit world."

"Do you mean witches, dark sorcerers?" blurted Nakosis.

Loka answered, "Anyone who can enter the spirit world as we do, Nakosis, can have either a good or a bad desire, just as do people in the waking world. It is their motive that determines whether people call them Shaman or sorcerer. This is also a world of great temptation. Once one understands it, one realizes that they can influence to some degree things and events in the waking world. At times some Shamans have used the spirit world as a place from which to inflict harm upon their enemies. It is told of a people who live at the shores of the great waters who have an entire lodge of Shamans who will work with evil spirits to cause their enemies to weaken. Then when their warriors attack, their enemy cannot defend themselves and are easily killed or taken as slaves."

"Yes," Chako broke in, "and these people are also said to be cannibals!"

Nakosis felt a cold shiver run down his spine. He asked, "But where do these 'evil' spirits come from? How is it they exist?"

Chako answered, "I believe that some are the spirits of these dark Shamans. I believe that because they have spent their life's energy in such dark matters that once they die their spirits go to where they are familiar. They try much of their days to be one with the dark world of the spirit that when they die they get what they strive for."

"You see, Nakosis," interrupted Loka, "Acts such as this disturb the natural balance in both the spirit world and the waking world. Whatever you do in the spirit world has an action in the waking world also. Every day and night there are forces around us, working for us or against us. Most of the time these are due to things we create ourselves. For example, someone may suffer from an illness that makes him or her feel weak and lacking life energy and we can see no cause for their suffering. This is often because they have upset the natural balance of their life. They have acted in such a way as to bring the illness upon themselves. But, you see, they are unaware of it and so cannot change the course they have set upon and so their problems only increase. If they have an unpleasant heart then they may grow even more unpleasant or even become violent or act crazy. What we must do is to find out just what it is that they have done to disturb the balance and then try to restore it with spirits help."

"Yes," Chako said, "and you must have respect and restraint within one's journeying. It is tempting, at first, to give into the great joy and to want to go as one would in a new and wonderful land. But there, Nakosis, there are more dangers than you can imagine. Don't think that you cannot come to harm there as you do in the waking world. As you can now see, there are powers in the spirit world that can inflict bodily harm upon you here in the waking world. But it is much worse should your spirit body be harmed when journeying. Why, you could even be trapped, unable to return to your waking body."

"Do you remember," said Loka, "back in the village I told you that to be a Shaman means to be equally in the waking world and the spirit world, to have this balance? To fall either way too far is to lose the balance. To survive, to serve the people and our mother earth is to always maintain this balance. We can only serve our people by journeying to the spirit world and then returning with help for those who require it. For a Shaman, too much of one is dangerous."

Nakosis had no idea of the potential perils that he faced. Until now he innocently thought that it was a harmless venture, something of a gift for few to enjoy.

Almost as though understanding his thoughts Chako added. "This is no toy. You would not give the sharpest spear point to a baby to play with and likewise this is a great gift that comes with a great responsibility."

Loka reached over and gently touching Nakosis' hand he looked into his eyes and said, "My son, you possess great ability. Neither Chako nor I had the ability to journey as you did when we began on this, our life's path. We know of no one who has so very easily slipped into the world of spirit as you have done. Until now I have been hesitant to speak so of it to you, in fear that you may not have the maturity to understand this gift. I worried that you might loose your humility, that you would become proud in a bad way."

Chako broke in, "Arrogance and pride is the worst danger for a Shaman, especially one inexperienced. It will inevitably lead to your death Nakosis.

Embrace this understanding and, with humility, continue under our guidance to see your full potential." Then Chako added, "And hopefully reveal the special task the spirits have so gifted you for."

Loka said, "It is plain for us to see in you, Nakosis, that you share in the Shaman's vision as Chako and I do after many years of learning. You have come by this naturally and in this world nothing happens without great purpose. Our world will soon change rapidly. This has long been prophesized. How it will come about and whether good or bad we cannot predict, for the outcome will depend upon the wishes of the people and our great mother earth and the spirits. But it is the duty of the Shaman to try to do what is best for maintaining the web of life."

"Regardless of the wishes of people," Chako interrupted, "because people alone do not decide the ways of our mother earth. To think they can do so is a great arrogance and, like pride to a Shaman, it will lead to destruction. Already we see changes in the people. Our peoples now enjoy great prosperity as never before. Our enemies leave us alone and we have bountiful crops as we never did."

Nakosis asked, "But how is this a bad thing?

"Oh, it is a blessing." said Chako, "But in such times people think that they are solely responsible for their fate. They enjoy great blessings and do not see it as such and so their arrogance leads them to think that they are not vulnerable. Just as a warrior cannot grow fat and lazy lest he suffer defeat."

"So you're saying that the people have become forgetful of the spirit world and because of such you now believe that they will suffer?" Nakosis questioned.

"It's not that the spirits require anything from us least of all supplication! Said Chako, "It is we who need to remain within the connectedness of all things, within this world and the spirit world, simply to be whole beings. We gather here, and elsewhere others like us gather also, in the hope that the balance will continue unbroken for future generations of all beings. It has been said that a time will come when the nations of men will forget their brethren. When they will become as lowly beasts, seeking only to satisfy a hunger to dominate other beings and will wage great wars over other men. If this continues they risk loosing their connection to the web of life."

"And if that happens," Loka broke in, "the prophecy says that earth mother herself will begin to die and all our brethren also!"

"Is such a thing even possible!?" Nakosis cried. "How am I involved in such things and if it is prophesized that such a harm can befall us then how can I, or for that matter you and others, stay the course of men as many as the lights of the night sky?"

Sensing his great sadness, Loka looked at Nakosis and answered saying, "I can't answer that for certain Nakosis, but I can tell you that it is also prophesized that there will be those entrusted to keep this balance and that they will be greatly tasked, but if enough stand to the challenge then the course of destruction may be averted."

"And," Chako added, "it is told of one who will be born again and again to take up the challenge, the one who will have the power to sway the hearts and minds of many nations! And so it becomes our task to hold the balance until the appointed time, when the earth becomes ill and we join the great healer of the prophesy and together once again bring balance and harmony."

Loka continued, "This is our belief Nakosis. This is why we live the lives we do, why we train ourselves in the ways of the spirit. We understand, as I believe you now do also, that our lives and the path we have chosen will continue when our bodies perish in this world. We will again return and again we will take up the

task the spirit world has chosen for us."

"So, then you believe I also have been a Shaman before - in another time, in another life?" Nakosis asked.

"Of course," said Chako "how else does one explain the ease with which you take to the journeying? You are simply continuing the work you left in your last life. Events have come to pass that have allowed you and Loka to join paths and I also to come to you. These things are the working of the spirits and we are but to act. Nothing happens by chance, my friend, all these things were meant to be. I can only believe that our coming together in such a way is a great portent for what is to come. Pray we are up to the task."

These final words left Nakosis speechless and pondering what his future could possibly hold. Only this morning he was basking in the newfound wonderment of an exciting world of unlimited possibilities and now he quite possibly faced the greatest and most dangerous challenge of his life. In fact, it would seem of many lives! This all seemed too much for his mind to grasp.

Sensing such, as Loka always seemed to do, he spoke up saying. "In such times, when I find myself over-whelmed by events, I seek guidance from the spirits. It is there that my path is again set straight and my vision again becomes clear. Let us together seek the answers."

Chako smiled that reassuring toothless grin and nodding at Loka together they turned their gaze to Nakosis who, despite their dire warnings, felt that he'd sooner be in the relative safety of these two great old Shamans than just about anywhere else - in either world.

Chako yawning said, "Let us take a little rest now. Our young friend has had much to ponder and we will see what we can discover later this evening."

Loka, needing no persuasion, rose and headed for his hut and his sleeping robes. Chako chose to wrap himself in a blanket and propping a large sack against a rock facing the fire he allowed himself to fall heavy against it, it's contents readily shaping to his body, as it seemed he'd done many times before. He simply sat silent, gazing expressionless into the fire.

Nakosis tried to follow Chako's example, placing his blanket over his shoulders and resting his back against a tree, but his mind was too full of the afternoon's conversation, too many vast and amazing possibilities to consider. The old men had said that we have lived many lives. It had been generally accepted that many of the animal spirits whose assistance helped in the hunt were, in fact, ancestors watching over their families, helping in their lives. But to now truly accept this as a reality was staggering. It meant that one could be as he was in the journeying - a raven, a wolf, an eagle. Perhaps, Nakosis thought, this is why we have animal spirit guardians. Perhaps it is we who have been these beings in a previous life. These things weighed heavy on his young mind and he was far too restless for sleep. Looking over at Chako he studied the old mans face. He seemed deep asleep, yet his eyes appeared as though they were still slightly open. His face was furrowed by deep valleys of time, and two scars plainly marked both cheeks beneath his eyes. They were too exact to have been accidents, he thought. What, he wondered would have prompted him to create them? His hair was long and gray and hung loosely over his shoulders as did Loka's, but Chako wore part of his hair in small braids with many decorative beads woven into it. A pair of large feathers also hung down the back, tied to a small braid, but perhaps most noticeable were the large brilliant blue stones he wore on both his necklace and as a bracelet. Loka, by comparison, was plain in appearance apart from his necklace of claws, bones and a few tattered feathers. So as to not disturb the old man's slumber with his restlessness, and also to seek some relief from the dizzying questions flooding his mind, Nakosis choose to remove himself from the clearing and to walk for a while.

He followed the trail through the forested bench for a ways and then, turning toward the river, he pushed his way through the deep underbrush until he arrived at the edge of the bench atop a high cliff overlooking the valley below. Several old trees had succumbed to time and fallen over the edge while others hung precariously by what roots still grabbed the earth. How like them we are, thought Nakosis. We are fragile and dependent upon our mother earth, clinging to her like these trees and eventually we too will see our last season and will fall, as trees, into the unknown of another existence. Do trees have many lives also he wondered? Indeed they continue to seed many other generations within the shadow of past ancestors whose decaying hulks continue to nurture new growth. Are we not more than simple trees? If, in the journeying, I can leave our mother earth and soar higher than eagles to touch the lights of the night skies then surely, he thought, we must not need to return here again and again as lowly creatures, scrambling beneath the leaves for insects, unaware of our great potential?

Nakosis rested his tired body against the mossy trunk of a great tree. Looking out over the beauty of the mountain valley, the mist and the gentle sound of the mighty river so far below and feeling the warmth of the afternoon sun bathing his skin he soon drifted off to sleep.

When he awoke it was as though he had only just rested his eyes for a heartbeat. Yet the sun, now partly hidden by the distant ridge, signaled the passing of much more time than he thought possible. Never before had he experienced such a deep and dreamless sleep that past as though but a moment of time had lapsed. He knew he must return to the clearing and to the two men who would share so much with him and yet he felt a deep contentment resting in the protection of the large and ancient tree.

"How long," he said aloud, "before you too, great tree, must take the fall over the mountain? How long do any of us have?"

The scurrying of a squirrel overhead drew his attention as it paused inquisitively to inspect him. Then feeling something on his leg he quickly responded, bringing his hand to swipe away the spider now crossing his thigh. But something made him hesitate and he instead placed his hand in front of the small creature, allowing it to walk over his palm. Then placing the other hand next to the first he watched as the spider moved from hand to hand as he gently lowered it to the forest floor. Although he could never explain why, he normally felt some fear of these creatures and had since childhood. Now, however, he felt a deep sadness for this tiny being simply trying to survive in the harsh world beneath his feet. How vulnerable their life is, he thought. Looking around him he imagined all the beings that existed within this small world of the great tree. Then of the many birds who nested and raised their broods of young within its branches. Over the countless years it has stood the test of time as the cliff edge slowly crept closer and it's great roots broke through the rock to hang in the air. How many animals rested just as he did today under its spreading canopy - bears, wolves and perhaps even a panther? All of them were now gone, their lives a brief expression of struggle and survival. Were the people no different? He thought of his father and mother and how hard and short their lives were. They too, no doubt, had dreams and plans that were shattered by unforeseeable disaster. What of them, were they now living lives as some other being? Did the cycle of life bring them to become something else, perhaps even this lowly spider? Was this even possible he wondered? But as much as these things weighed heavy on Nakosis, deep inside he knew the truth - life is an endless circle of power that never diminishes, but simply adapts and changes. He pondered all the suffering of the countless forms of beings around him and thought of their returning as yet another creature whose lives were fraught with danger. Such immense suffering in these lives he thought. He tried not to think of his parents returning as such beings, but he could not and the feeling of great unexplainable sadness overtook him and tears warmed his cheeks, as they had not done since he was a child. He wept as he could not recall and with each wave of tears his sadness deepened until he was sure his heart would burst. He raised his head from his hands and heaved a great sigh as the sun lowered his rays to illuminate the forest in a blanket of rich golden light. The sun seemed to speak to Nakosis, to somehow comfort him and in that moment he realized that death is also life. They are as inseparable as the blazing warmth of the sun is from the cool moonlight of night, he thought. Life cannot continue without death to renew it. He smiled to himself and he bowed his head to father sun and aloud he thanked him for his teaching. Straightening himself and gathering his things he turned back toward the cave and to the task the universe had set for him.

CHAPTER 7
HISTORY

When Nakosis entered the clearing Loka was warming himself by the fire. He was still wet from having just bathed at the pool. Chako was preparing something. They both turned and smiled at him.

Chako spoke up, "Did you get some rest Nakosis?"

He smiled and nodded, moving to take a seat before the fire. Chako had placed water into a large container beside the fire and using a pair of forked sticks he was removing stones from the flames and gently dropping them into the container. Each stone was about the size that would fit within a fist. After a moment he would remove the stone and switch it with another from the fire. In such a way the water was beginning to boil and with great care he was adding a mixture of crushed leaves and powders from his satchel, stirring the mixture gently with the stick, then, almost as an afterthought, or perhaps just for good measure, he rose and grabbed a handful of fresh berries and tossed them unceremoniously into the watery broth. Loka joined Nakosis in sitting beside the fire and watching the preparation.

"It smells very good Uncle." Nakosis said and was met with the usual giggling laughter and head nodding that never failed to also make him chuckle.

Soon Chako informed them that the concoction was ready. They gathered a couple of gourd cups and Chako proudly served them each a portion of the steaming brew only after first using the stick to shake a few drops to the directions and give thanks. Nakosis, having been surprised by the gourd Loka had given him upon awakening from his journeying, cautiously placed the cup to his lips, fully prepared for a pungent shock. Much to his surprise and delight it was a wonderfully sweet and flavorful soup. It was made from the large tuberous roots of a tall plant with bright yellow flowers. It grows wild in some of the meadows but the people grow it in large plots in the village gardens. Chako had flavored it with the addition of succulent young tree needles, sweet sap from the white bark tree, dried herbs from his satchel and, of course, the berries. Both Loka and Nakosis grunted their approval between deep gulps to a much-delighted Chako.

"So," Loka said, "tell us now of your journey Nakosis."

"Yes, yes please do," giggled Chako, serving more of the warm soup.

Nakosis was careful to recall the journey with as much detail as possible. He openly told of his feelings and the early effects of the cave, the rattle and the way he quickly drifted. The two men made no comments but nodded in mutual understanding, making agreeable sounds between their loud sipping from the cups. Nakosis then came to the part where he told of the vast barren land and both men ceased their sipping and for a brief moment they looked at one another. When he told of Panther, Loka nodded deeply and grunted in approval. When he finished he fully expected them to question him or at least divulge some deeper interpretation beyond what he understood, but much to his dismay they said nothing until Chako turned to him with his endless grin asking, "More soup?" If he had any thoughts he was not sharing them. Loka seemed at least to be considering the content as he looked at the fire.

Then he said, "It will rain tonight. I believe we have enough wood in the cave to keep the fire."

Then as if commanded, a quick gust of wind rippled through the forest canopy above them, bending the branches, signaling the coming change in weather. Loka handed the remains of the basket to Nakosis who politely refused, offering it instead to the giggling Chako, who delighted in downing the last of the brew.

He attempted to say, "The bottom is the best." as he drank, but in so doing much of the soup ran down his chin. As he tried to jump away from it Nakosis and Loka laughed but still not as much as did Chako. Nakosis was certain he'd never known anyone who seemed to always exhibit such a degree of contented happiness as this wonderful old man. Loka, while he had grown much more personal was, by comparison, more serious but still possessed of humor and great kindness. Nakosis smiled warmly as he watched the two old men picking up the gourd cups and the basket to rinse in the pool. Loka packed away the utensils and Chako retrieved his large bag and walked toward the cave entrance, followed by the other two. Before entering, Loka, having forgot, urgently asked Nakosis to "quickly, bring fire."

The two men stood in the dark as he entered with a flaming stick to light the bark torch Loka presented. Chako found the whole situation very entertaining and his laughter rang off the cave walls. He could lighten almost any situation, thought Nakosis. Once the torch had ignited the fire, Chako reached into his bag bringing forth a beautiful headdress of small iridescent blue feathers. There were small red feathers at the base of the blue ones and

Nakosis could see some of the rare and beautiful blue stones about the size of beads sewn to the dark colored band of the headdress. It was not grand like those worn for ceremonies by the leaders of society lodges, but Nakosis thought it was wonderful. Chako laid this and a drum, much larger than that of either Loka or Nakosis, upon the rock ledge. Loka was making the fire offering and had lit the purifying smudge of herbs and with his feather fan began the offering to the directions. Chako tied the headdress up around the top of his head, so that the feathers stood straight up, looking very grand thought Nakosis. Nakosis picked his drum up from the ledge and carefully unwrapping it he stood awaiting direction. Loka bathed Chako and then Nakosis in the sweet smelling smoke of purification. Then he did the same to the rattles and the drums. They then moved to sit crossed legged around the fire. Loka nodded to Chako and the old man, always so jovial, so full of easy laughter, now suddenly appeared a mountain of restraint, seriousness and power. Nakosis realized the importance of the undertaking and how privileged he was to be in the company of these great men. Chako raised his arms skyward and lifted his head toward the cave ceiling and in a somber tone he spoke an invocation.

"*We ask the great mystery to witness and to bless our humble offerings this night. We ask that the spirit of this great mountain, who protects us, give us It's blessing. We ask that the spirits of all our brethren smile upon us now and accept our offering and help to guide us in our journey. We ask our beloved mother earth to bear witness that these things we do we do not for ourselves, but for all the brethren in all the worlds and for the ancestors who dwell among us and in the spirit world also. If they find us worthy, may the spirits guide us and protect us and may we have ears to hear their council. May all beings benefit from our endeavors this night.*"

Then Chako threw a handful of powder into the fire causing it to flare high to the cave ceiling and with a loud voice he proclaimed, "For all our brethren!" Loka yelled this last proclamation also and before the echo of their voices fell back down around them Chako began to beat his drum. Nakosis was deeply moved by Chako's supplication. He had never before heard such words so beautifully and sincerely spoken. Now Chako's drum startled him as it was tremendously deep and its volume was unexpected. Loka had closed his eyes and joined in. Nakosis looked about, taking in the magical presence these two old Shamans now radiated as they drummed and chanted. Nakosis would have happily been just a spectator to the ritual, but none-the-less he beat his drum softly.

He swayed gently to the melody, unable to resist it's infectious beat. Something was drawing him in and he could not be only a witness. He closed his eyes and swayed side to side, his hand now drumming without his willing it to do so, his voice singing louder, now blending into the one ancient vibration ringing off the cave walls cascading down around them until the sound came from everywhere and nowhere, from inside him as well as outside. Nakosis began to visualize a spiral of color swirling and pulsating with the rhythm, now cone shaped and rising before him toward the top of the cave. In it was the red and yellows of the fire and the brilliant blue of Chako's headdress. Once again the familiar and welcoming call of Raven resounded in his ears and it gave him an immense feeling of familiarity and comfort. The colors pulsated and swirled as if possessed of life. It was unlike any fire he'd ever seen in that it spun with an unnatural force. Suddenly the light from the fire grew in great intensity, illuminating the cave like the sun itself. Nakosis had to shield his eyes and he heard a sound growing in intensity with the light of the fire. It was a haunting sound and yet vaguely familiar. As suddenly as the recollection came to him so too did the image within the flames –the dancing, fiery figure from his dream in the village. This time, however, it began to take shape; to have a much more defined form. The flames spun faster and began to blend into a maze of vibrant fiery hues and, before a startled Nakosis, a man appeared! He was completely formed of the fire and yet was not the fire. He was perfectly human looking now, but his skin still bore the brilliant color of fire. He was spectacular and the awe he generated in Nakosis surpassed his fear of him. His hair was long –perhaps to his waist and he wore it in many fiery braids. On his head was a headdress similar in design to that of Chako's. He was decorated with many bracelets and necklaces, but as they also were of fire color, Nakosis could not tell what they were. In his hand he held the flute that was, no doubt, the origin of the haunting melody that accompanied his arrival. He stepped out of the fire and took two very slow steps toward Nakosis. He was smiling in a very sincere and friendly way and Nakosis seemed to sense that he need not have any fear of this being, but he also knew that this was a spirit of immense power.

The fiery apparition looked at Nakosis and Nakosis asked without speaking, 'Who are you?'

The man of fire replied, also without words, 'You know who I am Nakosis. You only need to remember. You must seek me at the mountain of fire!'

Then he heard his name again and again "Nakosis! Nakosis! Nakosis!" The words grew louder and the fiery being and the cavern began to fade as the voice changed and suddenly Nakosis was back in the cave, lying on his back looking into the startled eyes of Chako and Loka. They were leaning over him, calling his name. His arms lay out at his sides, his drum beside him where it had fallen and come to rest. Loka had placed his hand under his head and was attempting to raise him up as Chako rushed behind Nakosis to help elevate him. He was sweating profusely and dizzy, his head swimming. He could only manage to bring himself up onto his elbows as Loka rushed to give him a gourd of water.

Chako was repeatedly asking him "Are you alright, are you alright?"

He could not speak but somehow he nodded and managed to communicate that he was not harmed. As he thirstily drank the gourd of water his voice returned and he immediately asked the still very concerned looking men, "Did you see him, in the fire?"

"Who do you speak of?" answered Loka "We saw nothing, my son, you quickly collapsed and were of the other world. We could not retrieve you."

"We thought you might be lost to us, Nakosis." Blurted Chako, who then proclaimed to Loka "I have not seen such deep possession! Is the boy alright?"

Loka nodded, not taking his eyes off Nakosis as he handed him yet another gourd of water.

Nakosis was now able to sit up and, taking a few deep breaths, shook some reality back into his still puzzled mind. After a brief moment, sure that he was indeed intact and unharmed the two old Shamans began serious questioning, demanding to hear every minute detail of what Nakosis had experienced. Their still heightened level of concern unnerved Nakosis and so he went to some lengths to appear exceptionally 'normal' to relieve their obvious alarm. They sat closely on either side in rapt attention, fixed upon his every word. He felt a little embarrassed receiving such personal attention from them but did his best to describe every detail of the swirling colors, how they manifested into the magical vortex of fire. Then, when he began to describe the physical being that appeared from the flames, Chako let out an unrestrained gasp and physically pulled away, trying unsuccessfully to recompose himself. His reaction caused Nakosis to stop talking and he turned to gage Loka's response and was met with a blank and befuddled expression.

"Sorry, my son, please do continue," said Chako who now looked seriously at Loka.

Nakosis finished the story and was met with more astonished looks when he told of the fiery being's request to 'seek me at the mountain of fire'.

The two old men stared at each other, as if each one expecting the other to begin commenting but instead a silent and unnerving pause ensued. Chako rose to his feet, turning his back on them and began pacing the cave.

It was Loka who spoke. "Nakosis," he said, "do you know who this 'fiery being' is?"

Nakosis shook his head and replied that he had no idea.

Chako had turned to stand before them. "You must have seen this being before. I mean you must have seen an image of him somewhere?"

Nakosis again nodded then remembering he said "Wait, yes I did! Back in the village when I was sleeping. Just before we left to come here I had a dream and he was in the dream. He appeared in a swirling fire along with the flute sounds, but he was not clear as now, nor did he speak."

Again the two men exchanged serious glances and it was getting very uncomfortable for Nakosis.

"What is the meaning of this? Tell me, who is this man?" demanded Nakosis, his growing concern now becoming obvious.

"This is no man," said Loka. "This is 'Hohapas' –the magic one! The first, Nakosis!"

Chako lowered his head at the very mention of the name and nodded in solemn agreement.

"The first what?" asked Nakosis. His moment of concern somewhat abated, Chako again sat beside him and that reassuring toothless smile once again lit up his wrinkled face giving some comfort to Nakosis.

"Why, the first Shaman, Nakosis." He said.

"What? Why have I never heard of him?" demanded Nakosis, not understanding why one so important would not have been sung of or his tales told at evening fires.

"His is not a common story among our people," said Loka. "It was only through Quansa that I came to know of him. It is usually only Shaman who learn of him and it is said that even the mention of his name carries his power!"

Chako now continued, "Yes indeed, he is more known among some of my people. You see the ancestors of your people came from the direction of where my people now reside. Of course, then no one lived where we do today. Both our peoples came from a far distant land, across many, many dangerous places. We are, you see, related, your people and my people. At one time we were one people. That is why we remain as brothers to this day."

"Yes," interrupted Nakosis, "I know we always call you our cousins in the low forest and I also have heard tales of the ancestors having come from a distant place, but no one seemed to know where that was."

"Ah ha," Chako continued, "the land they came from was so distant that it is said to have taken many seasons of travel. There are many stories among my people of how a great many of our ancestors perished in desolate places, some of extreme cold and extreme heat. They are said to have gone a great distance even before arriving at this foreboding land. But they knew that they had to cross this place to get to where they eventually would live and so they had no choice but to climb into the high mountains and there cross the plateau land that took many lives. You see, there was no way around before winter would overtake them and the land they had just crossed was a sea of sand and rock and afforded no protection and with little food they had to go on. There were a great number of people on that trek, men, women, children and the elderly with what food they could carry, hides, tools and weapons. It was hard to find game and plants to sustain so many after their food ran out. Many did not survive to see our new land. It was the Shaman at that time that led our peoples. His name was Takpas. It was to him that Hohapas came in a vision and, through him, ultimately led our people to these lands. Since then the Shaman was called Ho-Takpas. When the people crossed the great grasslands and came to the high wall of mountain they were hungry and tired and many did not want to go on. Indeed, some even stayed there in death. But it was said that it was Hohapas who led the Shaman through the air and showed him the way over the mountain and across the high land to the forests. Since that time I think very few Shamans have ever seen Hohapas. None that I have heard of have ever actually had him call them to him, until now Nakosis."

"Is Hohapas also Aan'ga, as he came from the fire?" asked Nakosis.

"Not really," answered Loka. "While Aan'ga represents the spirit of fire, Hohapas is able to become that spirit of fire, or water, or air, or earth also. He is the male counterpart to our Earth Mother. So, in a way, he is also the Earth Mother. It's a little complicated but it is said that he can be many things and can appear as many things."

"He is the power of magic that is there in all things," added Chako.

"Exactly!" exclaimed Loka, "That is how best to describe him –the magic in all these things, in all the elements. His is the magic power that gives life to all things that the Earth Mother creates. Earth Mother and Hohapas work together do you see? Together they are creation. Together they are one yet they are different, as a mother and a father together create a child yet are different. Since he is also called 'The great magic one', we also call him 'Shaman', as he is the source of all spirit power, Nakosis."

"So," Nakosis inquired, "When we have spirit guides or protection spirits then surely he must also be the source of these as well?"

"Yes, quite right." Said Loka, "but they have their own ways, just as you and I and Chako and everyone else have the same source yet are different people and act independently. Other than once in the great trek of our ancestors it is unknown for Hohapas to intervene or even commune directly with the world of men, even Shaman!"

"I don't know if you understand what importance this is. This is the greatest of portents, my young brother," Chako confided.

Never had Nakosis been called 'brother' by either of these, his elders, and in so doing Chako made him realize what an honor he had been given with his journey's vision.

"Why did our people leave their ancestral lands to begin with Uncle?" asked Nakosis, the question really directed at both men.

Chako continued, "There are said to be many reasons. People tell of fierce warriors who, in small bands, had begun attacking the villages, robbing and raiding the food stores. Others tell of drought that worsened each season until the crops would no longer feed our people and yet others tell of disease that took the lives of many. But it was all these things and also I think the people grew forgetful of the spirit world and so I believe the spirits abandoned them and so these things befell the people. Our ancestors lived much different lives than we do today. Yes, we were a great people with many, many villages and they had vast fields of crops. The land they lived on was very hot and dry but our ancient ones learned to make channels in rock to bring the water of many springs in the mountains to the fields far below. It was a great feat that some say took generations to complete. The people also raised animals and made marvelous warm blankets from the hair of these beasts. They built great villages of mud and stone within the very rock of mountains that were said to be the color of the setting sun. Truly they had great clans. Some tell of so many of our people that the villages, some a full days walk apart, were so plentiful that one could journey several days and see only our peoples. Between the villages were said to be vast fields of crops and the storehouses were always full of grains. Our enemies were few at first and no match for our warriors and so we had much peace. It was said to be a blessed time among all our peoples. But the rains started to lessen and the springs began to dry up. It is said that with each passing year the water grew less. The size of the fields became smaller and the people had to walk greater distances to tend crops that now had to be closer to where the water came from the mountain. Our enemies began growing ever bolder; raiding fields often, knowing the people could not watch all the crops. More of our people were killed in skirmishes with these raiders and the distance between the villages was getting dangerous to travel. As things worsened, the people grew hungry and so many were getting sick. As sickness spread from one village to another and people began dying, many were forced to leave and in small groups try to make for some place where they might find food and survive. Eventually the survivors abandoned the once great villages and moved together as their numbers became smaller. A great council was finally called and the people asked what they should do. They knew that their only hope was to keep the remaining numbers together to stave off attack and certain death from the fierce bands of marauders. Still, some clans chose to go on their own way. Some still had a number of fighting age men and they took their families and divided up the meager supplies and with their families they set out to try to reach the mountain forests. Whatever became of them is not known. Most of the remaining ones chose to leave together in one large group and try for a better land. It was at this time that a Shaman of one of the clans spent many days fasting, praying to the spirits for help and journeying. It was then that Hohapas was said to have appeared before him in vision and showed him the direction he should lead our people. After all the hardship of the trek and after our people finally arrived in the low forest, as you call it, we erected a rough village and began to rebuild our lives, but we were barely a shadow of our former selves. Too many had perished and much of our stores were lost. The ancestors again endured very hard times with the coming of their first winter. It was decided that for more to survive, the village would split into groups and each make a new village elsewhere in the forest with enough distance between them so that they could find sufficient game to eat. Your ancestors eventually settled far to the east in the foothills; my ancestors stayed in the low forest and one, the smallest group, was never seen again."

Nakosis had only heard watered down renditions of this story. Never had he imagined hearing such details as though actually hearing the ancestors themselves. No such complete stories survived with his people or at least if they did they were not described so fully.

He begged more information. "So, then we two peoples are what is left of our ancestors great villages?" he asked.

"Oh no," replied Chako. "There were still a few who did not wish to follow Takpas and the others."

"What became of them? Did anyone ever hear of them?" Nakosis asked, his curiosity now bursting.

"This is the interesting part, my friend," replied Chako. He leaned close to Nakosis and made it obvious with his tone of voice that he was about to reveal some great secret. "Those who stayed were Shamans from what remained of three smaller villages, their extended families and a small group of devoted people from their villages, only about thirty people in all. They said that instead of following the others, they would attempt to head for the sacred place of their ancestors. A place now almost a myth, said to lie in the far distant mountains, a place known as the Mountain of Fire!"

As though to punctuate the shocking impact of the statement, a brilliant flash of lightning burst a glaring white light through the small cave opening immediately followed by a roaring clap of thunder. The three men exchanged pensive glances, each lost to their thoughts. A sudden torrent of rain drew their attention as Loka, peering out the door, suggested they quickly bring their things into the cave. As the other two men gathered at the cave entrance a waterfall was now cascading over the low entryway, pooling on the hard packed ground and making it's way across the clearing.

"We must somehow get our things from the hut. Maybe we should wait and see if it stops." said Chako.

"This is just too much water for runoff. Perhaps somewhere above a stream has been diverted and now runs over our cave!" exclaimed Loka.

"I will get our things," offered Nakosis.

Being the younger it seemed the honorable gesture and one that neither of the older men seemed inclined to contest. As Nakosis lowered himself and prepared to make the dash through the curtain of water, Loka with a sudden moment of inspiration, said, "Nakosis, use the door covering!"

Nakosis grasped the woven mat that served as a door and as he raised it over his head he pulled slightly on the sides making it bow like an upturned bowl. As he bent to avoid the top of the opening he was forced to squat and the position greatly reduced his ability to balance or to move quickly.

Loka, chuckling at this sight yelled, "Run little turtle!" to which all of them burst into laughter. Chako gave his usual approving delight in repeated waves of giggling.

Nakosis burst through the door as fast as his legs could take him but the unexpected force of the water immediately drove him sprawling to the muddy pool now taking over their small clearing. The useless door cover was swept aside as a leaf in a strong wind and Nakosis, gasping in the sudden cold, bolted for the hut as Chako and Loka strained to see what was happening through the wall of water that was fast becoming their new door.

The hut was surprisingly sound and dry despite the pounding rain. The air now pulsated with great flashes of lightning and earth shaking rolls of thunder. The wind was sending large branches crashing to the forest floor and trees were bending like grasses. Nakosis was, however, deeply worried about the rapidly growing pool that seemed destined to consume the whole clearing if the water did not cease, and soon. Nakosis quickly grabbed only the most essential things, knowing that he would have to brave another run for the remaining supplies and questioning in his mind his ability to do so should the storm continue to intensify. Despite all his best efforts, much of the belongings were thoroughly soaked as he again passed through the wall of water that now hid the cave completely. He tried his best to survey the situation from the relative safety of the hut, to see if he could determine the severity or the source of the water, but the storm was now so intense that it was hard to see except for the frequent and violent flashes of lightning illuminating his way.

Once back inside, the other two men helped him to his feet and retrieved the belongings and quickly began to spread them by the fire.

"I have never seen a storm like this!" Nakosis yelled over the roar of wind and thunder. "I worry that the hut will be washed away. The whole clearing is becoming a large pond!"

Loka looked at both of them saying, "Well, for now we should be safe here in the cave. The land falls away from us so the water does not seem to enter here. There would be no use trying to wait this out anywhere out there." Chako shook his head in agreement.

"Well, I managed to grab what was left of the food, weapons and the blankets, but anything else we may have to do without I'm afraid. It may not be there come morning." Said Nakosis.

"That won't be too long in coming," said Chako, "we shall get comfortable and perhaps we can rest."

The evening had been very eventful, especially for Nakosis, yet it was the other two men who, having witnessed the events and having shared great concern for their young brother, bore the brunt of the exhaustion that now seemed to be taking them over. The three men huddled a bit closer to the fire and tried to find comfortable positions, since all they could do was wait. The sound of falling water echoed off the high cave walls yet it was, at times, surpassed by the roar of thunder and at one point the three men commented that it almost felt as though the mountain itself shook. They were ensconced in the cave, safe from the tempest beating relentlessly down upon the mountain but they were also prisoners until it ended. It was obvious no one would sleep this night and so they resumed the conversation.

"So, Uncle tell me about this mountain of fire." Begged Nakosis.

Loka too leaned in, unable to hide his growing curiosity.

"The story says," continued Chako, "That before settling in the red canyons of their villages, the people began life in a mountainous land bordered by high snow covered peaks. It was told that there, deep among those mountains, there were places in the ice and rock where fire came forth and water burst through our mother earth in huge clouds of hot mist that could burn a man in one touch!"

"How could fire and ice live together?" asked Nakosis.

"Yes it is so," said Loka. "I too have heard of such things, but I have never seen them with my own eyes."

Chako continued his story, "I also have not seen these things but there are those who have. There was once one in my village who journeyed very near there as a child. This was back when our peoples first settled in the low forest and the people scattered their villages some many days distance from one another. The village most distant was where he traveled to with his family to visit relations and to trade. While there he spoke of stories the villagers told of this place. They said it was some day's travel deep into the mountains. After they chose the place for their camp, some of the warriors explored the area and ventured into this place. It was said that they encountered strange creatures there, not men nor beast but both, like great bears that stood and walked as men and that had faces like men but whose bodies were covered in fur like a bear. Legend said that the Mountain of Fire lay at the far end of this wild land and that these creatures guarded its secrets. Even though they did not get close to these beings, the warriors were terrified by the sight of these creatures and the wild screams they made and they fled that place never to venture there again. It was said that when next people went to visit that village it was gone, empty, no one was ever found and we know not where they went. Perhaps the creatures killed them."

"Or perhaps," proposed Nakosis, "they went to join the others at the Mountain of Fire."

Chako nodded saying, "Maybe this is so. We may never know."

"Or perhaps we may come to know the truth." said Nakosis, revealing a little of his mind.

Loka, in a tense tone added, "Or someone could perish trying to find out!"

"I can't help but think that one so powerful as Hohapas, one whose name people are even reluctant to speak, would not protect someone he had called to his purpose…whatever that is." said Nakosis.

Shaking his head, making no attempt to mask his deep concern Loka said, "I hope you are right Nakosis."

CHAPTER 8
THE STORM

The violence of the great storm seemed to be waning but still the silvery ribbon of water filled the doorway of the cave and morning's light did not appear to be breaking through. The men had much discussion about it. They all agreed that it should be morning but without anything to give them some indication it could not be determined. They had not seen any lightning flashes nor felt the earth shaking thunder for a while and they decided that they should take their chances and venture out of the cave and access the storms damage. They divided the few bits of food remaining and ate while enjoying the last of the dwindling fire. Nakosis, it was decided would carry the heavier large bag and whatever others he felt his younger broad shoulders could bear through the falling water. The others would follow behind him, jumping as quickly as possible through the fast falling curtain of water. The three men packed themselves tightly together at the entrance as close to the water as possible while still not being immersed within it. The noise reverberating off the narrow point of the cave entrance was deafening and they had to yell loudly to be heard. Nakosis yelled that he would run and for them to give him a moment to get out of the way then Loka and Chako where to follow him.

Loka was enduring Nakosis' serious preparations and the young man's directions but finally said, "Boy, it's only water. I doubt we will melt. Get going!"

To which Nakosis threw himself out the door, disappearing into the wall of water. The waterfall was far more powerful than he could have prepared for and much greater than when he passed through it before. With the weight of the provisions on his back he was instantly driven to the ground and swept forward like a twig in a fast moving stream. The ground beneath him had become slick mud and he tumbled sideways, his arms thrashing about for something, anything to grasp as his feet struggled against the swift water for a foothold. As he spun around, his eyes briefly saw before him neither the clearing nor the trees surrounding it, but a great hole, a gaping chasm where but a day earlier they had sat around a fire.

Nakosis was being swept towards its edge. Abandoning the bag and everything else he bore he struggled with every bit of strength to throw his body to the side and grasp the paltry roots of an overturned tree and with great effort pull himself up and over the edge of the abyss. Already he saw Loka's hand pushing through the water testing its strength before he made his jump to what Nakosis knew would be certain death. He had to stop him! He was screaming Loka's name, but to no avail as he realized he could not be heard. Nakosis could feel the panicked drumming of his heart within his chest. He edged along the side of the rock close to the cave. The spray was now beating him heavily. Even if he could grab Loka's arm he would not be able to hold to the rock and they would both be swept down. His fingers bleeding, he grabbed onto the sharp slice of rock beside the cave opening and crouching low he threw himself sideways toward the wall of white, praying to all the guardians that it would not force him backward over the muddy side of the hole. He slammed through the water, crashing full force into a startled Loka, bouncing both him and a screaming Chako against the rock and crashing onto the cave floor. He was screaming 'Noooooo" at the top of his lungs. Poor Chako seemed to continue yelling even after they stopped rolling together across the cave floor. Nakosis was trembling with fear and although he could not convey it with words, Loka knew something was seriously wrong.

He instinctively grabbed for his spear, screaming at Nakosis "What, what, what is it boy!?"

"Don't go, it's gone, it's gone!" Nakosis finally gasped.

"What's gone, Nakosis?" demanded a troubled Loka.

Chako was still pulling himself up off the floor as Nakosis bent to grasp his arm and help raise him up.

"Everything," Nakosis said, still panting, "the whole clearing, the hut, the trees, all gone."

"Gone where, what are you saying?" Chako finally spoke as he inspected himself for damage.

"The whole mountain in front of the cave is gone," Nakosis was finally able to explain, "Washed away by the water. I didn't see how far down but I suspect right to the valley bottom. It is day but the sky is dark with clouds and still there is not much light. I worried that I would not be able to stop you, uncle." Nakosis said through trembling lips and, sensing his grave concern, Loka threw an arm around him and hugged him dearly saying,

"Thank you, my son, that was very brave of you. But now what shall we do?"

Nakosis considered the situation and decided that he might be able to reach the sharp rocky outcrop beside the cave opening and if he could get some sort of rope to them then they just might be able to pull themselves to the side of the waterfall. It was their only hope they decided. Loka and Chako would wait while Nakosis attempted to gather some vines or roots sufficient enough to reach the cave from the solid ground.

"But how will we know you weren't just swept away? Even if you can find the rope, Nakosis, how will you get it back into the cave?" asked Chako.

Loka decided he could push his spear through the waterfall into the air and Nakosis would have to try to get one end over the spearhead and Loka would then pull the rope into the cave and fasten it to both him and Chako. They would then have to crawl through the waterfall slowly, grabbing to the rock sides and along the edge of the mountain to where Nakosis could grab them, not jump through as Nakosis had done. The force of the falling water would be tremendous on the two old men, but it was either die in the fall or die in the cave.

Nakosis steeled himself and getting onto his knees and taking a deep breath he felt along the wall of the cave opening into the deafening noise and heavy weight of water. As Loka and Chako watched his body disappear into the falls they both beseeched the guardians to watch over them all. Nakosis pulled with all his strength to right himself against the tremendous force beating down on his back, his fingers digging for his life into the hard rock wall once again. He had but a foot's width of wet rock on which to find a toehold and move painfully along the rocky ledge. It was, thankfully, only about two bodies length to where the ground was solid, yet Nakosis could now see in the insipid light of a blackened sky, that a section of mountain had indeed slid to the valley bottom far below. He wished and willed himself slowly along, finally throwing his right arm out to grasp the large root now suspended in the wet air and pulling himself shaking once again onto the sodden fern covered ground. He rose to his feet gasping for air but knowing there was no time to waste. He realized also that the ground on which he now stood was being under cut by the eroding water and could become part of the valley floor at any moment. He raced like a mad man about the forest ripping at any roots that presented themselves. Many pulled up easily but were not of any length to be of use. He knew how to weave smaller roots and lengths of bark into a long sturdy rope by wrapping and twisting them into one long section, but there was not enough time. He was starting to panic and in a near crazed state he began screaming out load, running madly through the forest ripping up the mossy floor, his bare hands now bleeding profusely. He was like a starving bear digging for food. Then Raven appeared on a low branch right in front of him, not a bodies distance from him and cawed very loudly three times while glaring sternly at him. It startled Nakosis for just a moment but enough to make him gather his wits and to focus his attention. Then immediately he saw the vine on the tree Raven had only a heartbeat earlier spoken from. He quickly grasped it and pulled with all his weight and strength to watch bits of moss and bark fall about him as the long thick vine crashed to the moss at his feet. Racing back he worried if the two old men could withstand the pressures of the falls and whether the vine would hold both of them. Could they cling to the rock wall as he did, a strong and much younger man?

When Nakosis returned, Loka had placed his spear against the floor and wall of the cave and extended it out through the falling water where it vibrated in the pulse of the falls. Nakosis quickly tied one end of the vine to the up-turned tree trunk and fashioned a loop on the other. He extended himself as far as he safely could and slung the loop toward the waiting spear. He worried that Loka would be unable to feel the vine with the constant weight of the water bearing down on the spear. He made three attempts before lassoing the spearhead and it appeared that Loka still hadn't detected the vine. Then the spear slowly began to retract into the cave. The instant the force of the water hit the head of the spear the vine washed over the side. Nakosis decided there was no other way –he would again have to climb into the cave opening, again have to brave the water and deliver the vine rope to Loka and Chako. As he began to lower himself over the edge into the mud, the spear again appeared through the water but this time the two men had lashed a piece of firewood to the end so that it stuck out at an angle from the shaft of the spear. Loka was, no doubt, struggling in the cave to keep it upright against the push of the falls. Nakosis quickly scrambled up over the lip of the sunken forest and taking a deep breath and focusing his energy on the shaking spear he hurled the vine toward the water. Success! The loop landed squarely over the upturned stick and as he looked with great relief, Nakosis watched it being slowly extracted back to the cave. It seemed as though much time passed and Nakosis was becoming concerned that the two men had decided that they could not pass through the wall of water when a figure appeared. He assumed it was Loka as that had been the arrangement. He was crouching low to clear the opening but was also pushed to such a position by the enormous weight. Nakosis watched, unable to help, as the figure cleared the falling water and rose slightly, clinging precariously to the wet rock wall. It was Loka. He looked to where Nakosis stood and Nakosis could see the look of doubt in his eyes. Nakosis held the vine firmly in his right arm and stretched his left as much as he could in the direction of Loka, who was now straining to navigate this newly formed cliff face. He was advancing slowly, making sure of every footing, clinging with one hand to the rock, the other to the vine. Just then Nakosis caught a glimpse of Chako making his way through the waterfall. He emerged through safely and as he stood to his full height Nakosis looked with utter disbelief at the large leather bag slung across his shoulders! And Chako was not clinging to the vine as intended. Instead he simply maneuvered his slim frame along the rock like a bat moving across a cave wall. Nakosis waved his arms in wide circles about his waist, trying desperately to convey to the old man to tie the vine around him. Chako looked up with his big toothless grin and actually began to wave back at Nakosis! Maybe he has lost his wits altogether, he thought. Loka had made it to where Nakosis could thankfully get a grasp of his arm and pull him over the edge to the relative safety of the mossy ground. Loka heaved a sigh of relief and turned to see Chako crawl across the tiny lip of rock, his toes barely getting a foothold and no doubt being pulled away from the vertical cliff by the sheer weight of the large bag slung across his back.

"He'll fall, Nakosis!" Cried Loka.

"I know. He didn't tie the vine. What can we do?" Nakosis yelled, as he again scrambled over the edge, his now tired arm clinging to the vine.

Loka had leaned over and held on to Nakosis' arm as best he could. There was nothing they could do but watch. Chako was about half way to them when his left foot slipped from the wall. The weight of the bag now easily pulled him away from the mountain and to what was certain death, but Chako spun completely around with the bag, wedging it firmly against the cliff while he bent his legs under it. Chako looked up above him for a brief moment then studied his predicament and ever so slowly began turning around. It was torturous for the other two men to watch. In the most painstakingly slow maneuver, Chako moved his hands above his head, fingers groping the rock for the slightest grip. The big bag on his back was now suspended in space over the deep chasm, sure to be the cause of his end, the men thought. As they watched, Nakosis holding his breath straining his arm uselessly toward the old Shaman, Chako somehow managed to regain his original face forward position, still no longer using the vine that was to be his lifeline! He was now almost within reach of Nakosis' waiting hand, his fingers waving desperately in the wet air. No one could speak. Chako looked up from carefully positioning his feet on the ledge. He caught Nakosis' pained expression and still bearing his mad grin, he laughed out loud as he threw himself at the muddy bank, grabbing the awaiting arm. At that instant Loka and Nakosis pulled him up and over the edge. Chako fell to the forest floor, laughing like a child at play. The other two were simply too relieved to express their anger and so they too chuckled at the incredible ease with which he viewed whatever the world seemed to throw his way.

"Were you not afraid?" Loka finally asked.

"A little," replied Chako. "It appeared at one moment as though the bag would be lost." He said.

"The bag!" cried Loka, "Why you old fool, you can always get another bag." The anger in his voice was apparent, but also the relief in his eyes.

"But," Chako continued, turning to Nakosis, "you nearly scared me out of my skin!" Nakosis gave him a puzzled look. "When you burst through the water into the cave I was up close behind Loka, my foot on the rock ready to give a big push out the door. Then you came through knocking us down. It was so unexpected I swear by all the spirits, I nearly soiled myself!"

Loka laughed like Nakosis had never seen him do before. His face reddened and his eyes watered as he roared at the old man.

He managed to blurt out, "Now that I know you are prone to soiling yourself, I will be sure to always be the one in front - next we find ourselves in danger!"

Old Chako's wrinkled face lit up with his great toothless grin and he rolled on the ground in delightful laughter, the site of which caused the other two to do the same. Nakosis held his sides and wiped the tears from his cheeks and eyes. The laughter did wonders to ease their tension and once it subsided the men had an opportunity to survey the situation. They stood in awe looking at the great hole in the earth where once had been their hut and clearing. Giant trees leaned almost horizontally, and what once had been their small stream was now a waterfall, dropping almost to the river valley below.

"Nakosis was right, the stream must have been blocked and diverted by rocks moving in the rain," observed Chako.

"That would explain the great roar and shaking we thought was thunder," added Nakosis.

"We must move away. This edge is unsafe. Look over there at the other side," Chako cautioned.

They could clearly see large lumps of mud, ferns and small bushes that once were the topsoil of the forest falling down the watery sides of the great hole. Then pieces of rock beneath were breaking loose and tumbling down, the sound of their falling echoed up the face of the mountain. Trees that had stood for countless time now poised at the brim, their roots thrust into the wet air, awaiting their inevitable end.

"Quickly," said Nakosis, "lets move inland."

They followed the old trail through the forested bench. Many times the way was blocked by the great trees that had fallen in the storm, their huge branches forcing them to either crawl under or over the giant trunks. Chako commented that the storms' aftermath looked as if the gods had battled.

"We must make our village," said Loka. "I hope the storm was not as severe there also." He added, the grave concern unmistakable in his voice.

"We will not make the village by days end at this rate," said Chako, pointing to the many obstacles in their path.

"He is right." Loka conceded. "Perhaps we had best find a place to spend the night."

"Can we make the pool?" asked Nakosis. "At least if the stream was not destroyed by the storm we may still get some fish there."

"Ahh, a very good idea," said Chako, licking his lips in gesture, his appetite whetted.

"Yes, I think we can do that and there is a clearing enough for fire and to take our rest." replied Loka.

They moved slower than they imagined. The stress of the storm, their hair –raising escape from the cave, lack of rest and now the many natural hazards of the return journey were showing as great fatigue. They labored for breath and even Nakosis, although much younger, was finding the going hard. They stopped many times to recover. Loka was leading the way and would suggest the rest intervals and Nakosis suspected it was for Chako's benefit. Yet, the old man still seemed content and unconcerned. Nakosis reflected on the inner power Chako and Loka possessed. Few young men he knew in the village could endure as these two did. It was rumored that great Shamans don't have to sleep, that they go to the spirit world in trance and there they conduct their business as one does here during the course of the day, and then they return and do the same here in the waking world. Nakosis was beginning to believe there might be some truth to this story. Certainly neither of them had slept much since setting out from the village and although now extremely tired they did, in fact, seem to be possessed of unusual endurance. It was said that wherever a Shaman went his spirit guides and protectors went too, ever present within him ready to give protection. To harm a Shaman was considered a great taboo. Even a Shaman of the enemy would be accorded some respect, for not to do so would be to invite the wrath of his protector spirits.

The storm, it seemed, had rolled in from the flatlands where, unobstructed, it gathered tremendous power that it then unleashed on the mountains. It then moved further over the ridges into distant valleys, diminishing as it did. Loka was concerned that the river, like the stream above the cave, may have caused damage for the village. It was high enough to be safe from all but the worst flood. But Loka said that should many trees become jammed in the narrow passes, it could cause catastrophic flooding when it finally broke free.

His concern was somewhat relieved when they finally made it to the small stream and the pool and discovered that the waters appeared as normal. The thick black storm clouds had parted just enough to let the thin light of days end through the trees.

Chako now began to open the large bag as the other two looked on to see what he had risked life and limb for. He pulled forth the large blankets that had been left beside the fire to dry. Wrapped so carefully among them was Loka's ancient rattle! Loka's eyes lit up at the sight as Chako ceremoniously handed it to him, bowing his head in respect of the object. Before Loka could offer his gratitude, he also produced his large drum, laying it softly upon a rock then dug out and handed the smaller drum to Nakosis. Nakosis bowed his head and thanked him profusely as did a still very surprised Loka. Chako, true to form, simply giggled. In the bottom wrapped in the third blanket Chako pulled out his small shoulder bag containing his most important survival tools. Their faces brightened at the sight of the small satchel since they both knew what it contained. Chako giggled with delight when he brought forth his fire drill and the handful of shredded old bark tinder that the drill was always kept packed in. As well, there was a couple of small dried 'fire mushrooms'. These were actually a fungus that grew only on the white-bark tree. The bark of this tree was renown for making containers such as Chako used to brew the wonderful root soup, as well as many other practical things for the people, but also it was the best fire starter. These trees died from the top down and as they did the small crescent shaped fungus would also die and dry out. It made such good tinder that the people called it 'fire mushroom'.

Stepping up to take charge of the situation, Loka suggested that Chako put the fire drill to good use. He would attempt to gather some still dry wood and Nakosis would hopefully get some fish. Chako considered that worst was over and that they were now blessed by the spirits as all these things came together with relative ease. The three tired men sat back by a warm fire to fill their bellies and to perhaps explore the spiritual interpretations of the past events.

CHAPTER 9
PREPARATION

They talked about the great vision of Nakosis, especially the 'calling' of Hohapas. Both old men agreed that such a thing was an unprecedented occurrence, greatly eclipsing anything within their combined experience.

"We are just two old men," said Chako. "We have our spirit guides and our protectors and we have honored them all our days and our lives have been greatly enriched because of their presence. It is due to them that we have been able to assist our peoples in our small way. But THIS!" he exclaimed, shaking his head back and forth as though mystified, "THIS is a call from the gods!"

"The gods," Nakosis asked, somewhat confused.

"Why yes!" Chako continued. "Hohapas is no simple spirit, Nakosis. Some of our ancestors worshipped him. They said that while our Mother Earth appears in all the beautiful forms we behold every day and all the wonderful beings that are our brethren, Hohapas, being the magic force of Nature, could take shape as a visible being, a man, so that we can show proper reverence. Although, since the beginning time, only very few have actually seen him, his image has been passed down from the first of our Shaman. In all our stories, Nakosis, only Ho-Tapas is said to have seen him and that was when he pointed the way for our ancestors, causing the spirits to lift him like an eagle above the land to show the path. But even Ho-Tapas did not actually see him in the same personal way as in your vision. What to speak of being spoken to!"

"You said 'the beginning time', Chako? What of that time? Did people see him then?"

"Ahhh, that was a time of Hohapas' great power, when the world was much different than now. His magic was everywhere. The people at that time moved within the spirit world with every breath. There was no mist of separation as there is now. Then all the creatures could understand each other.

The people knew what the birds and the animals were saying. Not just how now we know sometimes what the different cry of a bird or call of an animal means, but I mean they could *really* speak with all their brethren in the animal world. The crops grew with almost no tending and every day the people lived with their spirit guides as they would with their brothers and sisters. It was even said that your spirits guides were visible to others and theirs also! Magic was very much alive in their world then, Nakosis. This was the power of Hohapas!"

"What happened and why now would Hohapas be letting me, of all people, see and hear him? Why not Loka or you, Chako? You at least know who he was...I mean *is*. You know of his history, whereas I had no idea who he was." There was a strain in Nakosis' voice and the two old Shamans could sense his apprehension at being chosen by Hohapas.

"That is for Hohapas only to know." Replied Chako.

Loka contributed his thoughts, "Nakosis my son, you, I believe, were chosen at your birth. I said at the time when the great sky fire appeared that something profound was to become of it and now this is coming to be. Everything in your life so far has brought you to this point."

"And what of my parents passing?" Nakosis yelled, then realizing he'd revealed such emotion he humbly lowered his eyes.

"Yes, even that too," Loka continued, "Your parents were my friends too Nakosis and I also grieved in their passing and for your loss. I too saw the pain in your heart and how well you tried to hide it. But now I see that in their moving on to their next life, you have become the man you are today. Perhaps, had they remained you may have been different, more like the other young men in the village. But you are not like them, are you Nakosis? No, and now with Chako's and my help your 'specialness' has been revealed. But also, like Chako said, we are just two old men. We cannot guide you much more, my young brother. You already walk more in the world of spirit and magic. We can maybe give you some small bit of guidance, but more from our years than our power. You know as we both do also what has to be done."

Chako shook his head in agreement and turning from Loka to look across the fire at Nakosis he said, "You must make the journey to the mountain of fire, Nakosis!"

"But how will I do such a thing?" Nakosis pleaded, "You know more about Hohapas than anyone and you said yourself that no one seems to know where this 'mountain of fire' even is." The young man's voice was trembling.

Hearing his trepidation, Chako stirred the coals of the fire and made adjustment to the wood, allowing a moment for the feeling to subside before he continued. "That is not entirely true. If one truly desired it then I believe it may be possible to find the mountain of fire. It wouldn't be easy, however. It would mean first finding the 'other ones', the other village. The people who long ago moved nearer to the frozen place said to be the beginning of that world. It is said that the mountain lies at the other end of that plateau, no doubt the same one of your visions, Nakosis. Hohapas has sent you some sign of the journey to come and he may yet give you more. The search could begin within my own village. There are still some elders there who may yet know something."

Loka intervened, "It is too late and we are too tired to make more sense of this now. Let us rest and in the morning we will make the village. There we can rest more and then with the spirit's blessing the three of us will devise a path to help our young brother."

Morning dawned warm and bright as though the tumult of the previous day had not occurred. Birds sang and every green thing was resplendent with drops of water, the air fresh and sweet. The morning sun filtered gently down through the canopy of leaves. They had all slept deeply, seemingly untroubled by dreams or visions and awoke feeling completely refreshed. They finished some fish and resumed the final leg of the path to the village.

It was Peeka who first acknowledged them, leaving the company of other young girls she ran up calling her uncle, looking oddly at Chako and Nakosis, she threw her small arms around Loka then greeted Nakosis likewise. He was slightly taken aback by the show of affection but it also warmed his heart. Others approached. The leader of the Wolf society's lodge was in the clearing and when he turned to wave a greeting to Loka, Loka signaled him to follow them to his hut. The village, it seemed, had been spared the ferocity of the storm, though the ground was still saturated in places, children playing in the puddles that had formed and angry parents collecting them, knocking mud from their clothes. The Wolf leader was barefoot, wrapped in a heavy blanket as though he'd only just left his lodge to relieve himself, not expecting to be headed off across the muddy village, but he would not hesitate to hear the words of his Shaman. His glance moved from Nakosis to Chako and back to Loka but he said nothing as they came to the Shaman's hut. Inside they all took positions in a circle on the floor. Loka entered last and leaving the door flap open for light and air, he took the Wolf leader's hands and they bowed their heads in formal greeting.

After being assured that all in the village were well and that the storm caused no damage, Loka turned to Nakosis, placing his hand on his shoulder saying, "Go now to your grandparents lodge and see that they are alright. They will also be concerned for you Nakosis, but please return here this evening. We have much to talk about." Loka turned to his old friend, "Chako, could you use some more to eat?"

That brought the radiant smile back to Chako's face and Loka yelled for Peeka as Nakosis ducked out the door and crossed the village to his grandparents lodge. As he stepped around puddles and the busy actions of playing children he smiled to himself at the gentle and peaceful life their village enjoyed. The crops were radiant in the warming sun and seemed ever more freshened by the heavy rains. Surely these people are blessed, he thought. What portent could his visions have that would disrupt this tranquil life? He did not like thinking that he could be the cause of some drastic alteration to the idealic world of the three villages. He almost secretly wished that it had not been him who the god had chosen. But then, he rationed, if it is meant to be then someone else would have been chosen and the outcome unchanged. No, I must accept this as Chako and Loka have and, like them, I must selflessly dedicate myself to the people, he thought. He only hoped that he was up to the calling. He knew he had no real training, that a Shaman undergoes a lifetime of teachings and gathering knowledge. He had only a brief instruction. Chako and Loka believe that a god had blessed him. He pondered the implication. Perhaps then my only course is to allow Hohapas to guide me, to give myself and to become open completely to the spirit world so that it will guide me and protect me. I do not know what else I can do, he resolved.

Lost in such thoughts he heard his name and looked up from the muddy ground into the deeply alluring eyes of Taku. His face brightened, revealing the joy he felt at the mere sight of her. She flashed a brilliant white smile and her eyes sparkled. How beautiful she is, Nakosis thought. As they drew closer Nakosis, never taking his eyes from hers, raised his arms as to invite an embrace. The gesture seemed to happen all by itself as though someone else was responding. He was a little shocked at his boldness but even more so at her reciprocating, as she wrapped her arms warmly around him. As he held her close he breathed her in, the sweet smell of her hair, the red flowers that adorned her braids, the smoke on her tanned dress and then just as quickly she drew back, looking around somewhat embarrassed at her leave of decorum. Nakosis also seemed a little taken aback, looking to see if others witnessed the open show of affection.

Now, with an appropriate gap between them she said, "How are you Nakosis? I...the village was concerned for you. I was told Loka had taken you into the mountain some place, perhaps to seek your animal spirits?"

Nakosis smiled and a slight chuckle escaped his lips. "More like they are seeking me!" he replied.

Thinking he must be referring to the incident with the panther, Taku giggled and in a gesture meant to acknowledge his humor she pushed her hand against his arm. The touch was only for a moment but the feel of her hand made him beam with an inner warmth.

"Well, hopefully no more visits from panther!" she commented.

"No" replied Nakosis, "a panther is the least of my concerns." She looked quizzically at him, not understanding the meaning of his words. "I only mean," he said, "that the spirit world is full of surprises," he sputtered, trying to dispel any further questions about his meaning.

"So, then you'll be learning more with Loka?" she asked.

"Ahh…well… not directly. Ahh…I will still be learning though, of that I'm sure."

"So the other one, the older Shaman, Chako, is he going to teach you, Nakosis?"

She was determined he thought. Still being vague but not wanting her to go he said, "Oh Chako, he has taught me many interesting things, to be sure." Then changing the conversation he said, "I was headed for my grandparents lodge. Where are you going? Are you in a hurry?" He thought that his tone may have been too pleading and for a heartbeat he worried that she might indeed have somewhere to be.

"No, not really" she said, the reply easing his concern and the relief no doubt evident in his smile.

"Perhaps then you could walk there with me. I thought I'd go along the river trail so I might bring some berries. Are there still any there?" he asked.

"Well, if I help you I think we could still find enough to fill this basket." She laughed, lifting a small bark container from where she'd held it by her side.

Nakosis had not even noticed it. Taku thought that he did in fact see the basket and made up the whole story about getting berries in order to accompany her to the river. The thought greatly pleased her. As they walked, Nakosis tried his best to keep the conversation away from him and where he'd been. He asked about her and her family and others in the village. A Shaman's journeying was not supposed to be discussed openly. A Shaman was to keep certain aspects of his spirit guides and guardians to themselves. Nakosis, because he was so inexperienced, revealed all to Loka so he could guide him and teach him. Chako also became a confidant for the same reasons, but now it seemed that the events were to prove to be of such importance that they would be openly discussed among the village leaders and wise elders. Could I tell her? Nakosis thought to himself. The elders would decide the proper course of action and determine how much the village needed to be aware of.

Village structure was such that everything was equally shared, food, as well as labor, were fairly and equitably divided among the many lodges. As there were many families, they all fell under the auspices of one of the warrior society lodges. These lodges were also societal houses of government based upon a common spirit animal such as the wolf, bear, eagle, or raven. They were not solely a hall of warriors, but more so the place where the elders would give council on all matters of the village. The name simply stuck from the more violent past when halls of warriors were the much-needed defensive front line in battle. Of course they still held that purpose.

Taku seemed to sense something in Nakosis. She had always had that ability since they were young children. It was part of what drew them close to each other. There existed a special openness and connection between them. When Nakosis lost his parents to the sickness he kept a brave and stoic face before the others, but when she sought him out alone by the river he could not conceal his grief and with her young arm around him he poured out his loss and wept openly in her embrace, as did she for his sorrow. She had made no mention of it to anyone. Then, Nakosis believed, that it was no coincidence that she be the one to bear witness to his miraculous encounter with the strange spirit panther very near to where they now stood. Taku strolled unspeaking beside Nakosis, noting how very, very slowly he walked trying to make the distance to his grandfather's lodge last a little longer.

As they paused by the berry bushes she turned to him and boldly reaching up and gently holding his face she looked him in the eyes and said, "My dear Nakosis, you cannot hide from me! What bears so heavy on your mind?"

"I must take a long and dangerous journey, Taku!" The words poured from his lips as natural as breath. There was absolutely no way he could continue the ruse, no way he could keep the truth from her. Taku kept his face in her hand and her eyes on his for what seemed an eternity. To Nakosis it was as though she was looking into his very soul. He could not determine a single thing from her expression. Finally, she allowed her hand to slowly slide down his face, her warm palm moved down his neck to rest for but a heart beat upon his bare chest while ever maintaining her eyes on his. She smiled her magnificent white smile. Her dark eyes narrowed and sparkled. She tilted her head ever so slightly, her tiny beaded braid brushed across her sandy colored skin and Nakosis grew weak at the knees at the beauty of her.

Turning and walking ever so slowly away she turned her head back and said, "Well, come Nakosis, tell me all about it."

They took a seat on a large gray log and Nakosis told his story. For what seemed a lifetime, the events of the last few days went by before the sun had passed half its journey through the sky.

Taku spoke barely a word other that to say, "Go On Nakosis, tell me more!"

Nakosis paused to get his breath, cupping his hands in the cold river to quench his thirst.

"Please, Taku," said Nakosis, "you must not repeat what I've told you. Loka feels that the people will think that there is cause for worry."

When he was done, she looked at him with eyes he could not read. That was the trouble with her, he thought. He never knew how she was taking the things he said. Finally after considering the story for a moment Taku rose, and with her arms clasped across her chest, she walked alone to the river and stood watching the water. Nakosis wanted to run up to her but decided against it. Better she gather her thoughts as is her way he surmised. Taku *always* spoke with carefully placed words, even as a child she always seemed to say only what was perfectly appropriate to the moment and she was *never* wrong. Nakosis thought her mind and her resolve was as rock steady as the White Mist Mountain. It was one of the things he admired about her and if he admitted it, he feared it a little also. There was not much she could not do if she so decided. As a child she was determined not to allow her sex to, in anyway, handicap her from achieving her full abilities. When she took up the bow she did so with such a concentration and determination that it amazed her father, who had given in to her persistence and taught her. Soon, much to the surprise of the young men, she easily surpassed them all in the village competition. And she did it with such skill, poise and grace that none dare make even a joking comment. Nakosis noted that it was an irresistible combination - a woman who had both stunning beauty and deep inner strength and wisdom. His only saving grace, he thought, was that most of the other young men were too intimidated by her to pursue her.

Taku seemed lost in her thoughts and Nakosis would have given anything in that uncertain moment to know what they were. It seemed an unduly long time that she pondered the situation. She turned twice to stare at Nakosis, only to turn again toward the river and resume her contemplation. The suspense was almost unbearable to Nakosis. In his mind he played out numerous possible reactions she might have and scenarios that could occur as a result. Finally Taku turned, clasped her hands behind her back and slowly and methodically paced toward Nakosis, as though finalizing one last detail of her decision.

Looking directly into his eyes, she tenderly placed her hands on either side of his face. "You have no choice, Nakosis." she said, still cradling his head in her hands. "You have been chosen. It is not for us to try to change the will of the spirits. They are the guardians and our people have always respected such things. I love you, Nakosis."

The words made him melt. In all his dreams these were the words his ears burned to hear and now that they had he was to leave this beautiful woman, his return uncertain.

Before he could respond she continued, "I will be here when you return Nakosis. And when you do the village will celebrate your return *and* our betrothal!" Nakosis could only stand dumb and speechless. "Until then you will be always in my thoughts and I will pray to the great mystery for your safe return." Taku reached up and kissed him tenderly on the lips, turned, and was gone.

Even when he came through the door of his grandparent's lodge and received their warm, loving embrace he was still in a fog and not fully aware of the world outside of Taku's beautiful smile. He must have appeared like a person touched, he thought, realizing he could not wipe the grin from his face. He felt now that no matter what his destiny presented he could endure even the worst knowing in his heart that he had the love of Taku to comfort him. He could not tell anyone of their betrothal promise, as none of the formalities with her parents had been properly attended to, but that was a mere formality that he would see righted upon his return. For now, though, it weighed heavily on him that he had to be the keeper of two great secrets. He took some solace in knowing that he could share the news of his bursting heart with Loka and Chako.

He was soon sharing a warm bowl of delicious stew with his grandparents and his visiting distant cousins from Deer River village. They did not visit often and so there was an atmosphere of festivity. As there was much catching up on the affairs of distant family, Nakosis' grandfather politely refrained from querying Nakosis about his time with Loka out of respect for the spiritual nature of his relationship. He knew that it would be a personal thing between Nakosis, his guides and his teacher.

The day was now gone and stars were replacing the last light of the sun as it dipped below the mountain and Nakosis knew he had to go to Loka's hut. He excused himself from the family, explaining he had other duties and that he would talk more with them tomorrow. As he walked the dark village he could smell the cooking fires, their smoke thick in the air, and he listened to the sounds of the village life around him, families talking of their day's labor, sharing meals, babies crying, dogs barking. The only people he met were the sentries who took turns patrolling the village, walking between the pitch torches that ringed the clearing. They said nothing but bowed their heads in passing.

Nakosis could see the fire glowing through the open door of Loka's hut. Chako's giggling was the first sound he heard and it immediately made him smile. He thought of the amazing events he had shared with these two, who not but a short time earlier were more like strangers. Now they are more like

84

my family, thought Nakosis. He stopped at the door and announced his arrival, as was the custom for one awaiting invitation to enter.

"Get in here Nakosis." was Loka's response.

He ducked in the doorway and was instantly pulled off balance by a very animated, giggling Chako who tugged him to the ground beside him. Loka laughed at the display and Nakosis could not help but do the same as Chako giggled on.

"How is your family little brother?" Chako asked.

Before he could answer Chako handed him a bowl of steaming hot venison stew.

"Had enough fish!" he commented.

Nakosis tried in vain to refuse, saying he'd previously eaten but it was useless to argue with Chako, so he pulled up a piece of hide and joined them at the fireside - eating. Chako threw his skinny arm over Nakosis' shoulder roughly pulling his young friend toward him in a warm hug that spilled hot stew over his leg, but Chako didn't care.

"The one who saved us!" he exclaimed as Loka laughed, adding,

"That he did! It was a great act of bravery, one that shall always be remembered."

Chako reached over, filling Loka's bowl. Chako was always delighted by the presence of food. It always seemed to make him overly joyous and it was heart warming to watch him enjoy a hearty meal.

As the food was finished and more sticks placed upon the fire, Loka cleared his throat. The others, getting the message, quickly emptied their bowls and settled themselves upon the hides and prepared to hear what Loka had to say.

He looked at Nakosis, "We have discussed it much, Chako and I." he said, "and Chako seems to believe that with the help of some of the elders of his village it may be possible to piece together the lost parts of the ancestor's story,"

Chako elaborated, "Yes, there are a few still alive who, when young, travelled to the location of the lost village. They went as children with a group of elders and they placed some offerings to the spirits of the people and prayed for them. They did not stay long. They were afraid that the beast people might discover them and so they left quickly, but they still have sharp minds and perhaps they will remember how to go there."

"Yes, but then what?" Nakosis asked, "You said the mountain of fire is across a barren plateau."

"Yes," Chako continued, "but it is said that the plateau world begins somewhere not far from the lost village and that the mountain of fire is on the other side of this place. If one found where this place began near the old village, then it would be easy to see what direction it takes and know where you would have to travel. Besides, I think once you were at the lost village you may receive some deeper sign."

"If it is their will that you should go there, Nakosis, I think they surely must help you. Said Loka adding, "Did you not say the same thing yourself?"

"Yes, but, it's just that… ah…forgive me…but… it just seems so uncertain uncle."

Loka continued, "The spirits do not work as men do, Nakosis. They only give us glimpses of their true purpose and let us know what is necessary. Sometimes we just have to have trust."

"Like when you threw yourself out the cave door!" Chako laughed.

"Maybe not the best example." Added Loka, as they all laughed at his easy, if not odd sense of humor.

Loka had been asked to visit Quick Waters village to assist in settling a quarrel among rival families that was disrupting the tranquility of the village and threatening to escalate. The nature of the dispute was uncertain but it appeared that a young girl was involved. Loka asked Nakosis to accompany him. Chako would remain in White Mist village in Loka's small lodge. As Loka's esteemed guest he would relish the attention of the others and especially the delicious meals they would ask him to attend. Chako had no argument about the arrangement. Nakosis would enjoy the opportunity to have some time alone with Loka and to talk with him further about his journey. He suspected that was partially the motivation behind Loka requesting he travel with him to the village. However, he knew his mind would be hard pressed to concentrate on anything but Taku. Chako and Loka discussed the problem in Quick Waters village, as Loka understood it, two young men had sought the affections of a particular young girl and had come to blows over their rivalry.

Chako laughed, shaking his head as he said, "A young man's feelings for a woman! What do you think of such things young brother?"

Nakosis, preoccupied with his own thoughts of Taku, suddenly realized he was being spoken to. He looked up to see both Chako and Loka staring at him, smiling. I can't hide a single thing from these two, Nakosis thought. He smiled, almost blushing and quickly blurted out the entire details of his and Taku's momentous event. He scarcely paused to breathe, feeling great relief at being able to share his incredible joy. The entire story was accompanied by constant suppressed giggling from Chako, who after Nakosis finished, turned to Loka and punching him on the arm declared, "So our young wolf has grown teeth eh?" Loka laughed partly, Nakosis thought, at Chako's comment and partly at Nakosis' boyish embarrassment. When Loka smiled, he radiated a deep and sincere warmth and reached across to grasp Nakosis by the shoulder congratulating and blessing him. Chako relayed his approval by his usual nodding and giggling.

The conversation soon returned to the search for the lost village. Chako would take Nakosis back to the village of the Low Forest People. Nakosis had never been there and were it not for Chako's presence he felt somewhat apprehensive about visiting a people other than his own. Chako was, for all intents and purposes, no different than anyone in his village, yet Nakosis now realized just how ill prepared he was for the incredible task that lay ahead of him. He had been trained, as had the other young men, with a survival skill set unsurpassed by anyone. He could fend quite well for himself in almost any wild situation. He had little fear for any natural beasts he might encounter. That was not his worry. He was uneasy about the unnatural beasts and unfamiliar peoples he may encounter.

"Who will be taking this journey with us, Uncle?" he asked. There was an uneasy silence in which Chako and Loka exchanged looks.

Loka answered, "You will have to undertake the journey alone Nakosis."

"Alone!" Nakosis cried.

Loka raised his palm to him explaining, "You know that it is the way of the people that at your age you would undertake the 'days on the mountain', fasting and seeking your spirit guides."

"Yes, but this is no 'days on the mountain' you are speaking of!" Nakosis interrupted. Loka waited a moment letting the young man regain his calm. Nakosis, realizing his lack of control apologized.

"No you are right, of course, this is more that just a spirit quest. But you are more than just an ordinary young man. Your spirits came to you - you did not seek them. You did not have any choice, Nakosis. Likewise, you have no choice now. You have been blessed, called by Hohapas himself to possibly fulfill an ancient prophecy or at least to fulfill your spiritual destiny. You have every right to be fearful of what you do not yet understand. Do you not remember I once said that I believed you would come to know much and fear little? This is that foretelling coming to be, Nakosis. We, each of us, have our own destinies. Most people do not have the fortune to even know their true purpose in life. I think some may be called to achieve greatness, yet they refuse to hear their call. They hold back from fear and lead 'ordinary' lives, never knowing what might have been had they only possessed the ears to hear and the heart to follow. You have no such obstacles, Nakosis. You have a power that neither of us has ever seen."

Loka indicated Chako who, now locking very serious, nodded in total agreement.

"You have the ability, all that remains, Nakosis, is that you find the courage. Trust in your heart that you are meant for this thing. Trust in your spirit guides, your guardians, trust that Hohapas will direct you, but mostly have faith in your own ability my young brother!"

Nakosis was greatly humbled and lowered his head. How could he not have the courage when these two men had so much trust in him? He knew that, if for no other reason, he couldn't let them down. He would find the mountain of fire and discover his destiny or he would die trying.

CHAPTER 10
BLACK FACES

Now it was morning. It was warm and fragrant as the mist rose off the river in one thick mass, wafting through the village as if it had a mind of its own like some ethereal being. Nakosis rose early before the first light of dawn, wrapping himself against the damp in a warm robe, he ducked out of his Grandparent's lodge and away from the snoring of his cousins. He strode quickly, determined, through the village to stop just behind the high wooden wall of a lodge across the dirt square from Taku's family dwelling. Smoke was wafting from the roof hole. Somewhere dogs were barking and villagers were rising to face the day. He would have to be at Loka's hut very soon but the urge to see Taku was too strong. He could hardly sleep since their last encounter. He just wanted to scream to the whole world of his undying love for her. The village should know they were betrothed, he thought, and if I were allowed a 'normal' calling it would be so. But deep inside he found the strength to stay the course and hold to his promise to Loka and Chako. 'You will return and marry that woman.' Chako had told him. He prayed it be so. The sun was almost up now and the heavy robe was getting warm. He paced outside the lodge - three steps one way then turned and three steps back to the corner to peer around it to see if Taku would emerge from the hut. No one had yet left. He was growing frustrated and threw the heavy robe against the wall of the lodge.

"Get up already!" he accidently spoke the words aloud!

From within the lodge a voice yelled out, "Who is there?"

Nakosis froze. He panicked and in the moment was unsure what to say or do.

"Who is it? What's going on?" Another voice from within the lodge broke in.

Nakosis heard rustling. Soon angry young warriors would emerge like wasps from a kicked nest. If they saw him they would not take kindly to this 'spirit boy' playing pranks. Nakosis grabbed the robe. It was caught on the log. Panicking, he jerked it free, the act causing the side of the lodge to shake and angry voices to issue forth. He ran quickly into the edge of the clearing, weaving swiftly between several dwellings before throwing the robe over his head and walking ever so slowly back through the square trying not to breathe too heavily. A few sleepy warriors, half naked, their spears in hand had ran from the lodge and gathered at the corner from where the noise had come. They were shooting glances around the still sleepy village. Nakosis walked purposefully toward them and as he strode past they tipped heads in greeting.

"What are you doing?" Nakosis asked trying desperately not to smile.

"Nothing" one replied.

"Just some silly children." Another responded.

Nakosis picked up his pace and when he was sure he was out of sight he laughed out loud. By the time he returned to his grandparent's hut he was absolutely giddy but was restraining it well. His grandmother had risen and rekindled the fire and was preparing some food for the still waking cousins. His Grandfather had already left to hunt for more food. Nakosis began packing his things. His Grandmother became upset, believing he was again leaving for a long while. He reassured her that this time he was merely going with Loka to Quick Water's village. Her eyes brightened when he said that Loka had requested he accompany him.

Looking at the two lazy cousins still wiping their sleepy eyes she turned to Nakosis saying, "Quick Waters! Wait, your cousins can travel with you!"

He hated to lie to his grandmother but he knew Loka would be furious if the two younger men went with them. Besides, aside from being quite lazy they were also very talkative. Nakosis imagined the journey and quickly stated that Loka was departing immediately. He, in fact, was late he said and couldn't keep the Shaman waiting!

"Besides," he added as a second precaution, "I believe he has some very special stop on the way that is to do with the spirits, very personal!" he added.

His Grandmother looked at him as though he were a stupid child.

"Yes, I'm sure it is!" she barked and almost hissed through her teeth at the two men stumbling from their robes to eat.

Nakosis leaned into the cook fire and kissed her on the cheek, "Sorry Grandmother."

She wacked him on the rear with the stick she held and smiled at him as he ducked through the door. He wasn't completely lying. Loka was indeed raring to go and a little upset that he'd had to wait until full light to depart. Nakosis didn't see Chako. He pictured him in the hut, no doubt enjoying a hearty morning's meal.

They left the village along the river trail, walking through the many fields of lush crops and then into the deep forest following the bench along side the river. Unlike the path to the cave, this trail was wide and smooth from being so well traveled. Along the path Nakosis took note of the many animals that also used this convenient route through the dense forest. Bear and deer left their marks in the soft black soil. 'How many people have placed their feet upon this very path as I am now doing?' Nakosis pondered the question. He thought of the many years since the villages settled here and the many generations of families who contributed their passage to the trail. How many were now gone, moved on, to where, to what other lives? He thought of the many animals also and of those who gave their lives to sustain the people. Of the deer whose hides made the moccasins to cover the feet that compacted this very earth he now walked upon. He thought about the village fletchers who made the perfect bows and arrows that enabled the people to hunt so proficiently, of the nappers who meticulously made the fine stone arrowheads and spear points. He thought of the earth herself. This is the 'connectedness' he realized, connected to the multitude of beings past and present and even future by the simple act of 'being'. His footfalls would now leave an imprint on the path and on the path of time itself. There is no act, no existence that does not have consequences, no matter how small. Perhaps in the future, long after I am gone another will walk here and ponder these things also. Perhaps it will even be me! I wonder, will a part of me have a 'feeling' of knowing about places?

As he looked about him, the morning sun had cast its brilliant rays down through the dew-covered canopy and the birds were heralding their passage through this splendid grove. Ahead, the first small falls of the Blue Fish River could be heard over the orchestra of birdsong. There were three falls before they came to the confluence of the Quick Water River. This was why the people had to travel by land and not by water. The people had knowledge of simple dugout canoes, but too little navigable waters to warrant the great labor involved in their making.

Loka marched forward, his eyes to the route ahead; turning unspeaking to make sure Nakosis was behind him. The falls were louder now and the air heavily laden with moisture from the thick clouds of spray. The red bark trees were abundant here, thriving in the lush environment and their thick trunks covered in deep layers of moss. Large ferns grew from the wide girths of their moss covered trunks, sometimes far up the huge trees to a height where a man could not reach. Nakosis marveled at such beauty. It had been a very long time since he had travelled this path with his father so many years past. Loka crested a rise in the path that afforded the first view of the falls. As he did so he fell immediately to the ground as though struck by an arrow. Nakosis gasped and rushed toward where he lay, but Loka had spun quickly to face the startled young man. He had a look of stark horror on his face. He slid his body down the muddy rise grabbing at the strap over Nakosis shoulder so as to pull him close. He uttered the dreaded word over the roar of the water -"Enemy!"

Nakosis opened his mouth to question, but Loka placed his hand over it, pulling Nakosis to the ground and almost dragging him through the thick forest floor, past the huge trees to where they could look over the falls and the Blue Fish River below. He pointed carefully, not extending his arm past the protective cover of ferns, to the far distant ridge on the other side of the falls. Nakosis stared intently for a moment before he detected the slight movement. There on the ridge a column of warriors was trying to navigate the slippery terrain and get to the river. They were still a ways off but Nakosis could see that they appeared heavily armed, their faces painted black.

Loka, holding Nakosis very close spoke, "They may have a scout ahead of that column. If so he must be close. They are still coming over the ridge and there may be a great many of them."

"I must run back to warn the village!" exclaimed Nakosis.

"No," said Loka, "I can make it to the village. I will run as fast as my old legs will take me. You must run for the Quick Waters Village as fast as you can. Alert them and bring their warriors. They will send runners to Deer Village."

"But it will take all day for me to reach them and then to return to our village. It will be too late." Nakosis argued.

"No," Loka countered, "Not if you meet someone on the trail. They can relay the message. You should wait on the trail for the warriors and return with them. If we can get our warriors out quickly we may yet have surprise. Now RUN Nakosis!"

Loka did not wait for a response. He yanked the large bag from his back and hurled it far off the trail into the ferns and with only his spear in hand he broke into a run for the village, not looking back. Nakosis did likewise, shedding his big leather sack. With only his shoulder bag and his spear, he took a deep breath, and leaning slightly forward, set off at a full run. His heart was pounding within his chest, not from exertion but from the utter shock of the moment. As he ran he spoke aloud for the spirits to help him. "Raven please help me, give wings to my feet," he uttered the words over and over with each breathe. It became his cadence chant. "Raven please help me." Then he'd take a few breaths and several long, even running steps then, "Give wings to my feet." In such a way he fell into a pattern that regulated his running and his breathing. This training that he'd learned many years ago and not given a thought about now came back to him. Runners could find the right pace this way and maintain it for incredibly long distances and over a very long time. The secret was to focus one's mind solely on the running and not to notice much else, even the surrounding terrain became secondary.

There was a tale of how in the old days a runner who, in such a perfect state of running trance, ran like a fox right through a camp of enemy warriors! They were eating around a fire and the runner flew up on them and through the camp with such incredible speed that it is said they were not even able to take up their arms and pursue him. They said such runners could travel all night and were possessed by the spirit of night creatures such as the owl. Nakosis thought of such things as he willed his legs to carry him forward, hoping that he too could somehow employ the magic of the spirits. He knew he was moving fast but he now visualized the Quick Waters Village as he remembered it when he last visited there many years ago. He pictured himself bursting like a lightning flash through the trees. His body actually felt empowered, his legs hot but not fatigued. His only distraction was Taku and the fear for her safety he could not completely shake. He managed to work his concern for the village into the running. He told himself that their safety depended on his swiftly making the village. He no longer noticed the trees nor even the trail. His focus became a tunnel, like a long cave and, just as he travelled to the underworld, this run became such a journey.

Old Loka did not have the youthful stamina that Nakosis did; yet he gathered every bit of strength both physical and spiritual to propel himself like an arrow back toward White Mist Village. This was his visualization. He imagined that he shot his spirit from a giant bow and was now travelling by its spirit power to this desired destination. He focused on the image of his hut, the one thing he knew best and in his mind he made it real and his entire spirit and life force was channeled through the forest trail toward the unsuspecting village. He ignored the pain in his chest, the throbbing in his old legs and the raspy strains to catch his wind and he ran on by sheer will.

Loka burst from the clearing beside the river where a couple of older men were fishing. Startled, they spun with their spears and Loka screamed with the last of his strength "Enemy!" As he fell to the gravel of the riverbank one of the men rushed to help him while without waiting for details, the other ran shouting the warning cry.

Within moments the village was being mobilized and panicked women where screaming for their children and ushering families into the larger lodges. Several warriors were rushing at full run for the river where Loka was upright against a log and being given water from a gourd. He sputtered out the details of the enemy advance. The Wolf lodge leader said that there were really only two possible places the warriors might cross the river, the falls being too dangerous for a whole column of warriors to safely navigate across the wet rocks. One was the narrows about half way to the falls, the other one here at the village.

"They would have to climb an embankment up from the river to reach the flat ground at the trail," the Wolf leader said.

His name was Hankas, a commanding figure, tall and as thickly limbed as a tree and as fierce a fighter as his appearance suggested. He led a group of several warriors who were all armed and ready for a fight.

"I'll take these men now and try to head them off at the spot." He turned to another warrior, "Send the best and fastest scout ahead and get their location. Keep the best runners on the trail to relay information. We must keep the men low until we can see them, we must have surprise! Engage them at a run, move so they don't know how many you are. Keep them there until the rest arrive!"

Hankas nodded to a sinewy young warrior who immediately took off like a deer at a full run, followed by three other runners who would each take up positions along the route to act as relay. Hankas ordered runners to the other lodges with the plan. Behind him was the sound of yelling and screaming as the village braced for battle. Warriors were now armed and streaming from the lodges, to muster at designated places to take up previously practiced positions. The village defense was quickly organized as many warriors lifted the wood stake barricades between the lodges and women ran to bring the animals within this newly designated area. Many of the younger women also took up positions on the barricades, arming themselves with slings, spears and bows. The larger lodges had storage shelves in the top, high above the living area below. These were accessed from inside by a ladder and there was an access door on the outside of some for loading stores from the fields. These doors were removed and archers took up positions in them behind the relative safety of the thick wooden walls. Among the archers positioned in these lofts was young Taku.

The village had a very good defensible position. Before anyone could reach it they would have to get over the banks of the river where warriors would set up defenses. Then they would have to clear the fields where they would be attacked through the cover of thick crops. This was, however, a last resort as no one wanted any enemy to get close to the precious fields. If the enemy did manage to defeat this position then the village itself presented a formidable defense. However, no one knew at this point just how many enemy warriors they were up against. Without the warriors of the other villages how long could they hold against a large and determined fighting force?

One of the runners was now racing along the riverbank toward the waiting Wolf leader. Loka was amazed at their ability to cover so much ground at such speed. By now he had regained his breath long enough to provide the Wolf leader with the full story and to inform him of Nakosis' desperate run for help.

"I pray that he is indeed blessed by the spirits," the Wolf leader confided to Loka, "The scouts say they have spotted the enemy across the river and that there are still warriors crossing the ridge!"

"What?" Loka cried. "Are they the flatlanders?"

"Perhaps," Wolf leader said, "We don't know, they look different than any flatlanders we've encountered. They wear breastplates and have black faces. Most seem to carry bows and axes. Lets hope they have not detected our scouts. We may still have surprise and with the spirit's blessings we might be able to hold them at the river."

Chako had appeared and rushed to Loka's side, inquiring as to his state. Loka assured him he was all right and quickly informed him of the situation.

The Wolf leader, looking very apprehensive, turned to the two men and said, "If the spirits give ears to your beckoning then I'd suggest that now would be a good time to ask for favors!"

He immediately ordered runners to take to the trail for Quick Waters village lest the enemy cut it off. He then ran for the village and the crowd of gathered warriors.

Nakosis had been running for a long time, but did not lessen his pace or his resolve. His cadenced run was trance like and he was feeling the effect as a dream-like state. He was aware of his muscles and breathing being strained yet it was as though they were not in control. He had twice tripped and once fell sprawling over a root that spanned the trail and he flew across the ground and onto his feet still running, not loosing his rhythm despite being aware of the warm blood running down his side. He had no idea where he was in relation to the Quick Waters village when he saw the girl. She looked up and startled she gasped and then let out a shrill scream. She was bent over the trail rearranging a bag. Nakosis had to will himself to stop lest he run right through the girl. She jumped to the side as a group of men and women came racing up the trail. An old woman ran to stand in front of the terrified girl. She was brandishing a knife, in her eyes a look of immense fear. Right on her heels a young man, very formidable looking, and an older man also very agitated and ready to do battle. Nakosis managed to halt his running and realizing he was still holding his spear, he threw it to the ground and fell to his knees, now panting as the effect of the run immediately became apparent.

He blurted out, "I am Nakosis, from White Mist; we are being attacked! Please get help!" He collapsed and the older man bent to help right him and gestured to the younger man to give him some water. He gulped at the gourd sputtering out words between mouthfuls. "Enemy warriors at the first falls... other side of river...how far to your village...must hurry!"

The old man said that they were not too far, having left that morning and he quickly yelled at the now stupefied young man to run. Again he had to tell him before he shook off the shock of what was happening and dashed back to Quick Waters Village. The people were a family headed to visit relations. They would accompany Nakosis back to their village, the father said, where Nakosis could rest and await word of the attack. Their village would send warriors immediately as soon as his son raised the alarm. He asked about the enemy but Nakosis had little to tell them. They too had relatives in White Mist Village and their concern was evident in their pained expressions. Once he regained his strength, however, Nakosis had only one thing on his mind and that was getting back to White Mist as quickly as he could.

"You cannot run back now young man! You will be no use to anyone if you are dead!" the mother said.

"Yes, please listen to her," the father added. "You must wait to go with the warriors from our village. If you must fight then better you lend support to their attack."

Nakosis had to concede to the logic of the old man. It seemed like much time before a young lean runner arrived, glistening with sweat.

He ran immediately to Nakosis, asking, "You sent the alarm?"

"Yes," Nakosis replied. He began to say who he was but the runner cut him off.

"Where exactly did you see them, how many in the enemy party? What did they look like?" he asked.

Nakosis spurted out the information as fast as he could and the runner turned on his heels and bolted back down the trail. Within moments he again returned at the head of a silent column of what appeared like very well trained warriors. The runner turned to look at the man behind him who simply nodded and the runner silently took off in the direction of the falls and the enemy warriors. The man stopped and Nakosis stood to meet him.

"I am Nakosis."

"Yes, I know you. I knew your father. I am Chasake, leader of the Bear

Lodge. We move now!"

Nakosis merely nodded and once again adopted the quick pace of the trotting column, taking position just behind Chasake. These Bear warriors had proven themselves many times in the contests and were very disciplined. In the past Nakosis, like other boys of his village, had resented the Quick Waters warriors when they sometimes bested his friends in the competition. Now, however, he was very grateful for their training and expertise. Apart from their breathing, they were almost silent in their movement. Their moccasined feet moved at exactly the same time so as to minimize the sound of many feet thudding at once down a hard trail. Even their spear carrying arms swung with precision. Nakosis swore that even their breathing was coordinated. It was the result of immense training, discipline and dedication. They all had covered their bodies in brown clay and wore no necklaces or talismans that would make noise when travelling. Nakosis had to admire the formidable and fierce fighting force they presented. Just the sight of this column gave him renewed confidence. Now if only they can be put to the test in time, he thought!

They did not stop. They did not speak nor did they drink. They covered ground like hungry wolves on the scent of a wounded animal. Finally the runner came down the trail from the other direction, he was at a fast walk and looking behind him as he advanced. Much to Nakosis' relief, the column finally stopped and the men all immediately assumed a crouched position. Hands on slightly raised spears and archers with arrows notched but bows slack. A gourd was passed and each man took only one drink of water. Nakosis and Chasake alone remained standing as he spoke to the runner in voices barely audible to Nakosis.

They turned to face him and Chasake asked, "When you saw them they were coming over the far ridge, across the valley, yes?"

Nakosis nodded, "Why?" he asked.

Chasake nodded to the runner who again headed off. "He located a runner from your village concealed in the brush. He had been watching the enemy and reporting to another. Thankfully your village has a relay of scouts on the trail and the enemy, it appears, may not know of the trail on this side. They appear to be trying to follow the river on the other side. I don't think they are aware of our people or perhaps they know not where our villages are."

"Well, surely that is good news," Nakosis said somewhat relieved.

"No doubt once they reach the narrows they will see the signs of where your people have crossed to set up the fishing traps there. Then they will know they are close and they will become wary and alert. But also, Nakosis, they are of great numbers. Your scout said that they have only recently finished crossing the ridge. They are strung out all along the other shore of the Blue Fish."

Nakosis knew suddenly of the dire consequences of engaging such a fighting force, even with the formidable Bear warriors of the Quick Water people. Deer River warriors would not be able to assist until the following day at the fastest run and by then it would be too late. They would simply be marching to certain death.

Chasake added, "Your leaders have planned to engage them the moment they try to cross. They think they may try at the first narrows. There they will have to climb a bank to get onto the flat ground of the trail. We do not know why, but ever since the great storm the river has been getting lower and lower. It is now not very fast or deep at the fish traps and the enemy could cross there easily. They are hoping to try to hold them on the bank. There are so many though, they could easily occupy those warriors there and send more downstream to the fishing narrows and on to the village."

Nakosis tried to get his mind around the seemingly hopeless situation.

Chasake, also considering options, scratched his head then added, "Maybe we could inflict enough injury upon them to make them feel that the fight is not worth their losses. And if our combined warriors could keep them engaged along the river long enough, the village could escape higher into the valley."

"Escape!" Nakosis said. "You mean abandon the village, leave the crops? Everything we possess is there and there are children and the elderly!" Now overcome with anger Nakosis yelled, "Who are these people? Where do they come from?"

Chasake proposed, "They look like they are nomads. They travel as though only to war. They have no supplies, no women, children or shelters. Perhaps they have heard about us from the flatlanders and came over the ridge hoping to find spoils, knowing the canyon was impassable. If they do have a camp somewhere it must be well over the ridge. They seem a determined bunch and not easily dissuaded!" He placed his hand on Nakosis' shoulder and said, "Perhaps you will want to take the trail back while it is still clear and be with your people, Nakosis. We will advance to the river and meet up with your warriors on the trail there and stay concealed until the attack."

Nakosis thanked Chasake and again ran for his life. He passed runner scouts along the way, relaying messages between the assembled warriors of the two villages. White Mist warriors were moving up the trail silently in single file and no one spoke as Nakosis flew past them. He burst onto the riverbank amid a scene of frenzy. The village was still rushing about in high alert. People were packing belongings and extinguishing cooking fires. Frantic mothers with children in their arms were running for the lodges, leaders barking commands to the warriors assigned to village defenses. Everywhere people were arming. Huts were emptied of every arrow and archers were placing full quivers beside their positions behind the barricades. Nakosis raced through the scene desperate to find Taku. No one seemed to know where she was. He ran from one lodge to another yelling her name. Finally he heard her voice answer him from her position high in the loft. He raced up the frail ladder, his feet almost not touching the rungs. As his head cleared the platform he saw that there were three other archers who took position in the opening and they had placed large wood pieces against small logs across the opening and were crouched behind this makeshift barrier. It looked to offer little protection he thought. He threw his arms around Taku who tried to maintain her stoic face in front of the three male archers. This was not a time for loosing composure or nerve. Nakosis realizing this, moved to stand beside Taku, surveying the approach to the village from their vantage point.

The enemy would have to leave cover and cross much open ground to make the village. They would be very vulnerable to well aimed arrows. Enough of them, however, and the lodge would be overrun. Taku asked Nakosis what he knew of the enemy and he could not tell her without possibly generating fear in the others. He said only that perhaps Taku should accompany him. She was determined, however, to hold her position in the loft where the lodge leader had requested she be. She was one of the best archers the village had and this was a long approach. Her near perfect aim at such long range would give them a great advantage. Nakosis knew, of course, that it was true and he knew also that despite being a beautiful young woman, despite the fact that she now consumed his very being, Taku was also a warrior, no different in her duty and obligation than any of her male counterparts. He also could not embarrass her nor cause her any loss of face. He said he was going to see that his grandparents and Loka and Chako were safe and he would return and take up position with his sling along side her. He wanted to kiss her desperately but decided against it, knowing this was not the time and he leapt back down the ladder, knowing that at least for the moment she was safe. Again he raced through the village seeking out his other loved ones. His grandfather grabbed him from behind as he was yelling into the open door of their empty hut. Grandmother was safely in the Wolf lodge with the others and he was headed for the barricades.

He told Nakosis, "Fight well, be brave, your ancestors stand with you!" and turned and was gone.

Nakosis found Loka and Chako in the old Shaman's hut. Loka was pleased to see he'd arrived knowing it meant that the Quick Water's warriors were dispatched.

"Yes, but I don't know how much difference it will make. "He said, telling them what he knew about the enemy and their numbers. "Chasake, the Bear Lodge leader, told me also that the water of the river is now very, very low at the fish traps. He said that for some reason it has been lowering ever since the great storm. It would appear that perhaps the spirits have not favored us as we thought. They seem to be favoring the enemy!"

Chako heaved a deep great sigh at the news and a grave look to Loka who seemed lost as to what to offer as encouragement.

"Nakosis," he said, "you must help us!"

"Me, what can I do? I am going to stand with Taku and if it is our last time in this life we will spend it together!"

"No, my son," Loka argued, "you must take one more journey and you must ask the spirits for help. Only you can reach them in time Nakosis."

Chako placed his hand on Nakosis' shoulder and with a sincere and pleading tone he said, "Remember what Loka said about having trust, Nakosis? This one time above all others you must trust in your ability and trust in the power of your guides. I'm begging you, Nakosis do this please!"

There was no way he could refuse. The urgency in their voices convinced him that he really had no other choice. Loka made some very quick offerings and purifications and allowed that the spirits would make exception given the circumstances. Chako spoke a passionate, heart felt, almost desperate plea for the guides to hear them and to grant their blessing and to guide their brother Nakosis.

"Give him the power to save his people," he pleaded. Nakosis took the drum Chako handed him. "I know, my brother, that we now ask much of you. But you are being called to the test now. You know how important this is and I know you know also that this is your greatest weapon. You must concentrate like never before Nakosis. Leave the fear of this place and time. Leave the approach of enemies and the smell of war that is in the air. Close your eyes and think back to the cave, Nakosis."

Chako and Loka began lightly beating their drum and rattle. Loka had closed the door and the hut was now dark. He left the offering smudge of herbs smoldering in the coals and the little hut was thick with the smoke of the sacred herbs and soon their drums beat as one. Chako and Loka began singing the sacred words in unison and Nakosis, eyes closed and swaying gently now, sang also. His reality began to shift away from the panicked world of rushing warriors, away from the dread sense of impending doom that permeated the whole village. Now he was only in the sanctity and silence of the cave once again. He saw the warm fire and the smoke rising slowly through unseen openings above. He heard the echo of a sacred song, of drum and rattle. He heard the familiar welcome caw of Raven. He felt himself floating.

The strange Black Face warriors aligned themselves silently along the thick brush of the opposite shore. Their scout had returned to the main force and pointed to an unseen spot down river. Chasake and the Wolf warrior, Hankas, lay unmoving in the thick fern cover on the other side observing the enemy's movements. They sent runners to amass two forces of their combined warriors along the river at the fishing trap and to remain there until the enemy began crossing. The archers were the front lines, concealed in a wide arch. It took them most of the afternoon to get into position without being detected, behind them more archers and men with slings, spears, clubs and knives.

Chasake said, "They will cross soon. If they know the village is near they will have to begin a running attack in the direction of the village or they will loose the light. It will be dark soon enough."

"Or perhaps they don't know of the village yet and are seeking a suitable place to camp and spend the night." Hankas hoped, he added, "Our scouts did not report seeing theirs cross the river yet."

"If they do cross they will see the signs of your people and quickly find the trail. Then realizing the day ending they will have to move quick to find the village and attack. Either way, if they cross we must charge them and hit them heavily!" said Chasake.

Hankas agreed. The enemy had now reached the spot their scout had pointed out. The worst fears were realized when they halted at the fish trap narrows. The scout was testing the depth as he stepped gingerly into the fast moving waters. Hankas commented that the river looked to be even lower than earlier in the day. Do they have some dark magic at work that can lower rivers he wondered? The word spread and the sound of the water covered the movements of the assembled warriors. Arrows were notched and fingers took up the tension on bowstrings. Silent prayers went up to the spirit guardians and Chasake prayed for his ancestors to be present and that he would make them proud.

Hankas said, "We must strike before the first to cross reach the bottom of the bank and we must kill all those still in the water while they're arms are busy holding their weapons dry. Then we must not stop. They will try to swarm us and we may not hold. Two other lodges lie in wait along the trail and at the village defenses. We can do no more!"

The Black Faced scout was now half way across. The enemy archers were poised, bows drawn, scanning the other shore for any movement. No one dare move. The scout had to cross safely or all surprise would be lost. He waded ashore, the water not reaching above his chest. He was easy to see now and Chasake could make out his features from his place of hiding among the thick ferns. The brown clay on his body added to his blending into the underbrush.

The scout was tall and muscular. His upper body was covered in an ochre red paint that was partly washed away in the fast river. His entire face was painted black, making his eyes appear large and wild looking. He wore a large axe on a belt at his waist and carried a long spear similar to the Three Rivers people, only the point was coal black and appeared longer. Across his back a bow and quiver of arrows, opposite his axe, he wore a large bone handled knife. His head was shorn, save for a small lock that appeared to come from the side of his head, tied up in what looked like a large knot. The scout was wary, ever looking at the trees above him, but his sight not penetrating into the thick underbrush that hid the anxious warriors. He turned his back and waved the first across.

Chasake braced himself. It would be he or Hankas who would strike the first blow and scream the attack signal that would launch the warriors against the enemy forces. The warriors began wading across but to Chasake's horror they were not coming all at once. About twenty warriors approached the water and began the crossing while others separated into smaller groups on the other side still under the watchful eye of their archers. Hankas had to admire this war leader -he knew what he was doing. The first twenty or so warriors were almost at the shore when the scout began climbing up the embankment, pulling himself up with his hands and feet. He was not far from the top within grasping reach of a hidden Quick Waters warrior when he suddenly stopped. He glanced to his right and then dropped back to the riverbank. The enemy warriors were assembling behind him on the rocks of the riverbank. He walked very slowly down the bank a short distance looking oddly at something. Chasake saw it first. It was a fish weir left from the last season upon the high water line of the bank. The scout raced for it and picking it up he immediately lowered his posture and brought his spear up scanning the forest. The others also were alerted and tense. He slowly walked past the weir and there he noticed the old worn path that led to the main trail. He picked up the weir and holding it above his head he clearly displayed it for the leader on the opposite shore. He signaled a command and another twenty began crossing as the first grouped tightly together facing the forest above them. These were well trained Hankas realized, as he also realized that this was as much surprise as they would ever get he pulled back his bow string until it reached his ear. He held and then released his breath as his arrow sought its mark at the heart of the enemy scout. The sound was deafening as hundreds of warriors on both sides of the river screamed their war cries and the strings of a hundred bows let loose a rain of arrows. Those caught in the river died almost instantly as the Three Rivers warriors had already targeted them from the hiding spots. The Black Faced leader was screaming commands, directing his warriors. Hankas could not understand their tongue. Chasake noticed a group of the enemy running fast back upstream.

"They may be trying to get warriors across the falls." he yelled at Hankas.

"It will be suicide," he replied, "but send someone to watch them. If Deer village gets here in time maybe we should have some of them up at the falls also."

Arrows were now ripping through the underbrush and striking into tree trunks all around them. The enemy archers were excellent marksmen and many of the Three Village warriors were killed or severely wounded. Still, many others, some with deep wounds, were bravely carrying the fight to the surviving enemy at the waters edge. Hankas saw enemy runners coming and going from where the leader had taken up a safe position behind a rock outcrop that suffered a steady rain of Three River's arrows.

In the village the din of the battle was now reverberating down the valley. Warriors poised at the river saw the first red streams of blood swirling amid the foaming water. As the sound reached the village fortifications a hush went up from the assembled warriors and prayers for their relations who were now falling. The Raven Lodge warriors were dispatched from the village to fortify those already in the thick of the fight. They ran like the wind up the river trail and as they approached closer to the scene of the battle they let go one tremendous war cry, letting their comrades, as well as the enemy, know of their arrival. The roar of the Raven warriors did distract the enemy archers for but a moment and it was enough for some of them to die under a hail of Three River's arrows.

The Black Face leader had sent a wave of enemy across the river as his archers tried to pin down those of the Three River forces. If they reached the bank they could assemble beneath its protective overhang, effectively out of reach of the village's archers, then make a concerted rush over the bank to attack the warriors holding the high ground. This would give the enemy enough time to pour their warriors across the shallow river.

Chasake's runners returned with word that the enemy had forces moving past the first falls. They were scouting for a way across to circle the village's warriors. Ducking as low as he could, a rain of arrows whizzing past his head, Chasake raced to where Hankas was consulting with the Raven leader to tell him of the new development.

The Raven leader said, "We must not be forced to engage them on two fronts. If they can place enough warriors on this side then we are in trouble. Those arriving from Deer Village will be running into them and cut off from our forces. There are enough of them that they could possibly get past both fronts if we divide our men any further! We don't want to bring the fight to the village!"

The runner again headed off to monitor the enemy advance upstream.

Nakosis was swaying now. He sat crossed legged at the fire but his upper body moved sun-wise in small circles. As he did he would utter small growl-like sounds that punctuated each revolution. Loka had ceased his chanting and now sat motionless watching young Nakosis. He still retained his ancient rattle and it continued shaking in his hand almost instinctively. Nakosis was somewhere lost to this world. The fire had long ago burned down to a few coals and ash, yet Loka observed many small bright orange flames now growing up from the dead fire. They grew in intensity and their brightness appeared reflected on Nakosis. His very body seemed to glow with the eerie ochre hue. The flames rose and to Loka appeared to begin dancing, swirling in time to the circular motion of Nakosis. Loka heard words beneath the growl as though there were two voices, but they were in no tongue he had ever heard. Loka tried to keep the rhythm of the rattle as he now attempted to shuffle back away from the dancing flames. He was aware that the drumming had stopped and as he glanced across to Chako saw the old Shaman was transfixed on the glowing image of Nakosis. Chako and Loka watched, speechless, as the fire now started to swirl as though caught in the funnel of a summer 'dust devil.' High up they rose. Loka was concerned about the small hut, yet he couldn't help but notice that despite the flames intense brightness they appeared to emit no heat!

Nakosis was within a swirling vapor, a funnel of ether racing around him at great speed. It appeared to reach to the end of the sky above him and he could not tell how far beneath him was the earth. Raven was playing in the whirlwind, soaring on his great black wings past Nakosis, very close and cawing. Raven's cry soon became laughter, joyous, roguish child-like laughter. He seemed, to Nakosis, to be in great delight, his shiny black eyes catching Nakosis' with each loop past. The wind made a deep, crackling sound like a pitch-thick fire over which a low throaty growl would come and fade, come and fade. Nakosis recalled Chako's words, 'Hohapas is able to become the spirit of fire, water, the air and even the earth also. He is called 'The Great magic.'

"Hohapas," Nakosis called and now smiled as though naming him made him more manifest, calling his great power. Up into the funnel Nakosis rose and now above the swirling vortex he looked down and saw the valley below. He saw the scene of the battle, the desperate struggle and the bloody river beneath him. Raven, his laugh now sounding sinister, stayed by Nakosis as they moved over the carnage. Nakosis now was aware that the vortex that bore him aloft was a funnel of Shamanic power, an unearthly, tremendous force that moved at his direction, taking him at will. He moved over the trail now thick with panicked, running warriors, up to the first falls. There he could see the warriors nervously watching the far shore and the enemy forces moving up toward the second falls. Above them, higher in the river, the last falls came into Nakosis' view. He couldn't believe his eyes. The last falls were the strongest because they funneled between two great pillars of bedrock that were extensions of the wall of mountain on either side. This place was known as 'Stags Leap' since an ancient legend told of how hunters once pursued a great stag that leapt across the abyss to safety on the other side. There beneath Nakosis, between the Stags Leap rocks, a mighty jam of trees blocked the waters passage to the height of several men. Behind it countless more trees piled up, no doubt victims of the great storm that washed away the cave clearing. They were the red bark giants, their thick mossy trunks stripped bare by the turbulent, eddying waters that now built up behind this dam. This was the secret to the river's low level!

Nakosis visualized himself lowering to the deadly foaming swirl of trees and black water. He watched his feet, expecting to feel the cold of the turbulent water, but instead the spinning power vortex penetrated the water as when one pushes a cup into a bowl of liquid. The water remained distant beneath him! The trees began to move toward him and the great black water started to boil around him as the vortex penetrated its surface. It was a terrifying thing made all the more so by Raven's even shriller laughter as he circled above. Nakosis became fearful that he would be sucked under and he hesitated. Immediately the water changed, no longer starting to spiral around him, becoming unpredictable and the trunks of trees began tilting toward him. Nakosis closed his eyes, thought of Taku, of his grandmother and grandfather, of Loka and Chako. He decided then and there that he would give his life if that was what the spirits desired of him. Abandoning any thoughts of himself, he closed his eyes and with immense concentration resumed lowering himself. The roar, the thunderous crackling surrounded him, and as he opened his eyes he was deep in the maelstrom. The only light was a spot of gray sky above and all around him the black, foaming death swirled. It began to move ever faster. Trees once defined were now a blur of indistinct shapes moving at incredible speed. Still, Nakosis concentrated.

Then it happened. The most vociferous roar Nakosis had ever heard as the great dam exploded in a massive geyser of trees and violent, roiling water. The funnel began quickly collapsing around him, dropping away like an avalanche. First the dam fell and then the great waters of the Blue Fish River stood like one mammoth wave on the upstream side before collapsing away around Nakosis. In the blink of an eye the mighty waters passed him in an enormous rush down river. Raven screamed at Nakosis. He turned to stare into Raven eyes. Then all was blackness.

It was the scouts who saw it first. Before they did it was the earth rumbling, unimaginable sound that took their breath away. They watched as a wall of water and trees burst through Stags Leap, completely engulfing the falls below. The enemy had no warning. They had time only to look up before they were dashed to oblivion. The scouts ran for the higher ground as great trees were tossed like a rock from a sling, catapulting through the forest with the speed of an arrow. Some of the riverbank, caught in the edge of the great wave, was whisked away under the enormous pressure, adding more rock and trees to the deadly wall of water and uprooted forest now plummeting down the valley below. At the fish trapping narrows the river was filled with the Black Faced warriors. Their leader was now in the open, safe from the Three River's archers who, vastly outnumbered, were now coming under a heavy barrage. He signaled the bulk of his men across the river to storm the Village warriors. Some of the Black Faces had managed to take the higher ground of the bank and were engaging the village warriors at close range with spears, axes and knives. The once verdant riverbank now ran with the blood of the slain and wounded. It mingled with the mud and made thick trails into the river's waters.

The fighting was so intense and the desperate screams of battle so extreme that at first no one heard the wave. For many it wasn't until the great trees came crashing through them that they were aware of it. By then it was too late. It was definitely too late for the enemy in the river. Those gathered under the bank were swept under the raging black tumult. Many Village warriors had sacrificed themselves, hurling their bodies and raised spears down the bank into the enemy warriors. They too were swept under. The trail was sheer pandemonium. The advancing Raven warriors and retreating forces collided as hundreds tried to escape the water. The runners were useless to try to advance a warning. Everyone now ran for their lives, for the higher ground in the forest. Before people could even manage to scream a warning, the water was already upon them, flooding the trail, bowling men over into the thick brush. Then just as suddenly it was gone.

The startled warriors quickly regained their focus and ran to observe the disastrous effect of the great wave. The flash flood waters were now returning back to the river. The bank was like one long waterfall, jets of floodwater poured over the edge and back into the river. Scores of enemy warriors littered the opposite bank, their twisted, broken bodies wrapped like a child's discarded doll around uprooted trees and over jagged boulders. A few survivors clung to roots and branches and were already being dispatched by Village warriors. The Black Face leader and most of those who had assembled on the river were sucked under the torrent and swept downstream. Many Three Village warriors were also washed away. More now lay injured and bleeding from their many wounds, some fatal. Runners were trying to navigate the slippery flooded trail to bring news up and down the line from the falls to the village. Anxious relatives besieged the runners for news of loved ones. Warriors of the Eagle lodge assigned to the village defenses had left the barricades and were engaging enemy survivors who were swept ashore near the village. Sporadic fighting was taking place among the fields of crops and in the near-by forest. Others had earlier been assigned to guard the canyon at arrow rocks in case the enemy tried for an attack from there. There was nowhere for the enemy survivors to run so they fought with all their strength, knowing they would likely die where they stood.

Runners made it through to Hankas to say that a full lodge of warriors had arrived at the falls from Deer River Village. Chasake had ordered them to go back upstream and to cross at the high narrow and to pursue the enemy at first light as night was now fast approaching. Despite the trauma, the village fell into a well-organized routine of tending to the dead and wounded. Women began cooking vast clay pots of food and the stores were emptied of dried meat as the battle weary made their way back through the barricades. The standing orders held and the village was still well protected, heavily armed barricades still in place. The fighting at the river near the village was ending after the Eagle warriors rushed to reinforce those already engaged. Enemy warriors were dispatched as quickly as they were located.

Up the river things were much more intense. Chasake and Hankas were desperately struggling to maintain some order among the many warriors. Overwhelmed with the emotion of the battle many had crossed the river intent on pursuing the retreating enemy force, their numbers now greatly reduced, their enthusiasm lessened. With much persuasion, the Raven leader managed to convince the other village warriors that they should return to the village to help their loved ones and their wounded comrades. His Raven warriors still fresh in the battle would take the fight to the retreating enemy. The Deer River warriors had crossed the river at the only other safe narrows above the Stag Leap falls. There they would remain until just before first light and then they would pick up the enemies trail back over the ridge. A few of their scouts, familiar with the territory, had moved off as silent as owls in the night to advance toward the enemy's trail.

Hankas made the decision to ease the village defenses somewhat and re-assign some of the warriors to help on the trail and the riverbank. The barricades and the warriors at the arrow rocks would remain but there were the bodies of the fallen and the many wounded to attend to. Torchbearers accompanied spearmen through the forest around the village and up both sides of the riverbanks; a moon would soon illuminate the scene of battle but for now it was completely dark. Throughout the long night the cries of the wounded and the mourning wails of bereaved relatives echoed through the village, mixed with the occasional screams of enemies flushed from hiding in the dark forest. It was an unpleasant and dangerous task. Every warrior knew there was nothing as dangerous as a wounded and trapped beast. The enemy surely knew also that there could be no one left alive to return to the village another time.

By dawn the whole battleground took on an otherworldly appearance. In the bright morning light and clear mountain air the red of the blood and smell of death were intensified. The hardest of men wept and vomited at the scale of the destruction. It was one thing to have to remove bodies ripped apart by the weapons of war, yet another to deal with those that were ripped to pieces by the shredding action of trees and rocks in a mammoth wall of rushing water. The gruesome work would continue for days. Raven warriors had followed up the other shore to join with the Deer River contingent. Their stealthy scouts moved like panthers in the faint moonlight to find and follow the enemy's trail over the ridge and now the chase had begun!

CHAPTER 11
AFTERMATH

Chako and Loka sat against the far wall of the grandparent's small lodge. They could do little more than they already had.

"He is no longer of this world I'm afraid. His fate is now up to him." Loka said with a voice strained by the stress of three days and nights of little sleep.

"Poor boy," Chako said quietly to Loka, "if he chooses to return he may be forever changed by these events."

Nakosis had fallen into the black of unconsciousness. When the great wave broke through the dam he simply collapsed as though his life force had instantly quit his body. He sprawled across the floor of Loka's hut, as Chako leapt to pull his arm from where it fell across the hot coals. His entire body was limp. He was completely drenched in sweat; his hair matted and stuck to his shoulders, his body so slippery that they could hardly maneuver him onto some hides. He was fever hot to the touch. Chako and Loka tried to revive him and to give him water. When nothing worked they sent Peeka running through the mayhem in the village to seek out Nakosis' grandfather or perhaps his two cousins. It was some time before his grandfather came bursting through the huts low door. He ran to Nakosis' side and quickly began turning him over, his eyes looking for the wound he assumed had been afflicted during the battle. Peeka came running breathlessly behind, tugging one of the Quick Water's cousins reluctantly into the hut. Without offering any explanation Nakosis' grandfather yelled at the cousin to help move him. Outside, at a nearby hut, a large hide was drying, stretched between poles. Grandfather ran and dragged it back. Together they pulled Nakosis outside and rolling him onto it, they dragged his pale and lifeless-looking body to their hut. Loka and Chako ran behind.

For three days and nights Nakosis barely moved from the sweat soaked bed. His fever continued and he occasionally would toss his head and mutter unintelligibly. Loka tried desperately to hear what he was saying but it made no sense. He assumed that wherever he was in the spirit world he was speaking to other beings in a tongue only they could understand. He and Chako had returned to their hut and drummed and chanted and journeyed through the night of the first day in an attempt to try to find their young brother and bring him back, but all to no avail.

The morning of the fourth day Chako rose and looked at Nakosis. He lay motionless but he breathed easily and slowly. Chako crawled over and touched his forehead. It was surprisingly cool. It appeared his fever had subsided. He looked over to where Loka lay asleep, exhausted from the long bedside vigil. He wanted to tell him but thought it best to let them both rest.

He ducked outside into the fading twilight. The air was cool and a beautiful large moon hung above the mountain as the last stars were fading under the warm glow of father sun's arrival. The smoke of many cooking fires mingled with the still lingering stench of the burned, bloodied clothes of the dead and wounded. Runners had yet to report on the latest advances of the pursuing war party. Families were still seeking the remains of loved ones far downstream, accompanied by warriors still guarding against enemies who may yet be hiding. The battle was won but the conflict would not be over until the last of the Black Faces had been killed. There would be apprehension and uneasiness for many days and the repercussions, the blow to the societal structure of the village, would last indefinitely. Things may never again be as they were for this village, Chako thought. His heart went out to these poor people as he thought of his own village so many days away. Were they safe? Had the Black Faces been there also? And what of that poor young man whose spirit is lost somewhere in the otherworld? What will become of him if he returns to learn of what happened?

Loka's ears perked and although his eyes were still closed he quickly awakened to the change in sound, the difference to the breathing and odd moans he'd been accustomed to monitoring these last few days. He sat up quickly and wiping the sleep from his eyes he shuffled over to Nakosis who lay staring at him with wide bewildered eyes. Loka yelled and Nakosis moved, as though to speak, as Chako ducked through the door and the grandparents quickly shed their sleeping robes to run to his side. Gasps of relief and tears of joy filled the small lodge and people began asking almost in unison about his condition.

Loka raised a hand and loudly he said, "Please give him some air, get him some water and give him time to speak if he can!"

His cousin, standing back behind the others, passed a gourd of water over those kneeling around Nakosis. Loka lifted his head and was relieved to see Nakosis trying to pull himself up on weak and wobbling arms to gulp back the first water in days. He gasped deeply and began coughing violently, the strain of which caused him to collapse against the soaked bedding, falling once more into unconsciousness. His grandmother began sobbing, but Loka assured her that it was a very good sign.

"His fever has broken and he has returned to us. Now he must rest a little more. He will awaken again soon. We must give him food but only a little, as with the water."

Chako beamed at his old friend Loka and grandfather placed his arm affectionately across Loka's shoulders.

"Thank you my dear friends." He said, also looking with swollen eyes to Chako. "I don't know what he would do without your care and guidance," he paused for a moment then added, "and your love. He will need all we can offer him in the next while - once he awakens fully and begins to ask. I swear I don't know I have the strength to tell him, after all that has happened to the poor boy."

Tears filled his eyes as he ducked out the door. Loka walked out with him, lending a comforting arm in support.

Hankas and Chasake had continued through the night, organizing and directing patrols and personally engaging in some intense fighting with small pockets of the enemy. The fighting was dire. The enemy had the benefit of surprise as Three Village warriors, illuminated by the bright bark torches made easy targets for hidden Black Face arrows and spears. These Black Faces fought knowing they would most likely not escape the patrols. They were determined to take as many with them as they could and their ferocity was alarming. Many Village warriors went to the afterlife that night, more from wounds later in the day. White Mist village literally vibrated with the tension and anxiety in the air; many had not slept in days. Hankas and Chasake, like so many others, simply collapsed amid the mud and blood, their battered bodies yielding to severe exhaustion. In White Mist village, lodges were transformed into places of the wounded, the dying and the dead. Families, who willingly surrendered their homes, now crowded into their relative's lodges and the combined shock and loss was both intensified and yet somehow they comforted one another. The field near the village was where some of the most desperate of the fighting occurred. Three Village warriors of the Raven lodge battled the Black Faces while family and relatives watched helplessly from the village barricades. Many had fallen there, from both sides. The crops in that field were completely trampled under a hundred bloody feet. The life of so many oozed into the earth creating a slick, red mud. Warriors fought and slipped trying to secure a footing amid the viscera of relatives and enemy alike. It was one of the most gruesome scenes. Many Raven warriors paid the highest price, determined to not let any Black Faces make it into the village. It was a last stand. It was there, in that field that the bodies were now being buried.

Those on the riverbank met a far superior force and still they dove head-long into the fray amid raining arrows and spears and many, though severely wounded, fought like cornered panthers.

A great council was now underway in the Raven lodge as the elders and war leaders consulted one another to get a more thorough picture of the battle and the aftermath. Recovery, disposal of the many dead, treatment of the wounded, food supply and mourning were the main topics. Just as the escaping enemy forces were being discussed, it was announced that a runner had brought word from the combined Deer River and Raven Lodge warriors. They had found the enemy. Details were sketchy but they were claiming victory over the Black Faces! A rousing war cry shook the rafters of Raven lodge. The assembled warriors smiled and embraced each other in a rare moment of celebration, as the ease of tension was apparent. A cheer for the victorious forces was reverberating through the village as word quickly spread. The enemy threat may have been finally eliminated but the damage was far from over. As the leaders conferred and related the scenes of the battle from their many perspectives, it was unanimously agreed that they were precariously close to being overrun by the Black Faces. It would have been a disaster, they all agreed, had it not been for the great wave.

Only now were many learning of the monumental dam at Stags Leap and it's mysterious collapse at the decisive moment. The Deer River warriors were still high above the falls when the great dam broke. They described the event as unearthly. The river they said was unusually high as though in heavy spring flood when suddenly it dropped like a rock from a cliff. Some say they could almost see the river bottom for a heartbeat and then just as suddenly it roared back up the valley and again down stream. The assembly gasped at the description and, though many questioned the mysterious source, they all knew that despite their losses in the great wave the village had been spared total destruction.

Nakosis had awakened. He was deathly pale and his eyes were ringed with red. He truly looked to be at death's door but he was coherent and able to sit up propped against bags and hides. A heavy robe was draped across his shivering shoulders. His grandmother and the others had kept up a constant rotation of moist hide rags to wipe his sweat stained body and kissing him gently on the forehead, she now took these away to the river to clean, leaving him with Loka and Chako as Loka had requested. Nakosis was parched, his throat burned, his tongue swollen to where speech was difficult. He managed to drink a gourd of water but Loka made him do so slowly. With Chako on one side and Loka on the other they together supported him as he drank. He now collapsed back onto his raised bedding and looked around at his surroundings, his eyes revealing his confusion. In a rough, faint voice he asked what had happened.

"What do you remember, Nakosis?" Loka asked.

"We sat at the fire in Loka's hut. Do you recall?" added Chako.

He paused for a moment, his mind trying to pull together the pieces.

"Yes…I…" then his eyes widened as his memory returned. "The Battle!" he cried. He coughed at the effort but continued. "What happened? I…I… don't re…me.."

"Yes, yes, yes," Loka interrupted. "Don't worry, Nakosis, the battle is over, the enemy was destroyed!" Loka leaned close. "Do you remember anything of your journeying Nakosis?"

Nakosis lay silent for a moment, slowly letting the memory return.

"I was in a great swirling." He said and then gradually, slowly, he recounted the experience as best he could. The details of the vortex and of the maelstrom of churning water brought hushed gasps from the two old Shamans. Nakosis was being fed small amounts of his grandmother's nourishing soup as he continued with what he could remember. He seemed to be regaining some strength but was still taxed to talk for very long. Loka made him pause, drink a little and breathe. Finally Nakosis turned and Loka and Chako both braced themselves for what they knew was inevitable.

"What of the battle? How is the village? Taku! I must see Taku! Where is she?"

Then, as neither man was quick to answer, he began to panic, his eyes widening, "She's alright, isn't she?" Nakosis asked, the anxiety evident in his quivering voice.

Chako and Loka exchanged looks, unable to mask the concern on their faces.

Loka spoke, "The village is safe Nakosis, thanks to you."

"To me, but I don't…"

Loka interrupted him, "Why yes, my friend, to you. It was you who, by the will of the gods, brought the great wave upon the heads of our enemy and by so doing our warriors were able to defeat them." Loka moved to position himself against Nakosis and he gently picked up his clammy hand and looked him in the eyes. His expression was grave. "Nakosis, the victory came at a cost to us all. Many brave warriors, men and women gave the ultimate sacrifice to save their loved ones and…" he didn't have to say more.

By his expression and the quiver in his voice Nakosis knew Taku was dead. His painful scream shattered the still silence of the hut. Outside, his grandparents held one another, a single robe across their old shoulders, tears staining their pained faces. Nakosis was insane with grief. His weakened state eclipsed by the sheer raw emotion of his anguish made him hard to restrain. His grandfather joined the two old shamans in holding him to his sick bed as he lashed and flayed amid agonizing screams of suffering and loss. He finally collapsed on his side and curled into a ball, pulling the worn robe up over his head. His grandmother tried to console him but he recoiled violently away demanding to be left alone.

Loka helped her to her feet and together they exited the hut. Outside old Chako could not suppress his sadness as tears streamed down his aged cheeks like tiny streams following the course of countless wrinkles. He turned his back on Loka and grandmother, not wanting to add to their suffering with his pained heart.

For two more days and nights Nakosis languished amid the old robes, their sick bed stench now filling the small lodge. He did not care, nor did he take food. He rebuffed any attempts at consolation. Finally Loka entered the hut and grabbing the old robe he yanked it off Nakosis curled frame and hurled it out the door into the dirt. Loka stood over the startled young man, his face wrathful and flushed with anger. It was a Loka Nakosis had never before seen.

He screamed at Nakosis, "Do you think you are the only one here who has suffered a loss Nakosis? Do you think that there is not a family in this village that does not mourn the loss of a loved one, a brother, a sister, father, son or daughter? Some families here have lost both a son and a father! And YOU!" Loka actually kicked Nakosis in his side! "You lay there in your self-pity thinking you are somehow so special that only YOU suffer a broken heart! How selfish you are! While you lay here wallowing like a scolded child, others must deal with what you only hide from! You say you loved Taku and you haven't even bothered to see her grieving family nor offer any condolences! You haven't visited her burial place to help with the passing of her spirit. Do you know what can happen to a spirit passed over in the chaos of battle Nakosis? How a person's spirit can be trapped in a realm of such torment and confusion, screaming for some direction, not knowing what happened or where she is? Imagine living one long terrible nightmare. You haven't asked how she died Nakosis!"

Nakosis was struck dumb by this uncharacteristic behavior. He couldn't stand being the target of such rage from his mentor and confidant.

"I...I... no ...I don't know, I'm sorry...I didn't realize..." He choked up, words could no longer come from his lips and his swollen eyes once more began to tear up. He began shaking uncontrollably. Loka realized what a weakened and vulnerable state he was in but still he maintained his stern expression.

"Well!" He yelled, "Are you going to help us to help Taku's spirit or are you yet not finished being selfish?"

Nakosis straightened himself, trying to regain some sense of composure.

"Yes… I …I...will help, yes of course Uncle, I'm sorry, I didn't know...I"

Loka threw a clean blanket at Nakosis. His voice now softened a little he said,

"Then here, get down to the river and get yourself cleaned up, you are not fit to go anywhere like that. When you've done so return here and eat and then together we will visit Taku's family and see to her afterlife."

Nakosis did not answer. He could not. He stumbled from the hut, pausing to steady his shaky legs and his spinning head as he focused on the direction of the river. Chako was waiting outside but Nakosis could not look at him lest he too berate him for his actions. He acted like he had not noticed him. He made it across the square and out of sight before he braced himself against a tree and vomited violently. Surprisingly, he felt a little better. He took several large deep breaths of the first truly fresh air in days and his dizzy head thanked him. Still he felt as one does after a strong fever. His head was light and things seemed slightly distant.

Chako approached Loka as he left the hut knowing how hard the performance was for the old man to do.

"Well, it worked!" Chako said, pleased with the result.

"Yes," Loka replied, "but I fear I have only replaced grief with guilt."

"Ahh" Chako said, scratching his head. He smiled at Loka saying, "I think guilt is much easier to deal with." The two old connivers smiled easy at each other.

"We've still a lot of work to do, my brother." Loka replied.

As Nakosis headed toward the river he was forced to traverse the length of the whole village. Loka knew this well. It was not the White Mist village he knew and loved. It had transformed into a scene of unimaginable suffering and pain. Everywhere huts seemed lifeless, yet people sat within mourning their loss. Children ran in the square and parents attempted to go about their duties, but with a sense of detachment. The large lodges were still filled with relatives and the injured and dying and their wails could still be heard from the open doors as he passed. There was a pall of rank smoke lingering over everything like the smell of death itself. Blood soaked rags and garments still burned outside the big lodge. As he staggered further he saw the field.

Everywhere piles of fresh dirt marked the graves of the fallen, too many for Nakosis to even guess their numbers. He knew too that his beloved Taku lay there somewhere amid so many others. People who only a few days past were jovial and laughing now stared silently at him as he passed. Some, enough in the moment, acknowledged his passing with a bowed head. Now the gesture seemed more than just customary. Now, it seemed to say 'we understand your pain also.' The ground around the path was still permeated with the red stain of battle. Had Taku shed her life's blood on this very soil, he wondered? Nakosis rounded the trail to face the riverbank as he had done since a child. He stopped cold, frozen in disbelief at what lay before him. The familiar place where he'd shared his secrets and professed his love, where he'd played, fished and swam as a child and also where he, not so long ago, had encountered the mystical panther was no more. The logs that had endured countless spring floods and summer droughts had vanished. Gone too was the gravel bench he'd so often walked and where he sat alone pondering the river's gentle flow. It had been scoured in places right to the now exposed gray bedrock. In many areas no soft earth remained. It too had been washed to points unknown down river. The once lush banks now appeared dead and lifeless. Broken trees and branches were piled like so much firewood at places where any outcrop of bedrock stopped their mad rush. Nakosis realized that it would never again, within his lifetime, resemble the river he'd once known.

He crept cautiously over the wet rock, his footing uncertain in his weak condition. He lowered his legs into the newly formed shallow pool in the bedrock and slowly began to cup his hands and wash his aching muscles. He was desperately parched and normally would have gladly drunk his fill from the cool water, but today the blood in the soil and the vision of carnage made him reel at the thought.

As he walked back to the village more people were awake and venturing about, trying to continue with their shattered lives. As he walked, pale and dazed looking into the stricken lodges and huts, people looked differently at him. Some he noticed could not meet his eyes and seemed to turn away. Others offered the respectful nod and one older woman obviously grieving over a loved one stood and faced him placing her hands to her chest and then extending them out toward him. It was called a heart blessing. It was usually reserved for very close family and revered elders. Nakosis, taken off guard by the intimate gesture, simply tried to offer a polite smile as he bowed and picked up the pace. He just wanted to return to the hut quickly now. The village was too unbearable for him and his own grief mingled with the reality of just how pervasive the loss was to everyone became oppressive and he felt himself panicking as he almost ran through the village.

Loka and Chako were seated by the fire, while his grandparents and one of his cousins were standing, and everyone stared at him as he entered. His grandparents quickly rushed to embrace him while his grandmother struggled to hold back her emotions. They all sat together at the fire as food was passed around. Nakosis finally managed to ask about Taku, fighting to retain a stoic face. Grandfather told him how she had been part of the wave of Raven lodge reinforcements sent from the village defenses to bolster the warriors on the riverbank. She was one of those brave souls who, screaming the war cry, leapt into the full enemy force on the riverbank just before the great wave came crashing upon them. She fell to an enemy spear.

"Her death was swift Nakosis," he said.

Her body was recovered the same day, miraculously thrown up on the bank where the trail meets the river. The same place Nakosis just finished bathing!   "Taku was a brave warrior, Nakosis, as are you also." He said smiling proudly at his grandson.

"Me?" Nakosis questioned. "I was here and did not join the others in the battle. Maybe if I had …" Thoughts of Taku dominated his mind.

Loka spoke up, "The whole village now knows what you did Nakosis."

"And at great risk to your own life, it would now seem." added Chako, nodding.

"But I thought we didn't talk…I mean …how." Nakosis had been unaware that knowledge of his experience had become known outside of the two old Shaman. One was not to openly discuss such things.

Loka alluded to the most likely source when he looked directly at the cowering cousin saying, "Someone with a very loose tongue must have spoken about what should have been kept among a very few!"

The cousin could not look at Loka, or for that matter anyone else in the room.

Grandfather turned to him and said, "Your brother has already returned to your village. If you do not wish to walk the trail alone then perhaps you should join the warriors returning to their families. They prepare to depart the big lodge as we speak."

The talkative, indolent young man grabbed his bag and uttering insincere thanks under his breath, immediately rushed from the hut. Nakosis now understood why the people appeared to be looking differently at him and why he received the heart blessing from the old woman.

"I know Taku's departing is a terrible thing for you, Nakosis, but you now have a responsibility. You must go to her family and we must prepare to undertake a passing-over ceremony so that the spirits of the deceased may move on unencumbered by past attachments to this realm. Come, we must prepare."

Loka didn't wait for Nakosis to answer but simply headed for the door.

Grandfather held Loka by the arm and thanked him. Loka placed his forehead to that of the old man indicating their shared understanding and respect. Nakosis helped Chako up from the floor and the three left for Loka's little hut.

Together Loka and Nakosis went to the hut of Taku's family. They stopped at the entry and Loka announced them. Nakosis was uneasy and not prepared to face the family for fear that his own grief would again overcome him, but for Taku's sake he knew he must now be strong and assume his duty. As they entered he was taken completely off guard when Taku's mother ran for the door past Loka and threw herself at Nakosis, wrapping her arms around him and burying her head into his chest crying. Nakosis hesitated for but a moment then warmly and gently he placed his arms over the trembling woman. She lifted her head to lay her tear-reddened eyes on Nakosis.

Raising a hand to wipe them she said, "I am so sorry my dear boy. We all know what you meant to each other."

Nakosis was unaware that her parents had even a suspicion of their affection but he then remembered Loka's comment about 'the whole village knows'.

She continued, "The day of the attack, just before word came, Taku sat right here and told us of your intentions to wed. I have never seen her so full of hope and life as in that moment." She paused to regain her voice. "It warmed our hearts to see such great happiness in our daughter and to know that you were the cause of such joy in her made us honored to bless your union Nakosis. I wanted you to know." Her tears ran unchecked and her husband stood beside her, comforting her as best he could. He looked down at the young man who now stood before him and studied him for a brief moment then, placing his hand upon his shoulder he said,

"Nakosis, I am not much for such words but I was pleased to call you my son-in-law. I shall think of you as such. You have my respect." He lowered his head and Nakosis did the same, out of respect, but also to shield the tears he could not hide.

He felt Loka's hand upon his shoulder as he said, "We are all still stricken beyond words and we must prepare now for the ceremony. Thank you for your kind words. I know Nakosis will cherish them as he does Taku's memory."

Nakosis could only say, "Yes, yes," as Loka herded him out the door.

His head to the ground they walked slowly toward the Shaman's hut as villagers looked from doorways at the 'wizard' amid their midst, the one who commanded the elements, the great Shaman who saved the people, the one who commands the spirits to do his bidding - Nakosis!

The rumors now took on fabled proportions. Loka and Chako alone knew the truth and they agreed that if the people had any understanding of just what Nakosis achieved, even their wildest stories would pale. For Nakosis, however, the odd glances and the looks of admiration mingled with fear were far from flattering. Loka explained that in such dire times as this, people's emotions run high and in their sorrow they often need a hero, one person of apparent strength or power to look up to or to lean on. Nakosis suggested they look to the war leaders who, as he said, 'did the real fighting'! He felt like an oddity, an outcast in the home that no longer resembled nor felt like it any longer.

Loka instructed Nakosis in the tradition of the ceremony and gave him certain responsibilities that Nakosis suspected were, in part, designed to keep him engaged so as to not dwell on Taku's passing. He was right, of course, but it was also necessary to help those spirits who, due to the tragic circumstances of their deaths, may still be trapped between two worlds, confused and unable to move on by themselves. Also, it gave much needed closure and solace to the grieving village. A great fire had been prepared near the burying field. Those who lost loved ones spoke of the good qualities or heroic deeds of the departed and told of their wish to see them move on safely into the otherworld. They said their memories would live on forever in the hearts and songs of their families. Their names would be given to future family members who would come to know their life's story and so their legacy would continue. Each family walked sun wise around the great fire, speaking their words to the assembled and at the end of each rotation they would throw in a pinch of sacred herbs prepared by Loka earlier. Into this mixture they would also add a small piece of their loved one's hair or a part of a favorite garment. This would help encourage any lost soul to depart this realm. Loka, Chako and Nakosis kept a steady soft drumming, muttering the words to invoke the spirits of the underworld to assist in the passing of any lost souls. Other villagers brought their drums also and joined in the drumming and chanting the sacred song. The bereaved were many and the fire lasted well into the night.

The effects of his grief, stress, lack of sleep and his days of fever were now starting to catch up to Nakosis, he thought. He was feeling tired and unfocused as he sat with his drum at the fire. As new family members took their rounds about the fire he would throw a bit of the sacred herbs into the fire and speak the few short words of invocation Loka had instructed. He tried shifting his position slightly to stay awake and focused. The whole village, no doubt, had eyes on him now since the rumors. 'Can't have their great magician dropping face first asleep at the most solemn ceremony in the peoples' history!' he thought and smiled to himself. Not outwardly though. He decided to focus his gaze on the flames as they were always trance inducing. Better to appear to be in some otherworldly trance than just ordinarily sleepy, he thought. The idea seemed to work. Nakosis let his eyes close just a little and let just enough of the firelight in to keep him from sleeping, yet give his tired eyes a rest. He rationalized, as he felt the drum slowly fall onto his lap, that no one would notice as many drums now beat like one great suffering heart of sorrow. It was a mistake! The last few family members had circled the fire, sending their relatives into the afterlife and now the drumming had taken on a life of its own as villagers poured their grief stricken hearts into the primal rhythm. They were dancing sun wise in one pulsating mass around the fire and around Loka, Chako, Nakosis and other villagers who sat around large drums that rested on the ground. Around and around them the procession circled. Loka and Chako were in a state of their own, eyes closed, being one with the rhythm. Everyone was now so possessed of the spirit of the ceremony that it went unnoticed that Nakosis had risen to his feet. He began to sway in small circles as the dancing crowd swept past. His feet began tapping out the rhythm on the hard dusty ground. Picking up momentum, he began dancing his own circle within the circle, his arms stretched out, his eyes still mostly closed he picked up his speed. The other dancers were automatically widening the ring further out around this young Shaman who they believed was expressing his own deep emotion, his own loss in this, his own small dance. They were wrong. There was no doubting Nakosis' grief or emotion but Nakosis was no longer the one dancing! The crowd started pulling away, widening the circle to escape the heat of the great fire that now seemed to intensify with the energy of the crowd. Perhaps it was the sheer moving mass of humanity creating the heat? Nakosis was now spinning, his feet leaving the ground. One foot would hit the dirt as the other rose up and his body would spin with an effortless, uncanny ease and grace. All the while his arms would swing extended like the magnificent wings of the eagle. A few at the outer edge of the great dancing circle were catching their breath. They were enjoying watching the dancers pass. Now though, many had their eyes on Nakosis. Soon anyone not captivated in their own movement had taken notice of the form of this young Shaman dancing in a manner unknown to them. Some speculated it was, in fact, a form of the eagle dance. Others insisted it was more a raven. No one, at first, noticed the fire beginning to bend as though a great wind was exerting force on its sides, funneling it up into the black night sky. It started to spin, slowly at first.

It was Chasake who said, "Look, the fire moves with the Shaman!"

Many of those caught up in the dancing began to slow and stop their circle about the now frightening spectacle of revolving flame. The fire had also taken on an otherworldly glow. Beside it Nakosis spun, like a leaf caught in a wind of spirit.   Loka was always sensitive to the fields of energy about him. He knew something was different and he looked up from his drumming to lay his eyes upon the form of Nakosis spinning madly, as though no longer bound to the earth, the funnel of fire providing a terrifying backdrop. He quickly and deliberately knocked over Chako as he rushed to Nakosis side. Grabbing him by the arm, he tried to pull him away from the growing flames. He had hoped to be as subtle as possible, stopping Nakosis' dance before more people took notice. Chako rose to assist, as did Nakosis' grandfather who had been watching his grandson through most of the ceremony. With grandfather's presence Loka yelled to Chako to keep drumming. Chako, now standing, resumed heavily beating his big drum; it's booming resonance setting back in motion the drumming that had begun to weaken in volume. As Nakosis was led away with Loka's blanket over him, the dancing seemed once again to continue as before. Some, undoubtedly unaware of the spectacle that occurred, would assume he was simply overcome by the emotion of the ceremony and being led from the fire supported by loved ones.

With the drumming and singing now carrying it's own momentum, Chako wove slowly through the crowd and rushed to catch up with the three men as they approached Loka's hut. They had a difficult time carrying the squirming younger man. He lay now on the floor, his eyes still closed, his mind not in the present, his limbs still jerking slightly as though still dancing, his head moving back and forth.

"What kind of evil spirit is this that has my boy?" Grandfather said.

The old man had stood his ground in the battle and had killed his adversary. He had proven himself as much a capable warrior as any of the younger men, but there was now unmistakable fear in his voice.

"It is no evil, my friend," Chako had leaned over between the two men, his hands on each of their shoulders. "He is the vessel of a power he has yet to fully understand. He just needs to be able to control it."

"I only hope he can before it destroys him!" grandfather replied.

They watched Nakosis for a good part of the evening.

"He is like a dreaming dog chasing rabbits," Loka observed, watching Nakosis' limbs twitching. Finally he fell into a still and restful sleep and the men seized the opportunity to do the same.

Come morning, Nakosis appeared quite normal, physically unaffected by the previous night's occurrence. The look on his face, however, showed that there was something deeply troubling him. Loka asked what he thought of the ceremony.

Nakosis thought for a moment before answering, "Oh no, I fell asleep didn't I? Taku's family! What will they think! I am so sorry. I couldn't help it! I..."

Loka had raised his hand. "Not exactly my boy," he said then he began to explain what had happened and how they whisked him away before too many became suspicious. Chako then told Nakosis that he must learn to control this colossal gift.

"This is no gift!" Nakosis spat the words, his frustration evident. "What gift possesses a man so? Perhaps it is a curse!"

Chako turned to Loka who waited for the emotion to ease a little then he explained, "It was not a curse that saved this village and the lives of so many, Nakosis. It is a power beyond your control at the present, but in time you will learn to control it and it will come to serve you even better in time of need. It is a gift from the gods!"

"Again I ask, why a god or spirit or whatever this is would choose me? I am not a trained Shaman like you or Chako. I am not a warrior like Hankas or Chasake. I have nothing to give and now I have lost the one thing I lived for! I am barely a man!" These last words were hard to utter and his voice cracked with the pain of having spoken them.

Chako placing a reassuring hand said softly, "You, my little brother, are far stronger than you know." Nakosis looked at his old friend as he continued, "Because you see, Nakosis, the great Mystery gives the hardest task to the strongest man."

As he walked the old familiar route to the river to wash away the sweat and daze of the previous night, he again thought of Taku. He had harbored the dream of leading a 'normal' life, married to the one he loved, treated like any other simple village member, but now the strange looks from the door-ways he passed told him this was not to be so. People he'd known his entire life, children he'd laughed and played with now looked at Nakosis with apprehension and spoke to him only with reservation, their eyes quickly looking away. What they were displaying, he realized was fear. Rumors quickly spread as events became exaggerated and Nakosis was starting to feel more like an outsider than a hero. Young children, always the least reserved, openly used pseudonyms for Nakosis like 'the fire spirit dancer' or, the one that hurt him the most, 'he kills with magic'. By the time he returned from the river he'd made the decision to undertake the quest to find the Mountain of Fire and finally, hopefully, find answers about his troublesome 'gift'. The village, he'd concluded, no longer had anything to hold him. He would miss the love of his grandparents but it was his time to leave.

Nakosis arrived at Loka's hut a different man than the one who left only moments before. Gone was the grief-shattered self-pitying adolescent and in his stead stood an extremely determined and anxious young man with the courage, will and spirit to begin the journey of his life. He commanded attention as he dominated the doorway. He dropped a heavy full pack on the floor and placing his arms across his chest he spoke with an air of confidence and self-assurance.

"So, now that the ceremony has concluded the village can surely continue without us. When do we leave for your village, Chako?"

The two old men were unprepared. They had only just discussed Chako's urge to soon return to attend the needs of his people and whether he'd be going alone.

"Ah,…well.." Loka struggled for the words, "I suppose we could leave soon Nakosis." He looked at Chako for some sign of confirmation.

Chako nodded, "Why… ah yes, yes, I… ahh…I could leave soon, yes," he stammered looking back at Loka.

"When?" Demanded Nakosis.

"I must give my gratitude and say my goodbyes to the village elders and there is also one more thing I would like to do. Hopefully it won't require more than two more days and we also must make our preparations." Chako deferred back to Loka who stood and spoke directly to Nakosis.

"You will spend the last two days with your grandparents no doubt? Who knows when you will see them again, Nakosis," he paused and added, his meaning obvious, "They are old Nakosis and they still love you very much!"

Nakosis realized as he lowered his head and nodded that he was being selfish, not considering the feelings his leaving would have on the two older ones who had been kind and caring parents to him for so long. Of course Loka was right, as usual. He would try to enjoy these last two days with them as much as he could.

After he left, the two old Shaman commented how the young man was a paradox of emotional extremes, one moment a typical teenager with nothing outside his immediate needs and the other moment a conscientious and mature young man. They concluded that such was typical behavior for one of his age and especially given the circumstances and the tragic loss he and the whole village had endured. It would be a long time before anything close to normal returned to the daily lives of the people.

Chako observed, giggling, "I am afraid I am too old to remember when I was like that!"

CHAPTER 12
THE QUEST

Nakosis had spent much time with his grandparents and reflected upon all they had done for him and he took the opportunity to let them know of his love and appreciation. He did so tactfully, so as not to sound like there was a possibility he might not return from the unknown. He wasn't fooling anyone though. His grandparents were also maintaining a calm outward appearance so as not to overly alarm the young man. Although they knew he needed all the support he could get to face his task, it still was hard for grandmother to not hold him fast and beg him to stay.

They had prepared a sumptuous meal the last night and had invited Chako and Loka to feast with them. This also offered them the opportunity to discuss the journey to Chako's village. Neither of them, despite their age and experience, had ventured further than the Deer River village. It was taxing on them to try to understand the extent of the journey their only grandson was about to embark upon but the two old Shaman, understanding their concern, tried to dispel their fears as best they could. Deep down, though, everyone knew that Nakosis was about to venture where no one in the history of the village had ever set foot before. Nakosis was especially aware of this, as he was noticeably quiet and absorbed in thought throughout the meal. He knew now that he had committed himself. He also realized that behind the closed doors of every village dwelling, people were, no doubt, also discussing the young Shaman. There was no turning back!

He excused himself and took one last walk through the village. He decided that he would not cower from the ignorance of others. He would not allow himself to feel in any way intimidated or offended by the fearful glances some gave him. He threw his robe about his shoulders and raised his head high and with a slow and steady gait he proudly walked through the village. His confidence so bolstered, he was taking some small delight in showing himself in such a way that he decided to completely walk every bit of public dirt in White Mist, perhaps, he reasoned, for the last time. He was putting himself up for display and he didn't care.

Almost without realizing it he'd arrived at the open door of Taku's family. He stood there unspeaking as the fact hit him and as her parents looked up he knew not what to say.

There was an uneasy silence for a few agonizing heartbeats until Nakosis cleared his throat and said, "Ah, I was just taking a walk...I... ah...will be leaving the village in the morning... and..."

It was Taku's mother who broke his stammering by rushing to the doorway and pulling him in by the arm. She threw her arms around him asking him to join them. Taku's father smiled welcomingly and grabbed Nakosis by the shoulder. He was a big and strong warrior and Nakosis was nearly jerked off his feet by the warm gesture. They talked very briefly as Taku's young brother peered giggling from behind his mother. Reaching behind the piled robes, blankets and containers of stored goods, Taku's father retrieved a bundle and turned to Nakosis presenting it to him with both hands as her mother began gently crying.

"Here my boy, we'd like you to take this with you on your journey. It will protect you and we know Taku would have wished it so."

Nakosis respectfully unwrapped the deer hide covering of what he could now clearly see was Taku's magnificent bow and quiver. He choked back the tears. He stared at it momentarily as he knew he could not immediately look into their eyes. He took a breath and sniffled back his tears, thanking them profusely.

"I think," Taku's mother added, "that her spirit will guide your hand should you have need Nakosis." At this she wept uncontrollably as her husband comforted her.

Nakosis left the hut and as he walked the remainder of the village he did so with less bravado, less haughtiness to his step. Taku's quiver over his shoulder and the powerful bow in his left hand, he strode up to the doorway of the great lodge. Inside many of the village elders and some of the families who'd lost their only son or daughter were still gathering each evening. They shared their communal meal and took comfort in one another's supportive presence. The ongoing preparations for the village's recovery were being discussed. Nakosis stood in the doorway, silhouetted by the setting sun, taking in the faces of those gathered. People he'd known and admired and many he'd called 'friend.' The assembly, all as one, turned and looked at this unannounced figure. Nakosis wasn't sure why he did it, but he had raised his right hand to his heart and out to those gathered in the gesture of the heart blessing. The seated warriors now stood and all bowed their heads in respect as the elders returned the blessing from where they sat by the fire. Then Nakosis turned his back on the lodge and left the village. The gesture had two meanings to Nakosis. It served as acknowledgement of his respect for the others and it also signified his official departure. Nakosis knew also that there would be some in the gathering that would give a sigh of relief at his leaving.

Nakosis had not slept well all night thinking of what unknown perils awaited him on this, his great journey. He spent a good part of the night trying to shake off recurring doubt and apprehension. He kept telling himself Chako's reassuring words, 'The Great Mystery gives the hardest task to the strongest man.' He lay awake for a long time staring at the doorway just waiting for dawn's approach. The waiting was almost harder than leaving, he thought.

He rose before the full light. His belongings had been carefully chosen and packed well in advance. Grabbing his things he left quickly, not wanting to prolong the inevitable. Loka and Chako were also awake and attending to the last details of their departure. They briefly discussed the day ahead. They planned to travel the river trail past the route to Quick Waters village and continue straight on to Deer River, where they would spend a day and two nights. Loka would attend to spiritual matters. Those who'd lost loved ones wanted the assurances that the fallen had attained the afterlife. The spirits of the dead soon dominated the conversation as they began walking the trail. Loka had confided to Nakosis that he could not guarantee the outcome of such ceremonies.

"The spirits of the departed are not ours to control." He said. "Sometimes they have too much attachment for this world, for the places where they lived, loved and died that a part of them can remain stuck neither in this world nor the other world." He added.

"So then," Nakosis asked, "they are ghosts?"

"Yes something like that. But I don't think the word 'ghost' best describes them. It creates fear in people like an evil spirit. The truth is most of these lost souls are never seen by people, they exist in a space that is in between, caught like a fish in a net that is suspended above the river –neither in the world of water nor the world of earth. Sometimes when we do these ceremonies the guiding spirits can come and help to take these lost ones back to the otherworld with them and so help them to move on to their next life, *but* we cannot determine what that life will be. This becomes the result of who they were in this life, what kind of person they were."

Chako contributed his insights, "Yes, and this comes down to what choices did they make while they lived, were they good people? Did they have reverence for Mother Earth and all the brethren? Did they offer respect to the spirits of those they killed for food? These sort of things say what kind of life they are born into."

It was becoming hard to walk and talk for the two older men, as the day was becoming increasingly hotter as the sun rose higher. They passed many people on the trail now. Since the battle, many families were travelling between the villages to visit loved ones. Loka commented that it was perhaps the one good thing to come from the disaster.

"People," he said, "sometime need hardship in their lives to reinforce the bonds between them. It is during such times that the love of relatives is strengthened and the strength of the community is made stronger."

Many warriors were on the trails also. Since the attack more watch posts were established at strategic points and all three villages were now more prepared and sentries and scouts were relieving one another by way of the trail. As people passed the three Shamans they would lower their heads with a reverent bow, but Nakosis noticed that they did not make eye contact nor did many speak any words to them in passing. Many feared the Shaman, as they believed that the spirits constantly surrounded them and as Loka had previously pointed out, people fear what they do not understand. He also speculated that all the villages, no doubt, knew the details of the events and that greatly exaggerated rumors had spread to them. He was preparing for an uneasy reception. A few days earlier he was filled with trepidation about his leaving the familiar surroundings of his life, but now he only wanted to get to Chako's village and his people. He was hoping that word of him had not yet reached those people. Deer River village was closest to Chako's village and it was possible that some traders from Deer Village had spread the story and the many rumors. He knew that, upon their arrival, Chako and Loka would inform the village elders of the details of battle and it's aftermath. Chako's people would also want to know about the Black Faces and possibly increase their vigilance, but they would not say anything that would incite any fear or animosity toward Nakosis.

No one made any mention of Stags Leap, nor of the events of the day of the battle. They stopped mid-way along the trail at the junction of the Deer River and the Blue Fish River. It was a spectacular spot and where the force of the two waters met a large wide pool was created that was separated from the main river by a great bank of gravel. It had been so for some time, Loka noticed, as there were numerous small willows growing up along its length. The three men took the opportunity to cool off in the refreshing waters. Usually the river was very cold, even in the warmest summer days, as it flowed down from the height of the mountains where snow remained all year bringing the cold with it. The pool, however, had soaked up some of the warmth of the sun and it was a perfectly refreshing temperature. Even Loka and Chako shed their garments and fully immersed their skinny frames into the glassy pool. Chako rushed into the water with total abandon and with childlike exuberance seized the chance to slap his hand upon the surface showering Loka who was only wading, cautiously, knee deep at the shoreline. Loka's shocked gasps and his stern reprimand caused Chako to giggle deliriously with delight. Nakosis doubled over in gales of laughter. Loka's attempts to appear stern and disapproving only intensified the humor of the situation until he also started laughing, shaking his finger at Loka as a mother to a child.

"I'm travelling with two boys!" he yelled at Chako upon which he received an additional splashing and waves of Chako's infectious giggles.

It was a much-needed respite from both the hot travelling and from the tensions of the past few days. They sat on a log letting the warm breeze dry them and cool their bodies. They didn't have time for a fire and so ate a little of the grain and dried berry cakes Nakosis' grandmother had prepared for them. Nakosis thought the break an opportunity to raise some questions.

"I've been wondering," he began, "about the 'Great Mystery'."

The two looked at him while eating their cakes, Chako nodding, as though waiting for him to continue.

"Well, I suppose I don't quite understand it."

Chako giggled and replied, "Yes, that's why we call it 'the Great Mystery'!"

Loka, quite out of character, burst into laughter at the comment, choking on bits of his bread. Chako giggling, slapped Nakosis hard on the shoulder. Nakosis also found the answer hysterical.

Finally, after they regained their composure. Nakosis refined the question.

"No, I mean, is the Great Mystery a spirit, like the guardians, because some also say 'Great Spirit'? "

"No," Chako continued, "Not like the guardians. They are indeed powerful, but we say *Great Spirit* to mean the power of creation."

This didn't help Nakosis who asked, "So are we talking about a person, I mean a being?"

Chako explained, "When we talk of the Earth Mother we refer to all the powers we see and hear and feel around us every day –the mountains, the trees, every one of our animal brethren, the rocks and the rivers. If there was a time when she did not exist, when she also came into being, then 'Great Mystery' or 'Great Spirit' means that which caused her coming, that which created all we know, even the spirit world also. Some like to think of this as being some kind of person or 'being' as you said, others believe that such a spirit has no form yet all form. Do you understand?"

"No form, yet all form?" Nakosis asked.

"Well, if such a power existed then some think that it is beyond our understanding and therefore beyond form, therefore we say great 'spirit' not great 'person'. But also if this spirit created all form then it can also take all forms. They think that if it were a person then it should also have a name. Who decides this name? To give such power a name is to try to understand the very thing they say we can't understand. Do you see? Then my people, your people, the flatlanders, the Black Faces who speak different tongues would all have different names and soon they would be talking in these tongues about something different! This, I think, makes the Great Spirit smaller in their minds, like something they could hope to control. People are funny, they name things thinking that to do so gives them understanding of that thing, but it only lowers that thing to each person's small understanding. You might understand something more than one person or less than another. Who's understanding is the right understanding? Then they believe that because this thing has a name that they now have a different relationship to it. They try to somehow own the thing. Other people are content to remain in awe and reverence and to say with humility 'I do not know!'"

Nakosis pondered this for a while then continued, "So what you say is that no one really knows whether there even is a great spirit, and if there is, then no one can really know exactly what it is?"

"Yes, that is what I'm saying but I believe, Nakosis, I *know* as do you also, that there are many other things beyond that of the waking world. You have experienced this perhaps even more than Loka and myself. Where these things come from is not really important. You can spend your life searching for that answer and neglect your gift and die never knowing the answer; or you can accept that these things are simply a part of all that exists, all part of the Great Mystery of life."

Loka now added his thoughts, "We believe that, yes, there is great power beyond our understanding. The waking world, the world above and also the underworld - all three worlds are alive by the same power, all the spirits, the guardians, even Hohapas is alive by this same power. It is through the spirits that this power sometimes comes to us and we are blessed by its presence."

Chako added, "Yes, and we acknowledge and respect the spirits because they come to us, they show themselves to us so we can see them. They are as messengers of the great power – the Great Mystery."

Nakosis considered these words for a while as the other two dressed and started picking up their packs. Nakosis hefted his big bag upon his shoulders and picked up his walking spear. They stood for a moment silently drinking in the splendid scenery of the two rivers and the breathtaking view of the mountainous valley spread before them. Nakosis wondered where beyond the mountain borders of his known world his quest would take him.

As they once again took to the trail Nakosis continued his question, "So, if the Great Mystery is the power behind all things, even Mother Earth and Hohapas is the power of magic, then he must also be the Great Spirit."

Chako and Loka looked at one another and it was Chako who picked up the challenge to provide the answer. "Yes, Nakosis but not directly so. Hohapas is, as we explained, a part of the power that is the Great Mystery, as are we all. It is just that the spirits dwell in a different existence."

"You mean the spirit world?" Nakosis said.

"Yes," Chako continued, "the spirit world. Although we journey there, it is also not a separate place apart from this, our waking world. All the three worlds exist as though within one world but in different ways. It is hard to explain. It is like when one dreams, Nakosis. When you dream do you not sometimes leave this world and fly with the eagles or run with the deer or live a different life, maybe love a woman?" The last part accompanied by his usual chuckles. Nakosis nodded. "So then, are you not also in your robes in the White Mist village asleep?" Again Nakosis agreed. "So then which is the right world? Which is the real world - the one of dreams or the one of waking? You see they are both real, Nakosis, they both exist together at the same time in the same place. You understand? So also the spirit worlds and the waking world exist in the same way. Through our practice we are sometimes, by the spirit's blessing, able to be in both worlds, to move between them. When you realize that the worlds are here around us as well as within us at all times then you see that it is no magic to be in either world. Anyone can do this. As we've said before everyone does so when they dream. We are just developing this ability within us, Nakosis, to be able to do so while also in the waking state. It is only that you have been given the extraordinary blessing of doing so with such great ease. The challenge you now face is not going to the spirit realm but to control when and how you do! That is also our challenge, to help you develop this ability. When you do, I cannot say what power you will find my brother."

Although it didn't seem possible the day grew even hotter, a thick and suffocating heat seemed to lay heavy over the valley. Leaving the river and its cooling breeze, they were plagued by the many insects that seem to thrive in the still, hot air. They trudged on, the trail now ascending higher into the forest. Loka said that they might soon find the going a little easier as the air would get cooler as they climbed higher into the forest and they may catch a breeze once they reached the ridge.

Chako only commented, "Yes, but there's the climbing!"

There was a good trail from Quick Waters village to Deer River village and it was relatively easy going through a small valley. As well, the Quick Waters trail from the main trail was not as steep. It was for this reason they reckoned that they did not encounter anyone on this leg of the walk. Normally they, like most others, would have gone to Quick Waters village first and then continued on to Deer River, but Chako had to return home to his village and so this was considered the faster way. The path was physically challenging and Nakosis was finding himself short of breath and the muscles in his legs were beginning to burn. He could only imagine how Loka and Chako were feeling; yet they seemed either to not be affected or else they bore it quite well. They stopped at what seemed to be a high point for a rest. A tiny spring afforded them the opportunity to drink their fill and replenish their empty water gourds. The trail from here on, Loka said, would be flatter and through the forest.

Regaining his breath, Nakosis asked Chako about his village. "So what is your village like? Is it much the same as our village? Where will I stay in your village? How long do you think it will take for you to find the information we need about the lost people?"

They had discussed the plans in Loka's hut previously but the two men knew that there was bound to be much apprehension and anxiety in the young man. He was, after all, venturing into unknown worlds, both physically and spiritually.

Chako raised his hand to stop the barrage of questions. "First, you will enjoy my village, my friend. Yes, it is in many ways like yours. Our people are related after all, but there are differences, yes. I don't want to spoil it for you nor do I want to give you a false image so you will simply have to have some patience. As for where you will stay, why, where do you think? Did you think I'd put you up in a grain hut?" Chako's customary chuckling accompanied the comment. "Why, no, you will stay with my family, of course!"

"Your family!" Nakosis said.

"Yes, my family. Why do you look so shocked? Do I look like a little orphan?" Even Loka laughed at this last remark.

"No, it's just that...I...ahh...I...thought that Shamans were not allowed families." Both Loka and Chako laughed.

"Not allowed...by who?" Chako demanded.

"Well," Nakosis looked over to Loka and Loka immediately picked up the topic, saving poor Nakosis any further embarrassment.

Smiling broadly Loka explained, "Don't think, Nakosis, that just because I live alone that it is some sort of rule for us, not at all. I have simply not received the 'calling' to raise a family. It is not in my nature. No, I have been quite content living the life I do. Chako here, on the other hand, has raised a very fine family and was happily married for many, many years."

Knowing the question waited unasked in Nakosis' mind, Chako offered the explanation. "It was the sickness, Nakosis - when I first met Loka and Quansa. You recall? I lost my wife at that time but, yes, I have a daughter and two sons and they also have a family so I have many grandchildren. I have my own dwelling though, of course. Lots of room, don't you worry," then he laughed heartily at the thought of Nakosis' statement.

"Well for some reason," Nakosis continued, "it seems that Shaman lead very lone lives, often having to be alone and find places of power to seek the spirits help, like your cave Loka. You were often gone, alone from the village for lengths at a time."

"Yes this is true," Loka added, "but no more than a man who must hunt for his family. Sometimes the hunter may be gone a very long period, especially in lean times."

Chako contributed, "Yes you are right Nakosis, but in my situation I had a hut just like every other family, but also one like Loka's so that I might undertake my journeying away from others, yet also be near. It is not that you *must* keep yourself separate from others, but there are times when you become so busy with the affairs of the everyday that you might neglect the spirits calling. Then sometimes you may need to go away for a day or more and regain your balance. You recall we mentioned that being a Shaman is all about maintaining the balance. This you can do within the fold of family and community if you only allow a certain amount of each day to make the connection with Mother Earth and your spirit guides. In fact, it is perhaps best to be where your help is most needed- among the people."

Loka nodded in agreement adding, "There are those who you, no doubt, have heard of that often choose another solitary path Nakosis. They stay isolated, usually in mountains somewhere. There are many tales of such people. They are generally misunderstood and people call them magicians. Perhaps they are but they are Shamans also. They have dedicated themselves to fully understanding the spirit world by continuous journeying. It is said that for some they are mostly in the spirit world and in this world barely a little. When you encounter such people you can feel their power immediately. They have chosen to work for the world away from the world."

"How is such a thing possible?" asked Nakosis, his curiosity aroused.

Loka explained, "You remember when we said that whatever one does in this world carries an echo that continues even into the next life and whatever you do in the world of the spirit has an echo in the waking world? Well, these men, and sometimes women also, will obtain the highest blessings they can and then in turn, they offer this to others. Some may undertake this life until such a time that they believe they have become the most beneficial they can and then they venture out and give the blessing of their powers to help others. A Shaman really has no power of his own, don't you see? He merely is a vessel for the power of the spirits – of the Great Mystery. You cannot hold it and store it in the way that one might keep grains against lean times. It is more like grabbing handfuls of water from a river that flows past you. You can take a cup and drink from it and you can hand some of it to one who is thirsty, but you cannot hold the river! The life force flows through you and all things at all times, so too the spirit power. You can learn to receive it and then you must let it go to help others. This power has to flow *through* you Nakosis. In doing so you can learn to let it fill your whole being, but you must give it out for it to flow, otherwise you do not receive it. People have tried to take this power, to make it their own. These are the ones who were sometimes called the dark magicians, but although they learned to become full with the power, they didn't give it out to help others. They used some to serve their greed while always trying to have more power. Then the power grows stale and rotten within them and ultimately it destroys them. This is also why we have said that humility is the most essential thing for a Shaman. The more power he or she has, the more important humility is because there is the temptation to want to misuse the power. Do you see now why this is so important, Nakosis?"

"Yes, Uncle I understand," Nakosis replied.

Nakosis could see that Loka had to stop talking and focus on walking. For a long while there was only their strained breathing, the occasional rustle of leaves in a much-appreciated wind and the steady buzz of countless insects. Even the birds seemed to be resting in the oppressive heat. It was indeed somewhat cooler in the forest but the air was so very still. Nakosis didn't mind the quiet. He used the time gainfully to assess the great teachings he had just received. There was so much for him to ponder, and ponder he did. He ran scenarios over in his mind of causes and affects and weighed these outcomes with his understanding of the 'echo' that accompanies every action. It was a staggering concept. The more he thought of it the more he understood the incredible depth to which it grew like unending roots of some great tree. There was, it seemed, not a single breath drawn in this life that did not have some effect. A whole new world opened to Nakosis. A vision of things now connected everyone and everything in a way he hadn't known. A thought occurred to him. He was reluctant to speak of it, as he knew that Loka and Chako were growing very tired and that they wanted to make the village before nightfall, but it gnawed at his mind and he needed to know. He waited until they had walked a fairly easy flat area of the trail for a while then he asked, "I've been thinking," he began.

"Ahhh, that was the blessed silence!" Loka quipped, laughing.

Nakosis smiled and continued, "Everything that happens, happens because of something else. Such as if I create some difficulty for someone I too will receive some difficulty, if not now then in my next life. Is that so?"

"Yes, it is somewhat like that, not necessarily one exact thing for the same. But yes, you get a good result from a good act, a bad result from a bad one, yes you are right."

Nakosis thought for a moment then asked, "So, why was our village attacked? Why was Taku, who was so young and caused no harm to anyone, killed in the battle also?"

They all stopped walking. Loka looked at Nakosis then turned and walked to a fallen tree. He hefted off his big bag and sat down indicating that this question warranted a rest break.

Once they were seated, he tried to explain. "You are quite right to ask such a thing, Nakosis. I am glad you did. It proves that you are learning. You see, it is not so simple a thing as you did a good deed yesterday so where is your reward today. The opposite also is true. Did you not see, as a young boy, someone who was not nice to others, a bully perhaps?"

Nakosis answered that indeed he had seen many such young boys in the village.

"They may also have had very good childhoods. They most likely were given many things from their parents and suffered no ill effect for their bullying?" Loka asked.

Again Nakosis agreed.

"So the result of their actions is yet to be felt for these people. Sometimes it doesn't happen in this life because everyone, each of us, carries the echo of both the good and the not so good that we have done in the past. Past, Nakosis, is not just last season, not just last life, but over many, many lives. Who's to say what we've done in the long ago? But everything now, both pleasant and painful, is because of the person we were before. Because of this a man might be the greatest father, brother, husband and friend to all and yet he may suffer a painful death, or worse, be forced to suffer the painful death of loved ones. Why is this we ask ourselves? It is because of the echo of past deeds. It doesn't mean that these people are in any way bad. In fact, as these echoes of the past deeds are heard in the new life, they diminish just as real echoes fade over a valley. So, if they continue to live a good life there will soon be fewer echoes to be heard in the next. When loved ones die, who suffers most? Is it the departed or the ones they leave behind?"

Nakosis replied, "The deceased have no suffering past their dying, yet the loved ones continue to suffer their loss."

"Exactly Nakosis," said Loka, adding, "So then, both echoes are ringing together –the lost one and the one missing them, but it is perhaps the one's mourning whose echo is repeating loudest." He waited for a moment then continued, "So, as to the village, again, who knows what events happened so far back in lost time that now, by some unknown cause, have chosen this time to echo from the pasts of so many, all at the same time. You must realize also then, that by this understanding, even the Black Faces must have some connection in this great unfolding! They too played a part in the great echoing. Taku's death, your parents' death, the passing away of everyone we will ever know or love is simply more unfolding of the echoes of our actions from this moment back to the lost time."

"So where does it all end then? Do we simply return to suffer the loss of our loved ones, to watch life fade before our eyes? What is the purpose then? If this is so, then life serves no reason. It is just a cruelty!" Nakosis was yelling now, his emotions and his lack of understanding making him obviously frustrated.

Chako interrupted, "You have just asked the greatest question and my boy; I think you know the answer. The purpose is to become one with the spirit that is all things, to live in perfect balance. It is said that one who achieves such a thing at the time of death creates no echoes of deeds and does not return to the waking world, or to other worlds. Their spirit guides carry them elsewhere."

Loka added, "Yes and it is also said that such people can even do so at a time of their choosing! They do not wait for death. Even, they say, some such beings return to the waking world in spirit to guide others just as it would seem that you, Nakosis, are being guided!"

They all reflected deeply on these last words and Loka finished, saying, "Come now, you should have enough to occupy your mind until we reach the village."

CHAPTER 13
DEER RIVER AND THE BEYOND

For the remainder of the day they focused on their walking and Nakosis on the weighty words of the last conversation. The sun was now descending behind the mountain and the cool breeze that heralded the coming of dusk was indeed a welcome relief, both from the heavy heat and the clouds of biting insects. They approached the village and several surprised sentries. They were not expecting to encounter anyone coming from this trail, especially so late in the day. The guards quickly recovered their composure and stern looks and as they nodded the three through into Deer River village, one ran ahead to announce their arrival. Children quickly gathered around the three men giggling and running around them as their parents called from their dwellings.

The first to approach them was an elder whose name was Sapaska. He walked across a broad square with his arms open wide and a warm welcoming smile as he approached his old friends. Behind him others now began to assemble. Loka introduced Nakosis and the old man gently held his hands as he welcomed them. The gesture was sincere and it did much to elevate Nakosis' expectations of their stay there.

The war leader, a colossal and imposing warrior who led the party against the retreating Black Faces, was the next to arrive. Everything about the man was an exaggeration of masculinity and bravado. Even his approach was a display, as he strutted like a rutting buck towards them. His head held unnaturally high and his chest and shoulders raised, his eyes wide. He had an unnerving forced smile, bordering on a grimace that made him look maniacal. He wore a great plume of feathers in his hair and carried an equally ostentatious ceremonial looking war club. Nakosis mustered every bit of self-control to maintain a straight face. Loka and Chako appeared unaffected as they were presented to each other. Sapaska introduced him as 'Washtaka- the one who killed the Black Faces!' Washtaka maintained his mask-like face. Sapaska first introduced Loka, then Chako who he announced was an honored guest from the low forest village, and then Nakosis, as was protocol since he was the youngest. Upon hearing his name, Washtaka's eyes widened just ever so slightly. He said nothing but simply bowed his head to them and opened his arms slightly as a gesture of welcoming.

Sapaska turned, still smiling and said to the war leader, "They should stay in the big lodge as our honored guests."

"No!" Washtaka immediately yelled. Then as though quickly trying to regain his self-control, he said, "No, that is…they must have their own hut … as will be fitting such distinguished guests!" he feigned a smile that again looked more like a grimace. It served to make him look a little demented, Nakosis thought.

Struggling a little at the response, Sapaska did his best to be diplomatic and suggested that perhaps Washtaka would see to it that a hut was made comfortable while they joined Sapaska in his hut for a meal. The war leader simply bowed slightly took a few steps backward, and quickly turned and disappeared into the large lodge.

Deer River village could have easily been a part of the White Mist village. Everything was similar, thought Nakosis; even many of the faces were familiar. The people here were accustomed to seeing Loka and, since the battle, exchange between the villages had increased greatly. Many families were brought together by the tragedy, as Loka had observed. There was an ongoing rotation of warriors also as the various lodges now hosted other warriors. Chasake and Hankas initiated a grand plan readily adopted by all the war leaders. It combined small groups of warriors from each of the villages to routinely make a reconnaissance of all three villages and surrounding areas from the promontories near the arrow rocks overlooking the foothills, to the high ridge across the Blue Fish river where the Black Faces retreated. This required that these warriors spend time on the move between each village and were relieved and rotated among all the lodges. This allowed for the men to spend time with their families, hunt, fish, tend crops and in the process it forged lasting bonds between the many warriors and their families. Some had become fast friends and were visiting the other villages more frequently since the battle. Nakosis need not wonder whether any news from home had preceded him.

Sapaska was a perfect host offering the men a sumptuous feast of roast venison and delicious flat cakes fresh baked over the coals of the evening fire. Naturally the talk centered on the Black Faces and the battle. As events were discussed and the many details unfolded the subject of the great dam breaking was raised. Nakosis had been trying to politely engage in the conversation but was being cautiously reserved, as was customary for one so young in the company of elders. Now he looked away from the faces gathered around him and stared at the fire, wondering how the talk would play out. Loka cleared his throat and made predictable remarks about what a blessing it was for our people and how the spirits blessed the warriors of Three River's villages.

"Blessed indeed!" Sapaska said, then so very matter-of-factly he added, "Why, wasn't it this, our very honored guest, the young Nakosis who I hear we owe our thanks to in this regard? Why is he not a real hero for all our people?" He was absolutely beaming with admiration when he spoke the words, looking at Nakosis for some acknowledgement to the comment.

It hadn't occurred to Nakosis that someone might actually be more grateful than fearful of him. It was so totally unexpected, however, that for a few heartbeats he could not respond. He shifted his eyes from Loka to Chako, who were both looking very pleased with the turn of events.

Finally he straightened himself from his slouching posture and gathering the most humility he could he replied, "Thank you so much for your praise honored Sapaska, but I myself did nothing. I was merely acting by the will of the spirits. They are the true heroes." Loka and Chako both gave Nakosis an approving nod.

Sapaska continued, "Three men of such great standing with the spirit guardians of our people! Here in our village –in my hut! Well, is it indeed not another wonderful blessing! We are so delighted to have you here. How long will you stay with us?"

Nakosis liked this old gentleman immediately. It wasn't just for having dispelled his tension and apprehension, it was also his complete openness and honesty. Few had seen past the deed to view the man and Nakosis was desperate for acceptance, even if for now it was just this one wonderful and gracious elder.

Loka responded while laughing at the embellished formality of Sapaska's speech, "Well my flattering old friend, we are pleased to accept your abundant hospitality…and this delicious venison!" He looked at Chako who, nodding and grinning, dove in for more helpings.

"Yes, yes, please eat, my distinguished friends!" gestured Sapaska, his arms sweeping across the fire and the cooking food. He never stopped smiling, Nakosis noticed.

Chako took the opportunity to finish answering. "I would very much like to stay and enjoy your gracious hospitality, Sapaska, but regrettably I must return to my village. I have been away for far too long. The terrible battle has stalled my return and I also would like to alert my people about those Black Faces. And I am taking my young brother here to visit my people." He grabbed Nakosis around the shoulder pulling him playfully toward him giggling.

Everyone smiled at Chako's affable and gentle character. Sapaska was, no doubt, about to deliver more flowing praise when a commotion began in the village square. Excited voices were raised and people began rushing about.

Sapaska turned to his guests, "Please eat more, please. I will go and see what is happening."

Within a short time he reappeared quite animated and overflowing with exhilaration. The party of warriors scouting the forested foothills near the arrow rock canyon had spied a small herd of the great shaggy beast of the plains. Their thick hides provided the warmest robes and heavy leather and the dried meat would replenish the seriously depleted stores of White Mist village since the many warriors had been fed from the supply of the village. These great animals occasionally fed in the wide rich meadows of the foot-hills, but had not done so for some time and the people would not follow the great herds out onto the open plains in fear of being caught by a larger num-ber of flatlander warriors. That was their territory and their lives revolved around following the great herds across the vast plains. There was more than enough meat to share among all the villages and so men were preparing to leave in the morning for White Mist and an air of celebration filled Deer River village as jubilant cries rang out.

Loka thanked Sapaska warmly for his wonderful hospitality but explained that they were all very tired from the long day's journey.

"Why, of course you are! How selfish of me to keep you from your rest! Please, please, let me show you your lodging. It is not really a fitting dwelling for such distinguished guests. Had we known of your arrival we would have prepared fitting accommodation."

Loka, obviously used to the nearly suffocating generosity of his old friend, simply smiled and shaking his head he replied, "Sapaska, my old friend, I'm sure anything will be just fine. Please do not worry so."

They walked across the square and many people had gathered around the bark torches that were now lit in a big circle. They were in a very joyous mood and eagerly discussing the coming hunt. Nakosis doubted that many of them would get much sleep this night. As they walked, Sapaska commented how much the villages needed this wonderful news at such a time of sadness.

"Such a blessing, such a blessing!" He repeated, always smiling. He issued a very long and formal goodnight to his 'distinguished guests' insuring that they would be served a sumptuous morning meal before he took his leave.

The hut was small but very comfortable robes had been provided. In fact many were piled deeply to provide a very soft bed for the three men. Chako threw himself upon them laughing and rolling like a little boy.

"Ohhh, how soft!" He cried.

Loka shook his head, yet could not resist laughing with Nakosis. As they settled in and set the torch to the wood provided, Chako opened up his big bag and acted like he was about to retrieve some great mystery from its leathery depths. Loka and Nakosis were his captive audience and he played it up, peering into the bag and saying,

"Ohhhh, what have I got here for someone special, for someone very, very *distinguished* indeed!" He sounded just like old Sapaska and Nakosis held his sides trying not to let his laughter be heard outside the small hut. Loka also laughed loudly, still shaking his head at his old friend's antics.

Chako raised his hand from the bag, revealing the top of a leather cylinder and Nakosis' interest was noticeably peeked as he leaned into the light of the fire to see what Chako possessed. Slowly, and with much suspense, he withdrew a beautiful leather container. It was wonderfully constructed with perfect sinew stitching up the length of its side and the lid was also made with great care and attention. It had a cap that extended down over the top. Along the cylinder's one side was the painted figure of Raven. On the other was Panther. Chako turned the lid to face Nakosis and Loka, and there on the lid was a representation of fire in brilliant sanguine colored ochre paint. It spun in a circle around the outside of the lid. In the center of the fire painting was the lid's handle. It was a leather strip attached to one of the large beautiful blue stones that Nakosis so admired on Chako. Immediately Nakosis looked at Chako's necklace and it appeared to be less one of the magnificent stones. Chako gently pulled on the handle and as the lid came free Nakosis could perceive what looked like dark feathers. Chako reached out and handed the cylinder to Nakosis.

"This is for you my *distinguished* little brother," he giggled.

Nakosis took the cylinder in his hands. He was spellbound. He had absolutely no idea of what was transpiring as he gently reached in and so very carefully drew up on leather ties that were protruding from either side. Slowly there emerged the blue black of Raven feathers. He looked up at the smiling, beaming face of Chako who simply nodded while Loka beamed at him across the fire. As Nakosis withdrew the item it was evident that it was a headdress, similar to what Chako wore except it was festooned with magnificent great Raven feathers.

"How...how...did you?..." Nakosis could not speak. He felt his throat choke up with emotion.

Loka, seeing this, came to the rescue asking, "Well open it up. Let's see it Nakosis."

He pulled out the headdress, laying it fully open across his lap. It was just spectacular, Nakosis thought. Dozens of perfect raven feathers stitched to a band of red died leather. At the base of each feather was a small blue feather where they attached, signifying Chako's blue bird spirit guide, no doubt. In the very middle were two large teeth and on each side of those, large bear claws. Nakosis laid the headdress in his shaking hands. He tried to thank them but his eyes were tearing and his voice quivered. Loka reached across and held him firmly by the arm as Chako rested his hand upon Nakosis' shoulder saying,

"I have asked the bluebird to watch over you and to give you his blessing. The two great teeth are from the skull of an ancient panther whose kind is no more. Do you know where that skull was found Nakosis?" He could only nod, wiping back tears.

Loka leaned in saying, "From the cave Nakosis! The very first time Quansa entered it he found the old skull in pieces. It must have died in that cave before the time of the ancestors. The bear teeth are from me." Nakosis looked and noticed Loka's precious necklace had become lighter. "I have also asked the Bear spirit to watch over you, my brother."

He could no longer hold back the flood of tears. The two old mentors slapped him on the back and also had to wipe tears from their eyes.

Nakosis thanked them again and again until Chako said, "Well, lets see if we guessed the size right!"

He reached out his hand and Nakosis gently handed the precious gift to him. Chako held it in place against Nakosis' forehead as Loka helped to tie the two leather tongs at the back of the young Shaman's head. Two pieces of red leather hung down the back across his shoulders and Nakosis only now noticed the tiny blue stones attached at their base as Chako brought them forward to rest over each shoulder.

"There, now you look very *distinguished* indeed!" It was Sapaska's distinct voice and Nakosis chuckled.

Loka smiled at him and nodded. "You look very striking Nakosis, but while this is so you must know that you do not wear this to impress others. Yes, it will let people know that you are a Shaman. It sets you apart from those who have chosen different paths. It lets others know that here is a man who has dedicated his life in the service of others, in the service of our great Earth Mother. It says you have discipline and dedication. It says you have no fear because you have trust in your life that the spirits will guide you and because you know that there is no death –there is only continuation. Life in connection, life in balance, helping all, that is your commitment, Nakosis, never forget it. Every time you place this on your head you reaffirm that commitment to yourself, to the earth and to all the brethren and the spirits too. It is no small thing. Do you understand, Nakosis?"

"I do." He said.

Chako reached over and undid the ties, letting the headdress rest gently in Nakosis' hands. "Put it away now," he said. "Like this, you roll it slowly, gently in a circle. Keep the feathers tight, roll the ties around, gently then lower it into the case like so. This you will respect and offer purification and blessings the same as your drum."

"And the same also for this, Nakosis." Loka said.

Nakosis turned to see Loka handing him a soft deer hide bag with a drawstring top. He knew immediately by its shape what it held. A rattle.

"Oh Loka, you shouldn't have…I..mean...you,.. you had a rattle made for me?"

"No my boy. I did not have a rattle made." Loka was smiling greatly at that last comment and now Nakosis was puzzled.

He took the bag, opened the drawstring and reaching in he felt the carved features. Loka's face revealed nothing. He smiled. As Nakosis withdrew the rattle he gasped and for a heartbeat he almost dropped it into his lap.

"Quansa's rattle!"

"Actually, you should know Nakosis that it was also given to Quansa from his teacher! As it has Raven on it, and as I have tried to teach you just a little, I think it fitting that you continue its journey. I know it will serve you well." Loka said.

Nakosis turned the exquisite ancient rattle over in his hands. Normally one's sacred items such as drums, rattles, feather fans, anything used ritually were not to be handled by another. When not used they were kept covered and protected until needed, at which time they were 'awakened' through the Shaman's entreating their spirit to be present. Such items, especially if very old, were thought to hold great power and in many circumstances people even feared them. For Chako and Loka to have given some of their precious sacred artifacts to Nakosis was an unheard of honor. It also conveyed their acceptance of him as one of them and conferred upon him their blessing as well as their expectations. While an enormous honor it was also a colossal responsibility.

"We will instruct you further in these things." Chako said, pointing to the items in Nakosis' lap.

Nakosis looked at the two men who sat beaming with pride and he said,

"I will do my utmost to honor this great gift and great blessing. I am forever in your debt."

"No, Nakosis," Loka replied, "you are indebted to the Great Mystery! Just try to be aware of the great connection at all times and we will be pleased. When things appear to be too great a challenge for you, when it seems that fate has thrown you more difficulty than one man can handle, just use these things Nakosis and our spirit and our spirit guides will be there to help."

Nakosis again thanked them many times over and as he began to choke up Chako broke the mood by asking, "Are you going to finish that lovely venison or shall I have to do it all by myself?"

The following morning Nakosis awoke upon the thick, soft bedding after one of the best nights sleep in a very long time. The morning sun had risen and both Loka and Chako were awake and had placed additional wood on the fire. Although the evenings were cool, the fire, while necessary for cooking, was more for comfort and as a deterrent for the many insects.

Sapaska was upon them almost immediately, his exuberance and his odd sounding voice breaking the quiet. It was, Nakosis thought, as though he was constantly about to sound some urgent alert. His voice was quite loud and shrill and Nakosis found him quite amusing, but a more gracious and charming host he had never met.

"Ohhh so verrry good! You are all awake! Yes, yes, I have a very nice morning meal prepared for you. Please come, come!" Sapaska raised his arms pointing out the door and stood there with that wide smile as the three hurried to make ready to leave.

Back across the square they went but not to Sapaska's hut. He led them directly to the large door of the great lodge. As they entered and Nakosis grew accustomed to the light he saw the imposing Washtaka seated by the large communal fire. Spaced around the fire were strategically arranged cushions of hides for the new guests.

"Please won't you be seated," Washtaka beckoned, extending his huge muscled arms to either side.

There was a spit of venison over the fire and several clay pots of other foods. A large flat stone at the fire's edge was heating flat grain bread; Loka and Chako immediately positioned themselves across from the war leader and Sapaska to one side, leaving the only place for Nakosis directly to Washtaka's left side. As he sat he couldn't help but stare at this man. He was unlike anyone he could recall from his village. There were some large and fierce looking warriors like Hankas, but this man was like two such people. A young man had brought additional wood for the fire as well as what appeared to be more pots of foodstuffs and then he silently left. It was becoming evident that this man was a person of great distinction in the village, beyond his fierce reputation as the one who defeated the Black Faces. Washtaka handed out bowls and ordered everyone to eat. As they settled into the meal he began extending his thanks and appreciation for having the three men visit.

He turned to Nakosis saying, "So, it seems we have something in common."

"We do?" Nakosis asked.

"Why yes, I couldn't help but notice the bow you carried yesterday. It is very fine workmanship, a warrior's bow to be sure. It is also one of my passions, although in battle I prefer my club" as he said so he reached behind him producing the great club that he had brandished upon their first meeting. He handed the prized weapon to Nakosis and as he did so Nakosis nearly let it fall due to the clubs surprising weight.

"Heavy, yes?" Washtaka commented adding, "Better to smash skulls with!" At this last statement he bellowed a hearty laugh that more resembled someone impersonating a laugh. The macabre grin now appeared ever more so when accompanied by the devilish laugh. As he leaned in toward Nakosis, laughing and retrieving his club, Nakosis noticed a massive fresh scar running up his right cheek almost from cheek to ear. It was well hidden with the black stripe of paint that he seemed to perpetually wear running horizontally across his face. This explained the wild 'smile.' Nakosis could only speculate that it must be the result of the Black Face's battle. Somehow, Nakosis felt much relieved to discover that his appearance was the result of some gruesome wound and not just a demonical or insane personality behind the frightening mask that was his face.

They discussed the bow and Nakosis told him all about Taku and how he had come to be in possession of such a fine weapon. Much to his surprise he found in Washtaka a sympathetic and caring listener. He was genuinely sad for his loss, recounting all the suffering the enemy had caused for the villages. He then began, as though by way of consolation, to detail the events of his warrior's defeat of the enemy Black Faces. He described in great detail how the scouts tracked and observed the enemy for days and how they prepared and coordinated their attack. He told of the ferocious fighting that ensued once the enemy realized they were being overrun. He spoke with tremendous respect of the bravery of the White Mist warriors who perished that day. It was evident that he had recounted the story over so many times that he now sounded like one of the storytellers repeating the old legends, but Nakosis was very grateful that Washtaka would take the time and effort to do so.

Loka and Chako were being engaged in deep conversation with the ever polite and proper Sapaska. They were discussing the spiritual preparations for assisting in the afterlife process, among other things.

Washtaka looked across the fire at the three older men and turning to Nakosis he said, "Come, my friend, let me show you my village!"

Nakosis felt like stretching his legs a little and was hoping for a break from the formality of the meal and so he eagerly accepted the invitation. The three men stopped talking as the other two rose. Nakosis excused himself, explaining he was being given a tour. Loka smiled and nodded at him as they left the lodge. Once outside in the warming sun Washtaka took a deep stretch, pulling his massive arms above his head and stretching out the powerful muscles.

"It can get stuffy sitting in the smoky lodge, don't you think? All that talking, talking, talking!" He shook his head from side to side and presented such a contradictory image to the renown fighting man that Nakosis couldn't help but laugh. He also found that he could not help but like this Washtaka, odd as he may be.

They toured the village. It was quite a bit smaller than White Mist but Nakosis had known it would be. Washtaka took Nakosis around the square, pointing out the various lodges and smaller buildings. It was almost a copy of his own village in that everything was arranged around a central square. Radiating out from this were smaller paths and another ring of smaller family dwellings interspersed with storage buildings. They had a lot of huts where large amounts of venison were smoking for winter storage. As well, there were many deer hides being fleshed, stretched, dried and tanned for clothing. It was obvious that these people depended far more on deer than did Nakosis' people and so it seemed only fitting for a village located on a river by that name. Nakosis commented on this fact and congratulated Washtaka on how much preparation his people had undergone for the long winter season.

Washtaka then took him to a big hut where a number of women had gathered for what looked like a communal garment making endeavor. The women were of a boisterous and friendly spirit. A few of the old ones made joking comments about Washtaka spying on the single ones to see who sews the best shirt so that he can pick a good wife.

"Look how good I can sew Washtaka!" yelled a very old toothless and wrinkled woman. The entire group laughed hysterically as many of the younger ones hid their faces behind the hides they were sewing as they blushed and giggled.

Washtaka laughed with them and made some remark about not being nearly man enough for the old woman. This caused more gales of laughter as they walked on. The on-going giggles could be heard for some distance. Washtaka was obviously much more than the sheer brute that Nakosis saw him to be upon their first meeting. He was very well liked and respected all over the village. He possessed a gentle sense of humor and humility, not afraid to laugh at himself. Nakosis was discovering a very different spirit than he'd ever thought in this mountain of a warrior. He brought to mind a teaching that Loka had given him a while ago and he'd forgotten until now. He had said that fearlessness was the mark of a warrior. But that this meant more than being fearless in the face of death. It meant also being fearless in the face of life. When Nakosis had asked what that meant Loka had replied 'Not being afraid to leave your heart vulnerable. Not fearing being open to the love and beauty around you, to open yourself fully to the world. To not hide behind your strengths takes the most courage. Some people use their power like a shield to protect their gentler natures because they fear that by revealing them they will be hurt. But it is only in revealing them, by letting them out that they grow, strengthen and they become a part of your power.' Watching this gentle giant roam about his village, talking with elders, laughing with the children and even cajoling with the women made Loka's lesson relevant. There was far more to some people than first impressions can reveal.

Washtaka insisted showing Nakosis one of his favorite spots. They walked through the village, Washtaka always nodding hello in return from everyone he met and smiling sincerely. He brought Nakosis past the last huts and upon a path toward a row of fields full and heavy with summer's bounty and soon they entered a small grove of trees. From down the path the sound of children's laughter could be heard echoing in the distance. Then they arrived upon a wide, white sandbank. Before them the Deer River flowed gently by, it's sandy banks widening to create a great deep pool at the foot of an incredibly long gently sloping waterfall that cascaded over the longest single rock Nakosis had ever recalled seeing. It had numerous dips and swells over a run that was easily greater than the furthest arrow could be shot. Several village children were hurling themselves into the top of the chute of water and joyously flying down its great length being bolstered aloft by the fast moving waist deep water. Nakosis could not believe the sheer length of the run, at the end of which was a man's height drop into the beautiful deep pool.

They walked a well-trodden trail to the top starting point to observe the gaiety of the young men and women of varying ages. Everyone beamed at the sight of Washtaka and the stranger. Many laughing young boys were daring Washtaka to join them. They watched as several young men showed off for the two important spectators making a group effort to ride the falls as one. Locking arms they all slid, butts first, into the fast flowing jet of water. They managed to successfully make it through the first big bump but, amid shrilling laughter, they all burst apart tumbling every which way upon flowing over the second rise. Washtaka and Nakosis roared at the antics when Washtaka turned to Nakosis and with a cavalier look said, "Well?"

Nakosis smiled but really had little intention of trying the water when Washtaka simply lifted him up by the waist like a bag of grass and slid the two of them head on into the water. He let go of Nakosis as soon as they were moving and his laughter could be heard above any sound the water made. Nakosis was bounced down the long waterfalls like a leaf upon a river current. All the way down he and Washtaka would pass one another, Washtaka screaming with the delight of a little child. By the time they surfaced from the deep pool Nakosis was laughing so hard he had to struggle to swim to shallower water, where he fell upon the soft sand holding his aching sides. Immediately, the two men were besieged by a bevy of screaming, happy children. They all piled upon Washtaka, who delighted as much in their play as did the children.

"Alright now you little weasels!" Washtaka cried. "Who among you little rodents can fetch us something to eat?"

The young ones instantly took off toward the village as though it were a contest to please the big warrior. Nakosis had not laughed with such carefree abandon in a very long time. He remembered when he too would play in such a way with the younger village children. It was only moments before the children returned, some with a few pieces of smoked meat, some a bowl of berries and yet another managed to wrangle some flatbread. Everyone sat on the bank of the Deer River enjoying the tasty meal that the children had pilfered from the local huts. It was painfully obvious that the children wanted to know whom Nakosis was but were being too polite to ask, so Washtaka placing his hand heavily upon Nakosis' shoulder offered an explanation.

"Do you know who this is?" he asked, knowing full well that they did not. "This is Nakosis, a great Shaman from White Mist village!"

The children all gave Nakosis a look of awe accompanied by all the appropriate gasps of surprise. Nakosis, blushing, quickly waived his hands in refusal of the accolade.

"No, no, no I'm not a great anything!"

"See, he is even humble like a great Shaman!" Washtaka was laughing now seemingly enjoying Nakosis' discomfort with flattery. "Now little ones, you must leave us or I'll ask him to turn you all into toads!"

They spun away laughing making exaggerated toad sounds as they fled.

Washtaka and Nakosis talked of many things. Washtaka spoke of his life growing up in Deer River, of his joy living in such a beautiful place. He talked about the warrior lodges and his rise to becoming a leader at such a young age –only seven summers older than Nakosis. Nakosis told him briefly of his 'calling' and how he came to be under the wing of Loka and now also Cha-ko. He could not tell him about his spirit guardians, about Panther, Raven and certainly not about Hohapas. Washtaka, of course, knew not to ask such questions but Nakosis so longed to be able to have a friend to confide in out-side of the two Shamans, as he had done with Taku. Nakosis told of his hav-ing to make a great journey as, according to the two Shamans, it was deemed to be his destiny. He desperately would have liked to reveal the details but settled with a somewhat vague synopsis of the journey. It wasn't a lie since he himself had no real inkling as to where the quest would take him.

When Washtaka inquired as to the main purpose of his quest, he had assumed it was totally spiritual in nature involving certain things only Sha-mans would know. Nakosis, however, revealed an additional purpose. When he and Loka had talked in the aftermath of the battle Loka had said, 'our world is getting smaller I think Nakosis. We have been blessed living here as we do in these mountains. The mountains shelter and protect us; they form a barrier to the outside world and to our enemies. They form the main defens-es making it hard for one who does not know the way to penetrate our little world. But, they also keep us prisoner in this world. These Black Faces are a warning. We had never before seen these people and suddenly they appear out of nowhere, a grave threat to our lives. I fear that there may be more strangers appearing. We know nothing outside of this world, the three villag-es and our valleys. I think it is good for you to journey outside these moun-tains, Nakosis, to see what waits on the outside world. It will be good for our people to know what we must prepare for. I think great changes are coming for our people, my friend.' Nakosis now relayed this insight to Washtaka.

He stared at the water silently in thought then he said, "Yes, this must be true. We have enjoyed such times of peace since the flatlanders first came and many of our elders said that they too believed that such days would not last. This is why the lodges have trained so hard for battle, because many knew these days would come. Perhaps we need to become closer with our brothers in the low forest villages. It is good you travel there my friend. It will ben-efit our villages." He paused for a moment and then, as though he had just received a great revelation he added, "Perhaps I should travel with you also! Yes, that would be a good idea, I think. Two people are better for such a jour-ney. I could help protect our great Shaman. Together we could have a great adventure!" Washtaka was beaming with excitement at the possibility of an adventure. He turned to face Nakosis and added, "Oh, but forgive me, I was not thinking. Perhaps this is a spiritual undertaking that you must undergo alone, like in a vision quest."

"No, no I...I think it would be wonderful to have a companion on such a venture, especially one such as yourself Washtaka." Nakosis answered excitedly.

He longed to not have to endure the hardship of such a lonely venture by himself, not having someone else to be there with him, to help in hard times and provide camaraderie. The idea of having Washtaka along beside him buoyed his hopes and optimism.

Smiling greatly at the prospect he added, "I will ask Loka and Chako about it, though," knowing that it would, no doubt, mean having to tell Washtaka about the vision of Hohapas.

Now, with their clothing nearly dried in the warm sun, they made the stroll back to the village. Nakosis didn't take any notice of the surroundings as the two men, now good friends, shared their imaginations as to where one could go and what one might encounter outside the familiar boundaries of their territory. By the time they reached the village square the two young men had thoroughly stoked the fires of adventure in their collective creative imaginations. Where he had suffered sleepless nights filled with trepidation and apprehension about the quest, now Nakosis was eager to embark into the unknown with the brave warrior, Washtaka, at his side.

They arrived at the big lodge just as the cooking fire was being stoked by one of a group of young warriors. A delicious smelling brew was simmering in a large clay pot. They all smiled and nodded to their leader and his new companion. Washtaka asked about the two older Shamans and was told that they had left with Sapaska, possibly to the Elder's lodge to discuss preparing for the passing over ceremony that evening.

"Good then!" Washtaka exclaimed, slapping Nakosis on the back, "So now we can relax and eat more!"

They took a seat around the cooking fire and, as bowls of soup were doled out, Washtaka introduced each of the several warriors in turn around the fire. Several others had taken their meals earlier and were now seated behind them on the many benches and sleeping platforms that lined the long wood planked walls. After circling the fire announcing names Washtaka looked at those seated behind him and simply waived his arm in their general direction saying, "And all these other ones too!" There was much laughter and joking about the fire and Nakosis delighted in the company of young men his own age. He'd forgotten how much he enjoyed a good laugh and the friendly banter and boasting.

One of the young warriors seated around the fire leaned in and asked, "Nakosis, friend, so you arrived with the two older Shamans?" Nakosis nodded and replied that he had indeed.

"Are you *him* –the one? I mean…the one who they say created the great wave? It is true, isn't it?" The warrior turned to the assembly and announced to all present, "This is the young Shaman they spoke of. He created the great wave by the power of his magic!"

The room fell silent for a heartbeat and then a chorus of hushed gasps spread through the men. Nakosis was immediately uncomfortable and felt, at that instant, like bolting for the open doorway.

Then Washtaka came to the rescue shattering the awkwardness with his booming voice, "Yes, of course it is him, you fools! And now he is the guest of this lodge and we should show him how we honor and welcome him as one of us, for he is a great warrior of the people!"

Cries echoed off the roof and the young warriors rushed to seize and raise a startled Nakosis to his feet and onto their shoulders. The cries intensified as the entire group made a sun wise circle around the fire before depositing Nakosis back in his original seat amid glorious laughter. Washtaka was literally doubled over pointing at a still shocked Nakosis.

"Your face!" He laughed. "You should have seen the look!"

All his comrades were now thoroughly enjoying the result of the surprise showing of respect and Nakosis was heartily laughing with them. The ploy had worked and Nakosis was being accepted among them. He welcomed the acceptance far more than he would have wanted attention for being a Shaman. He had so longed to be a simple member of a warrior lodge like the other young men of the village and now this afternoon was as close as he'd come. For the time being, while it lasted, Nakosis basked in the sense of belonging and acceptance. There was a lot of eating, exaggerated story telling and laughing. While this was a very welcome change from his usual routine of late, Nakosis knew it was but a short respite and that reality was soon to snap him back into the world of demands and responsibility. But for now a little immature fun was a much-needed break. His intuition was not off as Loka, Chako and Sapaska suddenly appeared amid the raucous laughter of the jubilant young men. The festive conduct and echoes of laughter came to an immediate halt, the warriors quickly trying to regain their manly and more mature bearing.

Loka was the first to speak, "Oh, I'm sorry we didn't mean to interrupt your fun my friends. Please, you needn't stop on our account. We were just looking for our friend." Loka was looking at Nakosis but was genuinely smiling and appeared to be happy to see his young friend sharing a laugh.

But it was Chako who definitely bridged the gap when he made straight for the pot of soup like a coyote for a mouse. "Ummmm, now THAT smells just wonderful!" Turning to the young men now circled about he announced with a perfectly serious face, "I am an expert on soup, did you know? Oh, why yes. My opinion on soup is highly valued all over the villages. Why, everywhere I go people are trying to convince me to taste their soup to see if it passes my particular tastes. I just might be persuaded to evaluate this soup if..."

Loka piped in, "Oh for the gods! Will someone please give the old fool some soup and shut him up!" They were like two old clowns. They made the lodge ring even louder with laughter as Washtaka, tears in his eyes, brought forth a bowl of hot soup for Chako.

The three older men took a seat with their younger brothers and the warriors drew into a tight circle around the visitors. It was such a great feeling of warmth, sharing and openness and Nakosis hated to leave, but he knew he had responsibilities.

Back in Sapaska's hut Loka and Chako discussed the ceremony.

Loka spoke, "It will not be like White Mist village. The warriors here fought a great and victorious battle. They thoroughly defeated the Black Faces, but there were many wounds suffered and they lost several men in the battle. Still there are some whose wounds may yet take them to the afterlife. So the families of the departed would like us to see to it that the spirits of the warriors are indeed going to their next life - that they will not cling to the place of their living. So again we will offer the artifacts to the flames and the appropriate chants."

Nakosis was looking troubled. He did not want to repeat the events that made his own people fear him. Not now, especially when he had made a good friend and had won over the acceptance of the many young men his own age.

Loka knew this, of course, and so he offered a plan. "People will expect to see you at the ceremony, Nakosis. You do understand this? Otherwise there will be more questions and that will lead to more speculation, more rumors, more exaggeration and further fear. You appear to have made a very good impression here, especially, it would seem, with the young warriors. Indeed, especially with the war leader, Washtaka. You must build upon that trust and respect. In the times to come it will be even more important that all our peoples, and Chako's people also, have strong bonds of kinship, trust and respect. As I have said, Nakosis, I believe our peoples will be put to the test in the future."

"Yes Uncle," Nakosis interrupted, "about that, there is something I wish to talk to you about."

Loka raised his hand to finish, "So, you must remember this tonight and you must be fully alert, not tired Nakosis. Are you tired? You must concentrate upon the words of the chant, upon the beat of the drums, upon throwing the artifacts and the sacred herbs into the fire and not allow yourself to be distracted, not into the flames or into yourself, but only on what is happening all around you. This way you will develop control of your senses. So, tonight Chako and I will drum and chant and you, Nakosis, will walk the fire. You will circle the fire with the families, walking in front of them you will lead them each in turn around the fire and you will place the items into the flame at the appropriate times. You will have to listen carefully to our singing so that the items are placed properly. Everybody will be looking to you to know when they should throw their offerings for Aan'ga to take to the ancestors. This will be an important task. You understand?"

Nakosis nodded. He also understood that Loka had deliberately placed him into a position of scrutiny by all in attendance and that he would have to be fully alert to the proceedings to ensure both that the ceremony was properly conducted and that the villagers were approving of Nakosis' performance and that nothing gave them warrant for fear.

Loka and Chako started to unpack some of the big bags.

Loka suddenly turned to Nakosis saying, "I'm sorry, what did you want to discuss, Nakosis?"

Nakosis explained in as articulate a manner as possible. He first told of how he explained to Washtaka about his journey, emphasizing his not divulging any secretive information. He explained how Washtaka, 'made a perfectly logical suggestion,' that such an undertaking would be better served by two people, especially given the importance of such a mission. Nakosis told of how he explained Loka's observations about a shrinking world and the need to know what lay elsewhere and how Washtaka was in complete agreement. He made particular mention of how such a joint venture would help, as his uncle had just mentioned, to strengthen bonds between the villages. When he was done he stood still, waiting for a reply. He did his best to try to appear neutral about the matter, but inside he was bursting for an approving gesture.

Loka simply replied with, "Hummmm," and looked over at Chako who revealed nothing in his expression. Nakosis thought for a moment that he may have detected a slight smile from Loka, but if so it was well concealed. Loka continued to slowly play with the big bag; he was obviously deep in thought. He turned and looked at Nakosis for some time without speaking, making Nakosis very uncomfortable in the process.

Then turning his attention back to the task at hand he said. "Yes, well, we shall have to give this some consideration, but now is not the time. We must get ready."

Chako called Nakosis and he turned half hoping it would be to hear words of agreement with his proposal, but instead he said, "And you will want to wear your new headdress, yes?"

Nakosis feigned a smile and replied that he would be delighted. In reality he wanted nothing more, at this moment that would draw even greater attention to him.

The ceremony was smaller, as there were not as many fallen warriors as White Mist and Quick Waters villages had suffered. Still, the suffering of the families and their desire to see to the spirits of their loved ones was equally as pronounced and the process was a serious and solemn occasion. Everything had to be done just right. Nakosis was prepared for a large fire in a dusty clearing. The fire, however, was in the center of a great stone circle that had been erected some time ago and it was obvious that it was used for ceremonial or communal occasions. It was in a clearing behind one of the great lodges that had been created for just such village gatherings. There were even some sitting benches made of split logs that were erected in tiers against a plank wall that circled half the clearing. Nakosis reflected that it was a marvelous idea and something that would make a valuable addition in White Mist village. Normally ceremonies were conducted in the great lodge and due attention and preparation could be afforded. This outdoor circle was very well prepared and formal in its creation and it possessed a definite air of sacredness. Nakosis was vey impressed and inspired and not a little nervous.

As they approached the village square they could hear the sound of many drums and singing. In the distance many torches were being lit. Sapaska and several elders met them outside the hut and escorted them to the great circle. As they entered from the square they saw that most everyone in the village was in attendance. The only ones perhaps not present were the sentries. A reed mat and hide cushions were placed for them to sit at the east side of the circle and many elders were seated around them. Many were drumming and singing the ancient songs. Nakosis looked splendid in his new headdress, it's beautiful black feathers reflecting an iridescent blue in the bright light of the fire. The family members lined up behind the elders and the Shaman. Loka and Chako began with the blessings and purification of the artifacts the family members had brought to be consumed by the flames. Then he and Chako began the invocation chants as they retook their seats on the raised hide cushions. Nakosis stood to their left and the bereaved lined up behind him. At the given signal when Loka gave him a nod, Nakosis began walking the first of the several families slowly around the fire and at certain intervals they would throw the items to the flames and Nakosis would say the appropriate phrases, adding the sacred, blessed herbs to help the spirits on their way. For the duration of the ceremony all eyes were on the dignified looking figure of Nakosis and the grieving villagers circling the great sacred fire. Being under such intense scrutiny by so many and having to concentrate on the performance of his sacred duty kept Nakosis focused completely upon the task at hand and achieved the desired result Loka had predicted. The last of the mourners were walked around the fire and then the somber mood of the crowd changed into a festive sending-off of the spirits with a joyous sounding rhythm that the entire crowd now participated in. All of Deer River Village, it seemed, now danced in one synchronized, pulsating ring around the fire. The dancers had many small deer hoof rattles attached to their ankles and the hems of dresses. Many more drums now accompanied the procession. It was beautiful to watch and Nakosis enjoyed doing so as he stood beside Loka and Chako. It now seemed more befitting that he uphold the solemn and decorous image that he appeared to present to the assembled crowd and so he held himself straight and proud as the rhythmic throng filed past.

He was just beginning to feel quite pleased with his performance and his maintaining such a ceremonial stature when he was quite literally swept off his feet, as though hit by a human avalanche. Before he could react or even scream he was physically carried fully a quarter way around the circle. By the time he could regain his senses he realized he was part of a wave of very animated warriors led by no other than Washtaka, who now held him by the waist on one side while another of the young warriors held him aloft from the other, all sang at the top of their lungs as they danced the great circle. As they made the first full round Nakosis caught Loka and Chako smiling at him, trying not to laugh as they continued singing. As they lowered him to the ground his feet immediately picked up the tempo and he lost himself to the great overwhelming ecstasy of the dance. He had no idea how long he danced for. He melted into the oneness of the dancers. He and they were one in spirit, one with the earth and one with the ancestors. The dance had become a primeval, kinetic, manifestation of spirit. The power of so many people moved by a common sharing and unfolding of spirit was an awakening for Nakosis. His limbs moved of their own accord. His body seemed to be able to transcend all boundaries of fatigue for the longest time. When finally the dancing wound down he was almost moved to tears by the experience.

He and Washtaka talked briefly and he said that he had yet to fully discuss their ideas with Loka but he hoped that they would see the practicality to the suggestion. For his part Washtaka said he was ready and committed and looking forward to an adventure, the gods willing. As they said their good nights, Nakosis slowly strolled through the torch lit paths of Deer Village back to the hut Sapaska had generously provided for them. On the way he stopped and drank in the cool night air and admired the thick blanket of lights in the night sky. He reflected upon the wonderful unity the village displayed and the tremendous openness and acceptance of its people. True,

White Mist was no doubt equally as hospitable to visiting friends, yet now it seemed like he was a stranger there. He felt very much at peace with these people and it made him realize how very alone he now felt. He hoped he could win Loka and Chako's approval to be accompanied by his new friend. As he walked he reasoned that this was, after all, *his* journey was it not? He was a man after all, not a child any longer. He could make his own decisions regarding his own life surely? After pacing, thinking and re-thinking the issue he had to admit that ultimately it was important to heed the words of his mentors. One did, after all, undertake spirit quests on ones own. Such a thing was necessary to have an understanding of ones self and of ones relationship with the spirit world and to get the blessing of a spirit guide.

"It is up to you," Nakosis said aloud, turning his head toward the night sky. "I'm asking you Raven and Panther to help me now." Then in a much quieter voice, he whispered, "Hohapas, if you want me to seek you at the Mountain of Fire then please help me to do so. I stand a better chance if I'm not alone."

CHAPTER 14
SHINING LAKES

Loka and Chako were tired as they sat by the tiny fire, but they were also still empowered by the evening's ceremony. They were discussing what a beautiful event it was when Nakosis came through the door.

"There's our little jumping rabbit!" Chako said as Loka burst out laughing.

Nakosis smiled and threw himself down beside the fire, sprawling on his side upon the piled up furs. He heaved a heavy sigh as he removed his headdress and carefully folded it up. Chako handed him a gourd and he drank it empty.

"What a wonderful evening!" He said after catching his breath. "And I didn't burn down the entire village!" He quipped.

The two men laughed, Chako adding, "Yes, that might have caused us some discomfort!"

Chako, true to form was re-warming the pot of soup he had been given from the warrior's lodge earlier. The same soup he had made such a fuss over and he now handed a bowl each to Loka and Nakosis. At first Nakosis didn't think he was hungry until the pleasant aroma hit his nose. His dancing marathon had apparently whetted his appetite.

As they sipped the warm broth Loka said, "Nakosis, I have been thinking about what you said earlier, about Washtaka. Chako and I have had a little time to discuss this and, as you know, you are facing a great challenge. It is usually a solitary undertaking – a spirit quest, but this I think is far more than your personal discovery of a deep spiritual awakening. The journey itself will teach you more about yourself than you ever knew." Loka sipped on his soup then continued, "It is necessary sometimes for a man to face the world alone, as it is alone that we will ultimately leave the world. If we can conquer our fear in life Nakosis, then at the time of death we will be prepared. If we do not face any great fears and challenges while living, if out of the fear of loneliness or of the desire for comfort and familiarity we neglect to heed the greater callings that come to all men, then we have wasted our life. You have been blessed to receive such a calling. To face this challenge makes one stronger and strengthens the connectedness that empowers us. Only then, once you are a complete person, one who fully knows himself- only then can you truly be of real benefit to others."

Nakosis knew where the talk was headed and he had to concede that Loka was right. No one underwent a spirit quest accompanied by another. It was a personal, deep bonding between the seeker and their spirit guides. Sometimes it is only when one is pushed to the ends of ones physical and mental limits that great breakthroughs come. It is said that is when true spiritual awakenings happen. The spirits come when you need them the most and when you have shed yourself of your attachments.

Nakosis sat with his head low, looking at the fire when Loka added, "However..." Sensing a hint of possibility, Nakosis' mood brightened as his hopes were raised and he looked up at Loka expectantly.

"However," Loka continued, "there is no denying that the chance of success is greatly improved by Washtaka's presence. As well, it would serve to strengthen the bonds between you and between our villages. Also, there is an additional purpose to your venturing outside our world and that is to know what dangers may await our people outside the protection of these mountains. Washtaka, as a warrior who knows how to gauge a potential threat, would be able to give his expert opinion."

Loka appeared to be weighing the pros and cons of the idea and his doing so was proving greatly frustrating for an impatient Nakosis. He had to try to influence his decision.

"Uncle," he began, "I fully understand the importance of solitary journeying, but I think we can all agree that there have been some very special circumstances in my situation. As you yourself said, normally one undertaking such a venture would have had to undergo many, many years of preparation before hand but, in my case, there is not time for this nor did you feel that I was unprepared to take on this burden. There is a great urgency that it be done and more than my spiritual awakening is at stake. Therefore, I believe it is only wise that I undertake this effort with as much guarantee of safety and success as I can, not just for my sake but also for that of our peoples. You have said that we do nothing for ourselves but all we do we do for the people and to help maintain the balance. I am prepared to give my life to that end if need be, Uncle. Washtaka, I believe, will help to see that I succeed to return to our people with the knowledge we seek."

Loka looked at Chako who, trying to suppress a grin, casually looked toward the floor. He simply nodded.

Loka looked directly at Nakosis, a broad smile lightened his face as he said

"You have spoken very well, Nakosis, you show truth and wisdom in your words. It is true that I ask a tremendous amount from you. As you say, it is a venture that could threaten your very life and, despite this, you have not shirked from that responsibility. You also show remarkable bravery and it is true that you have a very special gift that even many years of training could not achieve. You have the blessing of the spirits and, as we know, you have been gifted with the refuge of a very special guardian. It is largely because of this that I reluctantly place you in such a position. No ordinary man would I give this task to, Nakosis. You are right to want to use every opportunity to guarantee your safety. I think Washtaka will be a good help to you. I give my blessing for him to accompany you. Tomorrow Chako and I will talk with him."

Nakosis did his best to mask his excitement at the news. He maintained a stoic outer appearance merely nodding in agreement with Loka's decision. Inside he was giddy with happiness and relief.

Sleep did not come easy to Nakosis that night despite the relief of knowing he would have his new friend with him on the journey. He lay in his robes once again staring at the patterns the fire's dancing flames made upon the ceiling of the small lodge. He followed the tiny blue-gray wisps of smoke as they wove toward the opening above him, on and up into the cool night air. He tried closing his eyes and forcing images, fanciful and pleasant scenes of him and Washtaka traversing majestic mountain ridges and fording cascading streams with mossy fern covered banks. But other images forced their way in to him. Darker images. In the blackness of a cave, the reverberating vibrato of a lone flute spiraling around the rock walls, the melody becoming like a circle of sacred vibration. Then the unmistakable colors of fire began to appear within the spiraling sound, faintly at first, like a stain within the swirling music. Then the colors brightened and pulsated like a wind blown cook fire. Flames now began encircling a seated Nakosis. He could see himself as well as being within the scene. Never before had this vision appeared as it did now – all around him, spinning like a cloud of melodic colors. It made Nakosis feel uncomfortable, restricted, even imprisoned. Then as before the flames began taking form but, as they did so they ceased their perpetual spinning and in front of him they formed the conical spiral. The figure began taking shape within the flame and as it began to manifest, the being stepped out of the fire in the full and very real form of a man. Hohapas was not some ethereal creature of flame or smoke, but appeared as a living man not unlike any other, apart from an undeniable aura of power that radiated all around him like the glow of the rising sun. He smiled at Nakosis and in that instant any fear or apprehension Nakosis held was melted as snow before a warm spring wind.

Stepping toward him he said, "You need not fear me Nakosis for you and I are one. There is no separation between us. I will be the guiding voice within you who directs your course. You have only to listen Nakosis...listen Nakosis...listen Nakosis.."

Hohapas and the flames dissipated like valley mist. The haunting music echoed into silence and only the dark of the cave was left, faint light filtering down through the dark rock. Suddenly Nakosis became aware of another presence and he then heard the familiar chuckle of old Chako. Off to the side of the cave he saw the old Shaman squatting on the cave floor looking at him, laughing softly. The laugh then gradually changed pitch becoming the gravely cawing of Raven. As Nakosis watched, large black wings appeared behind Chako. His face became that of Raven and then he too vanished into the darkness.

Nakosis sprung awake with a start. As always he felt a little disoriented after these dreams, not quite sure which world he was in, which world was real. Both Loka and Chako were sleeping and the light of day had yet to show its face. Birds, however, were beginning their chorus of song, eager to start the day and heralding the coming sunshine. Bats were swooping like swallows of the night throughout the clearing, snatching up their last meals before surrendering their world to the light. Nakosis quietly threw his robe over his shoulders and stepped into the square. He wondered if Washtaka also slept uneasily, thinking of the coming day. He had responsibilities to his lodge that, no doubt, needed to be allocated to another. His family members would also want to be informed of his plans. He was obviously very strong both physically and also in character, but Nakosis had to wonder whether Washtaka also harbored fears and trepidation of the unknown that lay ahead for them. There was little movement in the village, apart from a couple of dogs inspecting the edge of a dead cooking fire. Although unseen, Nakosis knew guards would be manning their posts all through the night. In the dim pre-dawn light a form was moving far across the village square. It appeared like a ghostly silhouette, lumbering under a large burden as it advanced purposefully toward Nakosis. As the large figure neared, Nakosis heard the familiar voice of Washtaka.

"Pleasant morning to you my friend," he said softly so not to awaken others. As he drew close, Nakosis saw he was attempting to shoulder a large pack on his back while he walked. Rather than complete the task he now just dropped the big bundle on the ground at their feet.

"So, I'm assuming that we are good to travel?" He asked.

Nakosis was still a little taken aback, realizing perhaps that they were now indeed leaving to embark upon the great venture.

"Why, yes, actually. Loka has blessed our journey!" Nakosis responded.

"Are they awake yet?" Washtaka whispered when from within the hut a resounding,

"Yes, we are now!" boomed out the door.

Washtaka looked wide-eyed at Nakosis as he suppressed a laugh.

"Well, about time!" He laughed and ducking he entered the hut. He immediately began stoking the fire as though quite familiar with the two Shamans. Nakosis guessed that perhaps it was because of the familiar way that the warriors lived and their jovial camaraderie that Washtaka acted so very informal. Surprisingly Loka and Chako responded with equal ease, Chako asking if Washtaka was as good at preparing the morning meal as he was at tending fires.

Laughing, Washtaka answered, "No but my family is, at this moment, preparing a feast for us all and they asked if you would honor their humble lodge."

"A feast!" Chako cried, "I'm on my way!"

He then began making the others laugh as he pretended to dress in an exaggerated hurry. He certainly would have made a wonderful clown. thought Nakosis.

Washtaka's family consisted of his father, named Tantas, an aunt and uncle and their younger aged children. Like Nakosis, Washtaka had lost his mother when he was younger. When fishing from the rocks with a long spear she had fallen into the spring-flooded Deer River and drowned.

The lodge was warm and comfortable and had plenty of room for the guests to sit. Sapaska had come also and was his usual overly polite and formal self.

"Oh, I am so very happy to see you all! He said.

Chako stepped forward and taking his hands he said, "Thank you, Sapaska, you have been such a wonderful host and we are very grateful for your gracious hospitality. I will be sure to tell everyone in my village of the wonderful and warm people here in Deer village." Sapaska literally beamed with pride and a great warm smile at the compliment. Chako continued, "I sincerely hope that you will visit us soon. We have much trading to do soon, I believe, yes?"

"Indeed," said Sapaska, "once our hunters return from White Mist they should have many hides for warm winter robes and much dried meat from the plains beasts. They will, no doubt, be visiting your village, Chako, once they have prepared their goods to trade. Who knows, perhaps an old fool like me may even make the journey."

"That would be wonderful. We are brothers and our people should keep our friendships strong, especially now that our worlds seem to be changing." Chako was, of course, referring to the Black Faces and the need to consolidate their strengths.

Washtaka's father, Tantas, was unmistakable. He cast just as large and imposing an image and was in every way an older version of the son. He was also possessed of a disarming charm and wit that quickly had Chako and Loka warming to him. They discussed mutual acquaintances and reminisced about past ones. They all agreed that it would do the peoples of all the three rivers and also of the low forest much good to share in such sociable good times, the sharing of meals and conversation together. Washtaka's aunt and uncle bade everyone to come in and sit by the fire to take the meal. Tantas stepped through the men crowding in the doorway and grabbed Nakosis by the shoulders looking him in the eyes. The act startled him somewhat.

"Nakosis, it is an honor to have you in my lodge. My son has told me much of you. I can see why he insists on helping you on your journey. I know only the little he has told me, but I can see, my young man, that you are no ordinary man - nor an ordinary Shaman." He looked briefly over at Chako and Loka who were silent. Then looking back to Nakosis, still holding him by the shoulders he continued, "I know of what power you brought to bear upon the enemies of our people and this lodge is honored to have one of its own to be with you wherever the spirits take you both and know our prayers go with you." He then leaned forward and briefly touched his forehead to that of the young Shaman.

There was complete silence for a long heartbeat as no one seemed to know what to say and so Tantas, laughing at the awkward moment his formality had spawned said in a his loud voice, "Eat! You can't start a journey on empty bellies!"

The meal was spectacular but Nakosis couldn't help but think that perhaps Washtaka's family believed that this might well be the last meal they would share together. The meal consisted of rack of venison on a spit over the fire, a fine root stew fresh from the fields, seasoned with herbs from the surrounding gardens and forest, and fresh Deer River fish wrapped in a blanket of clay and baked in the coals of the fire and served on wooden planks. As the party indulged, Nakosis noticed that Washtaka's family had stuffed large amounts of smoked meat and fish into satchels for the four men to take with them. Chako will be very, very happy, thought Nakosis, smiling to himself.

"Well," Loka said, slapping his hands loudly on his thighs, "this is definitely one of the best meals I have ever had the privilege of enjoying and as much as I hate to leave it, we have a journey to make and we must have the light of day."

One by one they left the lodge, gathering just outside the door. Washtaka was the last one out.

Tantas embracing his son warmly said, "Handle yourself well, my son. Make us all proud. Come back to us safe." With that they turned and left.

Back at the hut, they packed their bags and loading them on their backs they passed the sentries at the west end of the village. Washtaka paused for a moment to say a few words as the others walked on. Washtaka's pack looked huge and Nakosis had no idea what he carried in it, but there was no mistaking the brutal looking war club he held resting over his shoulder.

The way led through a narrow valley westward through the deep forest on the other side of the Deer river. The path took them past the amazing long waterfalls that Washtaka had taken Nakosis for an involuntary ride over. As they neared the spot, Washtaka glanced over to Nakosis then nodding at Loka and Chako, then at the falls he said, smiling,

"What do you think?" Nakosis laughed out loud at the thought of Loka and Chako being taken for a surprise dunk over the falls. Then he quickly tried to suppress the laughter as they both turned back to look at him. When Washtaka tried not to giggle it only made things worse and for a short distance Nakosis had subtle bursts of giggles causing Loka and Chako to look at him like a man who has lost his mind.

As the trail wound away from the river it rose gradually to where they paused to look back over a magnificent view of the river valley. Behind the trees the village lay hidden from view, all but for the tell tale wisps of smoke from scores of cook fires. The forest began to take on a completely different look as the trail began to level out and wander through trees the size of which Nakosis had never seen. Giant trees with red bark so wide a girth at his shoulders that a dozen men could lock arms around them. Off the beaten trail, the forest floor was a luxurious bed of thick moss that grew up the giant tree trunks to the height of two or three men and rooted in it were huge ferns with serrated leaves that hung down like moist, green waterfalls. The tops of these trees were of such a height that Nakosis could not see them, only the boughs that formed a dark canopy far above the four men, dwarfing them like tiny insects. The woven crown of green formed such a thick barrier that sunlight only filtered through in brilliant shafts of golden rays. From far above the songs of a few birds filtered down, but for the most part it was strangely quiet. It was quite the majestic sight and imbued with a deep sense of sacredness. If the spirits played in Nature's garden, thought Nakosis, this surely must be the place. Chako, Loka and Washtaka, having all been here before were understanding of Nakosis' urge to linger for a little and drink in the splendor and awe that this place commanded. The three men seemed to take great delight and pride in watching his enjoyment of this ancient, luxurious paradise.

As they left the great forest and the trees resumed their normal proportions, the trail brought them to the edge of a narrow but very steep box canyon whose crowning jewel was a multi tiered waterfall that fell in cascading steps from the sheer rock wall at the canyons dead end. A cloud of thin white mist filled the grotto formed by the falls and rose like a ghostly vapor up the red rock to where the travelers stood. In the heat of midday it was a most refreshing relief to stand for a few moments in the cool spray and drink in the beauty of the scene far below. From this high vantage point Nakosis could see that the land was dropping away and they were descending gradually into thickly forested rolling hills that seemed to stretch as far as one could see. Ribbons of green/blue marked countless rivers and lakes that reached to the horizon. Rising from the myriad bodies of water were birds in such number that they appeared like a dark cloud on the horizon, their calls echoing across the hills. He knew this was the low forest.

By the time the trail carried them to the base of the mountain they were growing tired and due for a rest. Chako said that they could rest and eat a little, fill their gourds and that soon they would reach a nice site to spend the night. He led them through the forest on trails his people had worn bare for many generations. This was his homeland and there was no mistaking his renewed enthusiasm and the joy he displayed at being close to his village. Nakosis never imagined the low forest as having so much water. It could well have been called the land of water since, to his estimate, the water and the land was of about equal proportions. Rivers flowed everywhere and in places they widened into very long narrow lakes whose shorelines were a mat of beautiful floating flowers so thick that they looked like one could walk upon them. In places they all but closed the passage of water. Chako said his people were great makers of fine boats and used these almost exclusively to traverse the vast expanse that was their world. But since his village was not too far and was reachable by the land route there would be no need for boats. However, he said that his people would no doubt have to take Washtaka and Nakosis by boat to where they would need to go to seek the ancient home site of the people. This land had no high peaks, no breathtaking vistas of mist covered mountains, but it possessed a certain kind of calmness and tranquility that was its own primordial beauty. The waters were, for the most part, calm and peaceful to behold with very ancient looking gray, pitted rock rising from the flower-covered surface.

The trail was now very narrow and wound its way through areas that were rapidly becoming wetter as they progressed. In some places they were forced to navigate along strategically placed logs through shoulder height rushes and reeds as brightly colored birds with brilliant red and yellow wing patches signaled their passing with coarse songs similar to that of Raven. Large winged insects hovered along side them as though watching them, daring them to slip from the slimy wood walkway. Washtaka pointed out a large snake once and Nakosis wondered out loud if it posed a threat but Chako, laughing, said,

"No, no, only if it bites you!" Loka seemed to enjoy sharing his dark humor. Soon they emerged from the log walkway strewn with its watery obstacles to clamor up a large gentle rock face. On the top they discovered a flat expansive clearing of soft grassy soil with the opposite edge terminating in a steep bluff above a perfectly smooth reflective lake. The water was some distance below, about the height of three or four men. It was the perfect campsite. Islands dotted the shimmering, silver-blue lake and great herons, ducks and a variety of songbirds fed among the reed-choked shorelines. Chako pointed out the places where numerous travelers had spent countless evenings over the course of time, spread out around a large fire pit ringed by large rocks. The men began unburdening themselves of their loads and Washtaka wandered to the edge of the bluff, hands on his hips, drinking in the splendid colors as the sun dipped toward the forested horizon.

Nakosis leaned toward Loka and asked him, "So, how deep is the water off that edge?"

"Oh, the young people love to jump from there. It is one of their favorite places to swim." Loka replied.

A big smile dominated Nakosis' face as he said, "Excuse me, I'll be right back. I have something to do."

His quirky smile made the two older men curious and so they stopped unpacking to see what Nakosis was going to do. He walked up to stand beside Washtaka as he enjoyed the sunset.

"Beautiful, isn't it?" He asked as he acknowledged Nakosis beside him, not taking his eyes off the grand display of crimson and gold.

"Oh indeed," replied Nakosis "but not nearly as wonderful as this!"

At the last word, Nakosis threw his weight against Washtaka's hips, knowing he would need all of his strength to get the large man off balance. Washtaka was completely taken by surprise. He spun, his eyes wide and a high scream accompanied his look of panic that sent Nakosis into a delirious gale of laughter, but as Washtaka fell his huge muscled arm instinctively shot out to grasp something to stop his decent. That something was Nakosis' shoulder strap. For a brief moment the two stood poised, almost motionless on the edge as Nakosis waved his arms like a bird attempting backward flight. Then they were gone. Loka and Chako heard the pair screaming then the mighty splash as they rushed to the edge. Nakosis was kicking his feet frantically and beating the water with one arm like a wounded duck as he struggled to keep his bag above the water's surface. Washtaka was already headed for the shore where the rock face tapered to the reed-covered bank. From above came the bellowing laughter of Loka and Chako. The two men were bent over and pointing as they wept with delight at the scene.

Washtaka grabbed a hold of the branches of a dead tree that jutted out into the water and pulled himself up onto the rocky bank. He turned to watch Nakosis flailing about in the water as he struggled to shore. Washtaka was already laughing and extended his big hand to help Nakosis toward the tree branches. Nakosis handed his bag to Washtaka who, taking it, tossed it to dry ground and once again extended his hand to his friend. The rock extended beneath the surface making footing very slippery. Once Nakosis had a firm grip and had transferred his weigh to Washtaka's hand Washtaka opened his grip and watched Nakosis plunge backwards into the water completely submerging himself under the green surface before re-emerging with a startled gasp. This move proved greatly amusing for Washtaka as well as the two older men watching from the rock above.

"Well, I guess we both deserved that!" Exclaimed Nakosis, having finally managed to secure a grip on the tree branches and pull himself upon the rock. When they again climbed to the clearing above, Chako was still laughing. Loka, smiling, was shaking his head.

Loka commented to Nakosis, "So, I am thinking that did not quite turn out as you planned?"

"Not quite," said Nakosis, "but it was still worth it," he laughed. He then explained about his unplanned trip down the rock waterfall.

"Children, children!" chuckled Loka still smiling and shaking his head.

Chako was diligently pumping his bow drill to start a fire and seemed greatly relieved when Washtaka offered to take over the job. Nakosis dumped out and examined the contents of his small bag. All in all it faired quite well, the tight drawstring and oiled leather having protected the contents. The last rays of sun were bathing the entire clearing in a magnificent violet glow and the few wisps of cloud appeared like pink ribbons. The entire beauty of the setting sun was duplicated in the placid waters of the lake. Nakosis had witnessed wide vistas by looking out over the prairies from the high vantage point of the Arrow Rock Canyon but this was breathtaking beyond compare.

Soon Washtaka had a nice little fire blazing and the group set to making themselves comfortable for the evening, Washtaka and Nakosis finishing drying beside the growing flames. As the sun retreated behind the silhou-etted tree line and darkness claimed the furthest reaches of the wide lake, a small glow began to appear in the distance at the far shore of the lake. Nakosis saw it first and quickly drew the group's attention to it. As they rose and watched a second then a third glow appeared. It was clearly small fires, yet they appeared to be moving mysteriously along the water, following the shoreline toward where the group stood transfixed at this apparition.

"What in the spirits is such a thing?" Washtaka wondered as he instinc-tively reached for his great war club.

Chako began chuckling. "Fishing, fishing!" he laughed. Seeing the still startled looks on his companions faces he elaborated. "Men in boats are fish-ing. They carry big torches. A man in front holds a torch and the light attracts many fish for others in the boat to spear! They no doubt have seen the light of our fire and will come. Mmmm, we may have fresh fish for the evening meal!" His chuckling laugh filled the clearing.

As the torches drew nearer in the dwindling light they could make out the men in the boats. Chako called out to them and they responded in kind, re-lieved no doubt, to find their own village Shaman among the strangers. They pulled ashore near the fallen tree and the group scrambled down to meet them. The boats were clear now in the light of the torches and Nakosis could see that they were marvels of ingenuity, crafted not from hollowing a tree as he had previously seen, but by affixing bark to a large wood frame work. They revealed a highly developed skill and craftsmanship he had not expected.

Even though Chako welcomed the men ashore and introduced the rest of the group as his 'dear friends', the men still seemed a little guarded and eyed Washtaka and Nakosis with a distant caution, especially Washtaka's large war club. He made a point of deliberately placing it at the perimeter of the clear-ing next to his bag so as to show he was not a threat. Eventually, once seated around the fire, the men relaxed and as Chako had hoped they did indeed offer some of their fine catch for the evening meal. Pleasantries and intro-ductions were exchanged as the men sat for a while gathering the informa-tion about the strangers then said that they must return to their fishing and head back to their village. They would have a long hard night's work ahead of them. They would let the village know of Chako's return and of the three guests he brought with him.

As they roasted the skewered fish over the fire and recounted the day's travel, their conversation gradually came to the next phase of Nakosis and Washtaka's odyssey, a conversation Washtaka was very pleased to have. Cha-ko once again told the story of the migration of the people from a distant land where drought and fierce enemies had forced the collapse of a once great culture. He told of the perilous trek across parched barren land to finally arrive at a great wall of rock and how Ho-Tapas saw in his vision from above, as an eagle sees, the pass through to the lush forested lands. He recounted the tale of those of the original people who followed their leaders to the place of the Mountain of Fire, somewhere far into the unknown world, where it is said the people originated. This place was reachable; he said, from the lost village, the place of the people's first settlement. From this place one must find and cross a great barren plateau land. Washtaka listened intently, taking in every detail and glancing occasionally to Nakosis. He asked Chako how it came to pass that the people lost their memory of their first village in the new world and why it would be hard to find again. Chako told him of the long ago visit to the site of the abandoned village and of the fear of the great man-bear spirits who are said to live there. To this Washtaka's eyes widened. He would fearlessly face any man in battle, but he had an obvious abhorrence for taking on anything of the supernatural or spirit realm. He sat silently, dwelling for some time on this revelation.

Noticing Washtaka's obvious unease on hearing of such things, Loka encouragingly added, "Not to worry. You two will be fine. I have great faith in your outcome. Washtaka is a strong and brave warrior and Nakosis here has some very powerful allies. Don't you, my young brother?"

Nakosis was unsure of what to say since it had been agreed that he would not discuss the powerful visions of Hohapas.

"Perhaps it is time we talked about the one whose name we don't mention." Loka spoke without taking his eyes from Nakosis, who in turn looked to Chako for some indication of how to proceed.

Chako responded with his deadpan look of indifference but then he began to speak. He told Washtaka the history of Hohapas and his part in the migration of the people and then he explained about Nakosis' visions. He then indicated to Nakosis to continue, revealing to Washtaka the story behind the great wave and Hohapas' fiery appearance to the young Shaman. Nakosis also explained to the three men his latest vision of the very man-like appearance of the deity before their departure.

Washtaka was silent, stunned. He knew as much as any average villager about the world of the spirits. He heard how a Shaman moved between the worlds, but he had never heard such things and from not one, but three great Shamans. Suddenly, for all his brutish strength and his fierce reputation as a great warrior he felt somewhat a small player, grossly inadequate in a game that now seemed way out of his league. All along he believed that he was accompanying the young Shaman as his protection, his guardian, and this thought gave him great pride of purpose, but now he thought that perhaps it was he who was under a greater protection. Washtaka felt humbled and a little humiliated at his realization of the real power that his young friend seemed to wield at his command. In truth he had to admit that such a thing scared him. Finally after moments of silence Washtaka found words for his thoughts.

He looked at all three men and said, "I am truly honored to be in the company of men such as yourselves and especially to be asked to accompany you, Nakosis. I now realize that you carry the blessing of the power of a god. Of what help am I to one who can command the power of gods?"

Nakosis replied immediately, "No, no, no, my friend, it is not as you think. I have no power at all! I am simply like an arrow in the hands of the archer. The arrow can no more decide where and when it will go or whether it will even hit its mark. I cannot control the power, the 'gift,' in fact that has even proved to be a problem! But the power, the spirits, chose me. It is true that I am now learning how to allow that to happen, but please make no mistake, my dear friend, I have no more power than the person you see before you. That person most certainly could use your company and your help. I could not think of doing this without you, my friend."

Washtaka glowed with this praise, a broad scar-twisted smile brightening his face. Loka and Chako looked at each other and smiled approvingly in recognition of their young brother's maturity and understanding. Washtaka and Chako talked more about the history of the people. Nakosis was feeling the drain of the day's hike and wrapped in his robe he quickly drifted off to sleep.

Sunrise was just as remarkable to behold as was the previous day's sunset. A thin band of brilliant pink and purple lit up the distant shoreline from where the night fisherman had come. As the sun rose behind them, the line of color moved across the lake toward them until their clearing was bathed in the warm glow. Perhaps even more breath taking was the play of light in broad, golden shafts upon the smoke-like heavy mist rising off the still waters. They ate and quickly departed in a single line behind Chako. He said that they would soon reach his village. It was faster, he said, to travel by boat but a land trail completely circled their territory.

"Picture a very, very large lake," he said, "but imagine it is filled with a great many islands, some very large, some very small. All these islands have water flowing between them. The water and land are equally divided. That is our 'low forest' as you call it. But all around the shore of this great lake is a land trail. That is where we are now walking. That is how our people came to settle this place - first by following the shoreline. Finally, after a few days, they arrived at a beautiful place where a river comes down from the mountains.

You remember the wonderful waterfall in the canyon, yes? And it flows into the great lake. Where they meet the land juts far out into the water like two great fingers. Between it is a rock-lined bay with two great flat benches on either side of the bay. At the inlet of the bay, the place where the river comes, there is a long sand beach ideal for bringing the boats ashore. This is where our village lies."

At the beach or the benches?" asked Washtaka.

Chako paused in his stride and turning he smiled and said, "Why both! The village lies on both sides of the bay and, of course, the sand area."

"How big is this village? What is it like?" questioned Washtaka.

"Oh," thought Chako for a moment, "it is much like your villages but it is different. And also it is bigger."

For two more days they traversed the amazing shoreline of Chako's great lake. There was wildlife everywhere. Moose, deer, beaver, bear and water foul of every kind abounded. It was a water and forest paradise. Islands of heavy, thickly trunked trees were everywhere and many had splendid mosses hanging like greenish brown hair waving in the gentle breeze. On the second morning, as they packed up their camp, Chako announced that they would soon reach the village. The day was getting hot as the trail temporarily left the shore and meandered through the heavy woods. To his left Nakosis could see the shoreline had changed from trees that grew right to the water's edge with a band of reeds and rushes, to vertical rugged rock that rose steeply from the water.

At a point on the trail a second one split off toward the direction of the water. Loka insisted that it was worth a small detour. As they got closer to the water they could smell the moisture off a stiff steady wind that was a great relief. Suddenly they were perched high atop a massive cliff overlooking this watery green world far below them. Nakosis had not realized that they had been steadily, gently climbing for the entire morning. This had to be the highest point in this world. The water below was as far as a couple of the ancient giant trees were tall. It was a sheer drop and it made one feel dizzy looking out over the edge. The wind blasted the rock wall with a tremendous force and high above, coasting on the updraft, were two eagles. They glided effortlessly, never having to move their great wings. As Nakosis mustered up the courage to peer over and look straight down, the draft actually lifted his long hair straight up and he felt a force against his upper body.

"That is incredible." He said. "Has anyone ever fallen from this place?"

Chako and Loka laughed as Chako said, "Well, yes and no. You see there is a story. It seems there always is a story about such places. Anyway, the story said that long ago a distraught young lover decided to end his life here–off this edge. Apparently he said so to his young girl and with her screaming after him he ran to this spot and as she drew close he stepped off the edge." Chako then stopped talking as Loka could be heard chuckling to himself.

"That's it?" Asked Nakosis.

"What happened next?" Begged Washtaka.

"Oh, yes, well, you see, he was just a small young man and the wind was so strong that it blew him right back onto the top, right here where we stand. He landed at her feet and they wed and lived happy lives!" Chako, delighted with a perfect delivery of the story, laughed that infectious silly laugh of his and Loka, no doubt, having heard the tale many times, shook his head chuckling. Washtaka thought it was a great story. He was thoroughly enjoying the old man's sense of humor.

Loka then added, "I heard that she cried out to the gods as he jumped and when he came back she took it as a sign and that's why she wed him. Some say he did it deliberately knowing, or at least hoping, he would fly back and win her affections."

"Either she was something very spectacular or he was a very desperate young man." Said Washtaka, as he leaned his broad frame over the edge, delighting in the sensation of the updraft as it lifted his hair.

"Don't get ideas." Said Chako. "There isn't a wind strong enough to throw you back, Washtaka!"

They resumed the main trail and now knew that they were descending back down to the lake level. The trail made one more turn toward the rock edge and Chako had stopped ahead of them smiling and pointing. As the men caught up they stood looking down at silver-blue flickering waters and stretching out before them were the two huge jetties of land that formed the bay. The cascading mountain river now gently flowed out to meet the bay between the two broad arms of land. Brilliant white sand beaches were plainly visible. All around the scene was Chako's village. It was literally everywhere. Both jetties of land and the beach area was one massive village laid out like a gigantic half circle. Smoke from a hundred fires rose in faint blue plumes.

Chako said, "Welcome to my village, Shining Lakes!"

He and Loka were laughing at the startled look on the faces of Nakosis and Washtaka.

Loka said, "I wanted to tell you, but Chako made me promise. He wanted you to have this first view of Shining Lakes. Not what you were expecting?"

As they made the final descent down the trail toward the village they began encountering people going about their daily business, but there were no guards or sentries, and people merely stopped to stare, especially at Washtaka. Chako, of course, drew smiles and waves from villagers.

One of the first scenes they encountered was a vast area along the shore where dozens of large boats were pulled up on the sandy shore and dozens more were in various stages of construction. Men were busily hauling in their catch of the day. The waters of Shining Lakes obviously provided an ample supply of fish. Fish by the score were being cleaned and some dried in the hot sun, still others were being taken to the many smoke houses and still many more were destined for the day's cook fires.

As they left the trail and entered the village proper Nakosis could see that what looked to be a random scattering of many buildings was, in fact, a well laid out plan based around three great open pathways. The first, the grand thoroughfare ran parallel to the shore and the white sand beaches. Intersecting this were two equally impressive wide avenues that ran out the length of both arms of the wide bay. On either side of their great concourses were the many and varied buildings of Shining Lakes village. These great avenues were easily twice as wide as the big square in White Mist village and there was a steady stream of activity. People seemed to be constantly moving through engaged in various undertakings, men hauling burdensome loads of fish in large woven baskets and women carrying bundles of firewood, food and hides. Other men were working large sheets of bark that they used to build most all of the structures in the village. Their great lodges were easily twice the size of those in the Three Valley area. They were constructed of many long poles, their ends charred to prevent rotting and inserted into holes in the ground and bent over to form a half circle. Then they were expertly sheathed with the large bark panels, each overlapping the lower one so as to create a waterproof surface. Nakosis could see other smaller buildings that Loka said were smoke houses or storage huts.

As they began their passage along the grand way, a group of several people left a building and gathered to intercept them. They were mostly older men and women and they were smiling and waving at them. Chako ran up and everyone in the group each embraced him warmly then did the same to Loka.

One old man, warmly grabbed Chako's hands and touched foreheads then he turned and greeted Loka with tearing eyes saying, "It has been so long, my dear friend."

Chako waved Washtaka and Nakosis forward and introduced them. He motioned to the old man holding Loka by the arm saying, "This is Oneadagwa, grand chief of Shining Lakes!"

Nakosis did not know what to do. He was unsure of protocol and was quite frankly taken by surprise. This old man looked nothing like a person of such station. He was very ordinary. In fact, one could say he was *overly* ordinary. His feet were bare and he wore the simplest hide pants and no shirt. He had only a small bag, his power bag, on a plain leather tie about his neck and one lone eagle feather adorned his unbraided hair. Finally the chief took the initiative and stepped forward. He paused in front of Nakosis staring into his eyes, smiling for some time as though studying him.

Then he reached out and grasped his hands and holding them for a while he stood looking at him then finally said, "It is a pleasure to meet you, Nakosis. My village is your home. I'm looking forward to getting to know you." Then he touched his forehead to Nakosis' and turned to face Washtaka who, like Nakosis, seemed to have been struck silent.

He grabbed Washtaka's big hands and laughing he said, "Washtaka, I am also very pleased to meet you. My, but you are a big one! Please bend, won't you?"

Washtaka laughed and obliged the old chief by bending down to place his forehead to that of the chiefs. Oneadagwa then took both of them by the hand and gesturing down the great avenue he indicated that they should all join him in the long lodge.

As they approached the great lodge, those gathered outside made a wide path and the chief entered first followed by the others. They seated themselves on long wooden benches that lined the walls and another was brought up for the four to sit on facing the chief and the small group. The other members of the entourage were village elders and influential members of Shining Lakes and Oneadagwa introduced them all one by one. They, in turn, politely bowed their heads in respectful acknowledgement. Someone handed the chief a nicely decorated deerskin shirt and he dismissed it with a wave of his hand.

"So, please, you men have come a long way and you must be hungry?" the chief said beckoning the men to take from many dishes that were now being offered.

"Yes, of course we are hungry - for Shining Lakes smoked fish, ummm, yes!" Chako replied, his big toothless smile lightening the mood.

The chief laughed as everyone began to eat. Oneadagwa and Chako talked at length and Loka, Nakosis and Washtaka told the gathered elders about the Black Faces and the attack on the village. A somber and grave mood accompanied the hushed silence that followed the telling of the terrible attack.

Oneadagwa rose to his feet and addressing the three men he said, "Our hearts share in the terrible attack inflicted upon your peaceful people and the great loss of many of our brothers and sisters at the hands of these strangers, these Black Faces. We must discuss this more in great detail and see that our peoples are alert for any sign of these warriors. We shall make sure that we are not absent from each other's fires and that we strengthen the bonds between our villages. I will leave it to my son to make the arrangements and preparations. But, for now, please feel comfortable and safe here in Shining Lakes. Our village is your village, my brothers."

At the words a strong-looking young man rose to his feet and stepped forward. He had a look of nobility about him. His head was raised proudly and he wore an elegant garment draped over his shoulders. It was a short cape made of decorated deer hide and adorned with white fur strips and fine patterns in what appeared to be small, shiny pieces of shell. He held a splendidly carved staff at his side, it's crown adorned with the fine carving of an eagle head whose eyes were inset with more of the uniquely colored shell.

Oneadagwa stood and placed his hand on the man's shoulder and introduced his son, Teconas. Teconas stepped forward to greet Washtaka, Nakosis and Loka. As Loka stood to face him the proud looking young man immediately bowed low, extending his hands to Loka's in a gesture of immense respect. It surprised Nakosis who did not expect such humility. In turn, he offered a very formal welcome to Nakosis and Washtaka.

Then he faced the two younger men and said, "So, I understand that this is the first time you have visited Shining Lakes?" The two men nodded. "Well, then," said Teconas, "it would be my honor to show you my village - if it pleases you?" He smiled broadly at the prospect and looking at each other Washtaka and Nakosis smiled in return, eager to accept his offer.

"Yes, my son." Oneadagwa spoke up. "Please show our guests around and see to it that they are made comfortable. We older men have much to discuss and we will talk with you more later. You honor our lodge, Nakosis and Washtaka! Please, after you have relaxed we would greatly like to hear your council regarding these Black Faces."

Teconas nodded in the direction of the door and the three young men headed to explore the sights of Shining Lakes. The heat of the day was now at it's fullest and it seemed oppressively hot to Nakosis. He commented so to Washtaka who agreed fully saying that it must be the abundance of lake water that made the air so heavy with moisture. They proceeded along a perfectly straight and flat avenue that was wide enough for several men to walk abreast. On either side, long lodges, similar to the one they just left, lined the broad roadway, their fronts facing the passers by. Teconas explained that many families shared the great buildings. They were divided by partitions, giving both communal space or privacy as needed. As well they had much storage capacity.

At intervals along the grand walkway other smaller avenues branched off in opposite directions. Some of these terminated at plantations of the sacred

174

three sisters - maize, beans, squash, the smoking herb and other numerous plants. Some of the fields were almost as large as the village itself. Nakosis was amazed at the size of the crops he saw. Teconas proudly pointed out one vast field of maize that had to be the size of White Mist village itself. Washtaka said nothing as they walked, but Nakosis could see on his face that he too was impressed.

As they came toward what appeared to be the end of the long avenue, a small group of young men were crossing from one side to another. When they saw Teconas and the two strangers approaching they stopped their passing to speak. Teconas exchanged pleasant greetings and introduced Nakosis and Washtaka to the inquisitive youth. They had been looking the two men up and down gauging their worth as warriors, as is the way of young men. They had put on their best strong faces for the powerful looking Washtaka. Washtaka, for his part, had been quite used to such displays meant to intimidate and could somehow hold the most wild eyed look that revealed nothing of his intent, yet was in itself extremely unnerving to those unaccustomed to it. Nakosis was neither skilled in such displays nor did he ever desire to play such games. He simply smiled very slightly at everyone while maintaining eye contact and somehow this seemed to always give a similar effect. This had worked well for him ever since he was a young boy. When Teconas mentioned the two strangers names, however, the young men's expressions immediately changed. No longer looking upon the two as potential rivals or even as equals, they quickly lowered their gaze and bowed their heads in respectful greeting.

The most assertive looking of the group spoke up. "You are the ones who Chako travels with? The ones from the mountain people?"

"Mountain People?" Nakosis asked. Then realizing that he referred to the people of Shining Lakes as the 'low forest people' he answered, "Why yes, I am from White Mist and Washtaka is from Deer River."

"Yes," the young man said, "We know who you are, Shaman! We have heard recent word of your power over your attackers and also of the great Washtaka, war leader of those who tracked and killed the enemy. We are greatly honored!" His comrades all gave approving nods as they moved forward to meet them, now all smiling greatly.

"But how is it that you know these things? We have only just arrived in Shining Lakes and I...I... thought that no one knew of the attack on our people?" Nakosis questioned.

"Not so," the young man continued, "we received word almost immediately when some Quick Water's people arrived here just following the attack to see their relatives. Word has spread all over the village. It is all anyone talks of. We would very much like to hear the details of your great battle in you own words!"

Teconas interrupted, "As would we all, but my father and the council will be the first to hear it this evening. There will be much opportunity for discussion later but for now I have promised our distinguished guests a tour of Shining Lakes. Will you care to join us?"

Immediately the young spokesman stepped forward, extending his hands and introducing himself, followed instantly by the others. His name was Odai and he and the others insisted on carrying their guest's bags. When Nakosis slipped off his big pack and Odai saw the beauty of his bow and quiver he let out a gasp, unable to hide his appreciation for the weapon's exquisite craftsmanship.

"Yes, it is indeed a wonderful bow, is it not?" Asked Nakosis.

The group had to take turns inspecting it and offering their comments of appreciation. When another young man reached to take Washtaka's great war club, his powerful muscular arm flexed as his grip tightened on his club and as his eyes widened and his nostrils flared the young man quickly dropped his hand, knowing not to try to touch the warrior's prized possession. The whole entourage escorted them the remaining distance to the end of the wide avenue where they came to their lodgings.

Teconas said, "You can leave your belongings here. They will be safe." He looked at Washtaka's great club as he spoke and smiled. Washtaka reluctantly surrendered his club to sit atop his bag inside the doorway of the lodge. There was no one in the building but it was evident that, like the others, a number of people seemed to live in the dwelling.

"So," Teconas continued, "what shall we show our guests first?"

The group almost unanimously agreed on taking their guests to what they called 'the point.' Off they went, like a band of enthusiastic children on an outing. A well-trod path led from the edge of the avenue through lovely dense green trees whose sticky sap was very fragrant in the hot sun. The sap had left an indelible black stain on Nakosis' hand that he liked to hold up to his nose as they walked, it's earthy aroma lingering on his skin. Ahead through the trees they could see a band of blue water and, as they drew closer, the trees yielded to ancient gray-speckled slabs of pitted rock, some standing straight out of the water as though placed there deliberately. These great slabs were as tall as trees and formed a huge wall that dropped straight down into the most vivid clear blue water. Their vantage point was on the top of these rocky cliffs looking over a vast body of water dotted with islands too numerous to count. Some stood like green bowls atop huge pedestals of the gray rock while others gently sloped into the water, their thick foliage reaching down to touch the surface. Here and there could be seen a few sandy shorelines, some with boats on them. Flocks of birds constantly rose in great colored clouds that moved in tight formation as herons gingerly picked among the reeds and rushes. It was a green-blue watery paradise so very full of color and life. As they took in the panorama of water, islands and forest they realized that they were now standing at the end of one of the long fingers of land that formed either side of the deep bay that they had viewed from above on the mountain. Washtaka commented on how it looked so different now that they actually stood here. To their right, across the wide inlet, they could see the other 'finger' of land that was part of this vast network that comprised Shining Lakes. It was very impressive. Odai proudly pointed out that the other shore was home to an equal number of lodges and families in a layout that was a duplicate of the grand avenue they had just walked complete with additional fields and storehouses. In between the wide white sand beaches and small river was home to the boat building and the site of Shining Lake's great fleet of fishing canoes. Here, also, the catch was hung to dry or smoke and from there it was distributed down either arm of the village. It was a splendidly arranged and well-planned layout. It was a model of efficiency. And while fish was a huge part of their diet, the surrounding marshes and forests were thick with every type of game, except, of course, for the great shaggy beast of the plains.

Washtaka asked about defenses, as he hadn't noticed any sentries, lookouts or defensive positions or palisades. Teconas explained that his people were also spread out on some of the many islands that dotted their watery world. Apart from the circular land trail, the only way a large number of enemies could possibly pose a threat was if they came by water and he said,

"We are people of the water. There is not a ripple that our people cannot account for. Any outsiders moving anywhere on the lakes would be detected and their presence would be immediately known. We could launch a hundred canoes of warriors before they knew they had even been seen. The circular land route is so narrow and so treacherous that any number of warriors trying to get around the great waters to reach Shining Lakes would be know almost quicker and by water our warriors could cut off their only way out. So, you see, our water is our best defense!"

Washtaka nodded in agreement. It appeared that they had chosen a most perfect location and that they had become the undisputed masters of their domain.

On the walk back, the young warriors couldn't help but ask about the events of the battle with the Black Faces and Washtaka did his best to offer the most minimal of answers, out of respect for Oneadagwa, Teconas and the council. But as word had obviously preceded them, he did manage to offer a few small enticing bits of information but, for the rest, he said they would have to wait until after the meeting that evening. When one of the group asked questions about aspects of the battle, about the tactics or weapons of the Black Faces, Nakosis couldn't help but notice that the young warriors deliberately avoided asking about his involvement in the event. In fact, they would glance sideways at him and nervously look away. He realized that this was partly out of respect, since it was considered improper to discuss a Shaman's magic. Many of these young men were close to his age and, while they were exceptionally friendly and courteous, they still maintained a bit of a respectful distance with Nakosis. They also showed the fear that all people reserved for those who communed with the world of the spirits. He couldn't help but think once more of Loka's prophetic warning that people would view him with a certain apprehension.

One of the young men broached the issue by walking up beside Nakosis and asking, "So friend, what is it that brings you to our village? Will you be staying long?" All the others turned to hear the answer to questions they dared not ask. Washtaka and Nakosis exchanged quick glances.

"Well," Nakosis answered, "I... ah...am not really certain how long our stay will be. Much will depend on Chako. He has some plans that I am not yet completely sure of."

It was Washtaka who terminated the query by adding, "Nakosis is interested in hearing of the old stories of your people and Chako agreed to help him." He considered his reply to be reasonably believable and polite enough to not sound condescending yet still revealing nothing of their full plans. It was also, after all, not a lie.

The young man replied, "Maybe you'll hear of the Lake of Dark spirits."

Immediately it was obvious that he regretted the words that slipped from his tongue without forethought, as the entire group let out a slight gasp of disbelief. They all turned to glare at the young man.

"What, what is this lake you speak of?" Asked Nakosis, his interest instantly stimulated.

"Nothing," replied Teconas, still giving the young man a very stern glare. "It is simply childish legends, rumors, that we should not be repeating. It is not wise to speak such stories lest you bring the wrath of unseen things upon you!" The answer was as much directed to the now penitent looking young man as it was to the two guests.

"No, that is quite alright," said Nakosis. "We also have such stories among my people. There are tales of many things that are mostly said around evening fires to keep children close to their lodges. But sometimes there is a small truth hidden in such old tales and I have long had a fascination with these old stories. I rather enjoy hearing them whenever I can. So, please don't be afraid to tell me. I would very much welcome hearing them."

He was hoping this appeal might persuade them to overcome their fears or customary taboos and reveal the story behind a place with such an intriguing title as 'Lake of the Dark Spirits.' A few looks were exchanged and finally Teconas relented and the story unfolded, each member contributing a facet of the tale. Teconas deciphered the many contributions and eventually he reiterated the story.

"In the days of my great grandfather's youth, our villages were many among these islands. Shining Lakes was not yet the one great village, but was one of many small villages. It was here many peoples would gather during the height of the fishing and everyone looked forward to seeing friends and relatives. Somewhere distant from here it is told that there was a large island far to the west in the middle of a great lake where some of our ancestors first settled in a small village. They had wandered far and made their way through the mountains when they came upon this forested land and before them many lakes and rivers filled the horizon. They did well for themselves as fish and animals were plentiful and the land around the lake was very beautiful. Gradually they spread out, exploring this new land and settling in new villages, but one small group decided to stay behind in this, their first place.

One winter, however, was very hard. The cold and snow came very early. The berries all died and withered on the bush. The lake would freeze but only a little. It was not enough for walking on, yet too much for a canoe to travel. The men had a hard time reaching the mainland to hunt. They had to break this thin ice in front of the canoe with their paddles. This made great noise that echoed all around the lake and frightened the game away. The men had to walk further in the cold to find food and all the animals seemed to have left that place. The snow would fall very deep making walking very hard, but still the lake would not freeze solid. Even the fish seemed to be gone from there. They soon were using the last of their summer-dried fish and the men were going further and further to seek game. A few of them, two couples each with one child, decided to try to get to one of the other villages. It was a full hard day's paddle away in good weather. But it took them almost the whole day to reach the other side of the long lake, breaking the thin ice as they went. They had to camp under the trees in the snow that night and a strong wind came out of the north and across the thin ice of the lake. They took shelter under their big upturned canoe. They could not even get heat from their fire no matter how much wood they threw on it and the children were becoming very cold and all were now very hungry. They knew they now had to walk with their large canoe and their supplies some distance through the forest and deep snow to where they could again place their canoe into the next lake to continue their journey. It was an impossible task. They kept falling and tugging their canoe through the snow with their meager supplies and the young ones. The trail wound higher and they had to pull their big canoe up hill. The children were too weak to walk any further in the deep snow so the parents placed them in the canoe with their supplies and pulled and pushed it through the forest with all their strength. They soon saw the other lake far beneath them. The trail wound down to the water but now, of course, everything was under waist-deep snow.

As they stopped to catch their breath the canoe suddenly broke loose and, with its weight, slipped quickly down the long rocky slope toward the lake. The children were screaming and the men were trying to race after it, but they could barely move in the deep snow and watched helplessly as the canoe spun onto the thin ice and fell onto its side, spilling the robes and baskets and two young children out onto the thin ice. The people yelled at them to stay still, not to move or to grab the canoe as they tried to get to them. One man, jumping over fallen trees, disappeared under them wedged deep between steep rocks and cried out in pain as his leg snapped. The cracking of the thin ice could be heard over the cries of the children and the people trying to reach them. The canoe made a small turn and then the whole thing gave way with one big splash. The others had almost made the shore and the two young children were desperately trying to grab something to stay above the cold water. The canoe was on its side, filling up fast and starting to dip into the water as the remaining supplies floated out. One child was on the other side and they could not see it. The other was facing the shore and the child's mother now was crashing through the thin ice desperately reaching out to grab the young one, but the cold hit them both and the child slipped silently under the ice and the panicked woman, seeing this, lost all remaining strength. She turned briefly toward the others and slid under the water. The other child was nowhere to be seen. The other two were mad with their grief. They reached the shore and knew there was nothing they could do. There was no hope, yet still they called out the names of those children and their mother. They now tried to pull out the injured one from where he fell among the twisted dead trees and deep snow at the shoreline. His leg was badly broken and he could not walk. The remaining man and woman were tired and weak and the young wife desperately struggled to free her injured husband. He used every bit of strength to pull himself up from under the fallen trees to where he could help crawl as his wife and friend pulled him out of the hole he'd fallen into. By now it was growing dark and again the cold wind returned. They managed to retrieve a wet robe from the freezing waters but in the cold it was very hard to get a fire going. They huddled under the spreading branches of a great tree but found little shelter and warmth there. All through the night the injured man cried out and shivered from the cold and pain. By morning he had fallen into a deep fevered sleep. They gathered more wood and piled it on the fire and tried to dry out the wet robe and to warm themselves. They crawled about digging in the snow for anything to eat. They ate bark from the willows and needles from the green boughs. Heavy wet snow was falling and they found it hard to even see.

The woman, being so weak and tired became lost as she searched for something to eat. She called out her husband and her friend's names in the dark but heard only the wind and the sound of her voice echoing and her strained breathing. She somehow managed to crawl into a large hollowed log whose end was sticking out of the snow. She pulled at the loose rotting wood and squeezed her small body inside and wrapped her arms about her and fell into exhausted sleep. When she awoke the sun was shining and the storm had passed. She pulled herself out from the tree and found some withered dried berries and quickly ate these along with the dried leaves from the berry bush. She even ate the droppings from a rabbit whose tracks she followed with a stick held in her hand hoping she might strike it. No one, not even the woman, knew how far she had walked by the time she came to a lake. At first she smelled the wood smoke and her dulled senses immediately burst back into life. Even before she saw any sign of people she began screaming and running panicked in the snow. She stumbled upon the shore where two hunters had gathered around a fire cooking rabbits. She startled them and they said she had the look of a crazy person and at first they were afraid of her as they jumped back from their fire. She threw herself upon the cooking rabbit and the warmth of the fire. The startled men soon realized that she was desperate, starving and lost and she was soon able to tell them what had happened and she begged them to help her friend and her injured husband. The men wrapped her up in warm robes and piled much wood on the fire and bade her remain there while they went to find the other two.

They followed her tracks and found where she'd emerged from the old dead tree but the previous night's snow had covered most of her earlier tracks. The two men were good hunters, though, and after much difficulty they managed to trace her steps. She had crawled around mostly in circles through the deep snow and trees in the dark and they soon came to where the other two men had camped but they could not see anyone there. There had been a very large fire and the coals were still smoldering despite the nights snow. One of the hunters found tracks leading back to the water and there they saw that a hole had been smashed through the thin ice. A body was stuck under it just under the edge of the hole. They cut some long poles and managed to get a hold of the dead man and pull the body to shore. He had been stripped of his clothing. There was much blood in the snow all around the place. When they pulled the body out of the water the two men screamed in horror. They knew it was the woman's husband because his one leg was badly broken from where he'd fallen. But his throat had been cut and his body had pieces of flesh torn away. The two hunters knew that this man's body had been fed upon and as they stood in fear they both knew that no animal had done this. When they reached the spot where the canoe had sunk they discovered that someone had managed to retrieve it from the watery hole and had dragged it ashore successfully righting it. There was a clearly defined channel across the thin lake ice to where a clear ice-free channel flowed through the middle of the lake. This other man had killed and feasted upon his former friend, dried and stolen his clothing, and now he had managed to escape with their canoe across the water to where they could not track him.

The hunters were stricken with fear, for they believed that this man had been taken over by the spirit of a dark walker, a flesh eater! Such things are not of this world, nor of the underworld. The dark walker spirit, it is said, inhabit the wilder places, wandering without form and when they find the right person, especially one who has become mad, they take over this person. One taken in this way becomes a creature more feared than any in either realm.

They raced back from that scene and found the woman still huddled by the fire, still looking wild from her ordeal. When they told her the news she became crazy and screamed like a mad person. She hissed and struck out at the hunters and they were forced to bind her tightly in a bear robe and placed her in the middle of their canoe and they raced for their village. The two men paddled as though their lives depended on it. No doubt they wanted to get as far from that island as possible. Where they had broken the ice to the shore it had not frozen over and they made straight for the open channel of water off from the shore. Just as they reached the open water, the woman leapt up in the boat, almost tipping it over. The two men paddled desperately to keep it from tipping and the woman, her eyes wide with madness growled like a wolf at the men and then threw herself over the side into the water. They say she disappeared immediately, quickly pulled under the icy water. These two arrived at their village as others were preparing to take advantage of the warmer weather to fish. They were almost mad themselves with fear as they told the gathered crowd what they had seen.

A party of warriors was assembled and they set out the next morning for the island. They found the body on the frozen shore where the hunters had left it and they made a huge fire there and burned it. Then they set out to this island where the people had come from. When they came to the village there was smoke coming from their lone lodge, they saw much blood in the snow but they never found any bodies. It is thought that if one survived an attack by a dark walker, and had been bitten by one, then they too would become a flesh eater. They burned this place. After that, when a hunting party went to this place and made camp they said they heard strange sounds, like muffled screams deep in the night and heard things moving in the forest around their camp; and they all felt a fearful cold chill despite being beside their fires. They raced from that place in their canoes, carrying torches in the night. They would not even wait for dawn.

To this day no one goes to this place. They say it is now a place of many dark spirits and fearsome strange creatures are said to live in the forests."

Nakosis said, "I don't think I'm too eager to see this lake of yours!"

"Not to worry, my friend," said Washtaka, flexing his muscles and raising himself to his full height and showing his frightening wide-eyed war face. "I'll be with you, and if any of these dark walkers show their puny faces, we'll be the ones feasting on dark walker soup!"

The men reveled in this comment and Washtaka's show of bravado, their laughter completely undoing the somber mood left by the telling of the tale. Teconas had stood back and studied Washtaka from head to toe, gauging him as one warrior would another.

He then added, "I do believe that you could, my friend!"

Nakosis looked about at these young warriors and the admiration in their eyes for Washtaka. He realized that since he and Washtaka had become close friends that he now looked at him differently. He had come to know the man inside the large warrior's physique. He recalled, however, his first impression of him and how that had changed dramatically since coming to know the kind, jovial and loyal friend he had become. He had to stop and remember that he was also a very powerful and even feared fighter of great prowess and he was indeed the 'war leader who defeated the enemy' as the others were fond of introducing him as. Nakosis pondered the illusory nature of people's characters. Most, he thought, weren't necessarily what they seemed on the outside or upon first sight. Even Loka, now his great friend, teacher, and most trusted confidante appeared at first as somber, strict and even a little frightening. Now Nakosis knew of his sense of humor, his timeless wisdom and his deep compassion as well. And Chako, who from the beginning was almost Loka's opposite - playful, simple as a child at times and warm and approachable was also very wise and possessed great insight and could be deadly serious when he needed to be. This made him question his own character. How did others see him? He was aware of the fear that some viewed him with for his chosen path and also now from a reputation that was spreading through the village, no doubt, bolstered by outlandish rumors and embellishment. He took solace in knowing that his three closest friends truly knew his real being and they were what mattered. Loka had said once, 'What other people think of you is none of your concern.'

By now the group had walked the trail back almost to the village. The smells and sounds of village life filtered through the trees and mingled with that of songbirds and cicadas. It was now well past mid-day, yet the summer heat and humidity was oppressive. Nakosis had hoped that they would be diving from the great grey rocks into the blue placid waters of the bay. The group walked them back toward their quarters and as they approached they saw Chako and Loka seated just outside the lodge, it's door shaded by a very large leafed tree.

"Ah, there you are. Did you two see our lovely village? What do you think?" asked a smiling Chako.

"Yes, uncle," replied Nakosis, "Teconas and the others were very good hosts and the village is unlike anything I expected."

"It is amazing," Washtaka added.

The group was quite proud of their village and seemed very pleased that the two distinguished guests enjoyed their company. Chako laboriously rose to his feet, his legs stiff from the walking. He placed his weight upon his staff.

He waved the two men forward saying, "Come in and be comfortable. We have lots of room here in the back of my lodge for you. Please come and meet my family."

Nakosis had completely forgotten that Chako had a family, he was so used to seeing him in the same way that he did Loka – as a somewhat reclusive, solitary figure. They bade goodbye to the others, Teconas saying he would see them later on at his father's lodge.

Chako's lodge was much like the others they had seen in the village. It was separated into individual living spaces by dividers of wood and bark yet had a common aisle down its middle and boasted three fire pits in its center. There was a doorway at either end and each side housed benches, the bottom ones for sleeping and the top ones for storage. The roof had appropriate smoke holes. Chako's family occupied the first areas that faced the main avenue while Chako took the back area that exited onto a path bordering a large garden area. One by one he proudly introduced his family and each in turn was very warm and welcoming to the strangers. Their bags had been brought for them and were placed by sleeping platforms along the walls of the rear area of the lodge. The upper platforms were completely packed with belongings and possessions. Many hide-wrapped bundles, woven baskets and bark boxes lined the storage shelves. Above, thin poles reached across from one wall to another and they were draped with various dried and drying herbs and medicinal plants and other items. The skulls of different animals adorned the walls and the edges of shelves where there was any space. Nakosis found it very pleasing to the eye. It was fascinating just to take in this collection, as most lodges were very spartan and practical by comparison with little in the way of ornamentation or decoration. Nakosis assumed that much of what he saw was useful in Chako's world. It appeared that someone had to have moved much of the items to upper berths in order to free up the lower ones for their guests.

Chako's son and his wife were the perfect hosts. They served bowls of delicately flavored fish broth that had a slight smoky sweet essence that Nakosis had not tasted before. It was very touching to watch the loving way Chako would always place his gentle hand on his son's arm or shoulder whenever they passed him and his daughter-in-law looked to him as she would her father. Nakosis noticed that they never ceased to smile. It was extremely peaceful just being in their presence. They were also very quiet, not speaking unless necessary to ensure the comfort of their guests, then leaving the area to tend to the children while Chako visited with the others. Loka said that they would all be meeting with the village council later that evening at Oneadagwa's lodge to give them a report on the Black Faces.

He turned to Washtaka saying, "They will especially want to hear your opinion, Washtaka. Apparently word does indeed fly as though on the wings of an eagle. They know of the battle, but only second hand reports. You will be able to provide them with the truth about the enemy. I should think that the war leaders would be especially interested to hear your views."

Turning now to Nakosis, Loka gave a more solemn face. He placed his hand on Nakosis' shoulder and said, "Then, my little brother, I must return to our village within a few days. I regret my leaving, but now it is time for you to walk another path, one that Chako will see you well prepared for."

They looked at Chako who, as usual, smiled and nodded in agreement. Nakosis, despite the warm and friendly surroundings, now found his mind filled with thoughts of the lake of dark spirits. They unpacked their bags, shook out their clothes and hung them from the upper platforms wherever they could find space. Nakosis reverently hung Taku's great bow from the shelf above and removed the leather cylinder from his bag that housed the beautiful headdress. He stood silently, looking at it. He caught Loka watching him and when he turned to face him Loka looked at the cylinder and nodded. "Yes, you should." He said.

Nakosis removed the delicate headdress and lay it out on the bunk, carefully spreading the feathers and letting it 'breathe.' Chako handed him a smudge of sacred herb. They donned their finest clean garments and Nakosis now had the honor of blessing them all in the sacred smoke. Washtaka stood proudly between them receiving the scented offering, moving the smoke with his big hand, directing it over his heart, his head and down his body. He looked over to where his great club lay and back again to Loka and Chako. This he did more than once until finally Chako, with his customary giggle said, "Washtaka, my brother, you should carry your big club. I'm sure many want to see it. It is almost as famous as you are!" Then he laughed and Washtaka, though smiling his twisted smile, was blushing somewhat at the idea of his notoriety.

As one of the council, Chako's son accompanied them up the great avenue to the meeting. They looked magnificent in their decorated dress shirts, the beautiful headdresses and the looming figure of Washtaka with his great war club over his shoulder. Washtaka had mentioned that he did not know if it would be insulting to their hosts to bear arms in their lodge, thinking this might be perceived as a lack of trust. Loka commended him on his care and diplomacy, but assured him that this war club was as much a symbol of office as befitting a great war leader of his people as was a headdress or carved staff. It appeared to Nakosis that he now bore it with even more pride as it seemed weightless in his arm, as though it had a life of it's own.

As they entered the lodge they saw that a fire burned at its heart, despite the heat of day still lingering into evening. The air was redolent with the smell of smudged sacred herbs and smoke tanned hide clothing. The people formed a large half circle around the central fire with Oneadagwa in the center and Teconas at his side, holding the eagle staff that Nakosis realized was the totem emblem of their family. Seated around them were about a dozen elders, all donning their finest ceremonial clothing and accouterments showing their elevated status among the community, accouterments like finely decorated buckskins, ornate feather headdresses and a multitude of various necklaces. Two elderly ladies sat together, wearing long beautiful buckskin capes richly decorated with pieces of shiny, colorful shell and ornate delicate quillwork. They both seemed to wear very heavy large necklaces of what appeared to be claws, beads and some large very bright colorful stones. There must have been tiny rattles attached to their clothes or perhaps on their necklaces as Nakosis could detect a tinkling sound as they shuffled to better position themselves where they sat. They both looked the visitors over sternly and then their gaze fell upon Nakosis and it remained there. It was as though they were gauging him, studying him. Chako directed Loka to a seat and he took up one beside him pointing Nakosis and Washtaka to the spot on his other side. They were now seated in a line, hemmed in on three sides by the semi circle of the council of Shining Lakes. Others had quietly filed in through the door and were now taking up positions seated behind the circle and even a few stood against the wall of the big lodge.

When everyone appeared to have found their positions one of the old women rose to her feet and pulled a small rattle from behind her and began the blessing, making offerings to the directions and over the assembled crowd. Nakosis was stunned. She was a Shaman? He looked to Loka or Chako but they remained expressionless, looking directly ahead at the chief and council. She asked for the blessing of the Great Spirit on all who were gathered that he might guide their words to be truthful and wise, their ears to listen and their hearts to understand. It was very nice, thought Nakosis. The great chief looked at his son and Teconas rose to his feet and spoke. He welcomed them all one-by-one speaking their names by way of introduction to the group. Chako then rose at a nod from Oneadagwa. He looked about the room at the faces of his people and he extended a hand toward the other three saying how proud he was to have his good friend Loka once again visit Shining Lakes.

"We are also very honored to have among us two men who most of you will, no doubt, have already heard about. They both played important roles in the great victory over the enemy warriors who invaded our brothers' and sisters' land only a short time ago. I present my brother Shaman, Nakosis of White Mist village and Washtaka, war leader of Deer village." At this he reclaimed his seat as the assembly in unison raised a cry of respect for their guests.

Oneadagwa now spoke. "My brothers," he said looking mostly at Nakosis and Washtaka, "First let us all offer our deepest regret for those of your village who were killed or wounded in that awful battle and show our great respect for all your brave warriors who fought them." Again a cry rose from the assembly. "We have gathered here to seek knowledge of these enemy warriors who attacked you and to learn if we can help our Three Valley brothers in defending all our lands, should they or others ever return."

Teconas introduced the War Chief 'Tanku-pisa,' a grizzled looking man who, Nakosis thought, seemed far too old for such a position, yet he possessed the calm fierceness of one who has nothing to prove. He reminded Nakosis of one of those battle scared old stags that still take on the challenges of the younger elk and emerges victorious. Tanku-pisa offered Washtaka a bowed head of respect and received one in return. These two warriors then began discussing the Black Faces in detail, what they looked like, how they conducted themselves in battle and how they communicated during the fighting. Tanku-pisa wanted to hear everything, how did their leaders act when the fight turned bad, how did they retreat? Was it panicked or did they cover their flanks and their rear? Washtaka answered as best he could, explaining that the main battle had already been won, thanks in no small part to the miraculous power of his friend, Nakosis. The group uttered a subdued hush at the first mention of this. They all knew the stories but were reluctant to speak of it, as it was inappropriate to ask any questions of such nature. Washtaka said that the Black Faces were expert warriors, strong, fierce and disciplined and that they fought valiantly to the last man. He said that when his men finally caught up with them that it was the Black Faces who took the fight to them, attacking fiercely even though they were greatly outnumbered and in unfamiliar territory. He described their weapons and the way they fought. As he gave the account of the battle Nakosis could see the concern on the faces of the elders.

It was well into evening when the questions ended and Oneadagwa thanked his honored guests. The group rose to their feet and stretched their legs. Tanku-Pisa looked very concerned as he conferred with others of the council. He walked over to Washtaka and embraced him, as would a dear friend.

Softly he said, "My brother, I fear what would happen if a large war party of those creatures came to our home. If we could not meet them as one, they could wipe out village after village. Perhaps it must fall to you and I to arrange further councils with the other villages, with Hankas, Chasake and the others. I will organize our scouts as your people did and make sure we keep an eye on the further ends of our world. The Great Spirit has blessed us in this land as your people also have been blessed, but we have grown used to peace and plenty and even though we train our warriors well we must learn from you and your people. It is so very sad that your people had to suffer such a thing for our village to become more cautious, more ready for war if need be. I thank you, Washtaka, for helping us this day."

Teconas had walked over to join the two men. Washtaka was genuinely moved by the warmness of the revered old warrior and the many praises he received from Tanku-Pisa and the council.

Washtaka thanked Tanku-Pisa then said, "You have a big village with many boats and many good warriors. The water is very much your world and this, I think, is where your strength lies. These Black Faces are plains people. I don't think they have boats and even so they would never be able to move through these waters as well as your people." Washtaka looked at Teconas smiling and continued, "Teconas has said that not a ripple happens on these waters without one of your people knowing. I have not seen much of these waters, but it seems that without a strong knowledge of the many passages and lakes an enemy could easily become lost, what to speak of making a large attack."

"This is so," Teconas concurred, "Still, Tanku-Pisa is right, we must have our warriors patrol our lands."

"Perhaps then, brother, you would organize the young men into such groups?" asked Tanku-Pisa of the chief's son.

Smiling broadly, Teconas said he'd be honored to do so and then added, "Perhaps our honored guest would care to help me?"

Washtaka was very honored and did not want to reveal the real nature of their visit, as Loka and Chako seemed to purposefully skirt any mention of Nakosis, his visions and the urgent need to find the mountain of fire.

"I would be honored to assist in any way I can," Washtaka replied, adding, "at least until we have to depart. I am not certain just how long our stay here will be."

"Very well then," said a happy looking Teconas, "We will make arrangements later."

Nakosis had risen, somewhat grateful that he had not had to discuss his part in the battle. Chako was talking to the two old Shaman women and they all now turned to face Nakosis, as he stretched out his cramped legs. The two women were smiling now as Chako introduced them. Nakosis started to bow his head when they, each in turn, grabbed his hands and stepped forward to place their foreheads against his in the deeper, respectful way. He was both surprised and honored. Chako explained that the women were great healers and very revered members of Shining Lake's council.

"Healers?" said Nakosis. "So, you are also Shaman, like Chako?"

They all smiled and one of them replied, "No, my son, not like Chako, but similar. We work mostly with the gifts of the Great Spirit, the plants and herbs he has provided and, of course, we also invoke the blessing of the spirits to guide us in our healing work. But from time to time we must ask for the help of our beloved Chako. He, as you well know, my young friend, is blessed with the power of the spirit world and it would seem you also possess a very special gift. When our ways are not enough, then we must ask Chako to beg the spirits to help on our behalf."

"They are being modest," Chako said, "These women are great healers and seldom is there much that I can help them with. The Great Spirit guides them well."

The other woman had been staring at Nakosis, smiling, and she now spoke saying, "You are indeed very gifted, my son. The power is strong within you. I can see it even now, though it presently sleeps. Tomorrow Chako and Loka will bring you to us. We are here to help you and your friend on your journey, Nakosis."

He looked at Chako who, smiling at the somewhat startled look on his face said, "Yes, Nakosis, they are aware of your quest and they can show us the way to the lost village."

CHAPTER 15
THE TALE

As the crowd spilled into the long great avenue, their voices faded into the background chorus of crickets and frogs. A million fireflies flickered like tiny sparks among the silhouetted bushes. A few torches cast their flickering light outside the lodges creating pools of visibility in an otherwise very dark night. The people were obviously quite animated by the meeting as was evident by the myriad conversations now fading down the long, dusty street as each made their way back to their lodges. Nakosis was sure many would continue discussing the evenings' events well into the morning. Washtaka had been detained, still in deep conversation with the aging war chief and the others. He seemed to miss the companionship of his warrior brothers and the talk that only other warriors can truly share.

Nakosis asked Loka and Chako about the two women. They did not live in Shining Lakes proper Chako said. Families inhabited the many islands that made up the Shining Lake's community. The main village occupied the largest flat area where it was possible to maintain the vast village gardens that had so impressed Nakosis. However, many who were fishermen and hunters lived further out among the system of lakes, rivers and islands. It was on one of these further large islands that the women resided and it was there that they would go tomorrow. These women and a few other elders who lived there were part of the families who had the oldest ties to the lost village. Their families were among the last to leave that place. When they were younger they went to the site of the old village and they were sure, said Chako, that they could remember the route.

That night Nakosis slept poorly, his fitful slumber the result of bad dreams. He recalled the story of the dark walkers, his imagination providing all the gruesome visual details. Twice he awoke startled, sitting upright, sweating. He looked about the room and re-oriented himself to the surroundings and tried once again to regain sleep. The second time he noticed Washtaka had returned and was now asleep in his bunk, but he hadn't heard his arrival.

He took this as an indicator that he must have at least had *some* sleep. From the other room he smelled smoke and the pleasant aroma of the morning meal being prepared. He heard Chako playing with one of his young grandchildren and talking with his son and daughter-in-law. He could hear Loka engaging in the conversation also. Washtaka, quite out of character, was still asleep in his bunk. He woke up somewhat haggard looking as Nakosis was getting dressed.

"I did not hear you return." Nakosis said.

"No, it was well into night." Replied Washtaka. "I tried to be as quiet as I could. I talked with the others for a very long time about the preparations. I tried to leave several times, but those people are now quite worried about enemies. But it will prove to strengthen the family ties we all share. We will extend our village's preparedness to include Shining Lakes and we will organize their warriors as we have done ours. They have many able men and we have the skills and the organization of our warrior societies. Together we could be a mighty force that no one would dare fight."

Nakosis could see that Washtaka, despite his tiredness, was very much in his element when talking of such things. His whole life had been structured and prepared for just such an event. Nakosis now wondered if it was fair to ask him to accompany him on this journey. Perhaps his true calling was here, coordinating the two nations efforts and strengthening the bonds of kinship. Was this no less great a calling than that of Nakosis and whatever he may discover outside the mountains and forests of his world? He was already at the known edge of that world. These wonderful, friendly people of Shining Lakes were the last of his brethren he would see as he ventured further into the unknown. Again the thought brought fear and anxiety to him, but still it was *his* burden to bear. He must have bore the look of such thoughts with him as he sat to take the morning meal because Loka was looking at him in that all-knowing inquisitive way of his.

"Did anyone get much sleep?" asked Chako's son. "I don't think I've ever seen the whole village talking so into the night. I think many will be starting the day late!"

"Not to worry, my son," said Chako, "Nakosis and I are only going to the sister's island today. Perhaps you would take us there later?"

Loka looked over at Nakosis. "How are you today? You look tired. Have your dreams been troubling?" he asked.

"Actually, yes," he said, "thanks to some wild tales and stories." He looked at Washtaka who laughed a little.

"Ah, yes," said Washtaka, "evil flesh-eating ghosts!" He raised his arms high, looming over Nakosis, making a snarling face. Both of them laughed but Chako, looking quite unmoved by Washtaka's performance, asked what they were referring to.

Nakosis replied, "Oh, it was nothing, I think the young men were simply trying to test us with some old tales about some 'lake of dark spirits.'" Said Nakosis, still laughing at Washtaka who continued to make his strange faces.

"This is not a tale, my friends. It is very true indeed. It is not something one mentions in jest." Barked Chako. The family sipped their bowls, not speaking and it was very apparent that a nerve had been struck.

"I meant no disrespect." Said Washtaka. "I thought, as Nakosis said, that these boys were merely testing us."

"You are quite right, Washtaka. They were, no doubt testing you, yet there is said to be such a place and, yes, it is said to be everything the peoples' stories tell –and more. Best we talk about these things some other time." He looked at the small children.

They finished the rest of their bowls with little conversation. Teconas appeared and, announcing himself, was immediately invited to join them. His arrival was an opportunity to lighten the mood. He stated that he would very much like Washtaka to join him, Oneadagwa, Tanku-pisa and the others to discuss how to best make the arrangements for the plans they discussed on the previous evening.

Washtaka glanced to the others and Chako answered, "Yes, yes Washtaka, you must go and make these necessary arrangements. We have things to attend to that will require our being gone for a while. This should give you time to make all the plans and to send envoys to the other villages. Perhaps the people should meet at Deer River village, as it is central for here and White mist. Plans change, Washtaka, and you're involvement in this may be the key to our village's survival. All else will have to wait. Don't worry about our earlier plans. Go now and help them."

Washtaka rose and looked at Nakosis who could only nod his approval and then he was gone. Loka looked to Nakosis about to speak when one of the old sisters arrived. Chako jumped up smiling and bade her welcome, inviting her to join them. All nodded their respects.

"Thank you, but no, I just wished to say that I must stay in the village a little longer it seems. I must tend to someone who is not well and does not respond to the herbs I've given him. I know your plans, but the family has requested that I ask for you, Chako," the sister said.

Loka now spoke. "It is alright. If you don't mind, I will be happy to attend and Chako and Nakosis can leave with your sister and the others as planned. I must return to White Mist but I can afford one more day. That is if you think the family would not mind."

"Oh no, of course, that would be wonderful Loka, if it is not burdening you." She replied.

Chako still standing laughed and said, "Well, then it is settled. Thank you Loka."

Loka grabbed his satchel from the back room and prepared to leave with the old healer. He turned one last time to Nakosis who stood to meet him. He placed his hands on his shoulders and lowered his forehead to his and spoke softly,

"You will have trying times ahead, my son, but never doubt your ability and remember who is with you at all times - even when you least think it. When you need help the most you will only have to look inward, Nakosis. This is where the strength, your great power is hidden. Not elsewhere. Remember this and you will do well. Know you are always in my thoughts and I will ask the spirits to guide you, my brother!" Then he walked away. There was a painful silence.

Chako, turning to his son, said, "We had best get ready."

Nakosis packed his things in silence, more out of habit than actually paying attention. He was deep in thought and a little apprehensive about his future. He was truly feeling very alone now that both Washtaka and Loka were no longer there with him. Everything was now different. 'Nothing happens by accident. Everything has a purpose, a reason. Even the things that may seem inconvenient or uncomfortable at the time may have a good outcome.' Loka had once told him. He tried to remember this as he reflected on his feelings. It was indeed a truth that had revealed itself to him in recent events. He reflected on how being forced from the cave by the great storm led to them retreating back to White Mist. How he and Loka, being on the trail to the other village enabled them to discover the enemy and to change the course of events, even Taku's seemingly untimely death was very much the catalyst that propelled him down the path on which he now stood – at the end of his known world about to take a step into the unknown. He thought about his meeting Washtaka, who, he hoped, might yet still have an ongoing part to play in the journey ahead. He and Loka had talked about these things. Loka had said that it is so for all people, but that especially when one has looked deeply inward and has come to know their inner power, then these things become much more apparent. One can see the movement behind the events and one is more comfortable accepting things as they unfold, knowing that even if very painful they are leading them where they are meant to be on their spirit journey. He also knew that one could affect the waking world with their thoughts and actions both here and in the spirit realm. This was more than evident to Nakosis since the great flood of water that washed away the enemy Black Faces and the rising fire at the village ceremony. His confidence once again returned when he considered these things so that when Chako asked if he was ready he turned smiling saying, "Yes, Uncle, let us be on our way."

As they gathered at the shore a slight breeze across the lake made Nakosis take his shirt from his oiled leather bag and pull it over his head and shoulders. Chako's son, Washtago, had shouldered both his and his father's pack and he now dropped them on the sand beside the large cargo sized canoe. Nakosis still marveled at the skill and ingenuity such crafts displayed. He admired how they managed to secure the stitching so tightly and use the pitch to such efficiency to waterproof the seams. Teconas said that the village had a few very skilled craftsmen whose sole task was to build and repair these fine craft. They, in turn, apprenticed their sons in the trade and that it had been so for all time, he said.

The big boat was first righted and carried into the water and only then was it loaded. Despite their great hauling capacity and size they were still quite light and somewhat fragile when not floating in their element. However, overturned on a shore they provided excellent quick shelter. There were two such large canoes to transport the few people and their two guests back to their island. Bags were spread along the center bottom and Nakosis was directed toward the front of the great canoe and told where to sit. Washtago instructed him simply to paddle on one side of the canoe, as he would be steering from the rear of the canoe and others would paddle in front of him. They were staggered along the boats length. As they shoved off Nakosis felt an exuberance and sense of weightlessness as the sleek craft cut through the blue waters of the bay. He soon found his rhythm as he put his strong back into the paddling. They now moved at what seemed an alarming speed across the open water of the lake. Nakosis told Washtago that this was something he thought he could do all day long.

Washtago just laughed and said, "We'll see how you feel after today's paddle."

As they continued pushing the canoe into the blue expanse of the great lake, the once cool breeze was now refreshingly welcome to Nakosis as he began to feel the muscles in his back and arms start warming under the work. Soon, however, a light drizzle could be seen on the water not far ahead and they all watched as it moved towards them like a thin wall across the lake. Perhaps they would avoid it, thought Nakosis, but it was not to be. At first it was almost pleasant, easing the sweat that he was starting to create. In short time, though, it got heavier and with it the water began to roll as the wind started to pick up. By the time they were well into the middle of the lake, waves had formed and the rain was now driving, hitting the canoe's occupants like small pebbles. No one said anything, yet they all had begun paddling much harder, an unspoken intensity to their endeavor. Washtago had changed course, heading the canoe toward the middle of the great lake. He yelled to Nakosis over the sound of the rain to switch his paddling to the other side. He said that they must keep the boat turned into the wind, into the direction of the waves so that they did not hit against the side and force the boat over. They were now heading for an island that lay directly ahead. One of the other passengers had dug out a leather cape and draped it over Chako, who wrapped it over his head and shoulders as the wind and rain were now getting quite cold. Nakosis was keeping up well with the others and doing his best to not panic, but he was beginning to feel a bit anxious as the waves, now white with foam, were beginning to lift and drop the canoe severely. He sensed the urgency in the others also. They had been yelling between the two boats and both were now making a race for the shadow of trees that, in the growing fog, was the only visible sign of the small island. A sudden flash of lightning followed by an almost immediate roar of thunder and all stoicism was gone as everyone began yelling and urging the paddlers on. Nakosis could feel his heart pounding in his chest and in his ears and his lungs felt like they would burst. Another flash and clap and harder yet they paddled. They could feel the charge in the air as they finally neared the shoreline. The waves were beating hard against the fallen trees and rocks at the water's edge. The other canoe was now just ahead of them and reaching the shore. The lead paddler leapt from the canoe only to disappear beneath the waves and emerge startled and gasping. He grabbed for the side as another rushed to reach him and, for an instant, it looked as though the entire canoe was going to go over, but fortunately the momentum of the paddlers propelled the canoe forward and the clinging man found his footing and managed to safely pull the front of the boat upon the rocks of the shore. These canoes were of such value to the people that they would almost risk their lives to make sure they did not get damaged in landing, as well, it was now their only way of getting off the island.

The front paddler in Nakosis' canoe jumped out to guide the craft to a safe shoring. The greatly relieved occupants all heaved the canoes up onto solid ground and finding a flat space they quickly overturned them, taking refuge underneath while a brutally strong wind blew heavy rain and even sand, leaves and twigs about. The large carved paddles acted as braces upon which the canoes rested, slanted with their hulls to the wind. Once they all threw themselves under the canoe a nervous laughter erupted from under both overturned boats as they celebrated having cheated death one more time.

Nakosis wondered if such a thing was a regular occurrence to people whose lives were so entwined with the water and their canoes.

It was a long time before the storm passed. Nakosis spoke briefly with the old woman huddled under the big canoe with the leather cape over their legs. He asked about the sisters' island village and how far did he think it would be to find the ancient site of the ancestors. The old healer was called Namishta. She said that apart from herself, there was another older elder in the village who could provide more information about the history of the people and could remember the way to the old site. She had been on the lake where the village had been. Both she and her sister had been there with their parents when they were young, but they never went to the actual old village site. Nakosis asked why. Namishta replied that it had been long abandoned and there was therefore no need to go there, but Nakosis sensed that there was something that she wasn't telling.

By the time the storm abated enough to resume the trip the day was half gone. They would have to paddle hard if they were going to make her island by nightfall, so once back into the water they resumed their strenuous pace. Nakosis knew very quickly what Washtago meant about paddling all day. His muscles ached as never before but he kept up with the others. For their part, the other paddlers spoke not a word during the long day. They dug into the lake with their paddles and fixed their minds to the task and drove forward, making the big canoe ride across the water like a loon taking off in flight. As the waters calmed it seemed that the craft glided so smoothly that no discernable paddling motion could be felt, just a perfect smooth movement forward. These people certainly knew what they were doing in a canoe, thought Nakosis.

Darkness was fast approaching and as they rounded a point of land a beaver crashed its large leathery tail on the water's surface and the resounding echo reverberated all around the dark lake. There was a slit of pale yellow in the horizon and the tops of the trees glowed in the fading light. The wind had stopped altogether and biting bugs were making their appearance. Nakosis figured they would be camping some place soon when suddenly rounding the point, the lake stretched out before them, vast and smooth. Directly ahead a large island filled much of the horizon and torches could be seen on the shoreline as voices called out, their warm and welcome sounds echoing across the now watery blackness. As they pulled to a sandy beach, the paddlers made no attempt to hide their exhaustion nor to express their relief at finally being home among their loved ones. Nakosis also felt greatly relieved when he at last stepped from the great boat.

The entire village appeared to have turned out to greet the canoes and Namishta introduced Nakosis to all. Chako needed no introduction; apparently, as he was covered in warm embraces and his child-like laugh could be heard above everyone.

A younger woman stepped forward to Nakosis saying, "You must be hungry, please follow me." He looked over to the others but Chako was still laughing and greeting villagers he obviously had not seen for a long time. The young woman stopped after a few steps and waving her hand at Nakosis said,

"Well then, grab your bags and come!"

He stumbled after her, his legs still not functioning properly after a full hard day paddling in a crouched position. As he hefted his bag over his shoulder he felt the strain on his back muscles. She led him up from the beach to a lodge set in the tree line, a stones throw from the water. It was much the same as all the others in Shining Lakes, but smaller. Nakosis hadn't yet determined the size of the village and the number of its inhabitants and, as it was now dark, that would have to wait until morning.

As the warmth of the food and fire worked on the tired travelers, each one began dozing off and so all unanimously agreed to retire. The hardship of the day was evident as the weary crew tried rising from the meal. Aching muscles created many a mournful sigh as the paddlers stood and made for the door. Chako and Nakosis were not quartered in the main lodge, but in a small hut adjacent. It was however, well build, clean and comfortable and Nakosis deduced that it must have been used by the sisters for their healing and journeying, as the walls were festooned with artifacts similar to those found in either Chako's or Loka's homes. There were drums in cases, skulls and antlers, herbs hung from the rafters and boxes and bags. They had placed two sleeping platforms made from poles and taut willow webbing with heavy furs on top for a very comfortable bed. Nakosis was relieved and very appreciative to finally feel its cradling softness beneath his aching body. Sensing or suspecting he might be in a bit of pain, Chako gave him some shredded willow bark and instructed him to chew it and swallow the juices. They had a very small, yet comforting fire, more to keep away the insects but a slight breeze off the lake seemed to be remedying that problem nicely. The spot had been well chosen, Nakosis commented, just before he fell into a deep sleep.

He awoke with the most refreshed and rejuvenated feeling, as though having slept on air. His muscles felt tight but not hurting.

He dressed quickly and left the hut and a sleeping, snoring Chako and ventured down to the sandy shoreline to wash his face in the clear cool water. The morning sun was a pale ribbon of pinkish light over the farthest tree line. Birdsong filled the air and their myriad melodies were amplified across the expanse of water. Fish were jumping not far off shore in a thin mist that rose like smoke from the smooth lake's surface. This was a beautiful place. It afforded a most excellent panorama of the great lake, whose farthest shore was just visible in the distance. It appeared that a channel, a bay or maybe a river continued at a spot to the southernmost point of the distant horizon. He threw his hair back, feeling the startling cold of its wetness upon his bare back. To his left a jetty of rock reached far out into the water. By the way the brush looked it seemed that a path must surely follow it. He took his bow and quiver from the hut and decided to try his luck at fishing. The village was fairly silent and he would welcome the quiet time alone on the rocks. He also thought it would be nice if he could contribute something to the wonderful meals he'd been provided by these friendly people.

The fish continued to make small splashes very close to the last rocks of the jetty and it was here he decided to position himself. He chose his place carefully. The morning sun had yet to reach him enough to cast any shadow upon the water and he stood poised between two fallen dead trees whose branches spread out and into the water. He was as still as a rock, his arrow notched, a long thin string of sinew attached, the slack taken up in his bow-string. He watched the small fish jumping as larger ones moved closer to shore to feed. He kept his eye and arrow on just such a large fish and adjusted for the angle of the water. He ever so slowly drew the bowstring toward his ear. It was no easy task to pull the strength of a powerful bow slowly, not shaking under its tensed power, not moving a muscle unnecessarily. He was nowhere the marksman that Taku was, nor some of the other archers of his village, but Nakosis prided himself on his fishing ability with both bow and spear. When the big fish moved closest to the surface he loosed his arrow and watched it hit its mark as the dying fish leapt in a fury of spray. He instinctually grabbed the line with his right hand and began reeling the catch onto the rocks. It was a splendidly big fish, sufficient for a few people. He moved over to position himself further along the rocks away from where he had just shot and among more trees. This time he waded among the many branches to where the bottom of his great bow was still above the water and again he waited silent and still and his patience was quickly rewarded with another good-sized fish. In this way he soon had four fish to attest to his prowess as a fine fisherman.

"Nakosis! Oh there you are!" It was Namishta. She was walking with Washtago and one other younger man. "After the meal we must prepare to leave, Nakosis. There is another long day of paddling ahead for you, I'm afraid."

He returned to the hut to find Chako sitting in meditation beside the fire, his drum in his lap. He turned to leave when Chako spoke out,

"No need to leave, I am just coming now." He slowly rose extending his arm for Nakosis to help him. "I'm not used to sitting in that damned boat so long," he chuckled.

"Yes, I too felt it this morning and Namishta warned me already of another day in the canoe to reach the site of the lost village. Morning meal is cooking uncle. We should go and eat. I caught fist this morning." He said proudly.

"Umm very good." Chako said, "but I will not be staying with you at the lost village, Nakosis."

"What do you mean, uncle? I thought this was why we went to all the trouble! Why we travelled so far to get here!" he was completely astounded and visibly shaken.

"Nakosis, my boy. Not to worry. This is something you must do alone. Washtago and Namishta and a few others will accompany you to find that place, but they will return and leave you there. You alone must find out what the spirits have to tell you. You see it could be that our being there may hinder your chances, Nakosis. Some spirits are funny that way. They will speak to you, guide you and ultimately reveal your path to you if you alone are there to hear them. It is you alone who the great Hohapas has chosen to bless with his vision and you must now continue the journey. You know that most of us who walk the path of the spirits have spent many periods alone seeking their guidance and hearing their wisdom, often for many days at a time. This we do far removed from the distraction of others - deep in the forest or, as you know, in a cave. You have to seek out these places. They will present themselves to you when you ask the spirits to guide you to them. Sometimes they are not what you'd expect. We might choose a place of great beauty with splendid views, but this is sometimes not the way of the spirits. They choose differently. Sometimes it is also a beautiful place where waterfalls are, for example, but sometimes it is just some spot in the forest. Perhaps it is that this place may have been different in the past. If you are to journey to the underworld it may be a place where there is an ancient tree with very deep roots and openings in the earth like a crevice in old rock. This ancient village site may have been chosen because it was just such a place, chosen by the spirits and perhaps in the past our ancestors sensed this and so decided to make the village there"

"Could it also be a place where terrible things happened to attract certain spirits?" Nakosis asked, afraid of what the answer might be.

"Yes, it could be that also. Water falls to the lowest point of land does it not? Some flow from sweet streams high in the mountains, some flow through groves of old 'tanning bark' trees that carry a bitterness with them that makes the water brown. Our lives are a bit like the deep pool where all waters mingle, both sweet and bitter. If we want to drink we must have a little of both. In our practice, Nakosis, we get to sometimes separate the waters. But not if we don't drink from the pool of life."

There was a pause as Nakosis considered these words. "So as I must drink or die, I must also go to this place or my journey ends here, today."

Chako nodded and they walked in silence to the lodge to eat. Nakosis had sensed for some time that his would end up being a solitary quest. It scared him and he would try to dismiss it when the thought arose, but now it was certain. This segment of it, at least, would be his alone to experience. Some part of him felt oddly resigned to it. He had considered the words of encouragement Loka had given him. If the visions of Hohapas were indicators of his protection and power, then what could he possibly have to fear, Nakosis thought. Loka had once said that it was Nakosis' doubt of his abilities, of his own power and the spirit's protection that could prove dangerous for him. He'd said 'the spirits give you power when you believe they do. If you don't have faith in them, faith in your own power, Nakosis, then you will have none. You must always remember and trust in your power, especially when faced with the hardest trials. When you need your power the most then your trust is stronger and also your power is then stronger. Was it not so with the great water that killed the enemy?'

Seated by the fire were Namishta, Washtago and two other men. One was a seasoned warrior named Kahante. They would be accompanying the group to the ancient site. Through the door came an old woman, bent with age and leaning heavily on a stick and supported on each side by a younger man and woman. Everyone rose to greet her. She placed her one free arm around Chako and then greeted the others in turn with a big toothless smile. Despite her great age and physical disability, she had a radiant energy about her that Nakosis immediately liked. She touched her head to his when they were introduced and Kahante and his son hurried to find and pile up some furs atop a large bag to create a seat for the old woman beside the fire. Her name was Inipa. Nakosis soon realized that she was the clue to finding the old site.

"Yes, I was there when I was a girl." She said when Namishta posed the question. "I was with my father, mother and my older sister. We took our canoe and went with three other canoes. It was at the end of the warm season, before the cold. We fished and hunted birds on the way and we made camp twice, once to gather the seeds of the water grain at a smaller lake. My parents said that they used to go there more when they too were little children, just to honor the ancestors. But over time it had become harder to get to. The trail required having to cross overland a little ways with the canoes and it had become very overgrown and the water was thick with many of the flowering plants. Sometimes we used to gather their roots and roast them, but they made the travelling harder. There is much of the sinking earth there also. I remember we pulled our canoe over so us little girls could relieve ourselves and when we jumped onto the shore we sank to our knees! My father laughed so hard! We had to struggle through a ways to where the ground was hard enough to stand without sinking. There was good hunting and fishing near our villages so, over the years, the people just stopped going there. My father said that there was nothing there anyway but bad memories. I remember how we went there though."

The group soon reached a consensus as to the route to the old site. One of the hunters was familiar with the last lake where the portage was. From there it was only a matter of hefting the canoes over to the lake of the lost village.

Preparations were quickly completed and it was decided to set out immediately. Three smaller canoes were deemed preferable, as the portage would be easier. Kahante led the way, guided by the other older hunter Lutah. Nakosis and Washtago paddled the other canoe and Chako took a seat in the middle, atop a large bag. Most of their meager supplies were in the other canoe, but Kahante insisted that some of them be divided lest one canoe should tip or get damaged then all the supplies would not be lost.

Within an amazingly short time the party was crossing the sun dappled waters of the great lake. Nakosis was comforted to see clear blue skies as far as the horizon. Chako was too tired for much conversation, for a change, so the two young men focused on the paddling and the day swept by in splendid sunshine and the slight cooling breeze eased the heat of straining muscles. The strokes of the paddle, the repetitive motion in the warm sunshine all created a trance-like atmosphere and Nakosis very quickly allowed his mind and imagination to transport him elsewhere. He had been wondering about the days ahead and not without a little trepidation. He now had the confidence that he was up to the task of discovering whatever the spirits had to reveal and he felt a renewed optimism about his role in the mystic journey ahead. He seemed to acquire new energy as they plied the sleek craft forward, following the lead canoe.

As the sun was beginning to take his rest behind the dark outline of the forest, the lead canoe pulled to rest amid a dense growth of reeds and brightly colored water hyacinths. Washtago was cussing at the sinking earth that Inipa had described, as it now pulled and sucked at his moccasins and leggings as he and Kahante further struggled to get the craft ashore and across the muskeg to dry ground. Nakosis chose to stay back among the reeds and watch and wait until they had secured the way, not wanting to have to repeat their drudgery if he could help it. It appeared that the sinking ground was all along the shore area and with great reluctance Nakosis clamored over the bow of the canoe and struggled ashore with the cargo Chako handed him. He tried to make a rushed business of it but the muskeg wouldn't allow it. It set the speed. There was no moving any faster than a snail's pace, as he had to lift one stuck leg at a time and then the other. He could feel the weight of the bags pushing him even deeper into the slimy soup. Now each step was accompanied by a small rising cloud of tiny biting flies that went for his face and neck and any exposed parts of his body.

Washtago desperately searched for pieces of log or branches to lie down over the ground for Chako to step on. The idea worked but very temporarily. It spread his weight a little but then brown bubbles of goo would erupt around his feet and bits of branches and the whole mess would sink. After the day's hard paddle sitting with their legs unused this was a grueling exercise. The other two, having found secure footing, now came back to grab the bags and to help Chako over the rest of the muskeg. There were spots, Kahante noticed, closer to the base of the heavier bushes where it was easier to step, so they placed their feet down upon the tops of the thickest low bushes and, using them like stepping stones, they cautiously made their way to dry ground.

They settled on a location on a higher rocky point that overlooked the lake and the reed covered muskeg shoreline below. As it was more in the open there would be fewer of the notorious biting flies. They fell into an organized troop. Chako began gathering wood and starting a fire and retrieving the packs as the others hauled the canoes over the sucking ground they had just crossed to where they'd be secure.

"Good thing we have food," Chako said upon the other's return. "I wouldn't want to go through all that again just to try fishing!" He had already started a nice little fire and had rummaged through the bags to get a meal started. The older hunter was called Lutah. He gathered some boughs and a few armfuls of a low bright green shrub and threw them on Chako's fire much to Chako's displeasure.

"Not to worry. It will keep the biting ones away," he said as a pungent dark smoke rose.

They spent a restless night wrapped in robes, trying to avoid the hordes of bugs. They took turns maintaining the fire and keeping the smoking plants burning. By morning, they were ready to quickly break camp and get moving and away from the insects. While they packed camp, Kahante and Lutah searched for any signs of an old trail leading inland. It didn't take long before Lutah discovered where there had once been a small clearing. As well, some burned poles still lay on the ground. They would have once been part of the framework of a shelter. It was common practice to burn the poles to length and also to help preserve them from rot. He soon found where the most likely route of the old trail was. It was terribly overgrown with countless bushes, vines and bracken. Many thin willows and saplings now covered the trail. In fact Nakosis noted that one could actually see the direction of the old path by the colors of the numerous birch saplings and willows, their reddish colors stood out in contrast to the surrounding greens of the forest.

The group all looked at one another, realizing that they had a trek ahead of them. Kahante suggested that one of them should go on ahead to see how far it was and how overgrown. Chako said that they might as well all go, as there was nothing for the others to do except stand still while feeding the biters!

"At least we can push down some of these bigger saplings as we go," said Washtago.

So while Kahante went ahead the rest followed, clearing the larger obstacles and debris as they went. The trail appeared to rise somewhat and Washtago commented that at least once they reached the crest of the trail it would be downhill the rest of the way to the lake. It was as they were approaching what looked to be the top that Kahante reappeared. He was soaked with sweat and breathless from exertion. He grabbed a water gourd from the closest man and drank deeply. Then regaining his breath he announced that he had found the lake. They were half way, he declared. The going was no better but, yes, it was downhill. The island was far off across what he described as a great lake, similar to the one where their village was. They returned to the canoes and discussed the plans.

Lutah said, "If Nakosis is to spend time at the ancient village site alone, then it doesn't make sense to haul two canoes across this overgrown trail then back again and then we must return at the appointed time and again do this two more times. Perhaps he should just go alone."

The party was exhausted and this was the most logical suggestion, but Chako had reservations. He wanted to see the site also. He needed to be assured that it was indeed the ancient village location and he wanted to make sure Nakosis was well prepared for his vision quest. When he expressed his wishes the others knew not to question the old revered Shaman, despite their fatigue.

Nakosis didn't comment right away, but studied the situation closely and then he said, "I agree with Lutah. I believe I can handle a canoe well enough by myself. I can take one canoe over the trail, to the island and then after my time is done I can return." There was silence.

"You would have to take two trips on the trail," Lutah said, "you would need to take the canoe on one trip and the supplies on another."

"Well, I have all day!" Nakosis answered. The party looked at one another awaiting a sound suggestion.

Washtago offered, "I will carry the bag of supplies and you take the canoe. We can switch if need be."

"It will be too many in the one canoe for the return," observed Kahante.

"Oh, by the gods!" Chako barked. "We may as well all go! We'll camp the night on the island with Nakosis and then we can leave in the morning. The trail will be better for our return after we cross it twice!"

The crew began the arduous task of moving the gear and canoes over the rough terrain. The canoes were each light enough for one person to handle so Washtago and Nakosis shouldered the canoes as the other three, wearing bags of supplies, broke trail, pushing, breaking and hauling ahead as they went. At times they would stop and rest and notice the saplings bent by their passing springing back into position, unfettered by the attempt to flatten them. Nakosis felt guilty that these fine people were going to such extremes to accommodate him. He understood that many realized the importance of such spiritual undertakings but others, like Lutah perhaps, acted more out of a sense of duty than understanding. No doubt he was wishing he was at home with his family or out fishing rather than here on this trail.

The going was hard and Nakosis and Washtago stumbled often and the others scrambled to grab the precious canoes. If they were pierced by a branch or rock it would prove perilous. Several rest breaks and finally they saw the sun rippling across the vast blue waters below them. The sight gave them all a renewed sense of purpose and they quickly made the downhill stretch to the water's edge. The lake was indeed grand, as Lutah had described it. It spread in every direction and they could see the large island far in the distance. The struggle to transport the canoes and supplies through the dense undergrowth had taken the better part of the day. Kahante had observed that when it was a well-traversed route it would have only taken them a short time to cross. But now the sun was only a couple of hands distance above the horizon and Lutah suggested that they had best make time. "We can rest later but that island is a lot of paddles distant. We have to go." He pronounced.

The passage across the lake was fairly easy as the water was so placid that it was a perfect reflection of the entire surrounding forest. The number of birds taking flight at the sight of these intruders was completely astounding, even greater than Nakosis had seen at Shining Lakes. Moose crashed into the dense forest from where they had been eating the root of the water flowers among the thick reeds along the shoreline. A pair of large eagles circled overhead and the haunting call of a loon echoed across the water. The island was heavily treed and so wide as to block the view of the other side of the lake. It may well have continued to infinity, thought Nakosis. This was a truly ancient land, lost for some time to the people whose ancestors once called it their home. Everything about it radiated a sense of the primeval; even the trees seemed so much larger and older. Behind the dance of nature, the sounds and song of birds there loomed an all-pervasive silence, a dark and powerful force. Nakosis immediately thought of Hohapas. He had been able to keep his mind occupied by the mundane affairs of the waking world, but now, here, in this place where the power of mother earth was so ubiquitous he could not help but feel the magic, the personification of sacred power. As they neared the island he became very perceptive of the growing energy and more cognizant of the otherworldly presence that such places seemed to facilitate. He paddled without any connection to the movements. His mind was now as though it was another's. His body paddled, but his mind, his spiritual being, now focused elsewhere. The island, the trees, the rocks and the water of the great lake –all were alive with a tremendous force he could not ignore. It was as though they called him. It was not fearsome, nor foreboding. It was, in fact, like coming home.

CHAPTER 16
THE LOST VILLAGE

"The first peace, which is the most important, is that which comes within the souls of people when they realize their relationship, their oneness with the universe and all its powers, and when they realize that at the center of the universe dwells the Great Spirit, and that this center is really everywhere, it is within each of us."
~ Black Elk - Oglala Sioux

As they neared the island Nakosis could discern more features. The trees were huge, their massive trunks thick with dense moss. He reasoned that any ancient fires would have spared the island. As they drew closer he could clearly see a small cove banked on either side by forested jetties that formed a perfectly protected harbor shaped like a crescent moon. They instantly knew that this was the location of the old village site. It was the obvious choice. They pulled ashore with enough daylight left to make camp on the beach and explore the surrounding area for signs of earlier habitation. It didn't take long. Kahante yelled to the others at the boats and they all ran to where he stood within easy view of the water. He found many collapsed poles. They had been burned by a fire, yet the surrounding forest showed no signs of burning. The poles had once been the frameworks of a structure. As they looked further they realized that, like the overgrown trail, the clearing they stood in was at one time an open area. The willows and birches had taken over but one could clearly define an area that had once been cleared.

They explored the surrounding woods even further, driven now by the excitement of discovery. It was Washtago who yelled for the rest to come. There was urgency, even panic, in his voice that made them come with their spears raised. When they broke through the brush to where he stood, pointing, they saw the reason for his astonishment, a perfectly preserved lodge!

The men immediately began scanning the surrounding woods for sign of a presence. Chako walked right up to it and entered the uncovered doorway. He turned to the others and waved them in. The place was empty and showed no sign of recent habitation. The entire clearing was a dense mat of needles. Chako pointed out that the massive tree sheltering above must have kept the rain and snow from collapsing the structure. Perhaps, he said, the building had been constructed at a later time than the old village. It was small, well built and it's roof domed. A weasel scurried out from under some wind blown debris to stare at the intruders and darted about like a phantom. The men laughed.

"We should bring our paddles and use them to clear out this place and we can camp here tonight." Kahante said.

"Yes," Chako agreed. "It will also do well for you, Nakosis." He added with a wry smile, "It was nice of the spirits to leave this place for you!" Nakosis wasn't sure he saw any humor in the remark.

They soon had moved their bags, robes and gathered enough firewood to pleasantly warm the hut. Using the paddles they managed to remove dense mats of needles and moss and more than a few mice and squirrels also. As darkness approached, the glow of the fire made the place seem very inviting. Nakosis could not even see many holes in the hut's ancient roof. The men were ravenous and dug into the food they had brought. The exertion of the day had worked up very hearty appetites and no one spoke as the men devoured their meal.

Afterward, talk of the ancient ones became the focal point of the conversation. It was Lutah who, usually of few words, decided to illuminate the rest with his knowledge of the history of the people. For the most part he repeated what everyone had already heard about the migration and the grueling trek across barren dry land to come through the mountains someplace to eventually end up here, where they now sat in this hut. He did, however, add additional anecdotes and personality sketches to the story so as to make it riveting to hear. For such a quiet and verbally pragmatic man he proved to be a most excellent storyteller, a trait highly valued among the people. When he finished Nakosis looked at him for a while and finally spoke up asking Lutah,

"So, my friend what of these other stories we've heard. I mean about the dark walkers?" Chako spun as though hit. He glared his disapproval at Nakosis, but Nakosis would not be censored even when Chako hissed and growled. Instead, he spun uncharacteristically to Chako declaring,

"It is I, Chako, who will be questing in this place for five sun's time. It is I who wish to know the true story, the full story, of this place. As you pointed out, I have great protection with me at all times. It is not *me* who fears hearing the story. If it frightens the rest of you then you will only be scared for tonight and soon will be safe in your homes." He held his head high and his expression showed no emotion when he spoke.

For once, Chako, obviously upset at what he perceived as disrespect, had to yield to Nakosis. He sensed a rising power in him and the old Shaman knew intuitively to let the story be told. Lutah was at first reluctant, but he too yielded to the young Shaman's request and re-told the whole story as Nakosis and Washtaka had heard it. As with the other tale, he also added some additional embellishments and flairs. It was painfully obvious that such stories made the group nervous and almost unconsciously the men pulled their spears closer to them. The total blackness of night now, no doubt, added to their tension.

Lutah broke the silence that immediately followed by adding, "But these stories are only tales that no one can prove, you know. Yes, some people died in a bad winter, but that sort of thing can happen always, isn't that so?" he looked around at the heads nodding in agreement then continued, "The man may not have even done that thing. It may have been something else, an animal. The hunters may have been wrong. They were scared and scared people do not see things as they really are. Anyway, there it is! I told you what you wanted to hear, but I just want you all to know that I don't really believe these things and I am not to be frightened by old woman's tales!"

Chako immediately lent his support and added that he shared Lutah's sentiments. Nakosis just smiled and lay back on his robes and greeted a much-needed sleep. He slept like the dead, no dreams that he could recall and he awoke feeling completely rejuvenated and more alive than ever. He apparently was the only one.

The others were all awake and preparing to eat and already beginning to pack their bags to the canoes. Their faces bore their obvious unrest and unease like a mask. They quickly said their goodbyes to Nakosis and wished him well in his quest and left for the boats. Chako reminded Nakosis of the procedures they had discussed many times and Nakosis smiled and nodded. Chako still seemed a little uneasy, but Nakosis felt incredibly content and empowered by his surroundings, he simply wanted the others to leave so he could be alone to explore the energy he felt with every fiber of his being. It was his near blissful countenance, his smiling, relaxed persona that actually had Chako concerned. But it was now Nakosis' personal experience and Chako touched foreheads with him and gave his blessing. Then they were gone. Chako and Washtago looked back several times as they returned across the cool lake, the chill morning mist rising off the halcyon waters. They half expected to see Nakosis standing on the shore waving to them but he was not there.

The song of birds filled the clearing and their jubilant calls reverberated across the tranquil waters and echoed off the façade of tall trees. This was not at all what Nakosis had expected when he first heard the stories back in Shining Lakes. He had pictured a dead and fearful place. Certainly the forest was indeed dark and mysterious, but it was fully alive in every way. Birds and animals were prolific and yet, above all, was an undeniable power so strong that the air actually seemed to hum with its presence. To Nakosis, it harbored nothing malevolent that he could sense. He had removed his small drum from his bag and he held it in his hand as he walked along the shoreline exploring this world. He wasn't sure why, but he felt the need to gently tap on the drum as he walked, his steps in cadence with the gentle rhythm he now played. He smiled to himself. He spoke softly to the surroundings, addressing the trees, birds and rocks as he strode, as though they were old friends welcoming him home from a long journey. He would lift his small drum and tap a few beats at the largest trees, wishing them well, blessing them. Time seemed not to have any bearing on him. He had no goal to reach, no direction in which to travel. He was fully in the splendor of the moment and it was powerful. Chako and Loka had instructed Nakosis on how he should spend his five days on the old site. He was told to meditate, to use his drum or rattle and to allow himself to be open to any guidance the spirits might wish to bless him with. But to sit in silence and 'listen' for messages was not easy for Nakosis. To Nakosis, sitting in such a way was like eating with one's eyes closed - you loose a part of the experience. He preferred to have his eyes wide open and leap into the unknown. He never had to concentrate or focus on the spirits to hear their beckoning.

He made his way in this walking, waking trance, drinking in the serenity and beauty around him, breathing in the intense power of this place when he suddenly came to the far side of the island. He couldn't believe his eyes. The lake continued far into the horizon, the ancient forest rising and rolling on either shore in increasingly higher hills and there, far in the distance, towering above the thick white mist were snow-covered peaks! They dominated the distant horizon as far as he could see. It was a world of barren snow and ice. Just like the realm described in the ancient tales! Nakosis stood for some time absorbing what his eyes were taking in. If this was indeed the ancient village site, then it only stood to reason that there must be a route through the mountains that the ancient ones had discovered. Somewhere, over those frozen peaks and valleys lay hidden the 'mountain of fire' and his spiritual destiny. He now knew with certainty that this magical island, with its air of power and wonder was to provide the key to the rest of his journey.

He returned to his hut, prepared a light meal and blessed the dwelling with his smudge of sacred herbs. He had pondered whether this hut, being built away from the main clearing and under this magnificent giant tree was once used by a Shaman. He wondered aloud at how long it had been since the fragrant blessing aroma had filled the dwelling. He bathed himself with the blue/gray smoke, then all his belongings. He then went outside and began walking through the overgrown clearing to the sandy shore, waving the sacred smoke to all directions and asking the spirits to honor the ancestors who once lived and died there and to all the brethren in all the other realms, the animals, birds, insects, rocks, trees and to the great water that nurtured them all.

He felt a reciprocal wave blow over him like a great long awaited sigh, like the breath of Mother Earth herself. Nakosis felt warm tears on his cheeks and he fell to his knees on the sand of the beach, raising his arms high to the power that now filled his being. He decided he would build his fire on the sandy clearing, not in the hut, as the sky was brilliantly clear. He gathered wood and brought a burning stick from the fire in the hut and retrieved his bag also. This was as it should be he realized, under the sky, in the wind, the earth beneath his bare feet, the fragrance of forest, lake and the fire mingling in the clear air and within him also.

He thought back to the night in the cave and the wonderful evocation to the spirits that Chako had spoken. He now recalled those words. He stood facing the direction of the rising sun and then speaking he moved sun-wise around his fire shaking his ancient rattle with its beautiful Raven carved handle to all the directions. He raised his arms to father sky reciting the words,

" *I ask the great mystery to witness and to bless my humble offerings this day. I ask that the spirits of all our brethren smile upon me now and accept my offering and help to guide me in my journey. I ask our beloved mother earth to bear witness that these things I do, I do not for myself but for all the brethren in all the worlds and for the ancestors who dwell among us and in the spirit world also. If they find me worthy, may the spirits guide me and protect me and may I have ears to hear their council. May all beings benefit from my endeavors."*

Nakosis circled the fire, gently tapping his drum, slowly, methodically at first. He chanted the ancient words and felt the rhythm of the earth moving his limbs. His feet lifting in a shuffled step around the fire and his body slowly beginning to turn from left to right, right to left. An energy started rising in him like the uncurling of a great snake, it's power filling his being and the strength of it moving him as though he were a child's doll in unseen hands. His momentum increased as the drum beats quickened and he began twirling within the circle of the dance as he rounded the fire. He was unaware of either time or physical sensation. He felt not his legs nor the heat of the fire neither did he notice the setting sun, the brilliant rising moon and the blanket of stars above. He was no longer even aware that it was he who beat the drum. He was not the dancer, he *was* the dance and it was the primordial dance of the cosmos. The fire had not dissipated despite never having been stoked the entire day. Not only did it continue to burn, it did so with a light not borne of flame, a glow that outshone that of the now radiant full moon. From out of the luminosity there came lights of many colors, some tiny and less conspicuous while others shone with radiance equal to their source. This rainbow of lights spun around the fire pulsating with the twirling dance, following Nakosis like a procession of otherworldly auras.

Many spirits answered the call. They came from out of the forest, spirit of deer, wolf, bear and coyote, and his old friend and guardian, panther. From the air the great eagle, raven and even the mysterious owl spirit. The island shone like a hundred stars fallen to earth to honor all creation and the great mystery unfolded amid the fiery celebration of being. Nakosis was the apex, the center and simultaneously he was also the culmination of all the spirit beings. He became wolf, bear and deer, eagle and raven. He sensed their world, felt their lives, he understood their being and their inter-connectedness, their part in the great mystery. He now knew them all as never before. He wept openly as he passed the fire in each of the spirit's guises. He felt their immense suffering, the suffering of the sacred mother earth, whom it seemed man understood less with the passing of time. He understood how it was when the ancestors spoke all the being's tongues. He also felt Hohapas among the multitude of spirits. He was as a gatherer of spirits. He was Hohapas and was also all the other spirits as well. Nakosis realized that Hohapas *was* the magic, the life force in all of Nature. The mesmerizing song of his flute was the very vibration of creation, the pulse of life itself. It was in the rhythm of his heart, the beat of his drum, the waves on the shore and the beating of Raven's wings. The world of the waking was no more for Nakosis. He saw it as non- different from that of a dream. This world, the reality in which the veils of the supernatural, the unknown, were pulled back was more alive, more vibrant and energetic than anything he'd ever experienced. But he also understood that they were inseparable realities, not two worlds but two aspects of one reality that in truth exist simultaneously. Yet people have eyes, ears and senses for only one vision. When they, in their ephemeral flashes of insight, are blessed with a glimpse of the other reality they deem it mystical, magical, unknown and fearful. To Nakosis now it was abundantly clear that all things exist within one world, even the spirits. That one world was all encompassing. He did not have, as he previously though, one foot in the spiritual world and one in the waking world, but both feet firmly planted in a world that was now whole, complete, and the manifestation of the magic and creativity of the sacred mystery.

Clouds passed overhead, birds sang, the sun shone through, a light rain came and went, darkness fell, the brilliance of the moon flooded the island once more, the stars illuminated the blackness of space and beneath it all Nakosis was untouched by anything, unaware even of any external phenomenon. His legs were supported by the muscle and sinew of the deer, the courage and strength of the great bear coursed through his being, he was lifted aloft upon the wings of a great eagle, high above the island. He could see, far below, the tiny figure dancing, swirling, drumming, and circling the sacred fire. He saw the infinite rainbow of light that spiraled outward from the dancer and filled the cosmos, fading into every direction. He saw also the distant snow covered peaks rising above the verdant forests. Wherever he looked he was instantly there, soaring high above the ragged peaks and plateaus of the mountainous realm of perpetual winter. He gazed across the barren vastness to the distant horizon. He saw the rising plume of thick clouds issuing from unseen valleys, forests of lushness he had never imagined, plants he had never envisioned. Pools of water amid bright red rock bubbled and boiled and steamed hot vapor into the cool mountain air then cascaded down precipitous canyon walls into the bluest pools. The rock walls of the canyon were a wondrous blend of pinks and creams. Many places of this mountain were of the most unimaginable beauty and the power of it all was unmistakable –this was the mountain of fire! Nakosis now knew where the route lay.

It was not known how long he danced, how long he was with the spirits. When he 'awoke' to the other world it was not as his waking had ever been before. This morning he awoke beside the dead fire and looked upon the world with the eyes of one who has seen what most will never understand. When Nakosis drank in the surroundings it was with a sight that comprehended the totality of all things. He not only saw the trees, rocks, sky and animals but he *felt* them with senses he could not explain. It was almost as though he saw *through* everything, beyond their physical presence to their real identity, their spiritual essence. There was no separation between the object and the seer. He could discern the various things around him yet they were also a part of him, as one would see one's hands and fingers, and yet also different. It needed no clarification to Nakosis as it was completely experiential, but he knew others would never understand.

He ate a little food and wrapped his robe over his shoulders and sat upon the rocks of the jetty overlooking the cove. The water was placid, calm and reflective. He crawled over the rocks to the water's edge and there bent with cupped hand to drink. As he leaned out over the last boulder he caught a glimpse of himself in the mirrored surface of the lake. He stared for what must have been some time at his reflection for he did not recognize himself at first. His hair lay strewn across his head and shoulders and there on one side against his face a small streak of white flowed down to his chest. He calmly fingered the strands, pulling them up and examining them in his hand. A length about as thick as a finger, only on his right side was as white as the snowy peaks of the mountain of fire. For some reason he himself couldn't fathom, it didn't bother him at all. He soon realized that this was the side closest to the fire as he danced in ecstasy around it's blinding light. He chuckled as he looked again at himself in the water and then he laughed. He roared with laughter, his voice echoing back at him across the bay. He laughed more. He laughed harder. Now standing, he held the frosty lock up to the rays of the rising sun and delighted at the sound of his laughter. The echo made it appear like a group of men engaged in enjoying some bizarre joke.

Occasionally he would break his silent vigil with short laughs, but otherwise he sat simply, quietly, finding tremendous humor in the unseen forces that, to him, had engaged him in loving playfulness. He felt calmness, serenity and also power and confidence that made him completely fearless. He could not stop smiling. He knew the men were coming. He heard them long ago when they were still on the trail carrying the canoe. He knew they would approach him, speak to him, and ask him many questions. It didn't matter. Nothing really mattered.

Chako and Washtago saw him first. They were looking at the clearing, expecting to see smoke. Then they saw the figure huddled under a robe upon the rock. They called out but no answer came.

"Perhaps he is hurt." Said Lutah.

Chako feared something worse. He thought he might have suffered harm beyond that of the body. They pulled the canoes to shore and Kahante leapt from the bow helping an excited Chako to the beach. They ran up to Nakosis, still unmoving, seated upon the rock. As they came upon him he moved for the first time and Washtago sighed relief. When he turned to face the men they all suppressed a gasp at his appearance. The white streak was the most noticeable sign, but there was an unmistakable look in his face, a brightness and deepness to his eyes and calmness to his gentle smile that was deeply moving.

The four men sat on the rocks as Chako took his hand and asked, "Nakosis, what happened? Are you alright my son?" He smiled at Chako and placing his hand over his he said,

"All men will die soon enough. Life is but the blink of an eye in the time of the great mystery. Most men direct their lives by measuring the passing of time. I have experienced timelessness. Time, the measuring and marking of the rising of the sun and moon, are merely man's attempts at placing constraints upon the infinite. The Great Mystery laughs. It is not that the passing of days doesn't watch the slow decay of all men. Even death, with its seeming finality, is but a process, a rock in the trail of a man's journey to understanding the Great Mystery. I reflected on leaving my own body behind and freeing my being, my spirit, to dance with the infinite. I knew that the spirit exists, one with the Great Mystery, regardless of the body it moves in within the waking world. Eagle or mouse, it doesn't matter. Sprit is spirit! It is our choices, our ability to hear when spirit speaks and tries to guide us that determines whether we come back to this world or to our ancestors, or perhaps directly to become a part of the Great Mystery, never to return here. It is the great connection that is the secret. That is what all beings have to come to understand and embrace. It is my destiny and that of all beings to eventually come to know the oneness with the Great Mystery, to have one's waking existence melt like ice in the sun of understanding and to be free from the bonds of this waking world and all its suffering. I must seek this understanding. This is my destiny, this is what I know!"

No one spoke. Everybody sat silently, staring at Nakosis, waiting for him to speak again. Nakosis remained seated upon the rock, the sun warming its ancient, pitted features. He moved his hands across it's surface, smiling. He looked upon the reflection of the tranquil waters of the great lake. The call of Raven echoed across the cove and Nakosis chuckled. "Yes, my brother," he said softly under his breath, still chuckling lightly as though sharing a humorous moment in a private conversation. He then turned to the expectant men gathered around him and he looked smiling, lovingly at each one in turn.

Turning to face Chako, he said, "The mountain of fire is straight west of this very island, Chako. The spirits have shown me this place. I have seen it and I have also seen the way to go there. What purpose is served by my returning with you now? We have known my destiny before leaving White Mist and now the path is before me and I must take it, my old friend." He looked at the others and back to Chako continuing, "There is a game trail, it is clear and wide over there on the north side of the lake." He raised his arm to point. "Someone should take me over there now in the canoe and I shall be on my way. I will say goodbye to you all and may the sprits bless you and guide you as they now do me."

Nakosis finished speaking and stood up. Chako and the others rose. While the other men looked at each other, lost for words, Chako put his old arms around his friend and held him tightly. Tears were in his eyes as he said,

"My dear son, you are unlike any other man I have ever known. You are truly blessed and destined for greatness, Nakosis, and I have no doubt that you will be guided and protected to serve whatever task the Great Mystery has set before you. I cry only from the pain in my heart that I feel at your leaving. I shall miss you, my brother. Loka and I will be praying for you and we will be with you in spirit whenever we journey. Little brother, do not stray. Keep strong on the quest and have faith in the spirits. Loka and I are with you. This will test you far beyond anything you ever thought possible. Do not loose faith, my friend." Chako pulled back and wiped his teary cheek with his sleeve.

Washtago stepped forward. "Nakosis, my friend, I will be honored to see you to the mainland."

"Then we should leave immediately." Nakosis said.

He touched his forehead to that of his old friend and mentor and then picking up his big bag, shouldering his bow and smaller satchel, he turned and walked quietly to the waiting canoe.

As the sleek craft cut glistening ripples through the water of the small bay, the three men stood silently on the sandy shore watching their companion leave them. The dipping of Washtago's lone paddle and the echoing refrain of ravens and loons were the only sounds other than the soft muffled chant of the ancient tongue that Chako now sent in the direction of his young friend and brother Shaman. The canoe soon reached the opposite shore. Nakosis and Washtago embraced and bade each other farewell. Chako finished his ancient chant and looking across the expanse of the bay, tears in his eyes he said,

"May Raven and Panther protect you, may the Great Mystery bless you and may Hohapas guide your steps, my son."

They stood watching as Nakosis entered the dark of the forest and they could see him no more.

CHAPTER 17
TO THE MOUNTAIN

Nakosis used his hands to grasp the dense brackens and bushes of the shoreline foliage to pull himself up into the dark shade of the giant trees above the high water line. He climbed up a short distance to where he stopped and caught his breath. From here, unseen by those still on the island, he looked back to watch his old friend Chako still standing on the distant shore, now gently shaking his old rattle in his direction of travel. Nakosis knew he was sending blessings with all the power at his disposal. Nakosis smiled affectionately at his friend and his selfless gesture warmed his heart. He raised his arms, closed his eyes and lowering his head slightly, he said softly, "May the spirits serve you well and your guardians protect you. May we live to see each other again, my old friend."

Chako suddenly felt a deep warm wind come across the lake and gently blow over him like a comforting blanket on a cool evening. He smiled and wiping the tears from his eyes he chuckled lightly to himself. And then he laughed out loud, the sound startling the other men who were preparing the canoes for departure. They looked at one another and simply shrugged their shoulders.

Lutah commented, "Only they know their ways!"

Nakosis had soon made the crest of land above the lake and found the wide game trail. It was free of much undergrowth and afforded a clear view of the surrounding land and the water below. Animals were opportunists, he observed. Why would they not take the easiest route? He knew that it would take days to reach the base of the great mountains and there would not be much more left to this one. He would walk on toward the distant snowy peaks and then he was certain a suitable site to spend the night would, no doubt, present itself. It was different, he observed, 'walking in spirit', moving one's feet without mindful connection to the goal or outcome. He had total faith and no attachment to the results of his labors. He would try to remain completely 'open'. To do this did not require any strenuous activity or deep concentration. Instead it required quite the opposite. One had to be free from the constraints of thinking in an analytical manner, not deciding on where and when, not contemplating which path was right, but just walking with utter abandon, yet with complete trust that wherever he went was precisely where he was meant to be. He would become an empty vessel that the Great Mystery would fill. Night, cold, dark, sun, heat and rain were like the clouds of the dreaming world. Though they had affect upon his body they had little real significance. Still though, he needed rest and so, in the dusky light of day's end he came to a perfect little clearing atop a rocky ledge above the spot where a small spring gently trickled into the lake. It reminded him of a much smaller version of the place where he, Loka, Chako and Washtaka had camped on their first night in the low forest. He chuckled remembering how he leapt into the cold waters, dragging his friend in with him. He knew Washtaka was thoroughly engaged with securing the safety of the people and organizing the warriors. Smiling, he wished him well.

There was a brilliant moon appearing in the clear evening skies and he saw no need to restrict his appreciation of it with a fire. He ate a little of the provisions he found in his bag and spreading his robe about himself, he sat comfortably on the ground and watched the transition of day into night. He noticed with perfect clarity how the song of blackbirds and warblers gave way to crickets and the boisterous cacophony of frogs as the creatures of the day yielded up their world unto the night. Bats swooped in seemingly miraculous dips, turns and swirls after gossamer winged insects. In the distance, atop the moonlight ridge of the game trails, a mystical chorus of wolves echoed across the wide expanse of lake. The moon, now risen above the high ridge of great trees, illuminated the world of the night creatures. Something small, perhaps a weasel, darted about along the water's edge hunting for unwary frogs. The reeds and rushes and low bushes sparkled with the otherworldly flashes of a million fireflies. Nakosis loved this time. There was a special magic, a great power to the dusk. It was as though the full bright light of day held back the more secretive, more elusive, more intriguing elements of creation that chose to haunt this mysterious realm, especially under the aura of a full moon. This was the time when the veils between the two worlds had dissolved and the insipid world of the waking had been made more spiritually animate by the presence of night.

Nakosis, placing his back against the base of a large comforting tree, his thick sleeping robe around him, smiled deeply at the wondrous display of energy and life that abounded. He could detect the myriad life forces engaged in the primeval dance. They glowed in luminosities of varying intensities and faint colors like the ghosts of fireflies. He closed his eyes and the tiny glowing orbs remained faintly against the black backdrop. Then a faint blend of rainbow colors appeared, like a misty version of the great colors of the winter skies that sometimes appear from out of the cold north. He opened his eyes again and the rainbow was there still, softly, yet it permeated the entire view. It was dancing, vibrating behind all the multitude of glowing beings, growing in its power. He raised his hand to examine the expertly crafted weave of the fine sleeping robe that he now had wrapped himself in and he made a profound observation. A voice then spoke to him without words. It spoke to his heart and it told him that all he now saw was but like the many threads of one universal blanket. It is a blanket with no beginning and no end. It is being woven and unwoven continuously, from time without beginning. All life, all creatures were a strand of thread and the patterns they created were the weaving of their own design. They move, endlessly throughout the pattern, sometimes this color, sometimes that, none aware of the loom of desire and longing that bind them with the weft and warp of this endless fabric of time. Men especially think that they are free of the entanglement, that they are the weaver but they are only another thread, no less, no greater. This is their flaw and also their greatest suffering. They must see the oneness of all the blanket of existence and then they can untangle themselves, free themselves from the weave of life and leave the incessant circle in which they are caught. Nakosis realized that the blanket was woven from the threads of our own consciousness, our very own thoughts. Life after life, time after time, man has observed the blanket, marveled at it's beauty, complexity and constantly changed its pattern to suite his desires, all the while thinking that the secret to the blanket lay somehow in the arrangement of the infinite threads that made up its composition. But now Nakosis saw that, in fact, the secret lay not within the complexity of the blanket's weave at all. No, it was in the very minute spaces between the weave, between the threads, the very spaces themselves held the secret to liberation from the entanglement of the weave of life. As long as we continue to weave the threads of our own undertakings we bind ourselves within the complexity of the web of life, death and the suffering that accompanies it. It was a great revelation to Nakosis.

The most simple and now obvious solution to the entanglement of the circle of existence lay within his very own mind, his very thoughts were the loom that spun the threads of repetitive existence, of returning in the uncountable variety of forms that house the spirit. Thinking preceded actions and these actions carried an energy of their own that spun outward like ripples from a stone thrown in a pond. The ripples radiate out into another life after death and they even continue to ripple within the new form, carried on by the presence of spirit. It was all becoming very clear now. Thoughts, then actions in this life determined where in the weave he would be in the next life. The question now was how to be in-between the infinite threads of the weave of spirit, of the Great Mystery, while also being within the blanket of life? He held one corner of his blanket up to the brilliant blue moonlight and laughed while looking at the soft pattern along it's edge. He smiled as he pulled the beautiful woven sleeping robe over his shoulders and resting his head against the ancient tree he fell deeply asleep.

His dreams now took on a reality, clarity as never before. He could reach out and feel his surroundings and smell the air, fragrant with the scents of the lush forest and clear waters. In his dreaming world, the rainbow colored light of spiritual being permeated everything, illuminated all. It would reflect from the tiny glowing orbs of light that shone from every living thing. Nakosis understood that while every form of life glowed with its individual spirit presence, behind the grand performance, the magical dance of creation, destruction and re-creation was the ever-present connection of the Great Mystery. It wasn't that the Great Mystery was necessarily a separate magic beyond that of all other things. It was more that it was the collective magic of all things, the essence, the spiritual manifestation of the magic of sacred Mother Earth, of Hohapas also. In fact, Nakosis saw that even the sacred Mother was not independent of the omniscient magic of the 'great connection.' The Great Mystery was indeed great but it was, for Nakosis, gradually becoming less of a mystery.

The night had brought a soft, gentle rain. Sheltered under the boughs of the great tree, wrapped in his warm blanket, Nakosis was unfettered by the gentle drizzle. Morning sun's radiance upon the newly watered blanket of moss and ferns caused the air to burst with freshness and fragrance. Loons and ravens signaled their arrival unto the day and Nakosis fished at the water's edge. After his meal, he set upon the trail once more. He found the trail tougher going as it wound higher and steeper toward the distant foothills. He used his walking spear more as he leveraged his large bag higher on his back for better balance. As the day unfolded more rain fell and he was engulfed in a thick wet mist as clouds moved continuously down from the mountain. The cool freshness of the moisture was a welcome relief from the heat of the exertion under the weight of his pack.

Like all men of the mountain peoples he knew how to survive quite well with a minimal of tools and weapons, but as he was undoubtedly going to have to traverse the high wintery places, he had provisioned for these conditions by bringing along his heavy winter shirt, his thick winter moccasins and his fur lined leather mitts. These things along with his finely woven blanket, strips of leather cords for fastening, pieces of deer hide for patching and a little dry food were the only survival tools he required. The bag also held his small drum, the ancient rattle and the beautiful headdress. His small satchel contained his bow drill; a handful of fine tinder, a few bone needles and some sewing sinew, his small knife for skinning and cleaning and spare arrowheads. It also could be attached to his large bag if needed. When travelling, he would attach his bow and quiver to his bag with leather thongs. His bow was itself wrapped in oiled leather for protection, its sinew string unhooked to relieve tension. In this way he could leave his large bag at a chosen site and venture out lightly equipped with just his small satchel and his bow and quiver for a days hunting and fishing. All in all it wasn't too heavy for a strong young man and his spear helped him lift his frame over the rocks, fallen trees and debris along the game trail. His trusty spear would be his primary weapon should an enemy appear, but in this wild and ancient world he hadn't detected any signs of other people, nor did he detect the threat from dangerous predators. Nakosis had faith in his spirit guides to alert him to any danger and to protect him from harm. As such, he could focus upon his travel and the blessing of feeling his spirit at one with the magnificent world around him. As the day progressed he could feel a growing anticipation, a sense of exploration taking him over, like a child discovering a new cave or a waterfall. He needed to know what lay beyond the next visible point of his view and he pushed forward, propelled by this newfound vigor and curiosity.

The clouds were moving very fast now, flying past like flocks of great white and gray birds. Just ahead, through a small portal in the smoky mist, he caught a brief glimpse of sunlight, a brilliant ray of gold and green. He pushed himself upward, his hands clutching his spear near the ground and his knees almost touching the thick forest floor as he all but crawled to the high ridge above the trail. He could hear the beat of his own heart drumming in his chest and his breath grasping at the moist mountain air. Suddenly he reached the top and fell to his knees while releasing the load from his back. He stared out in complete awe at the scene before him. A broad valley, free of the clouds, was bathed in sunshine and it was a magical, wondrous world with a green lushness, as he had never laid eyes upon. The trees were different here. As the forest descended into the vast world below, the giant evergreens of the heights gave way to broad-leaved trees of great variety. They could easily rival any of the great red bark trees of the mountains in their height and girth. Their trunks were as wide as a small lodge and they towered above the dense forest floor. Clouds of birds lifted off from the canopies and their many songs echoed to where Nakosis now stood in wonder. Huge vines as thick as a man's arm wove around the trees like giant serpents. Behind this amazing vista was a backdrop of towering mountains. Snow capped peaks thrust out of the belt of clouds that hung just above the sun-soaked green world below. Unbelievable waterfalls, too many to count, appeared to come straight out of the sky as they plummeted from unseen sources high in the clouds. Tremendous plumes of mist rose from where they erupted into the luxuriant forest beneath them and wafted high and wide, mingling with the white clouds above the mighty canopy. In the shafts of brilliant sunlight every droplet seemed to be alive with tiny rainbows of light. Nakosis could see where this valley world spread into the horizon and seemed to disappear into low clouds at the foot of a more distant range of blue colored mountains. It was as though these mighty mountains were the guardians and protectors of this hidden world. This was completely unexpected and Nakosis realized that, as astounding as this world was, it was not the mountain of fire and he would somehow have to find a way either through or around this astonishing realm of trees, water and mist.

He returned to the trail and, following it a short distance to the crest of a ridge, he looked out to see if it offered a direction around the valley. It appeared to descend into the green world below. No doubt the deer that blazed this trail sought the cornucopia of succulent foliage in this lush paradise, thought Nakosis. He was right. The trail clearly made its way zigzagging down the overgrown mountainside to the valley bottom. Nakosis, his breath returned, now adjusted his gear and began the long descent using his spear for balance. Several times he slipped on the wet mossy path, sliding some distance before grasping a branch, root or vine to stay his fall. He desperately did his best to try to remain quiet, but the trail was exasperating as every other step was becoming precarious. With much diligence he gradually made his way to where the going was a little better, the ground somewhat easier to get a foot hold on.

The climb down took far longer than he had expected and he knew he would soon have to find a place to camp, but he would have to make the forest floor first. There was no way he could spend the night exposed on this game trail on the mountainside. Either by luck or the intervention of spirits he soon discovered that the trail ran somewhat parallel for a while, making a much more gradual decent into the tangled maze of dense forest. Many other smaller game trails appeared to come from many directions to join with this main trail and enter the forest at the base of the rock on which he now finally stood. He wanted to rest now that he'd made it down the slippery slope, but he had to push on to find a decent place to spend the night.

Entering this forest was like stepping through the doors of some great sacred lodge. The vibrational energy of life itself was so strong that Nakosis had to pause and offer his respect and leave a small offering of sacred herbs. He

222

asked that the spirit guardians of this wondrous place take no offense at his passing through and that they, hopefully, guide his steps. Someone must have listened, he thought, for it wasn't long before he sighted a tiny little clearing off to one side of the trail near a small trickling brook. He soon unloaded his heavy pack and in doing so felt a sudden lightness that, for a heartbeat, gave him the sensation of actually lifting off the ground. He stretched his sore limbs and arched his aching back, all the while keeping a cautious, trained eye on these unfamiliar surroundings. Nakosis could see shafts of daylight through gaps in the roof of green above and caught glimpses of sunlight on the distant slope, but it was growing dark quickly in the shadow of these great trees.

He arranged his belongings, keeping his trusty spear in arms reach and removing only his robe from the top of his big bag, closed it with the leather thongs again so as to be able to make a quick getaway should the need arise. He thought about his having beseeched the local guardians for safe passage and their seemingly quick approval at finding this perfect little clearing, yet he also reasoned that his own spirit protectors were perhaps best serving him by keeping him reminded of the need to always be prepared for any contingency.

He so wanted to have a fire to warm his aches and pains and to cook the fish he'd procured earlier in the day, but here in this great forest he soon discovered that, while he was within the lushest abundance of trees he'd ever seen, finding dead, dry wood was not easy. Everything here bore a thin coating of moisture. The steady rain that was directed here by the lay of the mountain and the prevailing winds made this place the humid paradise that it was. As well, the heavy mountain mists rolled down from the heights like a blanket of white to embrace the forest in a cloud so thick that it impeded visibility for even a short distance. Nakosis did manage to find a few dead fern fronds and a couple of dry twigs, enough to get a small fire going. It took much searching in the fast approaching dark to locate enough dry branches to be able to cook his diminutive evening meal. But the fire did offer some sense of security and comfort and its warmth in this cool, damp air was soothing on his body and he soon drifted into a much-needed sleep.

He wasn't sure if it was the snap of the branch or the blood-curdling cry that launched him to his feet, his spear in hand. His senses exploded to alertness and his heart pounded at the unseen presence. His every fiber strained to acquire some knowledge of the source, his eyes straining to detect anything in the blackness of the surrounding night, his tiny fire now nothing more than small glowing embers. He willed his body to freeze every movement and his heart to slow so that his ears might pick up the direction of some indicator of movement. He turned to face each direction ever so slowly so that anything watching would, hopefully, be challenged to locate him. Nothing! Could it have all been a dream? This thought was soon dispelled when again an unmistakable screech in the dark raised the hairs on Nakosis' neck. It sounded close this time but in these trees, he rationalized, the location was hard to determine. He knew of no owl or animal that produced this cry in the night. To Nakosis' panicking mind it resembled more of a deep growl than a human scream. It was more than unsettling. He stood with his back to the large tree under whose shelter he was sleeping and he held his spear at waist level and there he remained, listening and watching for the rest of the night. He had fallen asleep at some point and slid down the base of the tree to lay folded against its wide trunk. It was in this surprised condition that he awoke and sprung to a defensive standing position like a loosed arrow. Nothing but bird song and minute shafts of morning sunlight greeted his awakening. Only once he had ascertained that he appeared to be in no immediate danger did he allow himself to move and survey the surrounding area further with his tired eyes.

It didn't take him long at all to heft his supplies on his back and make a hasty retreat further from the spot. For the next while he wandered through the maze of jungle, both in awed by its splendor and grandeur and tense against an unseen, unknown possible danger. It was hard for him to gage direction since he could not get any visual bearings on surrounding mountains. For that matter even the sun was, at times, hard to place. He knew, from his initial observation up on the ridge, the direction he needed to go to reach the distant blue mountains. He was perplexed as to why, in his spirit journeying, he had not been shown this vast jungle from his magical flight. For the first time in a long while this caused him to have doubt as to his abilities or whether he was indeed 'chosen' by the spirits. As he sat to rest, he mulled these thoughts over in his head and just allowing this slight hesitation to enter his mind caused him tremendous agitation. He struggled with the thoughts of unworthiness and inadequacy. He was unsure of his spiritual destiny and now questioned his ending up in this place so far from his people and so alone. He had been filled with confidence and purpose back on the island. There was nothing he could not achieve with his spirits to guide and watch over him. But now, here, in this unfamiliar world, he began to feel alone and that allowed fear to enter his heart. As he looked about him, his breathing becoming faster, he imagined all sorts of things stalking him in this eerie forest. He recalled the tales of the dark walkers, cannibal beings of immense strength and powers. Was that the cry he'd heard during the night? His body was perspiring heavily now and he became aware that he was shaking. It was as though a wave of terror suddenly swept over him. He bolted from the spot, running into the thicket of vines and ferns. His only belonging, the spear, he desperately clutched. He'd abandoned everything else on the path. He growled and yelled at invisible things he imagined were hiding behind every tree and bracken, lashing out with his spear, shredding the foliage around him like a mad man. He railed at the guardian spirits whom he was now convinced had deluded him, luring him into their grasp like a spider into a web. He thought some creature was playing tricks on him, toying with him, keeping just out of his sight and spear range and so he dashed madly in circles, screaming and stabbing at every tree and bush until a loud snap as the shaft shattered against the massive trunk of a giant tree. One half spun back, deflected off the tree and the other half, still clutched in his hand, flew skyward as Nakosis tumbled forward, propelled by the action of his mad attack. He bore the brunt of the flying piece squarely in the face.

He knew not how long he'd lain there amid the wreckage of his tirade. His first sensation was of the wet warmth of blood on his face. He raised a hand to wipe it and stared in shock at the sticky redness of his fingers. He turned his head and looked about at the trampled undergrowth and the shattered spear at his side. He could barely recall his actions. Things seemed unreal and otherworldly. He pulled himself to his elbows and tried to reconstruct how it was he now lay prone and injured. Gradually he remembered his fear driven panic. As the delusional fog cleared, he felt pangs of guilt and remorse at his surrendering to such juvenile emotions. How did he allow himself to yield to such fear? Where, in fact, had such an overwhelming sense of dread come from? He had panicked and fled from nothing, no real tangible threat. Nothing had truly presented a danger other than in his own confused mind.

He realized that he had been so preoccupied with reaching the mountain of fire that he had not allowed himself the customary respite from the daily trek to dwell in the silence and solitude of his daily practice of sitting silently and 'listening' to the spirit world. He usually sat in this meditation for a few moments each day upon awakening and often in the evenings before sleep. Sometimes it didn't amount to more than an acknowledgement of something beyond himself, yet within himself, something deep and intrinsically powerful. Once he tapped into the tranquility of what Loka called 'dwelling within the spirit mind' he would try to remain there until the waking world intruded too much to ignore. Often, in this place, he would receive amazing insights and a deep understanding would come to him. His spiritual destiny would be made clear, his path defined. At the least, even if the spirits did not speak, he rested in a calm space unknown in his waking world. Nakosis now brought himself to his knees and took stock of the damage. He wiped the blood from his face with a handful of leaves and slowly stood up. He was not too dizzy. That was a good sign at least. He took several shaky steps to one of the multitude of tiny springs that dotted the forest floor and washed his face in its cold waters. Once the ripples had subsided he tried to see his reflection in the still part of the stream. He had a small cut on his forehead, but it was not bleeding profusely. He was noticing the beginnings of a large bump forming however. "Fool," he said aloud. He picked up the broken piece of his spear and examined the fine flint blade. Fortunately he wasn't aiming well when he thrust it at the large tree and the point had not struck. It, at least, was salvageable and could be re-attached to a new shaft, but this would eat into his time. He felt unarmed without his main weapon of defense and would now have to work on finding a suitable piece of wood with which to make a new shaft. This place had already proven hard to find even enough dead wood for a mediocre fire. Getting a good piece for his spear would be almost impossible.

Nakosis retraced his steps back to where he had abandoned his things on the narrow trail. In his mindless state he had run much further than he'd imagined. His keen eye for tracking led him through broken shrubs and trampled ferns. The trail was easy to detect. Nakosis was alarmed by the wild, scattered, rambling pattern he had blazed in the thick, green blanket of the forest floor. Soon he reached the spot on the path where he was certain he'd begun his fear fuelled tirade, but his belongings were nowhere in sight. He began to panic again but willed himself into a calmer state and pushed on further down the trail until he reached a point he knew, beyond a doubt, was past where he'd begun his mindless romp. Now he really became worried! His rational side kicked in, telling him that perhaps he discarded his things a bit further off the beaten trail and so he turned around and once again scoured the path for any tell tale sign.

As he approached the initial suspected spot, Nakosis stopped and ever so patiently scanned the ground for some indicator as to where he may have gone. It was then he saw the footprint. The clearly defined mark of a bare human foot! He lowered, raising the half shaft of his broken spear! His heart once again drummed the all too familiar beat of panic as he scanned the surroundings. Nothing moved and the steady chorus of bird song told him that no one was nearby. Now he fell to his knees, frantically looking for some hint as to the direction of travel the thief or thieves may have taken. It didn't take long for him to find more prints. It seemed like only one person. By the tracks they seemed to be slightly smaller than Nakosis and he could discern a slight difference in the soft black earth of the added weight of his belongings. The ground, being so thick with greenery, made the tracking easy once he'd discovered the thief's route. The thief stopped only a short distance from the trail and appeared to drop the bag and reload it before moving on.

Nakosis was filled with thoughts of the possibilities of what he might encounter and what he may have to undergo to retrieve his belongings. He could not continue without his precious bag nor did he wish to try to survive with half a broken spear. He knew, when he finally caught up with the culprit, that it might result in a fight to the death. He reasoned that he had no choice, but he prayed that he wouldn't have to. The thief had a good head start on Nakosis, as he'd lain unconscious for an undetermined amount of time, but the thief was also handicapped by the weight of the stolen possessions. Nakosis fought to keep his panic at bay and he slipped into a fighting, survival mode. He knew he'd have to overtake the thief well before darkness fell or risk loosing everything. He focused his stare on the ground ahead, his eyes easily following the beaten path of crushed and broken ferns and small growth. He now picked up his pace. The ground was, for the most part, somewhat flat as they were now on the forest floor.

Now he began a hunter's run, not too fast but a quick and steady trot. For a moment he flashed upon his race to alert the Quick Water's people about the Black Face's attack. To Nakosis this was now equally as important. Something caught his eye in the undergrowth and he froze, trying not to pant too audibly as he strained to see what it was from behind the cover of trees. He rushed to the spot and picked up his discarded satchel. Quickly he opened it and with a sigh of relief noticed its entire contents were intact. It must have fallen unnoticed from the back of the fleeing culprit. Reaching inside he retrieved his rawhide sling from the bottom of the small bag. He snatched up a few small stones from the bed of another one of the tiny creeks that riddled the forest floor, pausing to gulp a handful of cold water to salve his burning throat.

As he stooped to drink he heard a noise just ahead in the trees. He remained ever so still. Adroit and silent as the flight of an owl, he loaded his sling with a round stone while quietly moving forward at a low crouch. He'd done this so many times that he could load a sling while running, not miss a step and hurl it to its target with deadly accuracy. He positioned himself behind the trunk of a large tree and slowly peered around the thick gray bark. There were very tall ferns partly obscuring his view, but he could make out the form of someone crouched over his bag, removing its contents. Nakosis stepped away from the tree, held his breath as he raised his sling arm back and sent the stone to its target with such speed that the figure barely had time to begin turning when the stone caught him squarely in the back of the head, sending him sprawling across the big bag.

Nakosis now leapt like a frightened deer, half spear raised in his hand and in one great rush he pounced upon the still form of the prone thief. He was bleeding from the side of the head where the stone had hit its mark, his long black hair covering his face and upper back as he sprawled face down over Nakosis' possessions. Nakosis saw a large knife lying on the ground beside the enemy. He must have heard him set the stone to flight and reached for the knife just as the rock hit. Nakosis, holding his spear on the body in one hand, grabbed the figure by one foot and slowly pulled it back off the bag. Once he was satisfied that the thief was not conscious and was off the bag, he bent down and, grabbing his shoulder, he rolled the culprit over to get his first glimpse of the first human being he'd encountered, other than the Black Faces, that were not of his people.

What he saw made him step back several paces, his mouth open in sheer surprise! There sprawled out in the moss and bloodied ferns, was the body of a young woman. She was naked save for a breechcloth and the knife Nakosis had retrieved. Nakosis again scanned the surrounding terrain, certain that someone so lightly provisioned must surely have had others nearby or have a village very close. He quickly checked her condition and was very relieved to find that she still breathed. He had not wanted to have a violent encounter with anyone, much less a woman! He gathered some moss, choosing the driest he could find in this place, and after washing the clotting, dry blood from her wound; he bandaged her head with the dry moss and tied it in place with some strips of deer hide. He propped her up on his bag, raising her head into a seated position to stop the flow of blood. Satisfied this strange female would not pose a threat for a while, Nakosis circled the area quietly and covertly searching for any sign of the woman's possible companions or any other human presence.

The woman's tracks continued in both directions, past where he'd overtaken her. Cautiously Nakosis followed the weak trail to where a small bank just higher than a man had cut into a rise. Two great trees had succumbed to wind, erosion and time and had toppled to lay with their wide roots upturned on the top of the earthen bank, with their huge limbs resting on the ground slightly below. Their great trunks lay parallel a fair height above the ground. Someone, most likely the strange woman, had used this to make a shelter, piling branches and layers of large broad leaves across the fallen trees. It was surprisingly efficient. There was room to stand, height enough to safely have a small fire and the leaves were expertly layered so as to provide a waterproof roof above. Nakosis poked about the boughs strewn on the floor for bedding. There was a hastily constructed bow and a few arrows, several sticks of various sizes that looked to have been used for digging, a few small snares made from thin pieces of hide and a deer hide shirt that looked very hastily made by it's appearance. It was more just a skin with a hole in the middle for pulling over one's head and a strip to tie about the waist.

Whatever the reason for her being here, Nakosis concluded, she must have arrived with little to no provisions or perhaps she somehow was separated from others and became lost and stranded. He decided this was a safer place for both him and the stranger to wait out the night. He first carried the still unconscious woman and then his recovered belongings to the lean-to. Then he prepared a small fire and, after checking on her breathing, he left with his bow to seek food.   At least this forest yielded an abundance of game. It took him no time to procure a grouse and a rabbit. He returned to find the woman had fallen onto her side. When he rushed to right her she let out a slight moan. A good sign at least, he thought. He checked the bandage and was pleased to see that the dry moss had done the trick and clotted the blood, stopping her bleeding. He gently rinsed the wound and replaced her bandage, put more wood on the fire and set about cleaning the game. Until the fire was throwing more heat he carefully draped his warm blanket over her mostly naked frame. He couldn't help but notice that despite being a little thin she was in excellent shape and indeed quite beautiful. Her build was muscular and sinewy. Whoever she was she had been leading a very active strenuous life, much like the warrior women of his people, but she had a much darker complexion than the people of the Three Rivers. Her skin had a fine sheen and reminded him a little of a faint ochre stain. Her hair was raven black and shiny and full to her thin waist. The only decoration or ornamentation she wore was a lone skull of what looked to be an eagle, painted red and hung around her neck on a single plain leather cord strung through the eye sockets. Nakosis reached to examine it but stopped, realizing it may be her talisman and that he should respect it. With the girl now warmly wrapped and secure, Nakosis prepared the meal.

Night engulfed the little shelter very fast and a light rain began to fall. Nakosis was very grateful for the woman's well-crafted shelter. She hadn't moved very much and he was now getting concerned about her recovery. He thought about the situation and decided both him and this unknown, injured woman could use the blessing and connection of the spirits. He had neglected to keep his connection and now both of them were paying the price. He carefully unwrapped his beautiful headdress, respectfully groomed the delicate feathers, running his hands over the ancient teeth and great bear claws. He laid it upon his shirt along side Quansa's Raven handled rattle. He lit his smudge of sacred herbs and offered it to the four directions, mother earth and father sky. He bathed the headdress, rattle, himself and then the young woman in the sacred smoke and slowly began rattling. He asked the spirits to help this woman and asked that her guardians attend to her now and help her to return to the waking world. Nakosis donned his headdress and began the ritual he had now grown very familiar with.

When journeying he felt complete communion with the power of sacred mother earth and the inner tranquility that can only come when one is in to- tal harmony. This was where Nakosis was most at home, most himself, most complete. He sat by the small fire and swayed gently to the rattle's cadence, his eyes closed and his lips softly muttering the sacred words of the spirit's tongue. Loka had said that these were not words in the sense that we think of talking to each other. They had no meaning in the waking world. It was only when one had broken through to the other side and become one with the spirits that the words came naturally, of their own forming. One spoke them without conscious connection, the Shaman's inner spirit connecting through sacred tongue to the world of spirit around him. Chako had simply said, 'It is the words the spirits like to hear.'

He soon felt the familiar presence and call of his old companion Raven. Raven was usually the first harbinger of his entering the spirit world. It al- ways comforted Nakosis to hear his black winged brother. Soon the brilliant yellow eyes flashed before him from out of a mist of swirling dark. Panther was now here. The spiraling tunnel of dark gradually began to lighten and Nakosis felt the brush of a great wing against his face, a whirl of heavy wind buffeted him and a shrill, echoing cry resounded. Eagle! The lightness then quickly expanded and Nakosis broke through into splendid blinding blue sky. A voice came to him, speaking not to his ears but to his heart. It told him that his path was not his alone and that he would soon have a decision to make. While he should follow his spiritual destiny he must also remember that his life is in the service of others.

He awoke still sitting up, his body still gently swaying in a slow circle. His hand had ceased to shake the rattle, although he still held it. The fire was very low and above it's insipid glow, bats swooped in rapid circles. The waning moon cast very little light past the dense interlocking tree canopy above. He took a deep breath and arching his back he exhaled a few times to revive his external senses. He reached into his pouch and placed a small pinch of smoking herb onto the coals and gave thanks. He chucked a few pieces of small broken branches on the fire and when they burst into flame the tiny shelter came to life with the glow of the firelight. Nakosis turned to check on the young woman. She was gone! He spun around to see her in the darkened back of the lean-to, his blanket clutched tightly in her hands, holding it in front of her like some sort of shield, peering terrified from over its woven edge. The look was one of complete disorientation, confusion and panic.

He had no idea how long she had been awake and what she may have witnessed. He tried to imagine what she must have been going through and he tried to appear as unthreatening as possible. He turned very slowly and smiled at her. This had the opposite effect and she pushed herself further against the frail wall of branches and leaves. He stopped, removed his headdress and held out his hands; palms up to her, indicating he held no weapons. Then he ever so slowly dug out the gourd of water and stretching out he placed it as close to her as he could. Then, without looking at her he moved slowly to the opposite side of the fire. He took some of the cooked meat and laying it upon a large broad leaf he slowly placed it beside the gourd and retreated to the place across the small fire.

"You were hurt and I bandaged your head," he said, pointing to his own forehead then to hers. She reached up and felt the bandage, but her look remained puzzled. Nakosis continued, "I was very worried about you. I am happy you are awake now. Are you all right? What is your name?"

She reached for the food and water and ripped off a hunk of the grouse and washed it back with a long drink of water. She stared at Nakosis with a look of great astonishment.

Then much more slowly he said, "Do you understand me?"

She released her grip and let the blanket fall to her waist, her firm breasts protruding through the veil of her shining black hair and the firelight reflecting in her deep eyes. For a moment Nakosis could not but stare back, fascinated by her beauty.

She finally spoke, "You…you…were dead I thought!" She paused, gulping more water then she continued, "That is… I saw you… there in the clearing, lying on the ground. You had blood." She pointed at his forehead. "I kicked you but you did not move. There was much broken about you like you had fought with someone."

Nakosis didn't offer an explanation but asked, "How is it you came to be here?" What is your Name? I am called Nakosis."

She didn't answer. She grabbed at more meat and ate it fast. Seeing her pitiful excuse for a bow he wondered how long she'd gone without decent food. She was gathering her senses and looked about her taking in the scene and piecing together the events that placed him and her together in her lean-to. She looked to where her small bow was stashed and felt relief to see it still there. She was gauging Nakosis, studying him, determining his motives. He sensed this and smiled at her.

"Look," he said, "I didn't mean to cause you any harm. I didn't realize you were a woman. That is…I mean…I can see that you are, of course, a woman."

Nakosis pointed at her breasts and then immediately felt embarrassed and obtuse for having done so. "I just thought you were robbing me. I saw my things had been stolen and I came after you. I will not hurt you."

"You are a spirit talker!" she blurted.

"Ah…spirit talker?" Nakosis said. "Yes, I suppose you could say that. But I think it is more that I am a spirit listener!"

"Is that why you are here also? Have you come here to commune with the spirits? Are you on some quest? How is it that you are here in this forest alone?"

Not taking her eyes from this stranger, she pulled herself up and wrapped the blanket further over her shoulders and repositioned herself against the wall of the small shelter. As she moved she let out a soft moan and Nakosis immediately moved toward her asking if she was all right.

She smiled at him and raised her hand, "I will live spirit talker, don't be concerned." She had another piece of grouse and drink from the gourd and after heaving a sigh she began to explain the circumstances that caused their paths to cross.

CHAPTER 18
SHEENKA'S STORY

She placed her one hand over her chest and said, "I am called Sheenka. My people's village is several days journey from here. I lived with my father, mother, younger brother and younger sister. It is not a big village. There is one man there, a spirit talker like you." She thought for a moment and then continued, "No, he is not like you, Nakosis. You are a true spirit talker. I have witnessed your work. I was awake when you were with the spirits. I also heard and felt them. I, like you, have their blessing. You see that is why I am here. This man, our spirit talker, he is very powerful in our village, but he does not have the blessing of the spirits. Many people fear him and he has several men to do his biding. No one dare challenge him, lest their families suffer. He controls everything and he demands gifts and work from the others. These he shares with his men so they support him. The people have long suspected that he had no powers. Then once when my aunt became sick and the people called him to heal her he made some show of spirit talking, but he could not make my aunt well. He said it was because her family had not offered the spirits the right respect by honoring him with gifts. His men took most of their meager belongings. The family came to me because I have had the ear of the spirits ever since I was a young girl but, because I was not a boy, very few would acknowledge my gift. Our old Shaman, Holeeaho, saw that I was different and in secret he gave me some instruction, but could not publically acknowledge me. As I got older I found that the spirits spoke to me easier and more often. I would go into the forest alone and away from the village so I could freely journey as you do, Nakosis. It was through my journeying that my ability became clearer to me and the spirits made me see that I must use their gift for my people. So when my aunts' family came to me to help I went to her hut and I asked the sprits to help, just as I saw you do for me. When I was done and the spirits released me, my aunt woke from her fever and within two days she was much better. Soon everyone knew of this and the 'evil pretender' came and accused me of being a dark witch. He said I was the reason for the sickness in the first place and that the spirits had told him that I must be banished from the village or that the spirits would abandon the people altogether. My father faced him and refused and his men beat him terribly. I knew they would kill us all if I stayed so I agreed to leave. The next day they walked me to the edge of our village. My father could barely stand as my brother and mother held him up and they were all crying. The men stripped me of my clothes and the pretender would not let me take any weapons, food or clothes other than a small deer hide that my mother insisted they let me have. Only when my little sister ran up to hug me did she push my father's knife into my hand beneath the hide and I turned and ran." Sheenka then paused for more water. Nakosis moved closer to her, pulling up a seat of boughs and leaning in to hear more.

She smiled at him and continued. "I ran through the forest all of that first day. The pretender, his name is Kleeashto, but I don't like to say his name because I don't want to give it power by speaking it. He said his men would leave the next morning and they would track me and that if I was found before nightfall then they would kill me. I knew they would do other things to me also. After the second night I continued to move fast because I did not believe he would let me live." Sheenka paused in thought. Her face looked pained with the memory of the ordeal. "If I had been a man and faced him, then perhaps the other villagers may have stood with my family and it would be he who would have been banished."

Nakosis could hear the anger in her voice now as it quivered with rage and regret.

She collected herself and continued. "I don't remember how many days I kept moving, always looking behind, always expecting to hear the party of hunters.

I was the oldest child and my father treated me very much like a boy and he would take me hunting with him. I was always a good tracker and hunter so when I ran I moved in a crooked line, over rock and along streams to avoid leaving too much sign. I never went through grassy meadows, where my trail would be easy to see, always going around on hard ground. In this way I covered much distance, but as I was not heading in any direction I had no idea where I was. I could not get lost, as I had nowhere to go, so I just followed my instincts. Eventually I came to a high ridge and looked down upon this world. I remembered that my people spoke of this place. They sometimes called it the 'hidden valley of the Yeshta'. It is a place where no one of my village would ever come. To us it is a sacred place, but also a very fearful place. It is forbidden for people to be here. I knew I would be safe here –at least from the people." She looked into the darkness of the night and reached to place more sticks on the little fire.

"If this place is known to you, then do you know how to best reach the line of blue mountains?" Nakosis asked. "And what is the Yeshta you mentioned?"

"You have not heard of the Yeshta? Where are your people from, Nakosis? Tell me now, how is it that you also come to be here in this place if you also were not driven out or running from something?"

Nakosis smiled at her and said, "Ah, a question answered with a question. Very well. We'll come back to that and I will tell you about myself." Nakosis told Sheenka of his journeying, of his mentoring under the two great Shamans, of his visions and their directing him, driving him onward. He did not divulge the whole story, however. She needn't know about the Black Faces, Taku or too many details about his people or the villages. It was wise to reveal only what she needed to hear, he thought. He purposefully kept all mention of Hohapas a secret. He finished his abridged story with telling her he was trying to reach a place he knew only as the 'mountain of fire.' Sheenka let out an audible gasp at the mention of this place. Her dark eyes widened in surprise at his speaking of the mountain of fire.

"You know this place, Sheenka?" Nakosis was clearly excited at the prospect. She did not immediately respond and was now clearly agitated, but Nakosis begged her, "Please, it is important that I find this place. Please Sheenka, tell me what you know!" She raised her palm to him to stop his interrogative tone, turning from him slightly. "I'm sorry," he said. "You are no doubt still in pain and I should not ask so much of you now. Please rest."

"No," Sheenka continued, "it is not that, Nakosis. It is…well…you see…I also have had a vision. It came to me when I last journeyed in my secret place, away from my people. I heard the sweetest sound, like a songbird and a voice that spoke to my spirit. I understood somehow that this place, the fire mountain, was important to me in some way or, at least, that in time it would somehow become so." Sheenka looked seriously at Nakosis. "And now," she said, "The spirits have seen to make our paths cross. How else can it be?"

Nakosis nodded in understanding, adding, "Yes, it would seem to be the spirit's design to have our paths collide."

Sheenka chuckled and touching her bandaged head remarked, "I wish they would not have collided so violently!" She had a sense of humor at least, Nakosis reflected, smiling.

He leaned closer to her. "But, back to what you were saying. What is this thing you spoke of, the Yeshta, I think you said?"

Her eyes were growing very heavy and she opened them a little more as she spoke. "Tomorrow I will tell you more, but I cannot remain awake."

"Please, here" Nakosis said, removing his heavy shirt from his bag he placed the heavy sack against the wall and bade her to rest against it, helping her onto the bag. She placed her arms around his neck. As he lifted her slightly and shuffled her over the blanket dropped to the ground. Her closeness, the brush of her thick black hair, her sweet scent and the warm touch of her firm breast against his was so deeply sensual, so very erotic that he nearly dropped her. As he lowered her she held on just a heartbeat or two longer than necessary and when they released each other she looked him directly in the eyes and smiled. Nakosis had to turn away he was so moved by her radiant beauty and her affable charm.

She took the blanket from his hands and very, very slowly raised it over her breasts and gently let it fall across her shoulders, all the while not taking her eyes from him. He was uncomfortable and she knew it. Perhaps this one really is a

dark witch he thought. She certainly had worked some spell upon him.

"Goodnight Nakosis." She said. Then, before he could respond in kind she opened her eyes wide and sat up with a sudden urgency saying, "But tomorrow, Nakosis we must not stay here! We have to move at first light. You have made too much noise here." Then she was fast asleep.

Nakosis tended to the fire, secured the left over rabbit and piece of grouse away from prowling predators and rearranged his things before retiring. He lay there wondering about the amazing circumstances that brought her to him. 'Nothing happens without design,' Loka had said and so it would seem to be true. He thought deeply and long on her having a similar spirit calling and her having felt the pull to the sacred mountain. Part of him was displeased that she shared his vision. It meant that he was not as special as he thought himself to be. He held his tiny sacred power bag tightly to his chest, over his heart and he felt the presence of Loka and Chako guiding his thoughts toward the fulfillment of his spiritual destiny. A teaching from his old master came to mind reminding him that the greatest lesson a Shaman can have is humility. Then the last words the spirits spoke this very night was that he must remember that he was to be of service to others. They said also that he would have a decision to make. He knew that decision would involve Sheenka, but how he could not predict. He also thought about the woman's story, her expulsion from her village and her life long companions and family, everything familiar. He knew the pain of separation and the grief of loss and he felt a deep sudden empathy with this beautiful woman asleep in his blanket. Whatever powers that may have influenced the crossing of their paths one thing seemed certain to Nakosis and that was that he knew he would not abandon Sheenka, that their lives were inexorably tied by binds that transcend this waking world. He wondered no less about this mysterious thing called Yeshta. Then he too was asleep.

When Nakosis awoke it was with a sudden lurch from his prone position, upright and glaring at the surrounding shelter as though startled, but he had absolutely no recollection of having heard nor dreamed anything to warrant such an awakening. Sheenka was not there and he felt a sudden panic at not seeing her. He willed himself to remain calm until he noticed that Taku's bow and quiver were also missing. Now he gave way to an anger that sprang him quickly to his feet. He raced to get his belongings into the big bag, thankful that she appeared to have taken nothing else. He noticed, as he took a quick inventory that her deer hide shirt was also gone. "How could I have been so stupid?" he muttered to himself. "Sly as a fox that one was. Completely fooled me, she did." Just as he was pushing the last of his things into the bag he heard a footfall behind him and he spun, frantically looking for his broken half spear.

Sheenka stood before him, his great bow in her hand and a fresh grouse in the other. She casually tossed the grouse to the ground beside the fire and laid his bow and quiver by his large bag.

"Oh, very good, you're awake," she said, "and you're packed and ready to move. Let's eat this bird first, though. Then we'd better cover some ground."

Nakosis couldn't speak for a moment. Her actions were not expected. He was prepared to be angry. Sheenka looked up at him as she quickly plucked the grouse and placed it on the spit.

"Oh, I hope you don't mind." she said, pointing at the bow now unstrung and resting safe and secure once more. "That twig of mine is all but useless."

"Oh…no…ah…not at all." Nakosis stammered, unconvincingly. "Thank you for getting us the meal." He added.

Sheenka smiled and said, "We should eat while we move."

"What gives you cause for leaving so suddenly, Sheenka? You said you were safe from those hunting you here in this valley, did you not?"

She rotated the grouse on the green willow spit, obviously gathering her words. "You remember I said I would tell of the Yeshta? Well now is perhaps the best time." The telling of it seemed to make her very nervous and Nakosis noticed in her a heightened sense of caution and vigilance. "The Yeshta are said to live in the mountains around this valley. They are believed to sometimes hunt here."

"But," Nakosis interrupted, "who are these people. I have seen no sign of any people here at all!"

"Not people," she continued, "well, not really. They are half-people, Nakosis, half-man, half-beast, as tall as a great bear when it stands and as powerful. They look to be a man, but have bodies covered in dark hair."

Nakosis suddenly remembered the tales, saying, "Yes, yes I have heard of these creatures! The people who told me of the story called them bear men or man bear or the bear people, something like that. Do you believe these beings really live Sheenka?"

She shrugged her shoulders as she tended the roasting bird. "My people believe it, so much so that not one of them will come near to this place. It is told that they can rip a man in two with their hands!"

Nakosis suddenly became very excited. "If that is true then they are said to be the guardians of the mountain of fire." He stammered. She looked at him puzzled. He explained, "Don't you understand what this means? We are closer to the sacred mountain than I thought. Somewhere very near there is a way to the high world of summer snow. Across this place lies the sacred mountain. I have seen it in my vision, Sheenka!"

She placed the bird closer to the coals. "This is all fine, Nakosis, but you will not be so excited if we are discovered by the beasts. Your journey will end here, now, quick and bloody. We must go."

Nakosis was skeptical. "Has anyone of your people ever even seen one of these 'Yeshta'?" She grabbed one of the large leaves and pulling off a chunk of the bird she handed it to Nakosis.

"Yes." She said with just a little pride in her voice. "Once in my grandfather's time they hunted here thinking they had discovered a magic world of plenty, game so numerous and easy to catch, healing plants, plenty of sweet water and the winters were mild. Then on the third night they heard the beasts crashing through the woods around their camp. The hunting party was terrified as the tops of the trees swayed as the creatures bashed the trunks in anger like some massive bull moose in the rutting season. Their cries were deafening and terrifying."

"Cries!" shouted Nakosis. "What did the cries sound like?" There was a moment of silence as she studied his face.

"You have heard them?" she demanded. "Nakosis!" Sheenka was now looking angered. "Tell me!"

"I only know I heard *something*. I can't say what. An owl perhaps?" He said, knowing she knew better. He was becoming a little concerned himself. Again he asked, "So what did the hunters say the cry sounded like?"

"Like someone being tortured and growling like a bear at the same time. It was not a sound made by any man, it was something ghostly. The hunters kept a vigil through the night. The beasts seemed to stay from the light of the fire but they could see shapes in the dark, circling the camp. They fled at first light and as they looked back they saw the Yeshtas at the edge of the clearing. They said they were more than twice a man in height and completely covered in hair and that they moved very fast. Those men were never the same after that."

Sheenka was quick to extinguish the fire and Nakosis now decided caution was the better part of valor. "Yes, I think we'd better leave."

She was turning for the trail, eating as she went. "Where will we go?" She asked. "You said the spirits showed the path?"

"Yes," said Nakosis, "but mostly the direction. I did not even see this valley. In my journey the spirits pointed me toward the setting sun. We must reach the blue mountains. Then we should also be free of this forest and we can rest and ask the spirits for their guidance again."

The two moved fast, their pace quickened by the fear of an ancient legend. Nakosis reflected upon what Loka had said about people fearing that which they did not understand and how misunderstanding can lead to ignorance and violence. Perhaps the Yeshta weren't really all that sinister and hostile. Perhaps they were simply acting out of their own fear and ignorance. In Sheenka's story of the hunting party the creatures never actually attacked anyone, but only seemed to intimidate the men into leaving. Nakosis thought about his understanding of the universal connection with the Great Mystery - that is the common heritage of all living things. Should the Yeshta be any different? They were not excluded from the power of the Great Mystery. Perhaps then they could even experience the spirit's blessing in much the same way. These thoughts gave him some solace and relieved his anxiety.

Sheenka was taking the lead through the thick jungle. She had been here long enough to know some of the terrain. She moved with such a grace and agility over the dense undergrowth that Nakosis was having difficulty keeping up. Even without his heavier load, he reasoned that she would be a challenge for him. This, he reflected, explained her lithe and muscular physique. She was quite accustomed to running trails.

They walked uphill all day, climbing ever higher out of the wild green valley, where fate had brought them together under such bizarre circumstances. They rested at midday, taking a seat on the thick, mossy trunk of a fallen tree. They had made a high point that was long in ascending, due to the dense foliage of the forest floor and having to climb over and under a maze of fallen trees. They were afforded an unobstructed view of the valley for their great effort and exertion.

Sheenka stood silently surveying the majestic scene below them and appeared to be lost in thought, studying something about the view of the valley.

"What is it?" Nakosis asked.

She waved her arm about in front of her. "This view." she said, "It is familiar to me. I saw this view before, not long after fleeing my village. This is the way I came into this valley. My village cannot be too far from here." She appeared saddened, no doubt missing her family and angered at the circumstances that drove her away from them.

They both collapsed against a mammoth tree, panting and feeling the burning in their lungs and legs. They passed the gourd between them and when recovered they stood together to assess their progress. The blue mountains were still some distance but their hard, determined pace had advanced them considerably. They could now clearly make out many features on the misty blue range that completely filled their distant field of vision. Avalanche chutes, moraines and countless waterfalls could now be easily discerned from their green perch atop the rise. The glacial peaks, rising majestically above the clouds, glimmered in golden bright sunshine. The air was unbelievably fresh and cool and the warm sun bathed them for the first time since descending into the dark forest. Nakosis rummaged in the bag for the left over food and they sat eating in silence, drinking in the magnificent vista.

Sheenka turned, asking, "So what of us, spirit talker? Are we to follow our spirits together, to find this fire mountain?"

Nakosis didn't know how to answer. He had always considered it to be a solitary voyage, especially since his one companion, Washtaka, had been chosen to follow another calling. Now, however, the spirits had seen fit to place another on his path. Would she too end up leaving to pursue some other direction?

He thought a moment and answered saying, "I had always thought that the spirits had chosen this undertaking as a solitary quest for me. They seemed to apply their unseen hands to mould my life in this direction. First they gave me hope and happiness. Then they showed me loss and suffering. Then they placed others on my path, only to take them away. And now they have placed us together. Honestly, Sheenka, I cannot answer your question. It would appear that the decision for anything now in my life is little of my design or desire. I have learned that whatever my wishes, if they are not in accord with the balance of things, not flowing with the stream of the Great Connection, then the spirits intervene. I might not like their ways at the time. I may even rebel and, yes, even rage insanely against them, but I have come to bend to their will like the willows in the wind. To stay rigid against the will of the spirit world is to break and never receive the full power of their blessing. So, you must ask them yourself. As for me," He now turned to face her directly and moved to look into her dark eyes and feeling a sudden confidence he answered, "I know that for however long we travel together I will be very grateful."

She did not speak. She stared at him intently, her eyes inquiring, studying, analyzing and trying to interpret any feelings that may be masked behind the words. Then she raised her head, her eyes to his eyes, her breath against his face and she kissed him. Nakosis stiffened slightly, a little surprised but he had not pulled away. Instead he raised his hand to cup the softness of her cheek and pressed his lips fully against hers with a passion long in brewing. They slid toward the fern covered mossy ground, Nakosis fumbling to rid himself of the pack and weapons. They fell into each other's embrace with the wildness of unrestrained ardor. What Nakosis lacked in experience, nature provided and he pressed against her with an urge greater than anything he'd ever known. There was an animal-like wildness and beauty in Sheenka's nature. It had attracted Nakosis from the first. Now in the heat of their coupling, her unleashed primal passion shook Nakosis as no journeying ever had. She rolled him onto the wet ferns and dug her nails into his chest, her muscular thighs gripping him with remarkable strength. Her long black hair, wet with perspiration, clung to her shoulders and her firm dark breasts rose with her heavy breathing. Nakosis felt himself shudder and gasp in a warm burst of the most exquisite pleasure he could have ever imagined. As he did so, Sheenka arched her supple back and tilting her head skyward moaned loudly. He could feel her entire body spasm as her nails dug deeper in the flesh of his chest. He could not feel any pain, only an incomparable bliss. Sheenka collapsed across him, her head upon his shoulder. He placed his hands on her waist and pressed down gently on her hips as he moved ever so slightly beneath her. She moaned softly and raised her head to face him. She looked into his eyes, silently smiling for a while then kissed him passionately before righting herself, still clutching him firmly with her long legs.

"So spirit talker!" She laughed joyously at having called him that. "It appears we may be seeing much of each other!"

Nakosis was about to reply with words he thought would be meaningful, though still unworthy of expressing his strong feelings, when she suddenly stiffened and sat straight, her face stern, her eyes ahead. She slid quickly off him and indicated toward the forest. She was racing to grab her clothing and provisions. Nakosis did the same as silently as he could. Knowing what the look implied, he reached for his bow and quiver, throwing them onto his back first, even before grabbing his clothes. Sheenka nodded toward the trees beneath the rise and they quickly scrambled back down the slope for cover. Once they were out of site they quietly dressed, keeping an eye to the rise. Whispering into her ear Nakosis asked what it was that startled her.

"Not sure, something moving, maybe watching us. Up in the trees on the other side." She was clutching the half spear staring straight ahead as she whispered.

Then they both saw movement above the tree where they had just lain. In the thick of the forest something dark and shadowy moved ever so slowly. Then as Nakosis looked, Sheenka tapped his arm and gestured toward the far left. There too, a shape above the rise moved at the edge of the thickest growth. They both quickly scanned around in every direction, their senses struggling to detect any sign. It appeared to be two people stalking them, watching. Nakosis nodded his head further down the bank and they slid, keeping low to the ground, under the cover of the low bushes to a thicket where they could better be concealed. In a hushed voiced Nakosis asked if Sheenka thought it might be the hunters' still searching for her.

"No," she replied, "they would have given me up for lost and possibly dead by now. They do not wish to be away from the village. They are lazy men now that everyone else does their work for them!"

They exchanged worried looks and she said the last words they wanted to hear. "Yeshta?"

Nakosis had quietly strung the bow and placed his quiver of arrows by his feet. He reached for the gourd to wash the fear from their throats. Their hearts were pounding now and they were straining their eyes to try to detect the creatures' movement as they peered through the concealment of the heavy brush. Nakosis let out a subdued gasp that made Sheenka spin to face him. He was holding his big bag open and looking at her with a pained expression. She raised her shoulders in a questioning gesture.

He whispered, "My rattle. My ancient rattle, it's not here! He seemed to be more worried about this rattle than the impending terror descending upon them in the form of legendary beasts. Sheenka's puzzled and somewhat angry look conveyed her disbelief with an exaggerated gesture.

"You don't understand! I cannot loose that rattle!" He began to move and she dug her fingers into his arm.

"What are you doing? Do you want to kill us both?" she hissed under her breath.

The dark shapes were visible to them now, lurking, cowering behind the brush at the edge of the trees, atop the rise. They were definitely not people from Sheenka's village. To Nakosis there could be no doubt that they were, in fact, large dark beasts that resembled men. They were moving ever so slightly back and forth as though trying to get a better sight of the two terrified people.

Nakosis whispered to Sheenka's ear, "I don't think they want to hurt us. They did not attack and you said yourself they only frightened off the hunters from your village."

Sheenka's eyes were dark and her brow furrowed with both fear and anger as she hissed at Nakosis, "Are you wanting to take that chance and risk our lives for some old rattle!"

He held her arm gently and using his calmest voice he said, "Look, if they are as powerful and fierce as legend says, then why do they not simply crush us like ants? If they are the terrifying creatures of the stories then we cannot out run them and it is certain we cannot fight them and win, so what is there to loose? Besides, I don't sense danger from these beasts. I believe they are as fearful of us as we are of them." He let her arm go and laid down his bow and stood up.

"I hope you're right, 'spirit talker'! Well let's see if you can talk to beasts, too!" Sheenka said, standing also.

They emerged from the cover of the bush and walked out in front of it. She slipped her trembling hand in his and looked at him briefly before beginning a slow walk up the rise toward an unprecedented encounter and an unknown fate.

The couple advanced slowly toward where the creatures moved behind the cover of fallen trees and willows, each nervously watching the other. There was a spot midway up the rise where they lost sight of the huge beings and vice versa, due to the fallen tree and the low bushes. When their eyes finally peered above the tree where only moments ago they had lain in passionate embrace, Nakosis and Sheenka were looking into the startled face of a mysterious legendary Yeshta. The great beast must have grown bold in it's curiosity of the couple disappearing from sight and it advanced to just past the fallen tree standing, stretching up to peer over. Nakosis and Sheenka also had to stoop, their hands almost grasping at the ground to climb the short dip beneath the tree. In their haste to escape the creatures they had not noticed the steepness of the terrain. There was a heartbeat of utter terror as they realized the closeness of the giant. Nakosis felt the fearful grip of Sheenka's fingers as they bore into his hand and she swallowed a gasp, not wanting to startle the Yeshta into attack. Nakosis was frozen on the spot and, reacting as one would with the great bear, he spoke in very soft tones while taking a slow step away, but there was nowhere else to retreat without tumbling down the slope again. The Yeshta appeared equally unsure of its next move and a high-pitched, shrill whistle resounded from the woods. The creature turned only slightly, acknowledging what was obviously an alarm call from the other Yeshta.

Nakosis spoke very purposefully and in a very calming voice he said, "I do not know if you understand what I'm saying, but please do not fear me, great one. We mean you no harm."

The beast jerked and let out a short grunt. Its eyes were quite wide now and

Nakosis feared that it might either flee or attack. He slowly lowered himself toward the grassy earth, pulling a silent trembling Sheenka with him. They slowly sat upon the ground and Nakosis, moving at a snail's pace, reached out and retrieved the ancient rattle that caused their precarious predicament. All the while he kept repeating the same words, speaking softly to the creature. It seemed to relax once they were on the ground and no longer advancing.

Now, from this very vulnerable position, the Yeshta appeared even more ominous and gargantuan in stature. It was indeed very much a man, but a man of proportions unlike they had ever imagined and heavily muscled. It had a heavy coat of grayish hair covering its massive frame, but there were spots on its chest, thighs and arms where the hair was either worn or absent and a dark colored skin could be seen. It's face, however, was very much that of a man and it's burning eyes showed great intelligence as it now studied these two people seated beneath it. Its cheekbones were very high and it's nose broad. It had a large, powerful jaw and it had no fear of these two strangers, but seemed very curious of them.

Nakosis believed that their only other encounters with humans must have been at a safe distance. Nakosis looked up at the creature, trying not to make much eye contact, and being ever so careful to avoid any threatening gestures. He could not think of what to do next and for some reason the ancient words of one of Loka's chants came to him and he repeated it in a soft singing voice. The words were spoken at every ceremony's end and in the ancient tongue. Loka had said that it meant, 'May the spirits give their blessings.' As he did so, Sheenka turned to look at him. It was the first she'd moved since the creature appeared before them. He acknowledged her with a gentle nod, still reciting the ancient words. At the singing of the chant, the Yeshta emitted a long soft sound, seemingly placated by the words. Sheenka joined in, her voice clearly still shaking with fear, but her grip at least was more relaxed. A second soft call echoed from the woods and then a third! Sheenka was staring at Nakosis, but he did not look back. He was aware of the fact that there were more Yeshtas. The big one was obviously a male and he appeared very pleased with the lilting melody of the ancient words. Nakosis and Sheenka could hear the approach of the other Yeshta.

Nakosis glanced quickly and saw that they were moving slowly, cautiously toward where this highly unlikely group now rested. Soon the other two were squatted behind the great male at a safe distance from these strange singing beings. Perhaps, Nakosis thought, it was the ancient spirit tongue that spoke to them, easing their trepidation. The words seemed to have that effect on Nakosis as he succumbed to the gentle flowing rhythm and rhyme. As he swayed slightly to the pulse of the hypnotic chant, the ancient rattle rolled from where he'd laid it on his lap. It rolled onto the moss at his feet and the huge male Yeshta grunted with approval at the sound it made and he reached out to seize the precious artifact. Nakosis hesitated for a moment in the rhythm, carefully watching as the inquisitive beast picked up the old Shaman's rattle. Nakosis stopped chanting, staring, worried about the precious rattle in the Yeshta's huge hand. The big male held it in its palm and became thoroughly enchanted when it rattled as he rolled it in his palm. It was like an acorn in the hand of an average man. One tight closing of its fingers and the cherished rattle would crush like a mouse in the jaws of a wolf.

"Please don't!" The words were out of his mouth before he could think. His hand reached up to the beast. Sheenka let slip a soft cry. The startled Yeshta looked at Nakosis who sat, his hand extended toward the creature. Then the Yeshta looked at his own great fist, slowly opening it to look at the still intact rattle. He shook his hand once and a soft grunt showed its delight at the sound. Then he looked again at Nakosis.

They locked eyes and Nakosis again said, "Please may I have that? Please!"

The great beast lowered its hand and turning it slowly, gently let the rattle slip into Nakosis' palm. "Thank you, great one." Nakosis said and then looking briefly at Sheenka and the other two curious spectators, he resumed the chanting and slowly began to introduce the light shake of his precious rattle. The Yeshtas were thoroughly delighted. The other two, shuffled closer, but still behind the protective shield of the great male.

Nakosis wasn't sure how things would go, how long he could continue to keep this up or whether the Yeshta would just grow bored with them. He increased the rhythm slightly, closed his eyes and, focusing on the words and the rattle, he tried to forget about where he was, who he was with and whether there was to be a next moment. He again swayed gently and he could sense the presence of Sheenka moving and chanting beside him. He felt her spiritual energy begin to flow with his as when two discordant drums begin to beat in unison. There was an intense power to the union of their spirit. The Yeshta sensed it also. They moved gently to the ancient words, captivated and entranced by the spectacle, the play and movement of power. Nakosis felt their energy also. It was unlike any he had encountered. While extremely powerful and primordial it carried an echo of deep sensitivity. These beings, who appeared so primitive and lacked language as people did, had a much deeper connection with the sacred mother and the spirit world. They were overpowering! Nakosis, although succumbing to the will of the spirits, had always managed to remain somewhat in control of his direction ever since the incident with the village fire. But now, here, with these three great legendary beings, he was merely along for the ride. They were like a vortex of spirit energy that pulled him along within it, in a storm of the most incredible power. Nakosis saw the Sacred Mother Earth personified in the spirit of these gentle creatures. He could see the profound concord, the inseparable unity that existed between these ancient Yeshta and all creation. They were beings of pure magic. To Nakosis they seemed the true chosen embodiment of the spirit of Hohapas. He felt himself rising, floating on a constant wave of bliss. He had no words to describe the feelings he experienced. He had become one with the Yeshta's spirit and in so doing became one with the sacred mother. He began to hear the voices once again. It was a blend of many things, the voices of Raven, Panther, Eagle, Loka, Chako, and Sheenka. Then they began to subside and he heard his own voice singing the ancient song. Sheenka's voice also flowed within him like two clear streams melting into one. Behind their voices was a pulse of warm, droning sweet sound. It was the cooing like deep tones of the Yeshta. Other sounds diminished and their voices faded and Nakosis opened his eyes. The three Yeshtas, now seated in a half circle, were looking slightly upward, eyes closed and from their throats, this ethereal vibration faded.

It was now silent, save for the song of birds and the gentle flutter of leaves in the warm breeze. The Yeshtas opened their eyes and looked at the two people. Nakosis turned to face Sheenka and she was smiling. Tears flowed freely down her cheeks and she was staring, smiling widely at the Yeshta. Nakosis was too overcome to move or speak. What words would do this moment justice? Worlds had just melded, hearts, spirits joined as one within the Great Mystery. An understanding had been shared that escaped the parameters of language, even the ancient tongue. The Yeshta hummed a soft, barely audible sound of the deepest contentment. Nakosis looked into the face of this creature as though for the first time. There, in these beings eyes, he saw not the great formidable and fearful primitive beast of legend that spawned intense fear in people. He saw instead a spiritual being of the deepest compassion. The big male reached out his large hand and with the back of a great finger he softly, lovingly rubbed it against the side of Nakosis head. Nakosis reached up and gently touched his forehead to the creatures' great hand. As he did so, tears flowed uncontrollably from his eyes. Sheenka had moved closer to Nakosis, her arm around his side and she likewise had received the same blessing from the other of the Yeshta. The creatures slowly slid back from Nakosis and Sheenka and carefully, slowly rose to their amazing great height, standing twice as tall as the two humans. Nakosis and Sheenka stood and there was a difficult moment where Nakosis could not think of any words. For reasons known perhaps only to the spirits, he raised his ancient rattle, shaking it proudly toward the sky declaring loudly "Hohapas!"

Sheenka jumped and gasped in surprise at his sudden, exuberant yell. The Yeshtas turned their heads upward and issued the deepest most hair-raising roar. This was the cry most attributed to them. The most inconceivably loud and frightening call anyone had ever heard. Sheenka actually fell off her feet onto the trunk of the fallen tree. The Yeshtas, however, were far from angry. They seemed overjoyed about demonstrating their uncanny ability. Nakosis turned, helping up Sheenka and laughed. Once more he raised his rattle. The Yeshtas were like dogs waiting for someone to hurl a stick. It seemed that they were enjoying this little cross species interaction as much as Nakosis. Once more, after just a short hesitation for effect, Nakosis again yelled out the sacred name, 'Hohapas'. Almost before his yell finished the Yeshtas responded in unison even louder than before.

It was bizarre to witness such a thing, these ancient beings creating a sound so unnerving and terrifying from a moment of sheer delight. They stood for a few heartbeats then turned and swiftly and silently vanished into the woods.

Sheenka fell to her knees. Nakosis thought she might have fainted, but as he threw himself beside her he saw the tears of utter ecstasy in her eyes. She grasped him tightly, her arms unwilling to let go. She was attempting to say something but words escaped her.

"I know, I know," was all Nakosis could mutter. He knelt before her, brushing the hair from her eyes and kissing her forehead and her cheek, wiping her tears with his hand.

She looked into his eyes and stammered, "I…I…who…. would have ever dreamed…I….I "

Nakosis tried to say something, but instead he started giggling and then laughing. He laughed like a man who had lost his mind and Sheenka joined him. They both collapsed onto the mossy ground, lost in a world of emotion so unbelievable that no one would ever understand. There were no words to describe the rapture, the ecstasy of that moment when their worlds, their spirits, melded as one within the Great Mystery. Laughter seemed appropriate. They stood silently looking toward where the Yeshta disappeared into the trees, both half wondering if it really took place. Did something as truly amazing just really happen to them or was it all a dream?

It was getting cooler and night would soon be upon them. They had been oblivious to their external world. They descended back down the slope away from the scene of the most pivotal, poignant and profound moment in their lives. Back to where their belongings lay discarded on the ground at a time when they thought they were possibly taking their last steps in this lifetime. How incredibly long ago and far away that moment now felt. Neither of them had spoken.

Now Sheenka said, "The day is almost over. We know we need not fear the Yeshta so we should spend the night close by."

Nakosis agreed and shouldered the pack as they moved on through the trees to a flatter spot further down. They didn't have to go far until they found one of the multitudes of little streams gurgling down from the cloud-covered glaciers of the distant peaks. The setting sun bathed the mountains in crimson and violet. Stars were showing in the east against an indigo sky.

They started a fire and Nakosis quickly managed to trap a few large fish in the pool of the small stream and catch them with his hands. Sheenka and Nakosis went through the movements of setting a camp for the night but they felt disconnected from the mundane, from the activities of the waking world. Their movements were rote, dream-like. In the aftermath of the Yeshta's encounter everything else paled in comparison. Yet, they still basked in the residual radiance of the joining of spirits.

As they finally relaxed into some sense of 'normal' they managed to discuss more 'worldly' matters. Sheenka expressed her concern about the proximity to her village. As far as she could ascertain, they would need to figure out a way to circumvent the entire region near her people, lest they risk being sighted by someone out hunting. Most of the village was not a threat, as they were supportive of Sheenka and her family, but Kleeshto's men could be on the prowl. She figured that the way to the mountains, where the high land of summer snow began, was in the west, far past her peoples' valley. Her village was surrounded by rough mountainous terrain. It would be hard to navigate and remain undetected.

Nakosis stared into the flames watching the fish sizzle. He had been silent while listening to Sheenka, and now she knew he was thinking of the best next move. Perhaps the spirits would simply guide their feet and show him the right path, she hoped. Nakosis picked up a small stick and mindlessly poked at the fire's edge. He stopped and turned to Sheenka once, as though to speak, but returned to his ritual of poking and staring. Finally he threw the stick into the fire and rose to walk a few steps away. He stood motionless; his hands on his hips, then paced back and forth looking at the ground. It was trying for Sheenka to wait for his opinion, but she respected his abilities now enough to allow him to gather his thoughts. He turned and quickly returned to stand by the fire looking at Sheenka.

"You miss your family?" He asked, not needing a reply. "You also said that the village despised this 'pretender' and that, had you been a man, that perhaps they would have stood their ground. Then what?" She didn't understand and her look revealed it. Nakosis continued, "What would have happened if that was how it was, if the village turned against him?"

"Well, ah… I suppose they would disarm him and his men. The men are members of the village, people we played with as children. We ate together, hunted together and then when he came to be the Shaman everything changed, but these men would not do his bidding if he were overthrown. He is not a true spirit talker, Nakosis, but he does have some power over people. They are afraid of him. They only obey out of this fear. Why? What are you thinking?"

Nakosis sat beside her and taking her hands in his he smiled and told her his plan. "We don't go around your village, Sheenka. We go straight through it!"

"What? Have the spirits made your mind light, Nakosis?" Sheenka asked completely bemused by his proposition.

"No, listen," he explained, "what if we walked straight into the village, heads held high and we called this pretender to stand before the entire people and I, who no one knows, declare him to be the evil, false pretender everyone knows him to be. Do you think the people would stand with us?"

Sheenka needed a moment to consider this plan. It seemed so absurd, so impetuous that she found her mind visualizing it.

She answered, "Perhaps, if we were to sneak into the village at night when everyone is in their huts, I could see my family, tell them what we plan and allow them to carefully spread the word among the others we know to be supportive." She looked at him for a long moment then smiling she said, "It might work!" But then a solemn look overtook her and she added, "But what if he doesn't back down. As I told you, he has a very strong will. What if he doesn't back down and his men sense his fearlessness and stand with him. Then we will both die horribly, Nakosis."

He rose and paced again for a few long tense moments then turned. "If we can get to your family and tell the people to prepare a large fire in the village center. Do you have a central place where your people gather?" Sheenka nodded. "Well, just to be certain of the people's support have them wait until near dusk and prepare the fire. If he doesn't back down Sheenka, then I will make him. I will challenge him!"

"But how? In combat?" she asked.

"Of sorts, I suppose." Nakosis replied. "The spirits have given me a blessing. I seem to have a 'way' with fires."

Nakosis had a sarcastic smile and he exuded great confidence. Sheenka beamed with the possibility of being re-united with her loved ones and of the final, long awaited retribution of the pretender.

CHAPTER 19
HOMECOMING

Sheenka slept little that night. The day's events were simply too much for her mind to let go of. She relived the moment of passionate embrace with this incredible man, the otherworldly encounter of the legendary Yeshta and now the possibility of returning to her family and the overthrowing of the brutal despot who held her people in his grip of fear. How does anyone have such a day she wondered? The spirits worked more magic into her life in just one day than most peoples' lifetimes. How could she sleep? She was still vibrating.

They had talked well into the evening. With a belly full of fish, the warm glow of the fire, wrapped in his heavy shirt and the radiant Sheenka beside him, Nakosis fell quickly asleep. With Nakosis' woven blanket over her shoulders, Sheenka was pacing impatiently as the myriad scenarios played through her mind when she heard him snoring. She bent and gently kissed his forehead. She stood over him for the longest time, just watching him sleep. She looked back at the day again and again as though doing so would lend more believability to the events she'd witnessed. Not a single soul would be likely to believe it if she told them. None of these things would have been possible had all the many circumstances not brought her to the right place at the right time. Truly the Great Mystery is aptly named. To rest confidently in the understanding of it's unfolding was an experience that could not be caught in mere words. She felt the raised wound on her forehead and smiled. She caressed it as though it were the fading warmth of a lover's kiss, a small price to pay, she thought.

She had drifted off for a short while against the broad shoulder of a deeply sleeping Nakosis. She watched the pale pink line of dawn illuminate the clouds on the ridge of mountains. She felt a renewed awareness and energy despite the little sleep. This was her favorite time. Being attuned to the world of spirit, she also felt the enormous potential at the time when night and day overlap. This morning was different, though. Sheenka couldn't explain it but she felt as though she had more clarity and an intense sense of understanding of the great connection. The world looked different to her now. She once again took Nakosis' wonderful bow and quietly walked off to hunt.

When she returned he was still asleep and the morning sun had yet to liven the spot where they camped, so she stoked the fire and prepared the rabbit. It gave her enormous pleasure to be able to have the morning meal cooking before he awoke. After all, it was the least she could do for the man who just gave her the most incredible experiences of her life.

Sheenka watched the brilliant pink glow illuminate the opposite ridge and flow like liquid light down the rock-strewn slopes and meadows. In the morning sunlight she could easily make out details of the mountains not otherwise visible. Far off to the edge of her vision, about half way up one rocky slope, she watched a flock of birds descend into what appeared to be a wide cleft in the wall of rock. It was not a common thing. As she stood looking at this anomaly and the light moved further down the mountain she had the sudden realization that what she was watching was quite possibly a small hidden canyon, a way through the mountains, but to where?

A stirring behind her made her turn just as Nakosis shed the heavy shirt and yawned. He looked about him as he stretched, rubbing his eyes awake. He saw the rabbit roasting on the freshly banked fire and looked up smiling at the beautiful young woman standing statuesque before him in the morning light. She truly was a splendid figure, he thought. She stepped toward him, standing at his side, smiling down at him. Nakosis reached out his hand and touched her calf, feeling the warmth of her soft brown skin, her strong chiseled muscles. He slid his hand further up, caressing her powerful thighs. She trembled and sighed and bent slightly toward him and he reached up with both hands and pulled her into his open arms. They fell together across the heavy hide shirt with the warmth of the fire and the heat of their unrestrained passion.

Afterward, lying against his chest, Sheenka closed her eyes, holding his strong arms against her breast. She could easily have slept now, having been deprived of it during the night. Something was bothering her, however. Suddenly a scent jolted her back into reality.

"The rabbit!" she yelled and reached to rescue the burning meat from the flames. As Sheenka dove for the smoking meal she slipped, forcing Nakosis sprawling onto the ground on his side and sending the light sapling spit, smoking rabbit meat and all into the sputtering flames. As she worked frantically to retrieve it, with some of the meat and her dignity intact, Nakosis rolled in uproarious laughter. Once she'd managed to get the meal to the relative safety of the fireside rocks she too laughed, realizing how funny her

252

scrambling to save the meal must have looked. It was a tremendous release of pent up energy as the two lovers sat in the dirt, sharing their meal and their joyous tears of laughter. The meal was superb, Nakosis thought, despite of, or perhaps because of, the crisp charred crust.

They sat a while together after the meal, enjoying the call to action that the warm morning sun had upon the many creatures of the forest. The little gray jays, the 'camp robbers' made an appearance and waited boldly at their feet for any scraps thrown them. These cute little birds were constant and welcome companions to the camp of every deep wood's traveler, often eating right from one's hand. Then the ravens appeared, instantly evicting any other would be beggar from the area. With shrill caws they demanded the bones and remaining scraps from the human intruders as payment for crossing their world. Of course, both Nakosis and Sheenka held 'all the brethren,' as the prayer says, in the highest esteem and gave freely of whatever they didn't need.

They quickly broke camp, filled the water gourd and headed on their way. Sheenka said that while she knew roughly the way to reach her village it wasn't a defined path or trail. She was under extreme duress and fear when she last crossed this area and was running for her life. Just how long it would take before she came upon known and familiar territory she couldn't say, but it was decided that they should start taking more precaution in their movements and be more watchful. They decided to try to stay less in the open when they crossed the sub-alpine meadows and stick to the tree lines and in the shadows where they could see and not be seen so easily. Where possible, they would travel so that the sun would illuminate their way, yet be in the eyes of anyone approaching. They now also had their ears and noses trained to the wind for any approaching sound or scent that did not belong. They were both adept at being on the trail and knew how to navigate through even the most dense and dry ground with the utmost silence if need be. As well, when under such conditions, as it is with the best of hunters and warriors, one's other abilities also are heightened. The 'spirit senses' become attuned and intensified. When a really good hunter or warrior is near their quarry or an enemy something 'tells' them, often long before external senses pick up an alarm. In this mode they quietly passed half of the day steadily headed towards the direction of Sheenka's people and an uncertain outcome.

Many of the streams now began to get wider, steeper and faster as they descended into yet another lower region of valleys. Numerous rivulets and springs had run down from unseen sources high above the clouds to babble and gurgle over rock strewn moraines and fall over precipitous cliffs to eventually join forces on their inexorable march to the glacial lakes of the distant lowlands. Now these streams became tumultuous, churning chutes of water often deep in chasms of steep rock walls that funneled their power toward thunderous distant falls far below. Nakosis and Sheenka struggled through the thick wet undergrowth for the better part of the day, just looking for a place to cross such an impasse. Eventually, they found great trees fallen across the gorge.

Crossing was terrifying, as the girth of the ancient giant was so large that one could not reach around the sides and yet it's heavy carpet of wet moss provided no good gripping surface. Ferns, half as tall as a man, grew profusely from its surface. The combination of moss and ferns hung like a dripping verdant green veil from the sides and thick white clouds of mist engulfed the tree from the roaring stream so far below. As treacherous as it looked there was no other option. Nothing else had presented itself all day and so the two brave travelers took the chance. Nakosis sent Sheenka over first in case his weight, with the big pack, caused him to slip and pull the mossy surface with him. This logic was completely lost on Sheenka, who questioned his reasoning for a while before relenting and steeling herself for the crossing. She held her eagle skull totem tightly, closed her eyes for a moment and said a short, silent prayer. Then, kissing Nakosis firmly on the lips she said, "I love you spirit talker," smiled and stepped gingerly onto the fallen tree. She did not crawl as Nakosis expected and as much as he wanted to call to her to suggest that particular method, he daren't do so in fear of startling her. So he had no choice but to stand hopelessly on the edge, holding his breath, and 'willing' her across with every fiber of his being. Mentally, he called upon every possible invocation, every totem, guide and guardian he could think of. At one point about mid way she stopped and half turned to look back at him and smile. Whether this was to inspire confidence in herself wasn't certain, but when she again turned to continue she stumbled slightly, her arms flapping like a bird as she teetered to regain her balance. She straightened and stopped dead in her tracks, arms outstretched at her side. Nakosis held his hand over his mouth, biting into the flesh of his knuckles. Slowly she began moving again, step after heart wrenching step. Finally she reached the safety of the other side and Nakosis could no longer hold his anxiety and he fell to his knees in a great sigh of relief. Sheenka, the fiercely, stalwart woman that she was, simply smiled and raised her arm in defiance to the danger.

Sheenka wore the wonderful bow and quiver of Taku's strapped across her back on the crossing and Nakosis, admiring how stately she appeared, reasoned that Taku would be proud that such a woman now also bore the bow with such nobility and strength. Nakosis, however, now had the remainder of the gear, the big pack and the smaller pouch to bear across the precipitous jaws of death. The fact that the heavy mist obscured the actual view of the maelstrom churning so far below him was a blessing. Since he was on his knees, and had already said enough prayers for two lifetimes, he simply started crawling out onto the tree. He had secured the pack with additional leather cords and placed the as-yet unrepaired half spear inside.

At first it didn't seem so bad. Sheenka has flattened much of the ferns underfoot as they were not hard of stem and bent easily. He did not grasp the thick blanket of moss in his fingers as he worried it might just rip free of the bark surface. It seemed that his greatest challenge would be to keep the balance of the heavy pack centered over his back. He quickly realized that the slightest horizontal movement pulled greatly to either side. At the pace of a tortoise he moved a little further. He wanted to look up at Sheenka standing at the end of the tree, but he knew he dared not lift his gaze from the spot directly ahead of him. Neither could he attempt to look over the side, as to do either one, to move his head just that much, was enough to risk loosing his balance. The weight of the big pack bore down directly upon his shoulders and just a slight lifting of his head seemed to transfer the weight enough to pull him off center. It was absolutely horrifying. He forced his racing heart to calm by focusing on his breath and bringing his center back to balance. This he did during his quiet times when he would sit in silent meditation, not moving. Now, however, he could not stop the momentum that he'd begun and so he had the additional challenge of trying to quell his mounting trepidation and anxiety while maintaining the forward moving pace.

Sheenka sat, squatting on her ankles, elbows on her knees, her hands closed tightly together in fists before her, trembling. She wanted to look away but could not. Fear held her gaze captive on the struggling form of the man she loved. She knew he was in peril and dangerously close to plummeting with every painful forward crawl. She spoke soft encouragements to him, trying to convince him and herself that it was going well, that he was "almost there".

He had laboriously managed to make it two thirds of the way in what seemed to both of them to be an eternity. He heard her gentle words of confidence and looked up to smile at her and dispel the fear that was so obvious from her tone. Then he slipped! His feet went out from under him, his right leg slipping quickly over the side of the tree. As he struggled to counter the pull of the big pack, his opposite hand began frantically flailing at the air desperately hoping to grasp the thick moss as the weight of the heavy bag started to pull him over the side. His opposite leg was struggling to grip anything, but the tree was too wide to get a leg over the side. Sheenka screamed as she had never screamed before. She found herself crawling out onto the tree and realized that there was little she could do as it took all her appendages to stay gripped and not fall herself.

Nakosis managed to throw his weight forward with every reserve of strength he could muster. He stopped the fall but was prone, motionless, sideways across the tree with no means that he could sense of turning himself back in line without sending himself and the supplies to a watery demise. Sheenka was beside herself, yet she knew to not further increase Nakosis' risk of falling by being out on the tree herself, so she crawled back to solid ground searching for something, anything to reach him with, not knowing how she might help. She found a long length of thin branch, dead yet with sufficient springiness. She offered it out toward Nakosis, who was in no position to be able to take advantage of it. He ever so slowly turned his gaze, moving his head barely enough to be able to see her. He once again focused, calling upon every bit of strength, he dug deep inside and calmed his racing heart and cleared his head as best he could. He knew he had no way to move without a secure handhold and the wet mossy tree provided none. He thought for a moment.

Then as calmly as he could, he spoke to Sheenka asking, "So, just how good is your aim?"

"What? My what? My *aim*?" Knowing he would be deadly serious at the moment she said, "I…I… ah…yes…my aim is good, why?"

"Listen carefully." Nakosis instructed, "Move away, over further and along the edge to where it sticks out -do you see?"

Sheenka did as he ordered and raced to the spot of land that was a bit higher and jutted out just a little, about a few body lengths from the trunk of the great tree. She was now facing him at a bit of an elevation and was a little more parallel.

"Now," Nakosis said as loudly as he dare, "You must shoot an arrow in front of me. Do you hear? You must shoot it very hard Sheenka. Right ahead of my hand!"

"But… Nakosis… I…" she began and he cut her off.

"Do it NOW! I can't hold on much longer!" He yelled.

There was definite panic in his voice. Sheenka quickly brought the great bow up to bear in her left hand and in one skilful move reached behind her shoulder with her right and had an arrow notched, all within a single heartbeat. She took a deep breath then let it out slowly as she aimed at the place on the log not two hands distant from the man she loved. She pulled with as much strength as she could and, forcing the bow not to quiver under the enormous pressure, she let the arrow fly. The thud was audible over the constant roar of the falls.

"Again!" Nakosis screamed.

Once more she repeated the process and once more her superb marksmanship drove the arrow home through the dense moss into the thick bark of the ancient tree a little further ahead of the first. Now she raced to her original position in front of Nakosis, who as yet had not moved a hair. She once again brandished the thin stick, not sure what she'd do with it, but there was little else she could think to do to help. Nakosis knew he'd have one chance to get straightened with the assistance of the handhold the arrow would, hopefully, provide. He also knew there was an equally likely chance the thin arrow shaft could snap under his weight or brake free. He could not slowly creep toward it. It would have to be one swift hopeful grab. Taking any longer would not make the move any easier, he thought, so he silently asked the spirits for help and, taking a breath, he made a lunge with his left hand for the first arrow. He aimed for its base, where it impacted with the tree, knowing this would be the strongest point. As he did so, he simultaneously threw his hips and his dangling right leg toward the center of the tree. It worked! He was somewhat back in line with the tree, but still precariously close to falling. Some of the moss had broken away during the initial scampering to avoid the fall. As he gauged his movement toward the second arrow he could feel his hand sliding. The shaft of the arrow clutched tightly in his grip was starting to move! It was coming free! It seemed to bend very slowly. Nakosis stared unbelieving as it sloped gently towards him, as the arrowhead was being pried loose from the bark. Sheenka saw it also and was now on her knees in panic. Nakosis couldn't think about the next move, he simply took it, transferring his grip to the second arrow. The moment he did he didn't wait to test its strength, he immediately seized the opportunity to right himself fully, lest it also fall from his trembling fist. It held. Nakosis was now back in line and moving once again ever so slowly forward, left hand, right hand, left knee, right knee, in a tiny baby-like crawl on his belly, his hands clutching the arrows, digging their stone points into the mossy bark for grip.

Sheenka was stretched as far as her flexible body would allow. She'd hooked one foot under a root and her fingers were grasping for the first opportunity to grab him. As he slowly drew closer she got her hands on the back of his shirt and gently pulled until she reached the top of the big bag and then she almost lifted him completely onto the solid ground. Her strength surprised even her. Nakosis fell over on his side and grabbed the roots at his head, not wanting to let go. Sheenka was crying tears of both anxiety and relief and she threw herself across him, kissing his face repeatedly. They finally managed to get past the great tree's roots and sit up on a rock and allow themselves a moment to compose before going further.

Nakosis turned to her saying, "Now if you decide that the way to your people's village is really in the other direction you will be going back alone!"

Their nervous laughter did little to quell their trembling. Nakosis examined the arrows for wear and carefully placed them back into the leather quiver on Sheenka's back.

They pushed their way back downstream, choosing to move a little inland away from the edge of the chasm. The sun was beginning to set below the mountains and with a light rain falling they were now directly across from where they had stood earlier that day. It had taken all that time to travel the distance of a stones throw! It was extremely depressing for the two weary souls to realize how much they risked and what effort they expended to go such a short distance.

"We'd better find some place to rest." An exhausted Nakosis said.

He pulled the straps over his shoulder and let the big bag drop unceremoniously to the forest floor and immediately felt a rush that made him slightly dizzy, but greatly relieved. Sheenka looked about and picked a likely direction to begin searching for somewhere to camp. Her instincts told her to move away from the gorge and up to the base of the high ridge that was now blocking the sun. She was soon through the trees and against the base of a small cliff strewn with huge, jagged, gray boulders. She then heard Nakosis coming along behind her with the bag re-packed on his back. He trudged along behind her, leaving the direction of their travel up to Sheenka as he was far too tired to do much more than bear the burden of their supplies a little further. The light was fast retreating and the rain getting harder and they were soaked through their shirts. Sheenka pushed on around the curve of the cliff face and in between the great rocks. She heard water falling and as she rounded the next massive boulder she saw a tiny spring of water falling from above. There appeared to be an indentation in the rock face. Nakosis saw it too and the possibility of finding shelter in a now driving rain gave them renewed hope.

Her intuition was right. It was a grotto with an immensely wide opening, yet did not extend very far into the cliff. They hurriedly reached the protective shelter and Nakosis once again removed the heavy pack. He looked about and was pleasantly relieved to discover a large bundle of twigs and branches piled waist height upon a ledge at the back of the cave. It was the long-abandoned nest of a bush rat. They quickly set about getting the dry moss and twigs moved onto the floor and into a warming fire. Even after having been discarded by the rat for what seemed like a very long time, some of the wood still gave off a the pungent musk-like odor of the rodent's urine, which was its distinct mark. But it was a fire none-the less and on this particular evening it was indeed welcome.

Since their clothes were drying, wrung out and propped up on stones at the fire side, they made quick naked forays out into the surrounding rocks to gather whatever wood they could from under overhangs along the cliff face and raced back again to dry off at the fire. Despite the day's trials they seemed to derive a little enjoyment of the game this had become. They stood completely drenched, their shiny black hair stuck firmly to their glistening brown skin, rotating their bodies against the drying warmth of the fire and their comforting laughter brought life to the rock walls. Once some real wood had been piled on top of the old rat's nest material they were more than content with their fire and dug through the pack to retrieve what they could from the nearly depleted food supply. A little meat wrapped in large leaves; a few berries and some nuts would have to be the evening meal. Tomorrow they would replenish their little cache.

They sat back on the warm rocks, and the wood had dried sufficiently to now burn brightly and Sheenka detected something on the wall of the cave. She rose slowly, her eyes not leaving the spot across from her. Nakosis turned his head to see what had so grabbed her attention. She reached her hand toward the wall and turned to Nakosis to see if he'd realized the great painting that they were standing beneath. Indeed he had. It was in white, black and ocher. An unmistakable image of a man or being with a headdress and a thin stick-like object in his hand held near to his featureless face. His limbs indicated that he was in a dancing posture. Nakosis was now standing beside Sheenka.

"Hohapas!" He exclaimed.

Sheenka turned, "What? That was the word you sang to the Yeshta! What is it Nakosis? I was meaning to ask you but.."

He cut in, "You mean *who* is Hohapas, Sheenka!." Nakosis stepped forward and touched the painting and immediately offered his respect. Turning to Sheenka he began to explain all he knew about the mysterious figure on the wall. He used this opportunity also to fill in all the many gaps in the story of his life, of the nights and days spent at the sacred cave, of the powerful vortex that he manifested through the magic of Hohapas that destroyed the Black Faces and of the evening he caused great concern at a village ceremonial fire. He told her all the details of the lost village and his time on the island and the wonderful spiritual insights he'd attained at the blessing of the painted figure looking down upon them from the cave wall. He now divulged everything as the words poured from him.

Sheenka sat, her mouth open, her eyes wide. "That explains the strange glow I saw back in the forest when I first saw you. You were journeying and the fire and you, Nakosis, glowed as one. I thought it was because I had been injured and I had only just awakened. Now I see."

"Yes," Nakosis said, "it explains many things. It explains the Yeshta and their knowing his name, it explains our meeting and our bonding" Sheenka smiled. "It explains," he continued, looking into her eyes, "your vision, also for the pleasant music, the song you heard was none other than Hohapas playing his flute!" At which he pointed to the stick-like item in the cave drawing.

"Ahh! Yes!" Sheenka suddenly realized.

It all came together now. Their 'chance' meeting was pre-ordained by the very vision of a being she'd yet to know. They were not just two lovers travelling through life on an epic adventure. They were kindred souls joined by their common love for each other as well as a deep spiritual bond. Now there was a different element to their relationship. Sheenka sat back upon the warm rock and let her gaze rest upon the figure on the wall across from her. In the flickering light of the fire, Hohapas did indeed appear to be dancing in the fames. Nakosis took up a seat beside her, also pondering the circumstances of their meeting, their now being together in the knowledge of Hohapas and of their shared spirit world.

Sheenka was the first to break the silence of the warm sanctuary. "Ever since my last journeying and my being forced out of my village, away from my family, hunted like an animal by people of my own ..." she paused as the emotion of her recollection was overpowering for a moment. "Ever since then I have been afraid to really journey, Nakosis. Oh, I feel the connection at all times. How can one who has been so blessed not be aware of it, but I have not visited the spirit worlds as I once did." She turned to Nakosis and taking his hand gently in hers she asked him, "I think I would like to journey with you, my love, together as you did with your teachers. Will you be my teacher and guide me as Chako and Loka did you?"

He as a bit surprised and not a little embarrassed. Smiling and perhaps blushing a little he said, "I am not a worthy teacher. I have not even managed to control my senses. That time in the forest." He looked at the cave floor, feeling a little remorseful. "I gave in to fear. I thrashed about like a small child in a tantrum and ultimately knocked myself out. I was embarrassed that I acted so foolishly. A real teacher must have control over himself better than I do."

"Oh, my dear Nakosis," Sheenka said, "I have seen you do things I doubt any other man could ever achieve. What of the Yeshta? For countless generations our people have feared and avoided them and then you ...you Nakosis, you sit and sing to them and receive their blessing! Is this not a man who

could teach? You punish yourself for simply being human. Don't you see…
it is your humanness that I love Nakosis! Having fear like everyone does not
make you weak. It is also the source of your deep love and compassion. They
both come from the same place –your heart! Without your warm heart I
don't think you would be the spirit talker that you are. This also means that,
like me, like all people, you will be vulnerable. You just have to accept it, my
love."

Tears wet his eyes and he held her tight and kissed her. "It seems it is I
who is receiving a much needed teaching at this moment." Nakosis said. He
thought for a while then continued, "Loka once told me that a true warrior
was one who was not afraid to bear his heart, to be completely open. To
do otherwise is to loose the opportunity to grow and become a full human
being. I think, Sheenka, that I now truly understand this teaching." Then,
looking at the remarkable drawing of Hohapas he smiled at Sheenka and
said, "Hand me the big bag."

Lightning flashed across the now dark skies, almost like a proclamation of
the solemnity of the ceremony about to begin. Nakosis and Sheenka banked
the fire, the comforting warmth caressing their naked skin and illuminating
the haunting figure painted by some long-ago devotee of the primordial being. To Sheenka, there was an air of the sacred and the secret, the magical
and the marvelous in Nakosis' preparations as he lit the smudge of sacred
herb. She observed a difference to his character now as he waved the blessing
smoke over them, his headdress, the rattle and the drum. There was none
of the young man's jocular and casual comportment. This was, to Nakosis,
a deadly serious affair and the deeply reverent somber manner in which
he conducted himself made her a little nervous. She suddenly realized that
she had absolutely no idea what she was expecting. She felt a strange combination of apprehension and excitement, trepidation and empowerment. She
bowed her head respectfully as the fragrant smoke enveloped her. Taking her
hands, she directed the aromatic cloud over her head, down her shoulders
and across her body. Nakosis bathed himself in the offering and then paid
homage to the four directions and to earth and sky. He made offerings finally
to the spirit of the fire itself. He recited the words learned from Chako and
bade the spirits to give special guidance to their spiritual union.

As Nakosis donned his headdress, Sheenka couldn't help but notice his
silhouette reflected on the cave wall. As the shadows danced in the flickering
light she thought how he resembled the ancient depiction of the fiery Hohapas. They had discussed this cave and who might possibly have made the
image. It had to have been a Shaman who long ago used this place for his secluded practice. That meant that a village must have been within one or two

day's travel. It was most likely Sheenka's village. Before the pretender, the old village Shaman may have been the one who discovered and consecrated this ancient cave as his spiritual enclave.

In the black of the night the fire illuminated the grotto so that it resembled a single golden glowing eye within the dark façade of the cliff face. The thought of her family and friends being so close was comforting but on this night, in the warm womb of the mountain cave with Nakosis, she thought of nothing else as the comforting glow of the ceremonial fire and the deepening sense of the sacrosanct filled her with reverence for the journey they would now undertake together for the first time.

Sheenka took the ancient rattle Nakosis held out to her as he picked up his drum and began the methodical steady rhythm. He looked different to her now, more formal and somehow much older, as though embodying the very antiquity of the ancient rite. She had not undertaken any formal instruction in how to practice. As a child, she had received some secret guidance from the old Shaman and she sought out quiet places, removed from the prying eyes of her fellow villagers and sat silently, turning inward until the spirits 'spoke.' She now did as she had always done and listened to the drum and the rattle and allowed herself to fall into their trance. Nakosis likewise proceeded as he always had, but tonight he was distracted by Sheenka's presence. He wanted her to share the same marvelous experiences he had and was perhaps too concerned to be able to let his waking mind fall away. This would usually happen fairly quickly and often with no forethought. He would very easily give into the moment and be within the 'state' that was receptive to the will of the spirits. But now he found it a bit of a challenge to let the waking mind give way, to let his thoughts, his day-to-day consciousness fall away and dwell within the void.

He continued the drumming and from the corner of his eye he caught the image of Sheenka, eyes closed, face relaxed, rocking slowly to the rhythm, her hand gently shaking the ancient rattle. Realizing that she was easily succumbing to the spell of the moment he found it easier to do the same. He closed his eyes and focused on the sound of his voice, the rhyme of the ancient tongue, and the steady rhythm of drum and rattle. He briefly felt the glow upon his face from what seemed like a rising fire and then he was gone.

It was dark and from out of that canvas of void space faint images flickered, unformed figures, flashes of partial faces, eyes glowing and the rustle of black feathers, fur and claws echoed cries in a cave black world. Slowly one figure would start to manifest from out of the wild collage of ethereal images. This time it was the familiar glowing yellow eyes of his old friend, Panther. She moved forward as though emerging from out of a black night into the light of a small fire, only her magnificent eyes visible at first, telltale luminous specks in the dark. They looked through you, cutting right through any vestiges of the waking consciousness that came through the veil of the spirit world. That was her first act –to dispel any part of the Shaman that still clung to the other side. This was the part that felt fear at first contact. The Shaman would either go back, shocked into waking consciousness, or he would acknowledge that her fierce countenance was also his protection and they could continue. To Nakosis now, her face was welcomed with loving affection and the deepest reverence as though encountering a beloved teacher after a long absence. Panther led Nakosis to a spot of dirt. All around was dark, yet a faint firelight shone in the distant background. There was a small pile of debris, sticks and branches piled up, but few details to really discern what he was seeing. Panther dug with her paws at the pile, brushing it aside and stared at the dirt beneath and then turned her head to Nakosis and faded into the darkness around them, Now he was in a large clearing, beside a great fire among other people. He could feel their presence but they were not visible to him. He had one hand held to his chest and was speaking, but could not hear the words and the fire was burning hot before him. He then became aware of Sheenka beside him. She was all white and glowed like a full moon. She had strength, confidence and determination, but he sensed a defiant anger also. She was standing with him yet they were one in spirit, two flames from the same fire burning stronger in the presence of each other. Nakosis felt empowered by this union. There was a great presence among them. It was the source of Sheenka's defiance and her unwavering confidence and it inspired similar feelings in Nakosis. He basked in it. It was similar, in a way, to the sensation he had when he descended into the great maelstrom of swirling water that swept away the enemy warriors, an enormous feeling of inexorable power at his command. But Nakosis knew that such power was not his. It was only manifesting through him at it's own will and desire. He was but an implement for its might, yet for the time, wielding such power, being filled with its presence was indescribable. He knew also to be guarded against such feelings as to give in to the mistaken belief that one was invincible was to succumb to the ego and to erode all humility – the greatest obstacle to a Shaman. Loka and Chako had been very precise about insuring that Nakosis realized the importance of remaining humble. A Shaman cannot perform his assigned duty of helping others without developing great humility.

Something in him slowly pulled away from the euphoric sensation of dwelling within the powerful sensation of the moment. He now observed himself within the play of energies, rather than being only an unwilling participant. To his surprise and satisfaction he discovered that this was more rewarding and opened new vistas of experience that was, in fact, on a deeper level. He could see that as the waking world was full of illusion, so too the spirit world had its illusory nature. Nothing, it seemed, was truly tangible and solid. There was an underlying 'nothingness' to all that the senses could perceive, like a great cosmic joke. The secret, he realized, was to not become caught up in the belief that any of it was really real. There was, of course, a certain validity and solidity to the world. Things had cause and effect and actions created reactions, but underneath the play of these energies was another reality. He had yet to understand this fully but simply realizing this reality, comprehending this simple fact was more liberating, more empowering than any experience of spiritual power.

Nakosis stood by the fire, staring into the flames. He had returned to the waking world. He turned to see Sheenka sitting beside him across the fire. Tears streaked her face and she was looking up at Nakosis, smiling in complete rapture. She stood and slowly approached him, gently wrapping her arms around him and held him tight for a long while. They looked into each other's eyes and released their embrace and Sheenka, unspeaking, walked to the cave entrance staring out into the night. Nakosis offered his gratitude to the spirits and walked to stand beside Sheenka in the cave entrance. They stood silently together looking out into the night. The rain had stopped and the night air was unbelievably fresh and fragrant. A lone owl called out in the dark and stars flickered insipidly behind gossamer clouds. The sound of roaring water in the distant deep gorge far below them echoed up off the face of the rock wall. They sat on a rock just inside the shelter of the great overhang and discussed the evening's events.

Sheenka explained that her previous encounters with the spirit world had been more intuitive, an unseen hand directing her movements, an unspoken word guiding her, a nameless presence protecting her. The old Shaman had been sensitive to her 'gift' and instructed her in seeking out her spirit guides and she had come to recognize Eagle as one of her protectors. Seeking out the quiet and secluded place she had followed the old man's directions and quieted her mind and had come to dwell in the state of blissful connection of all things. But she had never before experienced the power she felt on this night. She said that she saw what Nakosis saw, but from the eyes of one observing, apart yet a part of it. She had no physical body so there was no sense of differentiation between being in a field of experience and watching the experience. His thoughts and emotions were shared, as if they were her own. As well, she had separate experiences. Eagle lifted her above the fire and above the cave. She described it as though the cave had no ceiling and she was observing from high above, yet she was also acutely aware of being seated beside Nakosis at the fire. She felt heat as the fire seemed to expand and then it appeared to engulf them both, but there was no sensation of burning, only an overwhelming feeling of great strength and invulnerability. This was when Nakosis had his sensations of being the instrument of great power. She said that next she was overcome with a feeling of deep compassion, of almost sorrowful proportions and she wept uncontrollably. That was when Nakosis returned to his waking consciousness.

They spent most of the remainder of the evening discussing the journey and unraveling the mystery behind its images. Panther was trying to tell Nakosis something and he was not sure of her instruction. They were now both beginning to feel the exhaustion that follows the emotional exhilaration of the vision and they could no longer stay awake. They both needed rest. Nakosis put more fuel to the precious fire and they spread out his big winter coat and the woven robe upon the soft dirt of the cave and they slept soundly.

When Sheenka awoke it was to brilliant sunlight outside their grotto and the songs of many birds. She was a little disoriented and felt heavy. It was hard to move, as though all her limbs had somehow gained much weight. She recalled feeling similar after dancing for the whole night during the many village ceremonies. Nakosis was awake and standing at the rear of the cave. He heard her move and turning he beckoned her quickly to come. There was urgency in his voice that caused her to forget her drowsy, weariness and rush to his side.

"What is it my love?" She asked as she placed her hand in his.

He pointed to the very rear of the cave where the rock funneled to a sharp indent at the floor level and a small pile of debris had collected. It appeared as though many years of wind and perhaps rodents had caused small twigs and leaves to naturally accumulate at the back of the grotto wall.

"In my vision," Nakosis said, "I didn't see it before and I wouldn't have given it any thought, except for my vision. Panther was showing me something, a pile of twigs that looked just like this. She dug at it with her paws and then just before she left she looked straight to me."

They both studied the pile and without speaking they began quickly removing the debris, chucking the handfuls of dead leaves, needles and twigs behind them until only bare dirt showed.

Nakosis looked at Sheenka as she said, "You said panther dug in the dirt?"

Nakosis slowly, carefully began to scrape the soil away. They both knelt, eagerly watching with anticipation as handful after handful was picked up and cast aside. Suddenly Nakosis stopped and turned to look at Sheenka, a look of surprise on his face.

"I've hit something!" he exclaimed.

As he gingerly used his fingers to remove the last dirt, a small piece of wood appeared. He slowly excavated a wooden board about the length of his forearm under which a small cavity had been dug. A bundle had been hidden within it. Nakosis carefully withdrew the package and turning toward the light he placed it upon the cave floor in front of them. It was a piece of hide, well oiled for preservation and tied in strips of leather. He unwrapped the hide and shook off the dust to reveal a necklace. It was several claws of the great brown bear carefully arranged between beads made from many sacred stones, white, red and blue. Sheenka gasped and jumped to her feet, her hand over her mouth.

"What is it? Nakosis demanded.

"That was the necklace of Holeeaho, our old Shaman!" she replied.

Nakosis held it out to her, watching the tiny particles of dust cascade to the floor of the cave in the sunlight. Her hands shaking, Sheenka reverently took it in her palms and turned toward the sunshine outside to study the old Shaman's amulet.

Placing it on the hide upon a rock, she told Nakosis, "Many in our village long suspected that Kleeashto had Holeeaho killed. Holeeaho had never recognized Kleeashto, but after Holeeaho mysteriously vanished, Kleeashto came forward and told everyone that he had received a vision from the spirits that he had been chosen to be our spiritual leader. He even said that the spirit's informed him that Holeeaho had returned to them, that he had wandered off into the mountains to die and that the spirit of Holeeaho actually came to him and instructed him to receive his blessing and to lead the people. Perhaps many would have opposed him, but because he said that Holeeaho's spirit had instructed such things, the people were reluctant to argue, out of respect for the spirit of the old Shaman. To speak out against it would have been disrespectful to Holeeaho. This pretender was very cunning. We all wondered why did Holeeaho not decree Kleeashto his successor before wandering off, why he did not give him this necklace, but no one dared to speak these thoughts. Now, of course, many wish they had spoken. Nakosis, if the people see this necklace they will all know that it belonged to our Shaman, our true spirit talker. This is truly a gift from the spirits. I think the spirits want this pretender gone as much as I do and they are helping us."

Sheenka was absolutely beaming. Nakosis could now see her inner spirit light glowing brightly even in the intensity of the morning sun.

Nakosis kissed her gently on the forehead saying, "We must eat, Sheenka, and then we must plan how we shall enter your village and challenge this imposter before his men have us skewered."

Since they only had one bow, they decided to forage together, keeping an eye out for both game and any sign of others. Nakosis found a choice piece of wood to serve as a new shaft for the spearhead. He used it as a walking stick as they proceeded along the base of the cliff. Sheenka, being as good with the bow as Taku was, kept it and the quiver at her ready. They found a small patch of succulent berries and loaded the small satchel with them, having left the larger bag in the cave. The cliff was gradually getting smaller as they followed the rock strewn ledge. Soon they found themselves on the top of a high precipice where the ledge terminated abruptly. The view was spectacular. Numerous rocky canyons scarred the rolling green forests carrying the waters of many glaciers to distant lakes. Sheenka noticed that just before the ledge ended the ground sloped off steeply down toward the river far below. It looked like an old deer trail. It had to be the track that Holeeaho must have taken to reach the cave. They decided to follow it a ways and after scrambling down precarious rocks and boulders they finally came to a place with more solid footing, amid trees. There was an easily discernable, but long unused path leading down the mountain. They exchanged hopeful glances, not wanting to speak out loud. Sheenka indicated with a nod that she wanted to proceed further and so they quietly moved through the trees. The trees were not very tall here and due to the rocky ground there was no undergrowth to obscure their view of the land dropping away from where they walked. They had very good vision of the whole surrounding mountainside all the way to the river below. They could see that where the trail appeared to lead, the river rushed out of the steep walled canyon. The same canyon that they were forced to cross over the great mossy tree that nearly took Nakosis' life. They looked at one another smiling as they both came to the same realization.

"Had we only known." Nakosis whispered into her ear.

They moved like snakes, slowly, deliberately, silently toward the river. Close to the bottom Sheenka stopped, lowering herself into the bushes as Nakosis, walking behind her instinctively ducked, not needing to ask, trusting her ability on the trail. He immediately began scouring the riverbank and distant tree line for any sign of warriors. Sheenka gently touched his arm and pointed ahead toward her left as she slowly began to raise the bow up. Then Nakosis saw it, a large turkey, so well camouflaged it amazed him that Sheenka noticed it. He remained motionless, fascinated, watching how she moved her lithe body, every motion a skillful combination of dexterity, strength and stealth. She never took her eyes from the quarry, as she seemed to instinctually place her feet silently toward the unsuspecting bird. Her hand slowly reaching an arrow, the muscles of her arm flexing under the bow's tension, her powerful legs holding her in a semi-squat, slowly flexing as she began to rise at a snail's pace, her torso perfectly unwavering. It was pure artistry to behold, thought Nakosis. She was a true predator, he thought, very much like panther.

The turkey never heard the arrow and Sheenka retrieved it without ever so much as a blade of grass moving to give away the fact that she was even there. Nakosis reckoned that she could have taken the bird on the edge of an enemies' camp and gone unnoticed, her stealth was so truly perfected.

They ascended back to the cave, not saying a word until they attained the ledge once again, at which point Nakosis couldn't wait to express his admiration for her superb abilities. She beamed with pride and blushed not a little and the sight of her child like joy at receiving such compliments made him laugh and embrace her dearly.

They enjoyed a marvelous meal by the small fire, knowing they were safe in Holeeaho's hidden sacred grotto. Nakosis had laid the spearhead in a small pool of water that had collected in a depression in a large black rock. He first noticed it when he observed some birds drinking and bathing in it. As the heat of the day slowly warmed the black surface of the rock, the water became fairly hot and the birds abandoned it. It would serve wonderfully for what he had in mind. The warm water softened the rawhide binding that secured the finely knapped spear-point to the broken shaft end. This he now carefully unwrapped and gently laid on a rock beside him as he sat by the fire. He used the sharp point to groove the end of the new shaft material. Then he carefully used the moistened rawhide to re-wrap the head onto the new shaft, laying it beside the fire, but not too close, to slowly dry. As it did so it would tighten considerably and harden to create a firm, strong bond. Then sitting back they discussed how they might enter Sheenka's village unnoticed, how to confront Kleeashto without involving his men and how they might rally others to depose him.

"If there was only some way of knowing for certain that Holeeaho had been murdered and that one could prove Kleeashto was behind his death." Sheenka wondered out loud.

"Perhaps he simply did just wander off to die?" Nakosis conjectured. "What if this pretender had nothing to do with it? If you accuse him, he will obviously just deny it and say that you are lying in an attempt to return to the village and simply displaying the necklace will prove nothing. In fact, if he is as sly as you suggest, he would probably suggest that possessing the necklace is proof of our guilt. He would turn the argument against you."

Sheenka spat. She cursed Kleeashto but knew that Nakosis was right.

"Why would he bury that necklace?" Sheenka asked.

Nakosis expressed further possibilities, "He had no successor and he somehow must have sensed that his death was coming. He also must have known that someday, someone, you perhaps, would one day find this cave and be guided by the spirits to uncover the necklace."

"Yes!" Sheenka exclaimed, obviously excited by some revelation Nakosis had failed to grasp. "That's it," she continued, "Don't you see? The spirits showed you the secret hiding place of Holeeaho's. It may even have been Holeeaho's spirit! Of course! Who else would have guided you so? He wanted you to discover it so we could finally rid ourselves of the evil one."

"Look," Nakosis said, placing his hand on her arm to calm her agitated mood. "You may be right, but still, it by itself is not proof of murder but..." Nakosis stopped in mid speech as a thought occurred to him.

"What, my love? What is it" Sheenka pleaded.

Pacing the cave a few moments, gathering his thoughts and words, Nakosis finally turned to her smiling and said, "Perhaps, if you are right, there may be a way we can learn more of this. If the spirits are truly willing."

She immediately knew what he meant and implied that she was very willing to journey with him to seek the answers she so desperately wanted. They prepared themselves as before, bathing in the sacred offering of smudge smoke and made the offerings to the directions, above and below, to Aan'ga the fire spirit and this time, facing the cave wall and holding the smudge to the painted figure, Nakosis begged the guidance to Hohapas directly. He seated himself with his back to the fire as Sheenka, across the fire from him, seated herself with his small Shaman's drum, gently tapping out the timeless rhythm. He had given her the sacred words in the ancient tongue and she recited them now, a mono-tonal chant as old as the people themselves, the words designed to invoke the very presence of the fiery god himself, the personification of Shamanic magic, Hohapas!

The chant reverberated about the rock enclave, each passing of the rhythm melding into the successive repetitions until it resembled a chorus of voices. Nakosis had stared un-blinking at the image painted above him. After he saw Hohapas walk from the flames as a man, he had been instructed by Loka to close his eyes and picture the fiery form as he appeared to Nakosis in his vision. Then he was to continue to hold that image in his mind as long as he could. This practice he would undertake daily until, upon closing his eyes, he could instantly recall every detail of the magical being in perfect clarity, until he appeared as real as a flesh and blood human being. He now closed his eyes and constructed in his mind the very glowing form that had appeared to him in a past vision. He mentally offered up the sacred words while imploring Hohapas to guide him in his endeavors. His shadow flickered upon the painted wall, dancing with the rudimentary image depicted there. The drumming increased and the words grew louder and echoes overlapped echoes until the words were no longer separate or definable but rather, had become a drone-like mantra of otherworldly tones.

Nakosis was swaying back and forth to the cadence, his head tilted slightly back as Sheenka, eyes closed, kept up the steady rhythm, allowing her consciousness to melt away from the worldly plane and become one with the sound. She continued the sacred words, although no longer even aware of body, words spoken nor the hand drumming. They were working independently, as though of their own volition. Nakosis was now fully in the underworld. Once again the golden eyes appeared as panther to lead him through the dark and cold of the earth beneath the rock of the mountain and into the jaws of a great cavern that overlooked a spectacular canyon of crimson, pink and purples as far as the horizon. A great hole had been made within the earth and lined with countless rocks like an endless round stone-wall, expertly erected by unseen craftsmen. Nakosis then descended into this circular chamber. Overhead, it had been roofed with golden pine logs and woven saplings and the earth once again covered it so that little light penetrated this sanctuary. A fire was burning, the smoke rising to exit invisible ports somewhere overhead. He now stood before this fire and as in the past he sensed the presence within the flames. He called out his name and soon the fire responded with the expected movement, swirling, spiraling flames congealing to form and shape. The now familiar figure stepped from the flames to face Nakosis. The being looked somehow a little older than Nakosis remembered and he could not help but notice that the fiery being had, like him, donned a white streak in his hair, just one small group of strands. Nakosis accepted this as a gesture of humor on Hohapas behalf. He was, after-all, supposed to be possessed at times of a child like playfulness.

Their eyes locked and instantly he heard the words within his head, although none were spoken. "The truth needs no justification. The truth speaks for itself and no argument of man can alter what is!" The fire rose higher and the glow illuminated the great structure. "You need not look outside yourself for any answers for you also are the truth. If you reside in it, it will flow through you and all who see you will know it to be so."

Then as quickly as he entered he was again pulled backward, the fire and the figure becoming a tiny distant spark within the blink of an eye. Distant drumming grew louder and louder. Then all he could hear was the ancient words, the rhythmic drum and the echo of the cave. He opened his eyes. He had returned. Sensing the sudden change in the energies, Sheenka also opened her eyes and they looked at each other and she ceased the chanting and slowly let the drumming slow down and finally end.

After making the necessary offerings of gratitude to the spirits, Nakosis told Sheenka, "I think having proof is not important. It doesn't change the truth and the truth will be easy for all to see when the need comes. We must just have faith that we will prevail, that we are right and that the spirits wish it to be so. If we can show this strength to the village, to the pretender and to his followers, then we will be successful. This is what I believe Hohapas has indicated to me." He smiled now at her and gently taking her hand he said, "And you will be reunited with your family -my little panther!"

"Panther, is it?" Sheenka laughed. Then picking up the strand of his hair in her hands she said, "Be careful about pet names, spirit talker. There is only one animal I know who has such a streak!"

They laughed heartily and he pretended to wrestle with her, but she was very quick and ducked her thin frame beneath him, tripping him to the cave floor. By the time he hit the ground she had pounced upon him, straddling him, playfully holding his hands to the floor,

"Panther is it?" she said once more and placed her lips upon his and kissed him passionately.

Nakosis wrapped his arm around her thin waist, sitting up, then lifting her as he stood. He carried her toward the cave entrance, her legs wrapped tightly about him, their lips never parting and just outside the cave, in the fading light of day, he sat her down upon a tall flat rock and they made love amid the crimson glow of the setting sun.

CHAPTER 20
RETRIBUTION

Sheenka believed that following the trail would have to lead them near her people's village. The discovery of the necklace proved that it was indeed Holeeaho who used the sacred grotto and it would had to have been within a few days travel from the village. She suggested that they ford the river and follow the trail, but from within the cover of the forest along the river bank and not walk on the trail itself. She believed that this river was the source of the many smaller creeks that wound their way through the valley of her people.

"There is one very wide but shallow creek that we all cross to reach the village from where we gather berries and the roots of the yellow flower plant. There is also a deeper pool where the fishing is good just a little further upstream. If I am right, then this river will become many streams not far from here and the most eastern will eventually border our village. Not far from the deep pool is where I had my sacred hiding place, where I would go to seek the help of the spirits. It is like this cave only much smaller, but it also is up on a rocky ledge where nobody has any cause to venture. We would be safe and undetected there and I could cross the creek and sneak into my family's lodge after dark."

Nakosis interrupted her at that comment saying, "You will not go there alone! They will kill you on site. I must go with you!"

Sheenka, shaking her head, argued, "No, Nakosis, no one will be expecting me. They probably think I am long dead. I can tell my family about you and they can spread the word to all the other families who support us. You, my love, must remain hidden and I will return before the dawn. Then we can enter the village together and challenge Kleeashto with the families behind us. I can learn everything we must know about what has happened in my absence. I will instruct the people to make sure that a large fire is lit in the center of the village. We should approach near dusk, as it will be more effective. You should wear the power necklace for all to see. Everyone will recognize it as Holeeahos. I will tell them that it is the will of the spirits that you were chosen to discover its secret hiding place and to avenge his death."

"No, Sheenka, I think I should keep the necklace covered under my robe or shirt until such time as it is necessary. My good friend and a wise warrior, Washtago, used to say that there is no benefit in revealing all your strength to an enemy. Always keep them wondering, keep some men in reserve for surprise. You cannot beat having the element of surprise."

Sheenka was listening to his words and could appreciate the logic of this approach but she said, "But you could wear your beautiful headdress and carry your drum or rattle so all will know you are a true spirit talker. You must challenge him in some way that his men will not interfere. You must force him to face you alone or loose face. But be warned, my love, he is not easily deceived, he will try to find every way to have us taken before he can be exposed. The villagers will not fight unless you can prove him to be a liar."

"I think it will not be as hard as you believe." Nakosis said. "His greatest weakness is his pride. He will be greatly angered and belittled and will want my head when I confront him, but he will be forced to honor the rite to challenge or else he will loose face either way. So he must confront me. Is it not your custom? For one in power to be challenged, to step aside or fight for the right to rule?"

"Why yes," Sheenka answered, "but usually in combat Nakosis, with axe, spear, a knife or a war club."

"Yes," Nakosis butted in, "But he is not a spearman, is he? He professes to yield the power of the spirits does he not? So it is with this that he must prove himself before the village and before me, his challenger." He stood and paced a little, thinking, then said, "I only hope your friends will stand with us long enough for the challenge to take place!"

They headed out before dawn, navigating the rocky slope and wading across the freezing river holding the bags, bow and quiver high above their heads as they carefully felt the pebbly river bottom with their bare feet. They picked a spot that looked the most promising, remembering that the old Shaman also had to have crossed somewhere close by. The water was terribly fast and reached almost to their chest, but soon they were across and hiding among the bushes of the opposite shore. They could barely make out any sign of a trail in such weak light and decided that for a short while, at least, it would probably be safe to follow the overgrown section of the path, keeping a watchful eye to the trail ahead. By sunrise they had covered a fair bit of ground and the trail showed no signs of having been used in a very long time. At times it seemed that it completely disappeared altogether. Suddenly Sheenka stopped and signaled to Nakosis. They immediately dropped to a low crouching position as he slowly crawled forward to see what she had discovered. There below them the river fell over a cascade of huge boulders, no doubt washed down from the steep canyon over eons of spring floodwaters. Then just as abruptly it forked into four distinct channels, each winding through the flat valley ahead. Sheenka pointed with a nod of her head to the furthest one and they slowly made their way along the top of the cascade toward the furthest creek. The water was much lower here and crossing was easy and made somewhat more so by jumping across the many rocks that spanned it's width.

When they had crossed and were safely out of view among the undergrowth, Sheenka whispered that they were now only half a day to the fishing pool and to Sheenka's secret hiding place. The travel was slow, for they moved as two warriors in the land of an enemy, being extremely stealthy, eyes peeled to the distant woods, feet avoiding the dry twigs, keeping low and within the cover of the deep brush. Nakosis had to be careful to duck due to the heavy big bag, making sure it did not catch and break any of the many dead hanging branches. To a watchful warrior, the simple crack of a twig would warrant attention. The sun was comparatively hotter now that they had descended into the lower valley and the tension added to their fatigue, but by afternoon they stopped on a ridge overlooking the creek below their position. Nakosis could clearly see the wide pool Sheenka had described. He wanted nothing more, at this point, than to lie in it's deep cool waters. They sat on the ground, catching their wind, carefully surveying the surrounding area for any sight or sound of people, but all was peacefully quiet.

Sheenka leaned to his ear saying, "There would usually be several young children swimming here on such a day. Come, follow me, the cave is not far from here."

They once again assumed their cautious pace, traversing the side of the mountain under the cover of the thick foliage, now and then getting a clear view of the river below. In one such open area a small slide of rocks had completely pushed the small willows and brushes down the mountain leaving a gap as wide as a large lodge. There was no choice but to cross. If anyone were looking their way they would surely see them. As well, all the stony rubble was just waiting to tumble noisily down the slope at the first step. They sat for what seemed an eternity, studying the terrain to determine the best approach to crossing and also scanning the distant riverbank for signs of any human presence. Nakosis picked a path across that did not require him contacting any larger stones. Instead he choose to place his feet upon the gravely sections between the larger boulders. He shouldered the big bag, tightened the straps securely and stepped out among the rocks. He placed one moccasin on the soft gravel, letting his weight slowly compress the small stones. He used his spear to transfer his weight slightly, keeping it on his downhill side. A few pebbles began to slide across the top of the bigger ones beneath, like a tiny gray colored wave. He stopped. Sheenka saw the slight movement but kept her eyes, for the most part, on the land below them, straining to see anyone before they looked up. Nakosis again began the cautious stepping, slowly, painfully making his way from one large boulder to the other. He tried to walk a path that allowed him to go behind, on the uphill side of the biggest of the rocks so when he paused he would be partially hidden by the boulders, but it wasn't always possible as some distance separated the largest stones. He now had managed to make it to the middle of the slide, approaching a fair sized boulder that he could hopefully get behind, when suddenly Sheenka let out a sharp hiss sound through her clenched teeth. It was similar to the sound a squirrel sometimes makes.

Nakosis dropped automatically to the rocky ground as he turned to her. She was wide–eyed and pointing down the mountain. He saw them, a group of about five. They appeared to be mostly young people, perhaps a couple of teenagers and the rest children. He quickly turned his back to the river, lay on his side and pulled his knees up to his chest and froze. He hoped that the big brown bag would at least partially hide him and appear as nothing more that another big rock from such a distance and angle. As feared, doing so moved a patch of the loose gray pebbles, which made their rattling way on down the steep slope. The tiny dark wave gathered momentum, dislodging a small rock and starting the feared slide that would undoubtedly draw attention. Sheenka crouched to the ground peering like an eagle from behind a boulder.

The last child in the string of youth stopped. He looked up at the sound of the falling rocks and was studying the slope, searching for the cause of the noise. Sheenka could see that he was not looking in their direction, he had turned his eyes to the top of the slide above their position, but his gaze was moving slowly down the rocks. She was sure he had to have now been look-ing directly at them. Nakosis could do nothing but remain in his position frozen to the spot, waiting for some signal from Sheenka. Then another of the youth approached the watching boy and Sheenka was almost certain that he too would begin scouring the slope, but instead he shoved the first hard to the ground and took off running. They could hear his laughter echoing up the mountain. The first boy picked himself up and began in earnest to chase the second through the woods in wide circles before they both took off in the direction of the pool. Nakosis could hear Sheenka's very audible sigh followed shortly by another hiss. He knew the signal and immediately rolled to his knees and made for the back of the boulder. He felt his heart racing as he looked about the opposite shore of the riverbank. None of the group of youth was visible. They all had moved on toward the pool, but others could be coming. He signaled to Sheenka that she too should cross quickly.

Not wasting a heartbeat she sped her way across the rocks not, at this point, caring about a few smaller stones giving way. When she reached the boulder they both made for the other side as fast as possible, watching worriedly down the mountain. They dove for cover behind the last large boulder of the slide and immediately scanned the river. Small pebbles were now flowing like a misty gray waterfall down the slope but, thankfully, no large rocks had broken loose. Now anyone looking would see what appeared to be only a naturally occurring, occasional movement. The ledge widened to form a narrow bench. From below it would have been invisible. They moved fairly quickly along the mountainside now that the ground was less precipitous, around a jutting outcrop and there it was. A small cave set back from where the bench widened considerably. It so reminded Nakosis of Loka's cave. He thought briefly of the bizarre circumstances that led to their near-death escape from the storm and the landslide.

Sheenka helped Nakosis off with his big bag and they ducked into her secret cave. It was small but it extended well into the mountain and provided more than enough room to stand comfortably. They unpacked the left over food and ate in silence as they leaned against the rocks of the cave wall.

Passing the gourd between them, Sheenka said, "I can head out soon. I can cross the river at a place I know downstream and be just outside my village before dark. I know these woods very well, Nakosis. You don't have to worry about me. As a young girl I used to run off and hide and no one could ever find me. They always asked where I went and I never said. I have many secret places around my village where I could not be seen, yet I could watch the other children. I can get right up to my families lodge."

He did not like the idea of letting her place herself in such potential danger, but as he did not know the country and as a stranger would be instantly spotted, he knew he had no other option than to go with her plan.

"There is a small spring just past the big rock." She said, pointing past the cave entrance. "I will go now." She kissed him and turned to leave.

"I will meditate on your safe return," is all Nakosis had a chance to say and she was gone.

Time dragged on terribly. Nakosis ventured outside to fill his gourd from the tiny spring and he peered out at the river valley below from behind the safety of the rocks and bushes. Nothing moved. Realizing she was now in the hands of the spirits and probably hiding near her village, he did the only thing he could. He sat cross-legged at the entrance to the small cave. He breathed out slowly several times and with his eyes mostly closed, he focused his attention on his breathing, feeling his heartbeat slow and the familiar calm overcome him. He did not want to make a fire just to use his smudge, so he made the offerings mentally. Once, when he was trying to learn the words to the spirit's invocation in the ancient tongue, he kept mispronouncing the words, at great frustration on his part. Expressing this to Chako, the old Shaman laughed and said that it didn't matter that he had the words perfect, but that his intent to be reverential was enough. 'If your intent is perfect, then the spirits would accept your offering and the words would come.' He had said.

Nakosis visualized the smudge smoke wafting over him, over Sheenka and he asked with the utmost reverence that the spirits heed his request. He sat in silent meditation calling upon his guardians and the spirit of Eagle to watch over and protect her. He decided that come nightfall, if she had not returned, he would don his headdress and his shirt and beating his drum he would march into her village and face the evil one. For now, though, he focused on sending her all the power he could muster. Whenever Nakosis meditated in this way, time was no longer of relevance. It was the same when he journeyed. He never knew how long he had been within the spirit realm. A day could pass and it would seem as though only a brief span of time had gone by. He might 'awake' feeling very hungry and thirsty, but while he was with the spirits he had no sensations of the waking world. It was so now, as his consciousness shifted to the deeper levels where the physical world had no hold. He visualized Sheenka, hiding among the rocks and the bushes and he imagined her covered by a protective light, a glowing spirit presence that enveloped her and protected her. He was still in this state when a sharp noise brought him to alertness. He remained in the seated position, but his hand reached out to seize the spear always within his grasp while his eyes looked to the cave entrance. He only then realized that it was now dark. A movement of shadow and then Sheenka was there beside him, kissing him.

"Here, my love, I have brought us some food, eat!"

She had pulled out some roasted venison meat from within a hide bag and the pleasant aroma made Nakosis' stomach gurgle with anticipation. After a diet of foul and rabbits, the venison was a welcome feast. He ripped off a chunk and began eating but his inquisitive look beckoned some information, so Sheenka, sitting on a rock across from him revealed the latest news.

"There is trouble in the village, Nakosis." She too grabbed some meat and chewed off a piece before continuing. "My people are at war!" She said.

"Who? Who are they at war with?" Nakosis asked, "I didn't realize you had many enemies. You didn't talk of enemies before."

"No," Sheenka replied, "We had troubles in the past with a neighboring people but those were resolved long, long ago. Oh, there were still some disputes over hunting and over the flint outcrops sometimes, but Holeeaho and the elders had always managed to resolve any differences without violence. But now Kleeashto and his men have started a war. They ambushed a small group by the river and killed the two men and captured their women." Sheenka paused, having some difficulty continuing. "Nakosis, Kleeashto's men are raping the one young girl in their lodge. No one knows if the other is still alive. What they have done will cause great bloodshed when it is discovered by their people. The village is on alert and there are sentries about. I had to be careful sneaking in." She paused to drink long from the gourd then she continued. "But now, more than ever, the people want to be rid of this pretender. Also, they have to be united to guard against the possibility of attack. My father believes that Kleeashto did this thing on purpose to force the village to fight."

"We can deal with this problem after, but what of those who would stand against him? Are they now still ready to oppose him, knowing an attack might come?" Nakosis asked.

"Yes," Sheenka replied, "they believe that war might be avoided if only he can be beaten, then the enemy could have their revenge on Kleeashto and his men."

Nakosis looked a little surprised saying, "They would turn those men over to the others to be killed?"

"Yes, I do believe they would. It would serve both parties. Ever since Kleeashto took power, the truce between us has been crumbling. He shows no respect to their people whenever they have entered our village and he has treated them poorly."

"So," Nakosis asked, "how shall we proceed?"

Sheenka suggested that she would sneak back into the village before dawn and make sure that everything had been arranged and Nakosis could approach the village from the main path and announce to the sentry that he is a shaman from a distant people come to speak to Kleeashto.

"What if the sentry takes me directly to his lodge? I will never be seen again."

Sheenka nodded her head saying, "No, not if all those who oppose him are standing at the village center waiting for you, knowing you will face Kleeashto."

Nakosis thought silently about it for a while then said, "You have faith, Sheenka, that the people will stand together if I enter your village?"

"Yes, I do. I will then make myself known also and I will stand with you and with the others."

Nakosis paced the small cave, thinking of the many scenarios that could happen. There was enormous room for things to go horribly wrong. The sentry could kill him before he ever got to announce himself. Other men could kill Sheenka before she got to say a word. She could be caught entering her village.

Nakosis sat upon the cave floor once again and said only, "I must think on these things."

Sheenka knew he would seek the council of the spirits and so she sat respectfully silent as Nakosis meditated once more. He closed his eyes and allowed himself again to enter that void between worlds where his sleeping and waking minds were combined, here the words, sights and sounds could pass through to him from all realms. He visualized himself walking down a dark path toward a flickering light. In the distance a figure stood between two large trees blocking the way and yelling demandingly at his approach. Nakosis moved steadily forward, oblivious to the figure before him. At his side he felt Panther's presence, her massive paws padding upon the ground in a defiant stalking motion, her fiery eyes piercing like an arrow through any who stood before her. Both Raven and Eagle swooped above him, cawing and screeching, diving down in front of him toward the path he trod, their great wings stirring clouds of dust before them. On his other side he now suddenly felt the spirit of the great Bear, the ground shaking at his step and his fierce growl making mock of thunder. In such a way Nakosis moved forward, a vanguard for the unstoppable spirit power that swirled about him. It was as though he had been engulfed in a vortex of protective power. All through this was the ever-present sense of fire. Enchanted flames danced, spun and swirled about the many spirit beings that accompanied Nakosis down the dark trail, casually brushing aside the faceless shapes of nameless people who approached like dead leaves in a tempest. The sense of power was intoxicating and unlike anything he had felt before. It was as though every magical presence was congealed into one mighty force and that force moved within and without Nakosis. Ahead of him stood a large fire. He could vaguely discern shapes about it but they seemed of no consequence. He reached out and, touching the flames, he spread his arms skyward and the fire shot like lightning toward the heavens as though commanded by his hand. The fire was he and he was the fire. He knew that it was the magical potency of Hohapas that he was now experiencing from both without and within. It was an indescribable exhilaration and ecstasy. He somehow managed to draw himself back away from the feelings of unassailable power. He broke the trance, sweating profusely and he was once again burning hot.

Sheenka had sat supportively beside him, quietly uttering the sacred words as he had instructed. She looked concerned when he finally turned to her. She took the deer hide and had poured water from the gourd to wipe his sweat stained face. The heat of his skin startled her, but by now she knew that at such times he wielded an enormous power that often left a sign in the wake of its presence. She also knew when Nakosis had been blessed with a visitation from the spirit of Hohapas, as the fiery god's heat remained with him for a while, but seemed not to affect him.

Nakosis drank from the gourd and poured some over his head. Shaking his wet hair and pulling it from his face he looked at Sheenka, smiling a little and said, "I know what I must do and you must have no fear. You must do as you did now and focus your will upon me and utter the sacred words. Do not let anyone distract you. Your strength will help me." Nakosis drank more water then said, "I will march into the village, Sheenka but I should do so tonight, now! We should leave now. When I enter your village all will know, everyone will leave their huts to come and see and you will enter undetected and see that the fire is lit. Nothing else need be done. Those who would oppose us and those who would support us will all be present and they will have to make a choice then and there."

Sheenka was shocked. "But, my love, this is too sudden, I need time to alert the others and ..."

Nakosis waved his hand, standing and said, "You said they are raping this girl? There may not be a tomorrow for her. No, all will come, the lines will be drawn and the end will be decided this night, Sheenka! We must hurry. I will dress and you will show me the way and then you will sneak in. The spirits are in a vengeful mood tonight, my love, and their power is beyond stopping this night!"

He looked different. His confidence was beyond rational, almost foolhardy. He had a mad look about his face and Sheenka suspected that Hohapas was yet with him. She only hoped it was so. Nakosis quickly donned his headdress, his deerskin shirt and leggings and wrapped his woven robe about his shoulders. He left his spear, both his bags and the ancient rattle behind in the cave, picking up only his drum.

As though sensing her wondering about this he said, "No weapons of the world of men are of any use to me this night." But he handed her the great bow and quiver telling her she may have need of it.

Sheenka moving silently out under the glow of the stars, made her way down the path that she had followed countless times over the years. She still harbored great worry, but the fortitude and sheer fearlessness of Nakosis gave her the confidence to do as he commanded. They were soon across the creek and standing in the middle of a wide trail beaten bare by the passing of many people over much time.

"This is the main trail into the village. Around the next bend there are large logs marking the entrance. There will be a guard there, Nakosis. He is bound to stop you. Are you sure about this, my love?"

He turned and laughed out loud, the volume made Sheenka recoil in shock as she spun in all directions to see if others may have heard.

Smiling he placed his hand upon her shoulder and sad, "I know he will try to stop me, my dear, I have already walked this path and I know the outcome. Have no fear for me but run now and be ready to enter the village. Disguise yourself and make sure the fire is burning well in the village center. Wait, I will be there quickly. When the people appear you can pass the word that the time is now!" Then looking suddenly very serious he commanded "Go!"

She set off at a slow run through the trees along unseen trails that only she knew and needed little light to navigate. She was soon crouched behind a large dead tree, not a stones-throw from the rear of her family's lodge. There was no one around, no sentries within the village proper, only at the outside perimeter where trails entered the clearing. She was not going to wait until Kleeashto's men had grabbed Nakosis. She ran up to the lodge within the darkness of the trees, staying within the faint shadows created by the brilliant starlight. She felt her way on her hands and knees along side the bottom of the hut's wall. She could hear the familiar voices of her father and her sister from within. She hesitated briefly at the corner of the lodge, studying the village square ahead of her. She was relieved to see that there was a small fire already lit at the center of the square. Quickly in one swift motion she ran across the front of the lodge and was through the hide door covering. As she burst into the light, her sister began to yell. Sheenka threw herself upon the younger girl, quickly covering her mouth and raised her hand to her lips to indicate silence before releasing her. She wasted no time, as there was no time left.

"It is tonight! Now! Quickly and quietly you must tell everyone. When you hear a commotion run out and pass the word. Nakosis is here now!"

Just then she heard the faint sound of a drum beating in the distance.

TO BE CONTINUED...